WOOSTER PROPOSES, JEEVES DISPOSES

WOOSTER PROPOSES, JEEVES DISPOSES

— OR —

Le Mot Juste

KRISTIN THOMPSON

Kristin Thompson

H

JAMES H. HEINEMAN

NEW YORK

1992

ISBN 0-87008-139-X

Printed in the United States of America

Text design by Beth Tondreau Design
Illustrations by Peter Van Straaten

H

James H. Heineman, Inc.,
475 Park Avenue,
New York, NY 10022

TO SIR EDWARD CAZALET,

without whose never-failing sympathy and encouragement
this book would have been finished in half the time—
because I would have known so much less
about Wodehouse.

CONTENTS

Acknowledgments / ix

Introduction / 1

1 / Professional Life of a Performing Flea / 16

2 / Writing the Same Story Differently / 59

3 / The World's First Consulting Valet:
Genre Transformations in the Series / 90

4 / The Psychology of the Stereotypic
Individual / 119

5 / Perfecting the Formula: The Short Stories / 159

6 / Where Every Prospect Pleases . . . .
The Novels / 204

7 / Postwar Experiments: Jeeves without Bertie,
Bertie on the Stage / 253

8 / *Le Mot Juste* / 275

Appendix A / Initial Magazine and Book
Publications of the Jeeves/Wooster Series / 331

Appendix B / A Timeless World? / 339

A Note on Editions and Sources / 347

Notes / 349

Select Bibliography / 377

Index / 381

ACKNOWLEDGMENTS

Either a love of P. G. Wodehouse's work tends to make people kind, or kind people tend to love Wodehouse, or perhaps these traits reinforce each other. At any rate, in the course of researching this book I have encountered many people willing to help me far beyond what any author, however optimistic, could expect. Eileen McIlvaine and A. C. L. Hall were most cooperative. Thanks also to the staffs of the Rare Books Room of Butler Library, Columbia University, and the Harry Ransom Humanities Research Center of the University of Texas at Austin (as well as to Janet Staiger, who introduced me to the latter). Barry Phelps, Richard Usborne, Ian Carmichael, Tom Sharpe, and Evelyne d'Auzac all put their expertise and recollections at my disposal. Elizabeth Cowie took me on a delightful tour of Herne Bay and environs, during which I learned a great deal about Jeeves's middle-class aspirations. Thomas Elsaesser kindly provided me with a tape of the BBC's recent documentary on

Wodehouse. Anthony Whittome generously allowed me to examine the records of the Herbert Jenkins/Barrie & Jenkins/Hutchinson publishing concerns relating to Wodehouse's British publications. Margaret Slythe not only facilitated my use of the collection in the P. G. Wodehouse Library at Dulwich College, but also gave unstintingly of her hospitality, time, and considerable knowledge of the subject. Lee Davis gave me access to other invaluable material and generously shared his expertise concerning Wodehouse's theatrical career. Thanks to Natalie Bernstein, Maxine Fleckner-Ducey, Mary Pinkerton, and Linda Henzel for reading portions of the manuscript and offering helpful suggestions.

I am particularly grateful to a number of people who worked with Wodehouse for granting me interviews: Christopher Maclehose, Scott Meredith, Hilary Rubenstein, and Peter Schwed.

James H. Heineman has dedicated a great deal of effort to preserving Wodehouse material and to making information about the Master available to enthusiasts and scholars alike. I am grateful to him for allowing me access to his collection, for publishing this book, and for his friendship.

Many thanks to the Wodehouse Estate for allowing me to quote without limitation from both published and unpublished texts.

A large portion of my research has been made a complete joy because of the hospitality of the Valdez family (Esther, Clemente, Richard, and Sarah Jane) and of Ernie and Pat Ellis. The entire project's scope would have been much narrower without the extraordinary and friendly cooperation of Sir Edward and Lady Cazalet—to the point where one thank you can only be said in the dedication of this volume.

Finally, a pip, pip to my husband, David Bordwell, who passed along a copy of *The Code of the Woosters* several years ago, remarking that I would probably enjoy it. He has cheerfully paid the price many times since by reading drafts of this book and offering innumerable valuable comments.

WOOSTER PROPOSES, JEEVES DISPOSES

INTRODUCTION

CLICHÉ MADE STRANGE

I've just sweated for three solid months in a roasting temperature and finished my masterpiece. It really is the best thing I've done, I believe, the only trouble being that it's a little like some of the others.

—Letter from Wodehouse to Will Cuppy, 1931

WHY WODEHOUSE?

Why is English humorist P. G. Wodehouse (1881–1975) still so widely read? As a product of the popular magazine boom just after the turn of the century, he was originally one of a large number of popular authors like Mary Roberts Rinehart, E. M. Dell, and Harry Leon Wilson. Yet the works of virtually all such contemporaries have retained only a small audience. The familiar row of orange-backed Wodehouse Penguin paperbacks greets us in any train-platform book kiosk in England and even in many shopping-mall bookstores in the United States. Enthusiasts of Rinehart or Wilson, on the other hand, must usually search library shelves or secondhand bookshops for aging copies of titles long out of print. Wodehouse's readership also includes a wide variety of people. Riding London's Underground, I observed a bowler-hatted businessman immersed in a Blandings novel, while a few days later I saw a teenager in punk gear reading one of the early school novels.

Moreover, there has long been a quiet but widely held conviction that Wodehouse is a major, even a great writer.[1]

Yet his work and career bear little resemblance to those of the more traditionally revered authors of his era—Woolf, Conrad, Joyce, Fitzgerald, Stein, and others. At a time when high literary modernism was being invented, Wodehouse opted for the traditional and the popular. In a 1961 interview, he hinted at his difference from such writers:

> "England is ridden by the caste system," Mr. Wodehouse said. "They've got terrible snobbery. Over here everybody is sort of pals together. I've always preferred America to England. I suppose it's really an odd attitude for a chap born in England. America to me has always been a romantic country. As a young man, I never wanted to go to the Left Bank, as the others did."[2]

So while "the others" headed for Bloomsbury and Paris, Wodehouse gravitated to Long Island and Broadway. Born into a middle-class British family, he adored his boys' school and began by writing sports stories for children's magazines. In addition to publishing vast amounts of ephemeral prose and poetry in the early years of the century, he became a lyricist for musical comedies, both in London and New York—collaborating most notably with Jerome Kern and Guy Bolton on the "Princess musicals" of the midteens. By 1915 he had established himself as a writer of comic fiction and nonfiction, and he continued to write in this vein for the rest of his life.

Wodehouse's decision to publish strictly in the popular-fiction magazines laid the groundwork for his neglect by most literary critics and historians today. What could there be to say about an author who contributed much of his best work to that bastion of middle-brow fiction, the *Saturday Evening Post,* who cheerfully accepted Sean O'Casey's designation of him as a "performing flea," and who boasted to interviewers of his devotion to a television soap opera?

This is not to suggest that other major authors of the era did not publish in the popular magazines. Especially up to the 1920s, works by authors like Fitzgerald and Dreiser did appear in mass-market journals like the *Post*. Many, however, found the formulaic requirements of this medium to be constricting. As one literary historian points out:

> Such authors as Sherwood Anderson and Theodore Dreiser convinced themselves that there was no means of compromise between their aims and the editorial requirements of such magazines. With only a few exceptions, authors of the thirties and forties have been printed in the popular magazines on their own terms only—which means, rarely.[3]

In contrast, regular publication in the *Post* was Wodehouse's goal, and after he achieved it in 1915, he never sought to move into the more prestigious literary magazines. He uncomplainingly worked within the constraints of editorial policy and even made them one of the bases of his art. Even when Wodehouse fell out of favor with the *Post* in the early forties and when the popular magazines declined after World War II, he continued to gear his work toward that fading market—producing work that, as commentators invariably note, changed relatively little over a sixty-year span.

Much of modern literary theory and criticism has moved to eliminate the traditional distinction which holds high literature to be automatically better than popular literature. Still, even if we do not base our evaluations on that distinction, we would not want to say that all popular literature is worth detailed analysis any more than that all writing aspires to be serious literature. (Any literary work can be useful to the study of popular culture, but that subject is beyond the scope of this book.) Wodehouse, however, provides a case where such close study is warranted. For one thing, he is by common consent a superb stylist; anyone who doubts this claim need only look at such passages as the opening of *The Code of the Woosters* or of *Jeeves and the Feudal Spirit* or the description of Bertie's cottage burning down that begins chapter 10 of *Joy in the Morning*.

Aside from Wodehouse's widely acknowledged technical skill, however, there are a number of reasons why his career and work are of interest today. Because of the high respect in which he has been held by many authors, his works have had considerable influence. Some of this influence has been on other writers concentrating on popular literary genres. For example, the traditional "silly-ass" British detective novel owes a great deal to Bertie Wooster (see chapter 3). Similarly, it is not difficult to detect in Evelyn Waugh's work an elaboration of Wodehouse's formula, turning it into high literature by stressing the tragic and grotesque possibilities in his humor.

Waugh has offered some of the most eloquent defenses of Wodehouse as a great writer, including the following:

> As a novelist he was always preoccupied by plot. He has created and peopled a whole world of pure imagination, extravagant, consistent, idiosyncratic in the full tradition of Malory, the "Faerie Queen," Gulliver and Alice; he has created a language as far removed from common speech as Racine's; all, it seems, instinctively and effortlessly while he has fretted about how to release a prize-pig from her kidnappers, how to draw sundered lovers together for reconciliation in the rose garden.[4]

As we shall see, neither the plotting nor the style were as instinctive or effortless as Waugh suggests, but the final effect was as worthy of attention as he claims.

The respect in which Waugh held Wodehouse can also be seen from their correspondence. After Waugh's first letter in 1947, Wodehouse replied, asking his correspondent to address him by his nickname, "Plum." Waugh replied that he could not address his "revered master" so familiarly and began his letters "Dear Dr Wodehouse" throughout their long friendship.[5]

In addition to his influence on other writers, Wodehouse is of interest in part because his career spanned an unusually long period. Beginning to publish professionally in 1900, he was still at work on the day of his death in 1975—a career of seventy-five years; the Jeeves/Wooster series lasted for sixty. The difficulties of maintaining a literary project for such a length of time present an interesting subject for the historian/analyst as well as for the general reader—especially when that project focuses specifically on play with the formulaic.

Perhaps the most compelling reason for studying Wodehouse closely, however, lies in his extraordinarily complex play with convention, repetition, and cliché. My main claim in this book is that Wodehouse was intensely aware of his own participation in the popular literary scene. He used the conventions of the popular literature of his day in a unique way: exaggerating and displaying clichés and repetitive formulas. Most authors with any pretention would be likely to avoid cliché or to use it to parody other literary works. Although there is an element of parody about Wodehouse's use of cliché, he is doing something far more ingenious with it. Specifically, he systematically uses familiar phrases, character types, and situations, foregrounding their formulaic nature until we are forced to notice them *as* clichéd. To borrow a term from Russian Formalist literary theory, he *defamiliarizes* these most familiar of literary conventions. As a result, he does not parody any one particular literary work; he parodies nineteenth-century literature itself.

The concept of defamiliarization lies at the basis of all artistic creation, the Formalists argued, since the main function of art is to renew our perceptions of things. As Viktor Shklovsky wrote in a famous passage:

> Habitualization devours work, clothes, furniture, one's wife, and the fear of war. . . . And art exists that one may recover the sensation of life; it exists to make one feel things, to make the stone *stony*. The purpose of art is to impart the sensation of things as they are perceived and not as they are known. The technique of art is to make objects "unfamiliar," to make forms difficult, to increase the difficulty and length of perception because the process of perception is an aesthetic end in itself and must be prolonged. *Art is a way of experiencing the artfulness of an object; the object is not important.*[6]

Any sort of literary device can be defamiliarizing, as long as it is fairly striking and original. But the repeated use of the same device robs it of its power to defamiliarize. It becomes *automatized*. As Boris Tomashevsky described literary devices, "to the extent that their use becomes automatic, they lose their efficiency and cease to be included on the list of acceptable techniques."[7] Clichés are extreme cases of automatization in that they can be perceived very easily; they are recognized rather than noticed. The cliché, then, would seem an unlikely device for a major author to make the center of his or her work—yet Wodehouse did just that.

He began as a professional author at a time when major changes were taking place in the literary world. Nineteenth-century traditions of high prose were being popularized by the tremendous boom in fiction magazines and novels that was well under way by the turn of the century. Wodehouse entered this growing market and by the 1920s became one of the most successful writers in the world. In doing so, he used minor genres, the popular-magazine short story and serial, to defamiliarize the clichés of Victorian and Edwardian literature, and as a result his work became subtly original. Most highly innovative authors overturn conventions through the introduction of daring devices and structures. Some also use clichés in new and strange ways. Wodehouse seems unique in the degree to which he eschewed anything obviously original, preferring to concentrate minutely on the conventional, the clichéd, and the repetitious. Like most popular writers who write quickly, he had his repertory of strategies and patterns. Yet unlike them, he made no attempt to use style or a veneer of realism to camouflage them. He does not, as one might expect, pull us away from the overly familiar but rather pushes us further and further into an awareness of the clichés at work in his narratives. Wodehouse uses a huge variety of tactics to make the dullest of outworn devices extraordinary and strange.[8]

Consider, for example, a passage from *Right Ho, Jeeves*. Bertie's cousin Angela has broken up with her fiancé, Tuppy Glossop, and Bertie uses reverse psychology, criticizing Tuppy in the hope that she will spring to his defense. But Angela has seen what Bertie does not—that Tuppy is eavesdropping from some nearby bushes; hence she pays little attention as Bertie tries to tell her what an unpleasant schoolmate young Tuppy had been:

> " 'Uncouth' about sums it up. I doubt if I've ever seen an uncouther kid than this Glossop. Ask anyone who knew him in those days to describe him in a word, and the word they will use is 'uncouth.' And he's just the same today. It's the old story. The boy is the father to the man."

> She appeared not to have heard.
>
> "The boy," I repeated, not wishing her to miss that one, "is the father to the man."
>
> "What are you talking about?"
>
> "I'm talking about this Glossop."
>
> "I thought you said something about somebody's father."
>
> "I said the boy was father to the man."
>
> "What boy?"
>
> "The boy Glossop."
>
> "He hasn't got a father."
>
> "I never said he had. I said he was the father of the boy—or, rather, of the man."
>
> "What man?"
>
> I saw that the conversation had reached a point where, unless care were taken, we should be muddled.
>
> "The point I am trying to make," I said, "is that the boy Glossop is the father to the man Glossop. In other words, each loathsome fault and blemish that led the boy Glossop to be frowned upon by his fellows is present in the man Glossop, and causes him—I am speaking now of the man Glossop—to be a hissing and a byword at places like the Drones, where a certain standard of decency is demanded from the inmates." (Chap. 14)

By the end of this passage, the clichéd passage (a slight misquotation from Wordsworth's "My Heart Leaps Up") has been pulverized, reversed, and turned into something strange indeed.

As this scene suggests, many of Wodehouse's standard phrases are quotations from or paraphrases of actual literary works. One of his most familiar tropes is "He reeled and would have fallen. . . ." This may seem just a stock Victorian catchphrase, but it comes from the scene in Bram Stoker's *Dracula* (published in 1897, while Wodehouse was in college) where Arthur stakes Lucy in her grave: "The hammer fell from Arthur's hand. He reeled and would have fallen had we not caught him." Wodehouse uses this line in many variants. The reeling character may avoid falling by clutching at a framed photograph or a passing dog. In *Stiff Upper Lip, Jeeves,* Bertie hears that Sir Watkyn Bassett wants to hire Jeeves: "I reeled, and might have fallen, had I not been sitting at the time" (chap. 5). Wodehouse never identifies the passage as being from *Dracula* or even as being a quotation; we are left to recognize it or not.[9] In other cases the source is given, usually by Jeeves. Either way, it is clear that certain phrases in the original works struck Wodehouse as clichés. He internalized the conventions and, in some cases, the exact phrases of what he read and rendered them in skewed fashion.

Aside from using the most familiar kinds of literary conventions and language, Wodehouse carried through his insistence on cliché by creating repetitious works. On the local level of diction, he uses much repetition in the conversation and redundancy between narration and dialogue, not to dull our sense of the language but to enhance it. At the level of plot, characters fall into a small number of similar groups and are often virtually interchangeable. Individual incidents and entire plot patterns come back over and over. One of the most intriguing things about Wodehouse is the fact that his readers are well aware of this repetition and yet delight in the return of familiar elements—elements that were usually not original to begin with.

One might argue that in fact most popular authors in such genres as the romance and the mystery use formulas and that their readers are conscious of the repetitive qualities in their works. Wodehouse's difference comes, I think, partly from the fact that he based the entertainment value of his writing so thoroughly on repetition. Moreover, though readers may delight in authors who work within cliché-ridden genres, they would probably not seriously defend them as great writers, as so many knowledgeable people have done with Wodehouse.

Wodehouse not only drew upon existing clichés but also built up a large set of devices that are essentially clichés internal to his oeuvre. The most famous of these within the Jeeves/Wooster series are undoubtedly Jeeves and Bertie's clashes over some gaudy piece of clothing to which Jeeves takes a dislike and which Bertie eventually sacrifices as a reward for Jeeves's help. As we shall see in chapter 2 in examining Wodehouse's writing methods, he organized his work around discrete, interchangeable units of language, character, and action, which he then recombined throughout his career.

Most critics and admirers have noted Wodehouse's use of cliché and quotation as a small-scale stylistic device.[10] Here I would like to suggest that the use of formulaic devices and structures pervades Wodehouse's work, forming what the Russian Formalists termed the *dominant;* that is, a central structure that organizes the whole work and forces all other devices, from the global to the local, to structure themselves around it. In the Jeeves/Wooster series, Wodehouse's most important works, the self-conscious use of the formulaic informs all levels: genre, narrative structure, character, and style.

In matters of genre conventions and narrative structures, I shall be analyzing how Wodehouse took several very specific genres and works of the turn-of-the-century era and recombined them into a distinctive formula of his own for the Jeeves/Wooster series. Most notably, he took character relations and narrational tactics from Doyle's Sherlock Holmes series, making Jeeves into a brilliant problem solver reported on by the less astute Bertie. Jettisoning the mystery element of the original, Wodehouse substituted a comic inversion of the standard romance, with the happy ending consisting of Bertie successfully escaping marriage rather than achieving the traditional final clinch in the last scene. This recombination of familiar devices creates a framework for a new set of conventions and for the play with quotation and cliché that pervades the series.

Wodehouse's main model, Arthur Conan Doyle, also wrote almost entirely for the popular magazines of this same era. (Indeed, the enormous success of *The Strand* after Doyle began contributing the Holmes stories shortly after the magazine began publishing in 1891 was a major factor stimulating the rise of popular middle-class fiction magazines.) It seems significant that Doyle is the other popular-magazine author of the time who is still read very widely today. (Probably a wider range of Wodehouse's work remains consistently in print, while readers of Doyle seldom venture beyond the Holmes stories and a few of the historical and fantasy novels; such a major Doyle book as *The Firm of Girdlestone* is occasionally reprinted but is probably read only by a small number of enthusiasts.) I do not think this is a matter of Wodehouse simply being prescient and realizing that by imitating an enduringly popular author he could himself gain lasting fame. Rather, in building his own art, he foregrounded those conventions that epitomized the popular, standardized literature of the late nineteenth century.

By and large, Doyle did not use these conventions in a systematically self-conscious way himself. That was Wodehouse's addition. He was not parodying Doyle or any other specific author. Parodies tend to lose their interest when the works or genres they are lampooning die out. Rather, Wodehouse is spoofing the originals by pointing up conventions and clichés that usually pass unremarked, and in doing so he created something of interest in its own right. Had the Holmes series faded into obscurity, it would make relatively little difference to readers of Wodehouse, as long as they understood the conventionality of the genres he worked in.

A self-conscious approach to writing, however, explains neither why Wodehouse is worth studying nor why he is still popular and respected today. Many authors, after all, use reflexivity in their work. Those who do so most extensively and consistently, however, are associated with modernism. Wodehouse seems a unique case of a writer remaining within the orbit of popular literature *and* exploring conventionality in a systematic fashion. While parody of literary convention is certainly an aspect of high literature—as in Jarry and Joyce—it still remains a subsidiary part of modernism. Wodehouse, on the other hand, largely avoids parody, while exaggerating the clichés of popular literature in a way rare in high literature. The very point of modernist literature is to destroy the conventional, not just explore or, worse yet, celebrate it. Moreover, high literature depends on the creation of originality and uniqueness. Wodehouse, on the other hand, offers one suggestion of how a modern, popular author can be original and yet remain a classicist. In his utter mastery of the conventions and his ability to add a sheen to them through an instantly recognizable brand of wit, Wodehouse might usefully be compared to another great popular comic master of this century, Ernst Lubitsch, whose Hollywood films of the twenties and early thirties similarly manage both to embrace the formulaic and to examine it at arm's length.

In sum, Wodehouse found a way of creating a richness and complexity usually thought of as accessible only to modern art. And because his humor is neither destructive nor parodic, his sophisticated but traditional approach remains widely accessible. It might not be too much to say that Wodehouse has achieved in popular literature something comparable to what Joyce did in the high-art novel, typically read now largely by professional academics and their students. Which is not to say anything against Joyce—but it is certainly not to say anything against Wodehouse either. He is perhaps the best argument we have for taking popular literature seriously.

APPROACHING WODEHOUSE

This book, then, will look at Wodehouse's work in a way that may shed light on the question of how an author can be a major literary figure *and* a product of the popular-magazine market.

First, it outlines Wodehouse's professional relationship to that magazine market.[11] As James L. W. West III recently wrote:

> If scholars or critics are fully to understand works of literary art, they must understand the commercial factors that influenced the composition and publication of these works. Ideally scholars and critics should know more about the literary marketplace of the author's time than the author would have known. The marketplace was only one of several factors that influenced the literary work, of course, and sometimes it was only a minor factor, but it was never absent from the author's thoughts if that author proposed to earn a living by writing. Commercial factors often influenced the published form of the work, and its success, more than the author realized.[12]

In Wodehouse's case, the constraints of the marketplace influenced his writing methods and the consequent form of his works in profound and evident ways, and Wodehouse was well aware of that fact.

Throughout most of his life, Wodehouse enjoyed remarkably stable publishing circumstances, with his stories and books coming out in the same magazines and from the same presses for years, even decades on end. The policies of the magazines in particular encouraged a formulaic approach to writing, one that fit in well with Wodehouse's tactic of emphasizing the use of cliché and repetition. His relationships with his editors and agents were also typically long-term and stable.

Wodehouse knew full well he was recycling a small number of plot formulas, as some of the epigraphs in this book demonstrate.

His working methods reflect that knowledge, as we shall see in chapter 2. Beginning with tiny scraps of ideas, often derived from previous works by other authors or by himself, Wodehouse reworked and combined these, using characters and incidents as movable pieces that could be substituted easily for each other; he finished the writing process by polishing his prose repeatedly, adding new clichés on the stylistic level as the last step.

The remaining chapters will analyze the Jeeves/Wooster series, beginning with the genre conventions upon which Wodehouse drew and examining the narrative formulas he built up from them. Chapter 4 looks at the characters as stereotypical figures and as units that function for certain repetitive purposes within the tiny set of narrative patterns Wodehouse had worked out. Those narrative patterns are the subject of the next three chapters, which deal with changes in the formulas in the course of the series: the short stories, the novels, and the anomalous postwar theater works and the one novel without Bertie. Finally, an analysis of the most localized use of cliché and repetition, on the level of style, concludes the book. Throughout, it should be apparent that Wodehouse's originality lies in the series' dominant tactic: its reflexive and yet classicist play with conventionality to create a distinctive type of humor.

PERIODIZATION

Wodehouse's lengthy career was marked by two long periods of considerable stability in his publishing situation: one lasting from the midteens to the end of the thirties, and one from the early fifties to his death in 1975. Before this there was a period during which he was developing as a writer and struggling to establish himself within the publishing world, and in the middle came an interruption caused by an incident during World War II. Wodehouse was briefly interned in Germany and then made a series of comic radio broadcasts there. The resulting uproar and its aftermath affected his career noticeably. The periods into which we can divide his writings do not correlate exactly with these periods of stability and breaks in his career, but Wodehouse's professional life did have effects on his work, and, as we shall see, there are connections between important changes in his career and shifts in his writing.

One pervasive myth about Wodehouse is that his writing never changed after he reached his mature style, that is, by the 1910s or 1920s. Frances Donaldson states that:

> Wodehouse did not develop in the way many writers do, and his books can be divided into two periods only—that of the school stories and that of the rest. . . .
>
> Once he had found his true form, Wodehouse never changed; and except perhaps in a geographical sense, one cannot relate different aspects of his work to different periods of his life.[13]

Writing in 1945, George Orwell saw three periods in Wodehouse's career: (1) the school-story period, up to and including *Psmith in the City* (1910); (2) the American period, from 1913 to 1920, when Wodehouse was living in the United States and setting his stories there; and (3) the country-house period, when he went back to English subjects for many of his stories.[14] Most critics and historians seem to accept the notion that Wodehouse was a static writer, for few attempt to discuss his work by period.

Although much depends on how one defines change, I believe Wodehouse's work did develop and its changes can be linked at times to his professional circumstances. Within the Jeeves/Wooster series there are several periods. Throughout this book, I shall look at the stories in relation to the chronology of their original magazine appearances. Wodehouse rearranged them for publication in book form, and many developmental patterns emerge when they are grouped in their original order. (The publishing history of the Jeeves series in appendix A provides a guide for keeping track of its many works.) My discussion will, however, be based on the texts as published in the books, partly for the reader's convenience and partly because these were apparently the versions Wodehouse intended as final.

The short stories can be seen as falling into three periods:

> *1. Early (1915–16).* Since the stories were intended from the start to be collected into books, they were written in batches in quick succession. These early stories came out just after Wodehouse's first big success at the *Saturday Evening Post.* In them, Jeeves is a relatively simple character, of average intelligence, who solves the problems by seizing on coincidences.
> *2. Middle (1918–25).* These stories develop considerably on the earlier formula. Jeeves becomes smarter, though he still relies on coincidence for solutions. Bertie becomes resentful of Jeeves at times, and the plots thus have more conflict and variety.
> *3. Late (1926–30).* By this point Jeeves is manipulating events from the beginning and seldom depends on coincidence. Bertie becomes more rebellious. Most of these stories are perfectly plotted.

Career stability does not, of course, automatically mean that an author will turn to this sort of formulaic, repetitive writing; far less does it explain how Wodehouse was able to turn that tactic into a complex, original formal system. Given that he adopted this formulaic pattern of writing early on and was soon successful with it, we can at least examine how his stable publishing circumstances encouraged him to move in this direction.

Wodehouse's stable situation at the *Post* and other magazines continued through the 1930s. The Jeeves/Wooster series was so successful that he promoted the pair to novels, turning out three during that decade. Even the turmoil of the war and the Berlin-broadcasts scandal failed to affect his writing significantly; he continued to do a novel a year, assuming that they would be published after the war. Thus the novels from *Thank You, Jeeves* (1934) to *The Mating Season* (1949) can be seen as defining one period.

After the war, however, Wodehouse's professional and personal circumstances changed, and we can see a distinct break in his writing. Boycotted by many magazines as a result of the broadcasts scandal, he wrote less. Postwar hardships in England made him think that publishers would not accept his idyllic world of rich Britishers and their servants. His solution was an attempt to salvage his most famous and lucrative character, Jeeves, or at least to create a Jeeves-like substitute for him. Hence he wrote a series of plays and novels featuring either Jeeves (in one version of a play, *Spring Fever*, in *Come On, Jeeves*, and in *Ring for Jeeves*) or Phipps (in other play versions and in *The Old Reliable*).

After Wodehouse's 1952 move to Simon and Schuster, which gave him a renewed stability, he returned to the old formula of the series, bringing back Bertie as the co-star. This period runs from 1954 (*Jeeves and the Feudal Spirit*) to 1974, when the last novel, *Aunts Aren't Gentlemen*, appeared.

Of course, given that the Jeeves/Wooster series lasted sixty years, its many consistencies are striking. This periodization, however, should make evident some distinct differences among the works—especially in the earliest stories and in the post–World War II period.

Wodehouse began his publishing career exactly on the brink of the new century, in 1900, yet he refused to move forward and adopt the avant-garde styles of that tumultuous period. He stood at the end of the Victorian literary era, and, as Bertie would say, saw it "steadily and saw it whole" (see the late poet Matthew Arnold). He rendered clichés to us as new-found wonders.

1

PROFESSIONAL LIFE OF A PERFORMING FLEA

I am only a public entertainer who has understood his time.
—PICASSO
(*Bartlett's Familiar Quotations*)

OBSESSION, ROUTINE, AND STABILITY

P. G. Wodehouse (1881–1975) was born in the same year as Picasso and died two years after the Spanish painter. He was born two years after Einstein, Stalin, and Trotsky, one year after Apollinaire, and one year before Braque, Joyce, and Woolf. He was part of a generation that created the radical changes of the twentieth century. Yet he also grew up at the end of the Victorian era and became a successful author in the Edwardian period. He loved his British public school and there was exposed to the classics and to the popular literature of the late nineteenth century. His only other early institutional experience was as an apprentice clerk in a London bank, which he disliked. He was never touched by influences that might have made him rebel against older literature and turn to new forms, as other major writers of his generation did. His perspective on the literature of his age let him see its conventions with a remarkably objective eye.

Throughout his life, writing obsessed him. He wrote whenever he could, and his closest friends were writers with whom he discussed his craft. Denis Mackail recalled that at their first meeting, Wodehouse

> immediately started talking about writing without a moment's delay. For this—apart from Pekes and cricket and football matches at his old school, with which he also seemed obsessed—was his own great, unending topic; and at all the evenings that we have spent together, I can't remember him ever lingering, for more than a few seconds, on anything else.[1]

After novels, the largest category of books in Wodehouse's library at his death was biographies and autobiographies of writers, which he had read and annotated. According to N. T. P. Murphy, writers appear as characters in eighty-two of his ninety-seven books. His stepdaughter Leonora described Wodehouse in the late 1920s: "He never seems to stop working; his idea of a holiday is to write a play instead of a novel, a short story instead of a musical comedy." Indeed, when Wodehouse was on holiday at Hunstanton Hall, which provided one of the models for Blandings Castle, he spent his days floating on the moat in a punt that he had outfitted with a chair and a typing table.[2]

During World War II, when there was a five-year gap in the publication of his novels, Wodehouse went on writing one a year. By 1945, when he had four unpublished manuscripts, he wrote to his friend William Townend:

> If you are a writer by nature, I don't believe you write for money or fame or even for publication, but simply for the pleasure of turning out the stuff. I don't really care if the books are published or not. The great thing is that I've got them down on paper, and can read and re-read them and polish

> them and change an adjective for a better one and cut out dead lines.[3]

Of course Wodehouse ultimately wanted his material published, but he did revise and polish extensively. The magazine versions were often further revised for book publication. He reread his own books, just as he did those of his favorite authors.

He seems to have been incapable of conceiving doing anything else besides writing. In 1950 he wrote to Townend:

> Do you regret not taking up a hobby of some sort? I find that I can do nothing but write and read. I am so uninterested in every side of life that it is a mystery to me how I have ever been able to do anything as a writer. I wish I could get genuinely interested in collecting stamps or something. . . . On the other hand, reading and writing fill one's time quite nicely.[4]

Even late in life, when he was having increasing difficulty getting ideas for novels, he never considered retiring. In 1974, after finishing *Aunts Aren't Gentlemen* and before beginning the project published posthumously as *Sunset at Blandings,* he wrote:

> Talking of ideas, I really believe I have come to the end of mine. I have always had this feeling in between books, but this time it looks like being permanent. I sit in the old arm chair and brood and I do get an occasional minor scene, but never anything I can build on. It doesn't matter to me financially, but how dull life will be if I can't write. I shall have to do essays![5]

Overall we get an image not of a man driven to write by his great inspirations but of one driven by his great love of writing to seek inspirations.

Wodehouse's writing was largely dependent on repetitiousness and the formulaic. The repetitiousness of his writing was fostered by two general factors in his publishing circumstances: first, he was largely a product of the flourishing fiction-magazine market of the early decades of the century, and second, during most of his life Wodehouse maintained highly stable relationships with his publishers. Such stability has been rare for serious authors in this century, as James L. W. West III points out:

> Writers are at their most productive when they have cooperative and savvy publishers who understand the mechanisms of the literary market-place, keep them solvent, and get their writings to the public. Such situations have not often existed for serious literary authors in twentieth-century America, however, and the increasing professionalization of American life, particularly of publishers and agents, has been partly at fault.[6]

The regularity of magazine publication may have been the source of Wodehouse's love of a regular writing routine, or it may simply have fostered his own inclinations in that direction. In either case, he throve in the stable relations he had with his magazine and book publishers. We shall see that routine and stability fostered Wodehouse's creation of that defamiliarizing play with repetition and cliché so central to his work.

PRE–1915: JOURNALISM AND THE MAGAZINE BOOM

Pelham Grenville Wodehouse was born in Guildford, Surrey, on October 15, 1881, the third of four sons in a middle-class family. His father's job as a magistrate in Hong Kong kept his parents abroad during most of his boyhood; the brothers stayed in England, at boarding schools and with relatives. Wodehouse's formal education was at Dulwich College, a respected public school. There he studied classics and participated avidly in the sports that formed the subjects of his early articles, stories, and serials. Among the authors his classwork led him to read were: Sophocles, Demosthenes, Aristophanes, Aeschylus, Plato, Aristotle, Pindar, Juvenal, Cicero, Virgil, and Lucan. He also studied Tennyson's *The Princess*. Other subjects included history, rhetoric, religion, and French.[7] Later, Wodehouse may have presented himself as loving trashy fiction, but his quotations from the classics show that this early influence stuck with him.

Wodehouse was initially expected to try for a scholarship to Oxford, as his elder brother had successfully done. Biographers have claimed that he was unable to go because, even with such a scholarship, his father could not afford the fees to send another son to Oxford. Evelyne Ginestet argues that Wodehouse received only mediocre marks at Dulwich and that his failure to go to Oxford may have been due to that fact and not to his father's limited financial means—though Wodehouse always gave the latter reason.[8] At any rate, in 1900 Wodehouse left Dulwich to become a clerk at the Hong Kong and Shanghai Bank in London, expecting to be transferred eventually to the Hong Kong branch.

Wodehouse never intended to become a banker, and throughout his life he ridiculed his incompetence in this job. Yet, ironically, during the same period, he maintained a private account book, detailing the writing he was selling and how much he was paid.[9] He lived alone in a small room, writing outside banking hours. Although he received many rejection slips, he also increasingly made sales. The notebook's fly leaf bears a quotation from one of his favorite authors, W. S. Gilbert:

> Though never nurtured in the lap
> Of luxury, yet, I admonish you,
> I am an intellectual chap,
> And think of things that would astonish you.
>
> (*Iolanthe*, II)

This "intellectual" image was far from the one Wodehouse later presented to the public, yet it was strangely appropriate.

The sales tally begins in February 1900, with a ten shillings, six pence prize for a contribution to *The Public School Magazine*; the last entry is for the same month in 1908. (Before 1900 he had published several sporting reports and a humorous poem in the Dulwich magazine, *The Alleynian*.) He cranked out stories, humorous articles, comic poems, sporting accounts, and other ephemeral pieces. *The Public School Magazine* was his mainstay into early 1902, with *The Captain* accepting stories from October 1901 on. By February 1902 he was getting three pounds for each *Captain* story and remarked, "My market value is going up!" In March he received word that his school serial, *The Pothunters*, was to be published as his first book. On June 30, he first wrote the humorous column "By the Way" for *The Globe* newspaper; he was soon asked to do so regularly. "On September 9th, having to choose between the *'Globe'* and the Bank, I chucked the latter, & started out on my wild lone as a freelance."[10]

Though his income fluctuated between five and ninety-two pounds per month over the next two years, he made far more than he would have at the bank. In late 1904, he wrote the notebook's longest comment:

> On this, the 13th December 1904, time 12 p.m. I set it down that I have *A*rrived. Letter from Cosmo Hamilton congratulating me on my work and promising a commission to write lyrics for his next piece. I have a lyric in "Sergeant Brue," another probably, in "The Cingalee," a serial in the *"Captain,"* five books published, I am editing "By the Way," *Pearson's* have two stories and two poems of mine, I have finished the "Kid Brady" stories, I have a commission to do a weekly poem for *"Vanity Fair,"* and Pocock has just got permanently on to *Pearson's* staff, so in future he will be on the spot.[11]

Wodehouse had begun occasionally writing lyrics for musical comedies. As a poet, newspaper columnist, novelist, and so on, he could consider himself a successful author, if on a minor scale.

Yet a glance through the journals or the *By the Way Book*[12] (a 1908 selection of Wodehouse's and Herbert Westbrook's columns) reveals that his work in this period was mostly undistinguished. The school stories are still read, especially in England, but few would claim that they show more than the occasional flash of his later style. Most scholars consider everything up to *Mike* (1909) or *Psmith in the City* (1910) apprentice work. (Even *Love among the Chickens* [1906], notable for its introduction of series character Ukridge, is familiar mainly in its 1921 revised version.)

Wodehouse was fortunate in starting during a boom in popular journalistic and magazine publishing. Years later he wrote:

> The dregs, of whom I was one, sat extremely pretty *circa* 1902. There were so many morning papers and evening papers and weekly papers and monthly magazines, that you were practically sure of landing your whimsical article on "The Language of Flowers" or your parody of Omar Khayyam somewhere or other after say thirty-five shots.[13]

This was no exaggeration. Wodehouse's account book records the publication in *To-day* of an article called "The Language of Flowers"; by this entry he noted: "'Ighly yumourous."

The British fiction magazine was an important literary factor in the nineteenth century, with such writers as Charles Dickens serializing their novels before publishing them in book form. But in the United States, popular-fiction magazines were scarce before the 1890s. Those magazines that did exist hardly encouraged original work; the lack of an international copyright law allowed American publishers to use British authors' works without payment. Similarly, if these publishers paid American authors for original stories and serials, these could be reprinted abroad free of charge. There were some serious short-story magazines in the United States, notably the *Atlantic Monthly*, beginning in 1857, and *The Nation*, founded in 1866; these fostered the work of such authors as Bret Harte, Henry James, and Mark Twain. By the 1880s, the short-story form was gaining wider respectability, and the British-American copyright law of 1891 led to the proliferation of American and British popular-fiction magazines that could pay reasonable fees with less fear of piracy abroad.

The Public School Magazine was started in England in 1898; it was Wodehouse's main early market. Its success led George Newnes Ltd. to bring out the competing *The Captain*, which published most of Wodehouse's early serials (reprinted as the six school novels, 1902–9). Beginning in 1891, the Newnes group also published *The Strand*, modeled loosely on prestigious American magazines like *Harper's* and *Scribner's*. Newnes initially avoided serials, trying to make each issue self-sufficient by printing only short stories. From the first issue, *The Strand* was enormously successful; its circulation quickly rose to a steady 500,000 monthly. One of the magazine's most famous series began when Doyle submitted a Sherlock Holmes story in the spring of 1891, boosting circulation and providing a model for *Strand* fiction. According to the magazine's official historian, "In inventing a new fiction character, Doyle had devised a new fiction form, the connected series of short stories, of about five or six thousand words each, that enabled readers to share the linked excitements of a serial without being committed to following each installment." Other popular magazines adopted this strategy. (The Jeeves/Wooster stories shared this approach.) *The Strand* began accepting serials in the first decade of the 1900s, partly to accommodate *The Hound of the Baskervilles*. By that time *The Strand* paid the highest prices for fiction of any English magazine.[14]

The rise of American popular-fiction magazines depended on several factors besides the 1891 copyright act. New printing methods, including the rotary press, facilitated the production of large editions; the growing railroad system in the late nineteenth century permitted cheap distribution, as did second-class mailing privileges created by the Postal Act of 1879. Mass distribution made magazines attractive to advertisers.[15] During the 1890s, fiction magazines proliferated. The success of *The Strand* (January 1891) led to profitable American imitations, including *Munsey's* (October 1891) and *McClure's* (1893).[16]

Most significantly for Wodehouse, the *Saturday Evening Post* flourished during this period. Linked tenuously back to a journal started by Benjamin Franklin in 1728, it changed its name to the *Saturday Evening Post* in 1821. It published significant nineteenth-century short-story authors, such as Edgar Allan Poe, Harriet Beecher Stowe, and J. F. Cooper. The *Post* declined after the Civil War and was at a low point in 1898, when George Horace Lorimer became editor. He remained at the *Post* until December 31, 1936, helping to make it one of the most successful American magazines.[17]

Lorimer revived the *Post* in various ways. He was very demanding in selecting the pieces to be used:

> No writer was bigger than the Post. If one chose to leave, there were always others to succeed him. Nor could he give any less than his best for the Post, because Lorimer would not hesitate to turn down the work of his highest-paid writers if he thought it fell below standard. He read every contribution as if it were the first piece the writer had submitted.[18]

The *Post* sent rejection slips to the likes of Rudyard Kipling and Willa Cather.[19] Similarly, lack of fame did not disqualify a new author. Wodehouse wrote in 1945: "I have always thought it conclusive evidence of Lorimer's greatness as an editor that he was willing to buy a serial by an absolutely unknown author."[20] In addition, the *Post*'s authors represented a wide range of the fiction market: from Stephen Crane to Marie Corelli, Theodore Dreiser to Irwin Cobb, William Faulkner to Mary Roberts Rinehart.

Wodehouse had other publishing outlets in the United States. *Collier's* was one of the *Post*'s principal rivals. Founded in 1888, it trailed the *Post* in popularity but received a boost in 1919, when it was taken over by the Crowell Publishing Co. By 1930, it was making a profit.[21] *Cosmopolitan* first appeared in 1886 and entered the Hearst publishing group in 1905. It was a somewhat more prestigious magazine than the *Post* or *Collier's*, selling for thirty-five cents during the 1920s[22]. Wodehouse contributed to it occasionally from 1910 to the 1930s.

The growth of such magazines created such a demand for fiction that the resulting published material inevitably became conventionalized. From the 1890s on, dozens of how-to manuals popularized the basic principles of prose writing for aspiring freelances. In 1915, the year when Wodehouse began both the Blandings and the Jeeves/Wooster series in the *Post*, a commentator noted how formulaic both high and popular-magazine fiction had become:

> It is not difficult to construct an outline of the "formula" by which thousands of current narratives are being whipped into shape. Indeed, by turning to the nearest textbook on "Selling the Short Story," I could find one ready-made. . . . The story *must* begin, it appears, with action or with dialogue. A mother packs her son's trunk while she gives him unheeded advice

> mingled with questions about shirts and socks; a corrupt and infuriated director pounds on the mahogany table at his board meeting, and curses the honest fool (hero of the story) who has got in his way; or " 'Where did Mary Worden get that curious gown?' inquired Mrs. Van Deming, glancing across the sparkling glass and silver of the hotel terrace." Any one of these will serve as an instance of the breakneck beginning which Kipling made obligatory.[23]

Wodehouse's success as a writer arose from his ability simultaneously to serve the needs of these magazines and to transform their common tropes.

Largely in response to the growing market in popular fiction, the institution of the literary agent grew up in both the United States and the United Kingdom during the late decades of the nineteenth century. Through much of Wodehouse's life, his long-term relationships with his agents were another important factor in rendering his professional situation highly stable.

After six years as a freelance, Wodehouse acquired his first British agent, J. B. Pinker, who handled *Love among the Chickens*. The choice was a revelatory one. Pinker was the second most important literary agent in the United Kingdom at this time. (The most important was A. P. Watt, established about 1875 and generally considered the first modern agent; Wodehouse would move to Watt's agency in the 1930s.) Having established his firm in 1896, Pinker at various points represented such authors as Henry James, Joseph Conrad, Arnold Bennett, Stephen Crane, Ford Madox Ford, H. G. Wells, and Oscar Wilde. He also, however, specialized in lesser-known figures. Pinker's advertisement stated: "Mr Pinker has always made a special point of helping young authors in the early stages of their career, when they need most the aid of an adviser with a thorough knowledge of the literary world and the publishing trade."[24] Pinker seems to have been successful in helping the young Wodehouse to expand his success.

Wodehouse had one of his few unpleasant publishing experiences with his first American agent. There the sale of *Love among the Chickens* was handled through A. E. Baerman, but Wodehouse's informal arrangements with him led to protracted problems about payment.[25] In

1909 Wodehouse took a trip to the United States, during which his second American agent, Seth Moyle, sold two stories, one to *Cosmopolitan* for $200 and one to *Collier's* for $300. This unprecedented success led Wodehouse to resign his job at *The Globe.*[26] He was moving out of journalism to concentrate on fiction magazines, and he was also to divide his time between the United States and England from this point on.[27]

A few years later, Wodehouse left Pinker to acquire a long-term British agent. He had collaborated with Dulwich classmate Herbert Westbrook on and off, most notably on the "By the Way" column and an autobiographical novel, *Not George Washington* (1907). Wodehouse and Westbrook also wrote a theatrical sketch in 1907, with music by Ella King-Hall. Westbrook and King-Hall married in 1909, and she became a literary agent. Wodehouse signed on as her client in 1912 and remained with her until her retirement in 1935.[28]

The period between 1909, when Wodehouse published *Mike,* the last of the school stories, and 1915, when he first had a serial accepted by the *Post,* can be seen as a polishing period. During these years he established professional habits that he would attempt to maintain throughout his life.

1915–1939: FAME AND FORTUNE

Wodehouse lived in America during most of the 1910s and enjoyed a considerable degree of stability in his working situation. During this period he created the series and the patterns of his mature work. In 1915, after having used a number of minor literary agents, he signed with Paul R. Reynolds, Sr., whose firm (later under his son, Paul R. Reynolds, Jr.) would represent him until 1947. Reynolds's first sale for Wodehouse was the serial *Something New* (British title, *Something Fresh*) to the *Post.*[29] In addition, in December of the same year, Wodehouse agreed to write lyrics for a Jerome Kern-Guy Bolton musical, *Miss Springtime.*[30] His collaboration with this team and others resulted in a series of musicals in the late teens and twenties that would keep him in the United States much of the time. Wodehouse's theatrical career was important in his life, especially during this period, but it is incidental to the Jeeves/Wooster series until after World War II. The Reynolds and *Post* connections were, however, crucial, for they coincided with Wodehouse's introduction of his two most famous series, both launched in America by the *Post* in 1915: *Something New* being the first Blandings novel (June 26–August 15) and "Extricating Young Gussie" (September 18) introducing Bertie and Jeeves.

The move to Paul R. Reynolds was a step up for Wodehouse. Reynolds, whose career began in 1891 and flourished during the boom in popular-magazine fiction, represented such authors as Robert Benchley, Willa Cather, F. Scott Fitzgerald, Sax Rohmer, George Bernard Shaw, Booth Tarkington, and H. G. Wells. He was the most successful agent for popular fiction, selling the *Post* nearly a quarter of all the fiction it published during the 1920s. Since the *Post* and similar magazines were giving the highest prices for fiction anywhere, some of Reynolds's clients must have numbered among the world's best-paid authors.[31] Remarkably, like Ella King-Hall, Reynolds agreed to a 5 percent commission rather than the standard 10 percent, since Wodehouse's clockwork output was so easy to handle.[32] Indeed, from 1915 to 1939, Wodehouse never received a rejection slip from the *Post.*[33] (He also published elsewhere—*McClure's, Cosmopolitan, Collier's,* and *Redbook*—presumably because his output was so high that no one magazine could handle it all.)

Wodehouse's association with the *Post* began at a favorable time. Lorimer had built up its circulation from 33,000 in 1898 to two million in 1913. Advertising revenues had risen from $8,000 in 1898 to $5 million in 1910; by the end of the 1920s, the advertising income was over $5 million annually—nearly 30 percent of the money spent on American magazine advertising.[34] Wodehouse's connection with the *Post* may also have helped him find a regular American book publisher, since George Doran was a friend of Lorimer's.

The George H. Doran Company had been founded in 1909 and published prominent British and American authors, including Hugh Walpole, Rebecca West, Mary Roberts Rinehart, Arnold Bennett, Irvin S. Cobb, and W. Somerset Maugham. In 1927 it merged with Doubleday, Page, the second largest American publishing firm. Doubleday had in 1925 founded a subsididary, Garden City Publishing Co., to bring out the firm's inexpensive reprint editions.[35] Wodehouse's first book with the George H. Doran Company was *A Damsel in Distress* (1919); with some exceptions, he remained with that firm (as Doubleday, Doran and later Doubleday & Company) until the publication of *Pigs Have Wings* (1952).

In Britain, *The Strand* had been carrying stories and serials by Wodehouse since 1905. There his book-publishing situation also changed in the late teens, and again the shift made his situation more regular and predictable. In 1917 he published *Piccadilly Jim* with the small private firm of Herbert Jenkins Ltd. Jenkins improved Wodehouse's British book sales considerably. While the earlier books' sales averaged around 2000 each, *Piccadilly Jim* sold 9000 in its first edition. As with Doubleday, Doran, one of Jenkins's tactics was to bring out the books' cheap editions himself and to keep reprinting them. Massive numbers of inexpensive copies were sold over the years. Anticipating the tactics of McDonald's fast-food chain, Jenkins listed the total number of each title printed to date, so that one may read, for example, on the copyright page of the 1934 twenty-first printing of *Piccadilly Jim* that it completes 236,000 copies. (Other publishers quickly followed this practice.) Each book went through several first-edition printings before appearing in a cheap edition. Herbert Jenkins died in the early 1920s, but the firm retained his name for decades.[36] It published most of Wodehouse's subsequent books in Britain. Thus during the second half of the teens, Wodehouse settled into a regular publishing routine that, despite a few shifts, was to last until 1940. This period from 1915 to 1939 saw the development of nearly all his major series. The only exception was the Psmith novels, of which three had already been published; one final entry in that series, *Leave It To Psmith*, was published in 1923.

The first among these actually to become a series was the Jeeves/Wooster saga. "Extricating Young Gussie" appeared in September of 1915, to be followed at intervals of a few months by five more stories. Then, aside from the publication of "Jeeves and the Chump Cyril" in mid–1918, there were no further Jeeves/Wooster stories until 1921–22; again, these appeared at a steady rate, sometimes as often as once a month. Thus the series follows the pattern Wodehouse employed during the 1920s, and to some degree into the 1930s. In general, his more broadly comic works were written as a series of stories, which would then be collected as a book. A few early collections brought together unrelated stories (for example, *The Man with Two Left Feet*, 1917). Increasingly, however, Wodehouse planned his books around a series situation or set of characters, as with the two golf collections (*The Clicking of Cuthbert*, 1922, and *The Heart of a Goof*, 1926) and later the Mulliner and Drones stories.[37] To minimize the lapse of time between the stories' initial magazine appearances and their collection in book form, Wodehouse concentrated on one series for a while: hence the periodic bursts of publication of Jeeves/Wooster stories.

He would certainly have been encouraged in this approach by the enormous success of his first Jeeves/Wooster collection, *Jeeves* (British title, *The Inimitable Jeeves*). It was one of only seven books that sold over a million copies in the United States from 1920 to 1929.[38] Given that it did not appear in the top ten fiction best-seller lists of any years, we must assume that it sold well mainly in its cheap edition. Still, as we shall see, *Jeeves* and the series that followed remained Wodehouse's most lucrative product.

Besides the short stories, Wodehouse wrote magazine serials that were reprinted as novels. These were usually romantic comedies without series characters, such as *Jill the Reckless* (1921) and *Big Money* (1931). *Something Fresh* belongs to this pattern, and here Wodehouse really seems not to have realized immediately that he could create a series. Even the second Blandings novel, *Leave It To Psmith* (1923), conforms to the romantic-comedy genre, since Psmith's courtship of Eve is the center of the narrative. Lord Emsworth really emerges as the central character of the series only with *Summer Lightning* (1929), the third Blandings book. Indeed, with this novel and *Thank You, Jeeves*, Wodehouse combined his two approaches, using his broad comic subjects as the basis for a serial rather than confining them to short stories. After the later 1920s, then, he had three major tactics rather than two; he could write clusters of comic stories, romantic serials, or comic serials. During the 1940 to 1947 period, when his magazine market disappeared, he wrote comic and romantic novels, but few stories; after 1947, when he had a much diminished magazine market, he wrote stories only occasionally. Of the fifty books Wodehouse published from 1910 to 1940, seventeen were collections of stories; of the thirty-four books completed thereafter, three were such collections.

That Wodehouse's writings reflect his magazine markets is not surprising. Although he published material in book form at every point in his career beyond the very earliest, his magazine markets changed considerably. Before World War II, magazine publication brought him more money and fame than it did later. In 1923 Wodehouse reported that the *Post* was paying $20,000 for the rights to his new serial (probably *Bill the Conqueror*). Paul R. Reynolds, Jr., recalled that in the late 1920s, Wodehouse was receiving around $40,000 for serial rights in a period when prices paid by the major fiction magazines ranged from $7500 to (rarely) $50,000. The Depression affected the market, and the *Post* declined in size as its advertising revenues dropped, but the reduction in serial and story fees was surprisingly small. In 1933 the *Post* paid $35,000 each for *Heavy Weather* and *Thank You, Jeeves.*[39] About this time, it was offering $4000 per story; Wodehouse had bids of $5000 to $6000 from other magazines but preferred to stay at the *Post.*

The fiction magazines' huge circulations guaranteed Wodehouse a large audience. His books, on the other hand, did not sell spectacularly well in their first editions. Predictably, the Depression hit book sales harder than it did the inexpensive fiction magazines. In 1933, Reynolds, Sr., contracted Wodehouse to Little, Brown, moving him temporarily from Doubleday, Doran. Little, Brown did not improve sales, and with *Young Men in Spats* (1936), Wodehouse returned to Doubleday, Doran. His book sales never reached high levels, demonstrating the degree to which Wodehouse was a product of the boom in fiction magazines. Reynolds summed up Wodehouse's situation in 1934:

> His books sell from 10,000 to 12,000 copies in the original edition and the same again in the cheap edition. His enormous popularity is of course mainly in the magazines rather than with the book buying public. He is one of the highest paid

> writers in the country, if not in the world. We were getting for him approximately $1.00 a word before the depression. We are now getting him from the magazines alone $5,000 for a 6,000 word short story; this is irrespective of book, syndicate, motion picture and foreign rights.[40]

The claim that Wodehouse was among the world's highest paid authors may well have been true. Sax Rohmer was getting $40,000 from *Collier's* for a Fu Manchu serial, and Wodehouse's *Post* fees reached this level by the late 1930s. The highest the *Post* had ever offered for serials was $60,000 to Mary Roberts Rinehart (in the teens and again in 1933) and to Booth Tarkington (in 1931). Even the less prestigious magazines paid Wodehouse well; in 1935 *Redbook* bought *The Luck of the Bodkins* for $28,000.[41]

The situation was similar in the United Kingdom, where the magazine sales were also more lucrative. In 1923, *The Strand* paid £1250 for the rights to a Wodehouse serial. A single short story in *The Strand* fetched £425 as of 1935, while a book advance from Jenkins was £800. The only major change in Wodehouse's English position came with the retirement of Ella King-Hall in 1935. Wodehouse went over to the oldest and most prestigious British literary agency, A. P. Watt; in the 1890s, Watt had represented such authors as Wilkie Collins, Arthur Conan Doyle, Rider Haggard, Thomas Hardy, Bret Harte, Rudyard Kipling, and William Butler Yeats. As with Wodehouse's other agencies, the firm agreed to a 5 percent commission.[42] Again it was to be a long-term relationship; the firm still represents the Wodehouse Estate.

The 1915 to 1939 period was certainly the height of Wodehouse's fame and earning power; some have argued, not without reason, that the years from about 1925 to the mid-1940s also saw his most consistently excellent writing. He was particularly prolific, publishing forty-five books in the twenty-six-year span from 1915 to 1940. During this time he was also deeply involved in the theater, working on the books and/or lyrics of thirty-three plays, mostly musicals.[43] Moreover, he twice worked as a Hollywood script writer, in 1930–31 and 1935–37. Apparently his regular publishing schedule allowed Wodehouse to work very efficiently.

During this period, Wodehouse traveled a great deal, dividing his time between the United States and England. He and his wife Ethel were fond of the resort towns of France as well. When, during the 1930s, Wodehouse was having tax troubles in the United States and England, he went to Le Touquet for an unusually long stay to establish a period of residency abroad. All this did not slow Wodehouse's output, but it helped cause an event that was to change his life significantly. In 1934, shortly after arriving for a two-year stay in Le Touquet, the Wodehouses bought a house there; six years later they would be in residence when the Germans occupied the town.

The event that caps this period in which his fame was at its height occurred on June 21, 1939, when Oxford University awarded Wodehouse an honorary doctorate of letters. The honor seems to have puzzled Wodehouse as much as anyone, and there was some controversy over whether it was deserved. (Some suggested that the whole thing was a joke.) Perhaps the award signaled a dawning academic appreciation of Wodehouse's work—but if so, it came too late. About a month later, Wodehouse returned to France. (His last visit to England occurred later that year, when he briefly came back to attend a cricket match at Dulwich.) The scandal over the Berlin broadcasts overshadowed Oxford's gesture.

1940–1947: THE WAR AND ITS AFTERMATH

Accounts of Wodehouse's career have typically turned a great deal of attention to his capture and internment by the Germans in 1940 and the scandal that erupted after his Berlin broadcasts of 1941. Even today there are people who know Wodehouse's name only through the association of his supposed collaboration with the Nazis. By now, however, the belated release of secret official documents and the diligence of biographers have provided strong evidence that Wodehouse was guilty of no more than bad judgment in doing five comic radio programs in Germany. While his internment and the broadcasts scandal posed great personal problems for Wodehouse, their immediate impact on his writing output was surprisingly small.[44] It was not until

1947, when Wodehouse moved to the United States, that he discovered how strong the prejudice against him was and how much it was affecting his career.

Wodehouse and his wife tried unsuccessfully to leave Le Touquet on May 20, 1940, but they were still in residence when the Germans occupied the town on May 22. As a result, Wodehouse was rounded up along with all French and foreign males under the age of sixty. They were shipped out of France to prevent their fighting for the Allies. Wodehouse went through a series of internment camps, the last and longest period being in a camp in Upper Silesia.

On June 21, 1941, Wodehouse was unexpectedly released from the camp. He would have been released officially on October 15, his sixtieth birthday. As Frances Donaldson points out, the reasons behind the early release are not entirely clear.[45] Wodehouse's friends and associates had been sending letters and petitions trying to pressure the Germans into letting him go. Since the United States was not yet in the war, German officials may have given in to this pressure. Possibly, however, they released Wodehouse in order to get him to broadcast for them, an action that would have some propaganda value. No evidence suggests that Wodehouse agreed to broadcast as a condition of his freedom. Whatever the cause of his release, the Germans kept him on a short leash. He was assigned to stay at the luxurious Hotel Adlon in Berlin, at his own expense. According to his later accounts, he and Ethel lived partly by selling her jewelry, partly through loans from friends, and perhaps from the numerous translations of his works being published in countries that still had diplomatic relations with Germany.

The internment might have had little effect on Wodehouse's career had he not done the broadcasts. On June 21, the day of his release, Wodehouse was visited by Werner Plack, a friend from the periods in Hollywood who had returned to Germany when the war broke out. He proposed that Wodehouse do a series of broadcasts to America. Wodehouse agreed and did five weekly programs (June 28 to August 6, 1941, all monitored and transcribed by the BBC). They described his experiences from arrest to release, all in a comic tone. He wrote them himself, apparently without censorship.

Wodehouse always explained his agreement to do the talks as stemming from a desire to respond to friends in America who had sent him letters and packages and to whom he had not hitherto been allowed to reply. Indeed, the last broadcast ended with a thank you for this correspondence. Nevertheless, the act of broadcasting over German air waves was technically a violation of British law. Moreover, the broadcasts became a subject of attack and debate. The first and most damaging assault came on July 15, when the BBC broadcast a denunciation of Wodehouse as a Nazi sympathizer. The official behind the attack was Minister of Information Duff Cooper, who seems to have considered Wodehouse guilty of treason.[46] The denunciation, which was riddled with errors, led to lengthy debates in the press. A similar debate raged in the United States, where many newspapers and journals depicted Wodehouse as a Nazi sympathizer.

Wodehouse quickly realized that the broadcasts had been a mistake, but there was little he could do to change public opinion as long as he was under German control. By September of 1943 Berlin was being bombed, and officials there let the Wodehouses go to Paris. From that point until their move to America, the couple lived in Parisian hotels and apartments. During 1943 and 1944 the British Government carried on an investigation, under Major Edward Cussen, to determine whether there was any basis for trying Wodehouse for treason or some lesser offense. The Cussen Report (September 28, 1944) cleared Wodehouse, but it was not made public until 1980. Inquiries by Thelma Cazalet-Keir (a member of Parliament and the sister of Wodehouse's son-in-law) failed to elicit any official assurance that Wodehouse would not be tried if he returned to England. He never did.

The question of Wodehouse's political stance remains. Was he a Nazi sympathizer, or anti-Semitic? Most modern accounts defending him stressed his naiveté, assuming that he was a dupe who did not understand what the Nazis stood for. A discussion of these points is in order, since many people seem to believe the old rumors.

The available evidence suggests that Wodehouse made the broadcasts in the belief that he was simply doing a job of writing and trying to contact friends and fans in the United States. Both public statements and private correspondence show that he regretted the decision once he realized its implications. His behavior does not mean, however, that he was totally naive and unworldly; there are indications that he knew something about National Socialism and its goals. There is also evidence that he was not anti-Semitic.

Several writers on Wodehouse have pointed to a passage in *The Code of the Woosters* to show that Wodehouse was satirizing fascism well before his internment. The villain, Roderick Spode, is based on Sir Oswald Mosley, organizer of the British Union of Fascists. (Coincidentally, Mosley was also interned—by the British—in 1940.) Bertie's memorable denunciation of Spode and his Black Shorts party may indicate Wodehouse's attitude:

> "It is about time," I proceeded, "that some public-spirited person came along and told you where you got off. The trouble with you, Spode, is that just because you have succeeded in inducing a handful of nit-wits to disfigure the London scene by going about in black shorts, you think you're someone. You hear them shouting 'Heil, Spode!' and you imagine it is the Voice of the People. That is where you make your bloomer. What the Voice of the People is saying is: 'Look at that frightful ass Spode swanking about in footer bags! Did you ever in your puff see such a perfect perisher?' " (Chap. 7)

An oblique 1938 denunciation of a British fascist is not enough, of course, to show that Wodehouse understood the situation in Germany (though the phrase "Heil, Spode" suggests that he recognized the link between Mosley and the Nazis). There is, however, a more specific satire on Hitler and his advisors, published by Wodehouse in *Punch* in late 1939. The premise is that the author is reporting a meeting at the Wilhelmstrasse:

> The front office was full, as any room would be that contained Field-Marshal Goering. I noticed several groups, all torn by dissension. I joined a couple of Generals who were chatting in low voices by the umbrella-stand.
>
> "Don't seem to get us anywhere, these conferences," one was saying. "Just a waste of time."
>
> "It's those bright ideas of our beloved Leader's that hang

> things up," assented the other. "I do sometimes wish he would leave military affairs to the military."
>
> At this moment the umbrella-stand moved from its place and arrested the two speakers. The Gestapo never sleeps and Himmler is a master of disguise. A few minutes later the Fuehrer bustled in.
>
> "Well, here we all are," he said. "Now, about getting this war started. Anybody any suggestions?"
>
> "I was thinking—" said Ribbentrop.
>
> "What with?" said Goering, who had a great gift for repartee.
>
> "Now, boys, boys," said the Fuehrer indulgently. "Cut out the cracks. We're all working for the good of the show. Here's a thought that crossed my mind as I was coming here. Let's destroy Britain."[47]

Hardly devastating material, yet it indicates that Wodehouse knew the major players in the Nazi hierarchy and deplored their militarism. Later, when he agreed to do the broadcasts, he probably did not realize that they had any connection to the Nazi political system.

No charge of anti-Semitism would presumably ever have been leveled against Wodehouse had it not been for the broadcasts scandal. Again, the evidence is in his favor. Robert Hall has argued that Wodehouse was considerably less anti-Jewish than most of his contemporaries among Edwardian authors. A few of Wodehouse's characters have Jewish names and are in professions stereotypically associated with Jews, but they are not treated in derogatory ways.[48] The Cohen Brothers provide an obvious example of what Hall is talking about. Dealers in secondhand clothing, they appear in several stories, displaying an astonishing ability to provide the characters with whatever bizarre outfits the exigencies of the plot demand. In *Joy in the Morning* they supply Boko and Bertie with costumes. In an extended scene at the Cohen Brothers' emporium in "The Ordeal of Osbert Mulliner," the dialogue bears no hint of vaudeville-stage Jewish dialect or other ethnic humor. David Cannadine compares Wodehouse to two authors of his generation, Sir Henry John Newbolt and John Buchan, both of whom also grew up with the "playing-field morality":

> Wodehouse's work, both early and mature, lacked the moralizing tone of Newbolt's and was not disfigured by the anti-Semitism which makes Buchan such embarrassing reading today. Nor is the exultation of war, the love of success, or the glorification of Empire to be found in his books.[49]

Indeed, there is no evidence of anti-Semitism in Wodehouse's works or private life.

Moreover, his extensive work in the musical theater brought him into close association with talented Jewish musicians relatively early in his life—most notably Jerome Kern and the Gershwins—and there is no hint that his love for this aspect of his career was tainted by prejudice. He was, for example, a close friend of Ira Gershwin while living in Hollywood.[50] Later on, a letter to Townend during the Exodus affair of 1947 indicates that he felt the British Government had acted wrongly:

> Aren't the Jews extraordinary people. They seem to infuriate all nations, as nations, and yet almost every individual has a number of Jewish friends. I was totting up the other day and found that, apart from my real inner circle of friends (numbering about three) most of the men I like best are Jews—e.g., Scott Meredith, Ira Gershwin, Molnar, Oscar Hammerstein, Irving Berlin . . . and a lot more. But, my gosh, what idiots the British government are. At the very moment when it is vital to have good relations with America they go and pull that Exodus stuff and club Jews and put them behind barbed wire and so forth. I should have thought it would have been infinitely better to let the poor devils into Palestine. That trouble at Hamburg has simply played into the hands of the anti-English here. But officials in every country are always dumb bricks.[51]

None of his writings suggests that Wodehouse participated in the Berlin broadcasts because of Nazi sympathies or anti-Semitic beliefs.

The turmoil surrounding the broadcasts initially had remarkably little effect on Wodehouse's writing. He was working on *Joy in the Morn-*

ing when he was captured but was unable to take the manuscript with him into the camps. He did, however, manage to get paper and rent a typewriter; he wrote all of *Money in the Bank* while interned. When Ethel joined him in late July 1941, she brought the *Joy in the Morning* manuscript, and Wodehouse finished it in Berlin. Apparently she also either brought his books and files of notes with her or had them shipped.[52] With this material available, Wodehouse continued to write on a regular schedule. He finished six novels between 1940 and 1947, though only one was actually published during the war. (See accompanying chart.)

DATES OF WODEHOUSE'S WARTIME WRITINGS

TITLE	PERIOD WRITTEN	DATE PUBLISHED (US/UK)
Money in the Bank	1940	1942/1946
Joy in the Morning	1940–41	1946/1947
Full Moon	1942	1947/1947
Spring Fever	1943	1948/1948
Uncle Dynamite	ca. 1944–45	1948/1948
The Mating Season	1942, 1946–47	1949/1949

SOURCES: David A. Jasen, *P. G. Wodehouse: A Portrait of a Master* (rev. ed., New York: Continuum, 1981), pp. 179, 183–84; "P. G. Wodehouse's Statement to Major E. J. P. Cussen," reprinted in Ian Sproat, *Wodehouse at War* (New Haven: Ticknor & Fields, 1981), p. 193; letters, Wodehouse (Paris) to Sheran Cazalet, 27 March 1946 and 27 March 1947; Wodehouse (New York) to Benoit de Fonscolombe, 28 Nov. 1947; Wodehouse (Paris) to Jack Donaldson, 17 Aug. 1945, Wodehouse Archives.

Despite the controversies and the interruption in Wodehouse's publishing schedule, there were no upheavals in his professional relationships with his agents and book publishers. Throughout, A. P. Watt remained his British agency; although Paul R. Reynolds, Sr., died in 1944, his son carried on the business. When regular publication of his novels resumed in 1946, they were issued by his prewar presses, Doubleday, Doran and Herbert Jenkins. Apparently because of the scandals, both presses were reluctant to publish Wodehouse during the war; the only new novel to appear between 1940 and 1946 was the American edition of *Money in the Bank* (1942, Doubleday, Doran). Jenkins kept the cheap editions of his earlier books in print, devoting much of its paper ration to them.[53]

After the war, the English edition of *Money in the Bank* and both editions of *Joy in the Morning* sold unusually well, perhaps because no new Wodehouse book had appeared in years. Their high sales, combined with the favorable reviews that greeted them, bolstered Wodehouse's confidence. Hearing that a BBC radio reviewer had lauded *Money in the Bank,* Wodehouse wrote to him:

> You can probably imagine how I felt when I heard of your talk, for it was not without diffidence that I agreed to the publication of the book. I saw myself rather in the position of a red-nosed comedian who has got the bird at the first house on Monday and is having the temerity to go on and do his stuff at the second house, outwardly breezy and cheerful but feeling inside as if he had swallowed a heaping teaspoonful of butterflies and with a wary eye out for demonstrations from the gallery. And now comes this applause from the stalls, thank God! Bless you.[54]

The New York Times Book Review praised *Joy in the Morning* and Wodehouse elatedly sent Townend a copy: "Terrific, isn't it? The one paper that matters is the New York Times."[55]

In contrast to his ongoing relationships with agents and publishers, Wodehouse faced a reversal in his dealings with the fiction magazines. No short stories of his appeared between late 1940 and mid-1947. One nonfiction piece, "My War With Germany," appeared in the *Post* just as the broadcasts were being made (July 19, 194l); like them, it was a humorous account of camp life.

Wodehouse had run out of luck in tying his writing to the *Post*'s fortunes. In 1941 the magazine was deep in a slump that had begun with the Depression. Profits had fallen steadily, from $24.2 million in 1929 to $902,470 in 1942. After Lorimer's 1936 retirement, editor Wesley Stout failed to solve the *Post*'s problems. Issues shrank, and the price went from five to ten cents in 1942. Stout was also responsible for publishing a controversial article, "The Case Against the Jew"

(March 28, 1942), that cost the *Post* subscriptions and advertising revenues.[56] This was the sticky situation into which Ben Hibbs stepped when he replaced Stout as editor on March 15, 1942. Hibbs is generally credited with turning the *Post* around: reviving its Lorimer-period respectability, raising subscriptions, increasing advertising revenue. He began to downplay fiction, emphasizing war reportage and other nonfiction instead. During his two decades as editor (ending in 1961), circulation doubled, from 3.3 million to 6.5 million, and advertising revenue more than quadrupled, from $23 million to $104 million a year.[57] Few would claim, however, that the literary quality of the *Post* at any point after Lorimer left was up to that of the 1920s and early 1930s.

It seems likely that the controversy surrounding "The Case Against the Jew" made Hibbs shy away from Wodehouse's work. He might have perceived "My War With Germany," with its humorous, tolerant treatment of the guards in the internment camp, as another profascist statement. The controversy over the broadcasts, however, was undoubtedly the main reason that Wodehouse was blackballed by the *Post* and many other magazines for years. The scandal and this ostracism by the magazines affected his book publication, if not their writing, as well. In 1944 Paul R. Reynolds, Jr., wrote to him: "We did not give your novels to Doubleday to publish as a book because we questioned if it was an opportune time to have them published and we didn't like to kill any chance of a serial sale by having them in book form."[58]

The Strand's situation was somewhat comparable to that of the *Post*. It still had a high reputation but had not made significant profits since the early 1930s; during the war, paper rationing forced a price rise and a size reduction. Circulation continued to drop, and few submissions came in, as the American fiction magazines could pay more. In an attempt to revive the magazine, Reginald Pound was made editor. Pound has claimed that Wodehouse did not submit his stories to *The Strand* because of the reduced format:

> Occasionally readers asked why we had no more stories from him. I was glad not to have to make that editorial decision, for I was never able to read Wodehouse's stories or to under-

> stand the ecstacy they roused in others. Their appeal to pre-war readers of *The Strand* was apparently irresistible. I could only see it as a phenomenon of extended immaturity, an effect of the more enclosed forms of English education.[59]

It may be, however, that Wodehouse, always sensitive to agents' and editors' attitudes, avoided *The Strand*. His lengthy association with it had already come to an end with "Bramley Is So Bracing" in the December 1940 issue. He never published there again.

The British Government's refusal to assure Wodehouse's safety from prosecution should he return to England made it apparent that his future lay in America. For one thing, Wodehouse longed to return to the theater, and, with London closed to him, he planned to revive his Broadway career. On May 13, 1946, he applied at the United States Embassy in Paris for a visa and received it by mid-July.[60] He planned to go to the United States in October to work on a revival of *Leave It to Psmith* (first dramatized 1929); as a prospective production was delayed, however, he and Ethel stayed in France. Wodehouse finished *The Mating Season*, which he had worked on at intervals since 1942. The couple finally went to America in April of 1947, Wodehouse having been commissioned to adapt Molnar's play, *Arthur*.[61] His problems resulting from the Berlin broadcasts, however, were far from over.

1947–1951: POSTWAR UNCERTAINTIES

During these years the aftermath of the wartime scandal profoundly altered Wodehouse's professional life. Observing the American literary market firsthand, he realized that the fiction magazines were declining and that the prejudice against him among editors was widespread. Similarly, as he again attended Broadway plays and dealt with theatrical producers, he recognized that the conditions under which he had achieved his first successes had altered radically. Political and cultural changes also convinced him that fantasies of English country life would no longer interest readers. The result was a brief crisis in his career.

If we recall that *The Mating Season* was finished in early 1947 and then note that *The Old Reliable* was not written until 1950, we can see an unprecedented gap for an author who had written at least one book a year for decades. The only other book published during this period, *Nothing Serious* (1950), was a collection of ten stories from various sources.[62] Thus Wodehouse was, at least on the face of it, less prolific in this period than at any point since he started writing professionally. He actually spent much of his energy working on plays, in a vain effort to revive his theatrical career. He also made one substantial alteration in his professional relations.

Shortly after his return to the United States, Wodehouse changed his American agent, an action that was to have a major impact on his publishing circumstances for the rest of his life. Paul R. Reynolds, Jr., recalled an incident from the late 1930s:

> Wodehouse was one of the highest paid writers in the United States but he never understood the business side of his writing or the function of the agent. In 1939 the *Saturday Evening Post* offered $45,000 for a Wodehouse serial, the same price as they had previously paid. I went on to Philadelphia and told Wesley Stout, the editor of the *Post*, that if he could not pay $50,000 we would have to approach other magazines. Stout agreed to this price. When I told Wodehouse he was delighted at what he called the *Post*'s generosity. When I told him of my statement to Stout that it was to be $50,000 or we would go elsewhere, Wodehouse reproved me. He said he would not think of leaving such a generous magazine, and that my father would not have acted that way. Wodehouse adored my father and always did what my father wanted. I was a new personality whom he did not like.[63]

This is the only suggestion Reynolds gives as to why Wodehouse might have wanted to leave the agency after the elder Reynolds' death in 1944.

It is possible that Reynolds, Jr.,'s reaction to the broadcasts scandal inadvertently alienated Wodehouse. During the broadcasts the agency cabled Wodehouse to stop doing them, but he cabled back that he had to fulfill his contract for five radio talks. Reynolds concluded:

> I have often wondered if we could have done something to mute the damage that Wodehouse did to himself. This country was still neutral and perhaps we should have tried to go to Germany and talk to him. Perhaps we should have hired a public relations firm to try and counter the hostile press.[64]

Reynolds does not mention the break with Wodehouse in 1947, but the latter's new agent, Scott Meredith, né Feldman, *had* taken the tactic of "countering the hostile press"—not by hiring a public relations firm but by working, even before becoming Wodehouse's agent, to present the author in a better light.

Feldman had been an author before the war, writing mostly for the pulps, though he sold some material to magazines like the *Post* and *McCall's*. He recalls his fiction as being mostly imitations of Wodehouse. At one point before the war, Wodehouse wrote to compliment him on his work. The two had a brief correspondence that was broken off by the war. Feldman went into the military in 1943. In 1944, after he reestablished contact with Wodehouse, he started a campaign of letters to magazines and newspapers designed to clear Wodehouse's name. This aggressive approach contrasted considerably with the attitudes of Wodehouse's American and British agents and publishers, who advised him to keep a low profile and wait for the effects of the scandal to blow over. Wodehouse's correspondence suggests that he favored public explanations as a way of clearing the air. Hence his own attitude was closer to Feldman's, but he went along with the wait-and-see approach for a few years.

Shortly after Feldman got out of the service, he became an agent, renting a tiny set of offices and using the name Scott Meredith. By this time Wodehouse was in the States, but Meredith did not invite Wodehouse to become a client, partly because he was ashamed of his small operation and partly because he did not want Wodehouse to think that he was using their friendship to pressure him.[65]

In 1947, as Meredith was getting established, Harold Ober, a partner in the Reynolds firm, left to form his own agency. Wodehouse had promised Ober that if Ober ever left Reynolds, he would come over to Ober as a client, and he did so. Ober's first assignment was to place two stories. Both were turned down by *Cosmopolitan*, and Ober sent Wodehouse the rejections slip with an unfriendly letter suggesting that perhaps Wodehouse should consider retiring. Wodehouse took the letter to Meredith, who read the two stories that evening (which he dates as May 16) and resubmitted them to a different editor at *Cosmopolitan*. They were accepted immediately, and Meredith had a check for Wodehouse on May 18. Wodehouse became Meredith's client, and Scott Meredith, Inc., still represents his estate.

Meredith also pursued his campaign to restore Wodehouse's reputation. In 1949 Pocket Books issued *The Best of Wodehouse*, edited by Meredith; his introduction was an appreciation and brief career sketch that ignored the wartime period. Meredith also says he called and met with magazine editors to clear up misconceptions about the Berlin broadcasts. Despite these efforts, the rehabilitation process moved slowly. Only seven short stories were published from 1947 to 1951, and these appeared only in American and Canadian publications. No Wodehouse short story appeared in a British magazine until 1957.

The delayed return to regular magazine publishing seems to have affected Wodehouse's writing in a way that wartime events never had. His letters indicate a slowing in his fiction writing and an increasing hope that some of his theatrical projects would find producers. In late 1947 he wrote to his French translator:

> My affairs are moving slowly, as I expected them to do at first. I have sold a couple of short stories, but I doubt if I shall make much out of the magazines, as their whole policy seems to have changed. They now want heavy, serious stuff about life in the swamps of Carolina and that sort of thing and won't look at my English dudes! But I'm not worrying about that as I think I can get along quite well without the magazines. Nothing has happened yet about the various plays which I have worked on, but something is sure to come off soon or late, and meanwhile I have a very lively proposition, to wit a revival of a famous musical comedy of 1921 called Sally, for which I have written a new set of lyrics.[66]

Several months later, he told Townend that a revival of *The Play's the Thing* (1926) was in rehearsal and would soon open in New Haven. The revival of *Sally* (1920) had also been cast.[67]

Wodehouse's theatrical career did show some signs of resuscitation in 1948. *The Play's the Thing* ran for 244 performances in New York; a new play by Guy Bolton and Wodehouse, *Don't Listen, Ladies* opened in London in September and ran 219 performances. The latter, however, was to be the last new Wodehouse play to open in New York or London during his lifetime; moreover, *Sally* ran only thirty-six performances in New York. By mid-1949, prospects in the theatrical world had faded. Writing to Townend, Wodehouse told of being hired to doctor a thriller play to make it funny, like *Arsenic and Old Lace*: "It's very pleasant working for a firm that appreciates one's stuff."[68] Still, being a script doctor was a far cry from the glamorous career as a playwright and lyricist that he hoped to revive.

Wodehouse also realized that the Broadway theater had changed considerably since he had worked in it. In 1947 he wrote:

> Another thing which is rather preying on my nerves is the theatrical situation. I miss the old-time manager, who seems to have completely disappeared. In the old days I would pop in on Flo Ziegfeld and find that he wanted lyrics for a new show, and then call on Dillingham and get a contract for a musical comedy, but that's all over now. As far as I can make out, you have to write your show and then go about trying to interest people with money in it.[69]

Nevertheless, he remained keen on playwriting, and the "lull" of the late forties in his publishing is explained largely by his concentration on the theater. Despite the two successes noted earlier, most of his projects remained unproduced. Wodehouse never adapted to the new theatrical situations in New York and London. He had no regular theatrical agent, preferring that he or Bolton negotiate with producers.

One play project from this period relates directly to the Jeeves/Wooster series. It is the one in which Wodehouse persisted the longest and which ultimately led him back into writing novels. This project involved a series of adaptations of his novel *Spring Fever*. One of the many versions transformed the lead character, an English butler, into Jeeves; the novelization of another version became *The Old Reliable*, with the Jeeves-like Phipps as the main character.

Wodehouse wrote the novel *Spring Fever* in 1943, and he began turning it into a play in 1945, while living in Paris.[70] The play went through numerous drafts, some set in England, others in America. By 1949, the fourth version centered around a butler: "It is practically a play about Jeeves, though I give him another name."[71] At various intervals, George Abbott and Milton Shubert expressed interest in producing it.[72] Beginning in 1949, Wodehouse turned the play into *The Old Reliable*, but he also kept rewriting the script. He entered into tangled negotiations for either Edward Everett Horton or Joe E. Brown to play the role of the butler. After Horton did a read-through of the ninth version, Wodehouse reported: "They want me to make the butler Jeeves!"[73] He abandoned other work to rewrite yet again, and I shall refer to the play's tenth draft as the "Jeeves version" of *Spring Fever*.[74] Though Wodehouse nursed the project along, by January of 1952 he reported that the Horton deal was off.[75] He and Bolton then went after Joe E. Brown, rewriting the play several times as *Phipps* and *Kilroy Was Here*. It was apparent by 1953 that the new negotiations were fruitless, and the play on which Wodehouse had worked for eight years was abandoned.[76]

Wodehouse also tried another approach to creating a Jeeves play. In April of 1950 he wrote to Bolton: "I think the idea of the play is terrific. Do get going on it as soon as you can and send me a rough scenario so that I can perhaps add stuff. . . . I think your bookie idea is wonderful."[77] In the summer of 1952, Wodehouse and Bolton finally got together on Long Island to write *Come On, Jeeves*. By mid-July the play was finished, and Wodehouse immediately rewrote it as a novel. In March of 1953, *Ring For Jeeves* was in press, but negotiations for a production of *Come On, Jeeves* dragged on. By early 1955, Wodehouse reported that it was slated for a three-week run at the Liverpool Repertory, that the BBC had plans to produce it, and that "a tour is being arranged." He had hopes of a London presentation. In fact, the only staging of *Come On, Jeeves* during Wodehouse's lifetime was a provincial one, at the Guilford Theatre, June 20–25, 1955. Wodehouse hoped that some discerning London producer would be in the audience, but no such "angel" appeared. A British publisher brought out *Come On, Jeeves* in 1956, and Wodehouse continued to hope for a production, as references in his letters indicate.[78]

The play was Wodehouse's last serious attempt during the immediate postwar era to return to the theater.

The use of an English butler in *Spring Fever*, added to the strange separation of Jeeves from Bertie in *Come On, Jeeves*, offer another aspect of Wodehouse's postwar crisis. Significant political and cultural changes led him to doubt whether his prewar subject matter would still be acceptable to readers. As early as mid-1945 he expressed worries about the future:

> My trouble is that I already have five novels waiting to be published in England, so that any thing I write now will presumably appear around 1950, and I find it very hard to imagine what the world will be like then. I mean, it seems a waste of time to write about butlers and country houses if both are obsolete, as I suppose they will be. I can't see what future there is for Blandings Castle, and I doubt if Bertie Wooster will be able to afford a personal attendant with the income tax at ten shillings in the pound. It looks to me as if the only one of my characters who will be able to carry on is Ukridge.[79]

Wodehouse followed political changes in England. Cazalet-Keir lost her Conservative parliamentary seat in the 1945 elections, and Wodehouse's letters deplored the formation of the "welfare state." The notion of the gentry impoverished by heavy property and income taxes became an important concern. In late 1949 Townend wrote that

> England is full of old castles that are either empty save for two or three rooms occupied by the family or else have been taken over by the state as homes or institutions or hospitals . . . either that or they are falling into ruins. Most owners of these huge mansions are trying to sell and can't. Nobody can afford to keep them up.[80]

Only a few months later, Bolton sent Wodehouse the idea of an impoverished peer becoming a bookie, and a "white elephant" ancestral home became central to *Come On, Jeeves* and *Ring for Jeeves*.

Wodehouse tried to solve the problem of postwar subject matter in two ways. First, since the British upper classes seemed to be on the way out, he took to using American settings. Second, since Jeeves was his most popular and lucrative character, Wodehouse sought to place him in a more plausible postwar situation. Pursuing the first strategy, Wodehouse set the first two novels he wrote after the war (*The Old Reliable*, published in book form in 1951, and *Barmy in Wonderland*, 1952) in the United States. The one place he could conceive where people could still afford English butlers was that bastion of the nouveau riche, Hollywood. In 1948, he shifted the action of his *Spring Fever* play to Beverly Hills, with a story in which a silent movie queen employs an English butler; this later became *The Old Reliable*. *Barmy in Wonderland* returned to the milieu of the New York theater, which had formed the setting for *Jill the Reckless*.

Wodehouse's second strategy sought to maintain Jeeves as a viable character. If a rich wastrel like Bertie could no longer afford Jeeves, Wodehouse seems to have reasoned, then he would have to jettison Bertie. The years 1947 to 1951 contain two attempts to place Jeeves in a more plausible situation: the "Jeeves version" of *Spring Fever*, where Jeeves becomes a Beverly Hills butler, and *Ring for Jeeves*, where he goes to work, again as a butler, for an impoverished nobleman with a crumbling, expensive family home.

Wodehouse's desire to find plausible postwar subject matter seems to have lasted throughout the crisis in his career. Once his situation began to stabilize in 1950, he returned to his more accustomed situations. According to Scott Meredith, the prejudice against Wodehouse among magazine editors eased considerably during 1951, and after 1960, the effects of the scandal were virtually undetectable. Meredith considers the main breakthrough in the rehabilitation of Wodehouse's career to be when *Collier's* became the first major fiction magazine to accept one of his serials after the war. On May 6, 1950, Wodehouse wrote to Townend that Meredith had just sold *The Old Reliable* to *Collier's*. The bad news, Meredith had told Wodehouse, was that he had only obtained a $20,000 fee—half what Wodehouse got in the 1930s: "Well, you can imagine the promptness with which I accepted. Apart from the fact that $20,000 is a lot of money, the price didn't really matter. The important thing was to get a serial into a big magazine."[81]

His rising fortunes seem to have helped dispel Wodehouse's doubts about subject matter. In 1951 he told a friend: I absolutely agree with what you say about setting my stories in England, and I am going to do so from now on, though I think it will make the stories unsalable to the magazines over here. I don't feel at home with an American setting."[82] Soon he was at work on a Blandings novel, *Pigs Have Wings,* and shortly after that he brought back Bertie.

Wodehouse sought to cover over his period of uncertainty. While planning *Performing Flea,* he wrote to Townend:

> The two things I want to avoid are (a) the slightest hint that I was ever anxious or alarmed or wondering if I have lost my public and (b) any suggestion that your books have not done so well lately as the earlier ones did.
>
> As regards (a), I naturally poured out my hopes and fears to you, but I don't want the public to know that I ever had a doubt about my future. I want my attitude to be a rather amused aloofness, like Bernard Shaw's when he was attacked so bitterly in the first war. You know what I mean. "Very silly, all this fuss and indignation, but they can't expect an intelligent man to take it seriously."[83]

The idea that Wodehouse bounced back quickly after the wartime scandal passed into his public image. Still, a revealing moment in a television interview for the BBC in 1971 (when he was ninety) suggests how much it had affected him:

> INTERVIEWER: But the climate of opinion about you changed pretty quickly after the war, even before the end of the war, didn't it—I mean . . .
> WODEHOUSE: *Did* it, do you think?
> INTERVIEWER: Don't *you*?
> WODEHOUSE: Oh, I thought it took some time.[84]

The wistful tone in which he says the last line speaks volumes.

1952–1975: SECURITY

In 1953, *Bring on the Girls*, Wodehouse's and Bolton's collaborative theatrical memoirs, was published by Simon and Schuster. From that point until 1975, Simon and Schuster brought out about one Wodehouse book a year. Herbert Jenkins Ltd. continued to publish his books in England. Despite the decline of the magazine market, the ease of his relations with his agents and book editors helped place Wodehouse in a congenial situation in his old age.

Simon and Schuster had begun as a small press in 1924. Its initial success came with *The Crossword Puzzle Book*—the first book of this type ever published—a few months later. The firm gained respectability in 1926 by signing Will Durant to write *The Story of Philosophy*. From 1927 on it also aquired a reputation for publishing humor, with titles like Frank Scully's *Fun in Bed*, Eddy Cantor's *Caught Short*, Bob Hope's *I Never Left Home*, Bennett Cerf's *Try and Stop Me*, Shepherd Mead's *How to Succeed in Business without Really Trying*, Eric Hodgins' *Mr. Blandings Builds His Dream House*, and cartoon books by Peter Arno, Charles Addams, Al Capp, H. T. Webster, and Walt Kelly. Scott Meredith knew Simon and Schuster's strength in this area, and he succeeded in placing Wodehouse's books there.[85] Wodehouse's editor, Peter Schwed, had started work at Simon and Schuster in 1945. In 1944, Richard Simon and Max Schuster had sold the firm to Marshall Field, but they stayed on as managers. Field, a bibliophile, interfered little in the firm's workings and was content with a small profit. After his death in 1957, Simon and Schuster was sold back to the original partners, but when Wodehouse first went there, the laissez-faire, low-profit policy of the Field era was in effect.[86] Schwed knew Scott Meredith and, like Meredith, was already a Wodehouse fan. Meredith, Schwed, and Wodehouse became close friends.[87]

Such congenial circumstances were important for Wodehouse, since his books sold so few copies that many publishing houses would probably have been unwilling to keep him on. There is, I think, a general assumption that so famous an author as Wodehouse must have enjoyed high book sales, but this was seldom the case during this period. Each cloth edition usually sold at least 10,000 copies during the early

1950s, and by late in Wodehouse's life the average was closer to 15,000. The insignificance of such sales can be gauged by the fact that another comic series Schwed edited during the same period, Walt Kelly's *Pogo* books, sold around half a million copies each. Similarly, although *Jeeves* (the American title of *The Inimitable Jeeves*) sold over two million in the Pocket Books edition (published in 1939 and reprinted dozens of times), subsequent Wodehouse titles sold far fewer copies in paperback. Wodehouse's books of the 1950s, 1960s, and 1970s did not always come out in paper in the United States.[88] The phenomenon of the cheap hardback printing had shifted into book clubs, which were not a factor for Wodehouse.

Simon and Schuster's cost schedules reveal how small the income generated from Wodehouse's books was. The "Proposal to Publish" form for *The Ice in the Bedroom* (1961) suggests a first run of 10,000 copies. The book was to retail at $3.50, with a profit per copy of $0.315. If no further printings were done, the profits would be under $3,150 (assuming that some review copies were distributed). A similar form on *Stiff Upper Lip, Jeeves* (1962) shows a lower income yet. The book's first run was to be 8,500, with a cover price of $3.75. With estimated net sales of $17,220, costs of $14,860, and fixed costs of $2,320, the profit on the first printing would be a mere $40. Presumably such a low print run would enable a second printing; still, given that total hardback sales at this point were only a bit above 10,000, the total profit must still have been small. Wodehouse's royalties were 15 per cent; assuming that this is on the cover price, his total royalties per title would be somewhere between $5,625 (on sales of 10,000) and $8,438 (on 15,000).[89]

Schwed considers that he was largely responsible for Wodehouse's lengthy stay at Simon and Schuster. During this period, major changes occurred in the firm. At Simon's death in 1960, Schuster and Leon Shimkin bought his shares, and in 1966 Shimkin bought Schuster out, completely controlling the firm, which absorbed Pocket Books to become Simon & Schuster, Inc. Coincidentally, in the same year that Wodehouse died, 1975, Gulf & Western bought Simon & Schuster. At that point the firm's sales volume was about $44,000,000; by 1983 it had reached $210,000,000, According to Schwed, since 1975, Simon

& Schuster has become much more "bottom-line conscious" and would probably not take on an author with Wodehouse's sales potential today. His tenure there resulted partly from the fact that he was a prestige author and partly because Schwed and other staff members were fans.[90]

During the 1930s, Wodehouse's books had sold in this same 10,000 to 15,000 range in first edition. At that time, magazine publication provided the bulk of his readership. In this later period, however, lingering prejudices and the shrinking fiction-magazine market meant that, although most of his serials and stories sold easily, some had to be submitted repeatedly. "Jeeves Makes an Omelet," for example, was published by the *Toronto Star Weekly* after garnering six rejection slips from such magazines as the *Post* and *The Ladies' Home Journal.* (This was an improvement on one 1950 story that had to be submitted twenty-four times.) Wodehouse took his blackballing by the *Post* to heart, yet despite a string of rebuffs he consistently asked Meredith to submit his material there. The only new postwar story published in the *Post* was "The Battle of Squashy Hollow" (June 5, 1965). Hibbs had left in 1961, and Meredith got the new editor to commission the story. Wodehouse was elated by this publication.[91]

From 1955 to 1970 twenty of Wodehouse's pieces appeared in an unlikely place: *Playboy.* Fans may have been bemused at finding Wodehouse among the nudes, but it was a lucrative market. While the average short-story or essay fee for this period was $2,500 to $4,000, *Playboy* paid about $15,000. Most of his periodical publications, however, were in small magazines and Sunday newspaper supplements. The major fiction magazines were in serious decline, succumbing to competition from popular news magazines like *Time* and from magazines for specialized audiences. For example, *Collier's,* whose 1950 acceptance of *The Old Reliable* helped revive Wodehouse's career, was already in trouble at that point. In 1953 it went biweekly, and in December of 1956 the last issue appeared.[92] Magazines depended on advertising revenues, and a large circulation meant higher production costs. Advertisers were deserting the mass-circulation fiction magazines for television and special-audience magazines—like

Playboy. Nevertheless, Wodehouse stuck to old habits by trying to publish everything in magazine form.

In contrast, Wodehouse was known by a higher proportion of the British public. In 1953, Malcolm Muggeridge became editor of *Punch* and invited Wodehouse to contribute regularly; Wodehouse wrote many essays up until 1966. He stayed with Herbert Jenkins Ltd., being the firm's most prestigious and lucrative author. Sales were not large but provided regular, predictable profits. Though Wodehouse's books came out in Penguin editions beginning in the early 1950s, there was a small demand for hardcover reprints. Various editions of many Wodehouse titles have been kept in print by Herbert Jenkins and the larger firms that absorbed it.

Late in Wodehouse's life, that small private press was undergoing the process of merger and enlargement that has continued in the publishing industry. Jenkins was bought by Crescent Press and became Barrie & Jenkins (at which point Christopher Maclehose came to the firm and began editing Wodehouse, the first book to come out under the new imprint being *The Girl in Blue*, 1970). After Wodehouse's death, the Jenkins name disappeared as the press became part of the Hutchinson Group and then of the larger Century-Hutchinson. The latter has kept the books in print, though more for prestige than for profit. According to Hilary Rubenstein, Wodehouse's last representative at A. P. Watt, in the later years the British market probably provided a greater share of Wodehouse's income than did the American. In the 1960s and 1970s, television rights became particularly important. The BBC series "The World of Wooster" (1965) and subsequent adaptations also boosted sales of his books in Britain and elsewhere.[93]

As in the United States, Wodehouse's dealings with his last agent and major editor in the United Kingdom were facilitated by the fact that both admired his work. Rubenstein describes himself as having been "a passionate Wodehouse fan" from age seven to fifteen; he resumed reading Wodehouse's work upon becoming his agent. Christopher Maclehose, who edited most of Wodehouse's late novels, had been a fan while at Oxford and had reviewed some of Wodehouse's books.[94]

These various relationships with agents and editors led to a productive old age for Wodehouse. His secure publishing relationships again reinforced his inclination toward routine. Meredith has described his own role in the typical Wodehouse project. Shortly after delivering a book, Wodehouse would call and inform Meredith what the next project was to be; Meredith would then notify Peter Schwed. When Wodehouse delivered the manuscript, Meredith's agency would set about selling the serial rights while Simon and Schuster had the manuscript read. The negotiations between Meredith and Simon and Schuster were usually disposed of in one brief meeting. Meredith says he never returned manuscripts to Wodehouse for changes or made suggestions, even for single-word revisions—though he did ask other authors for minor or major revisions. Wodehouse would sometimes drop by Meredith's office to discuss plots, mostly during the planning stages.

According to Peter Schwed, the one-book-a-year schedule was not imposed by Simon and Schuster. The firm had two publishing seasons per year and could have done one book by him in each had he wanted to write more. (Indeed, publishing vagaries occasionally meant that two Wodehouse books came out in one year, with none in others—as when *Plum Pie* and *The Purloined Paperweight* came out in 1967, with no Simon and Schuster publication of Wodehouse in 1966.) Two books in one season would have exceeded the demand, so if Wodehouse had come up with three in one year, one would have been delayed.[95] Despite his earlier prolificacy, however, Wodehouse seemed to settle happily into this slightly slower writing pace.

Once Simon and Schuster received the new Wodehouse manuscript, the formalities of its going to press were minimal. Schwed and perhaps another member of the editorial staff would comment on it briefly. For example, the 1959 Editorial Department Report on *How Right You Are, Jeeves (Jeeves In the Offing)* contains one brief complaint from MLR, opining that the book is not as good as *Cocktail Time*: "It's once again silly old Bertie and I fear me his world no longer exists." Schwed adds:

> I too think it would be just as well if P. G. were to lay off Jeeves for a while—once every three or four years would be enough (after writing that I just looked in the catalogue, and

> he hasn't done one since 1955, so *there*, MLR and PS). But apart from such qualms as people being fed up with Jeeves, I have no other reservations. This seems to me top drawer post-war Wodehouse, and I'm glad to have it.[96]

A comparable report in 1962 is briefer yet; Schwed wrote: "*Stiff Upper Lip, Jeeves* is a typical Jeeves-Bertie Wooster, and it's a gem. Enough said."[97] The fixing of print runs and estimating of costs, profits, and so on, were simple matters as well, since Schwed had a clear understanding of Wodehouse's small market.

The situation was similar in England. Rubenstein says that Wodehouse never consulted him on projects. The books were contracted to Herbert Jenkins in sets of three. A. P. Watt received the manuscripts, which were read and sent along to Herbert Jenkins. Rubenstein might deal with mistakes involving technical matters, such as references to law and insurance, but he made no suggestions for other changes, except occasionally concerning the titles.[98] Similarly, Maclehose says that he made only a few tentative suggestions for changes. Occasionally he and Wodehouse discussed the titles, as when Maclehose suggested *The Honour of the Bodkins* but deferred when Wodehouse wanted *Pearls, Girls and Monty Bodkin.*[99]

Of the people closely connected with the writing of the novels, only Schwed consistently made suggestions, and often Wodehouse accepted these. Schwed frequently came up with different titles for the books on the assumption that what would be appropriate to the British market would not necessarily attract American readers. Hence, as in the earlier periods, many of the British and American titles were different. More significantly, Schwed caused the ending of *Much Obliged, Jeeves* to be changed for the American edition. Though he admired the book, he disliked the ending, where Jeeves simply says that he has torn the pages about Bertie out of the Club Book, and Bertie thanks him. Schwed objected that Jeeves would not damage the Book "without a rational explanation," and he drafted a longer, Wodehouse-style ending. There Jeeves says that the entry on Bertie is unnecessary to the Book, since he assumes that he will remain permanently with Bertie, there being "a tie that binds." Wodehouse worked Schwed's version into the ending of the American edition. His suggestion for an alternate title was also adopted: *Jeeves and the Tie That Binds.*[100]

In 1955 the Wodehouses moved permanently to Remsenburg, on Long Island. Bolton already lived there, and Wodehouse had often visited him to work on their projects. Ethel had purchased a house in 1952, and they used it in the summers until 1955. Thereafter Wodehouse visited New York City less frequently and eventually stopped traveling except for short car trips. He took to watching a soap opera, as well as baseball; television may have compensated for his inability to attend the theater. His life became highly routinized, and he delighted in outlining this routine to interviewers.

One thing that disturbed the relative serenity of the Remsenburg years was the 1965 success of the BBC "World of Wooster" series. This success surprised Wodehouse and led him to turn yet again to the theater, writing two plays involving Jeeves and Bertie.

In 1950, Wodehouse became convinced that Bertie Wooster could not be transferred from the printed page to any form of dramatization. He described to his step-granddaughter the event which created this conviction:

> Isn't it disappointing! The National Broadcasting Co. were planning to do a Jeeves series on the radio—thirteen weeks to start with, and I should have got about £100 a week out of it. We tried out the first of the series the other night before an audience at the Belasco Theatre, with Ray Noble playing Bertie and Arthur Margetson Jeeves, and it was AWFUL. So the deal is off for the moment. We are now trying to attack the thing from another angle. I have advised them to cut Bertie out of the series altogether and only have Jeeves. I don't know why it is, but Bertie, when he gets off the printed page isn't the least bit funny. . . . I think what we ought to do is have Jeeves come over to America and get employed in an American family. I think American audiences will accept an English butler but they don't want the Bertie type of young man.[101]

This is exactly what Wodehouse was doing in 1950: putting Jeeves into an American situation, both as himself and in slightly altered form as Phipps. He also kept Bertie out of *Come On, Jeeves.*

"The World of Wooster," however, changed Wodehouse's mind. He wrote to his friend Lord Walter Citrine in 1965:

> I was a bit apprehensive at first, though I had the feeling that Ian Carmichael would be fine as Bertie. (Denis [sic] Price I had never seen). But Frank Muir of the BBC, who came over here on a visit, came down to Remsenburg and ran two of the episodes for me. . . . I thought both sketches were fine.[102]

The series rekindled Wodehouse's desire to do a Jeeves play, and now he was willing to use Bertie. He proposed to Bolton that they revise *Come On, Jeeves* with Bertie replacing Bill Rowcester: "A Bertie-Jeeves play would be a natural after the hit the TV things have made."[103] The result, *Win with Wooster,* was an extensive revision of *Come On, Jeeves.* The idea was to replicate the casting of the BBC series. By the spring of 1966 there was a possibility of a London production, but Carmichael balked at being typecast as Bertie, and Dennis Price was unavailable.[104]

Wodehouse and Bolton were determined, however, and by late summer of 1966 they decided to turn *Win with Wooster* into a musical. This project lasted for several years and went under a number of titles, though it was copyrighted by Bolton and the Wodehouse Estate as *Betting on Bertie.* Protracted negotiations for a production periodically raised and dashed Wodehouse's hopes. By early 1968, the London theatrical producer Harold Fielding (who did *Half a Sixpence* and *Mame*) was interested. Wodehouse and Bolton had linked up with Robert Wright and George Forrest, composers of the pastiche scores for *Song of Norway* and *Kismet.*[105] Ian Carmichael was a possibility for Jeeves and Derek Nimmo for Bertie.[106] The production seemed set when suddenly, in 1969, Fielding withdrew from the project.[107] Wodehouse and Bolton continued to revise and seek a producer.

In 1972, Andrew Lloyd Webber and Tim Rice, fresh from their success with *Jesus Christ Superstar,* expressed interest in doing a Jeeves musical. Wodehouse noted prophetically that he suspected it "would be a flop," but he and Bolton negotiated.[108] By late 1972, however, Wodehouse was eager to make a deal with Webber and Rice; at this point, it appears, the famous duo was simply to rewrite the music for *Betting on Bertie.*[109] Once the deal was made, however, Webber and Rice embarked on a musical based on Wodehouse's earlier books. The result, *Jeeves*, played London briefly in 1975, shortly after Wodehouse's death; as he had predicted, it was a flop. *Betting on Bertie* has never been produced.

Despite the disturbances caused by these negotiations, Wodehouse kept working for the rest of his life. He had honed his tactics for decades; some of the jokes and clichés that he had worked out sixty years earlier still cropped up in his prose.

One last major event occurred at the beginning of 1975, when Wodehouse received a knighthood. Biographers have represented it as a sort of official exoneration of Wodehouse after the British Government's long silence on his innocence in the Berlin broadcasts affair, and there seems to be no other way to interpret it. Newly available letters reveal the lengthy gestation of the honor. Lord Walter Citrine, long a friend and admirer of Wodehouse, wrote to Prime Minister Harold Wilson in 1967 suggesting Wodehouse was due an official honor and pointing out that he was eighty-six years old; Wilson agreed to follow up on the idea. Citrine wrote again in early 1968 proposing that Wodehouse be made a Companion of Honour, but Wilson found that there were too few vacancies. Only in 1974 did the knighthood become possible. In 1984, Wilson explained to Citrine: "In fact, as you know, although the suggestion in 1968 was not possible, when I returned to No. 10 in 1974, it was possible to proceed, in the usual way, a recommendation for a knighthood."[110] What changed between 1968 and 1974 is a matter for further research, but Wodehouse duly became Sir Pelham Grenville Wodehouse in the honors list of 1975 (along with fellow humorist Sir Charles Chaplin).

Wodehouse died of a heart attack on February 14, 1975, in a hospital. The draft of his last, unfinished novel was beside him. He did some work on it on the day of his death.

2

WRITING THE SAME STORY DIFFERENTLY

Nobody is more alive than myself to the fact that, going by the book of rules, I do everything all wrong. I never have a theme, and I work from plot to characters and not from characters to plot, which as everybody knows is the done thing. The men up top, so they tell us, start with a group of characters and then sit back and let them do what they feel like doing. And the catch in that is—suppose they don't do anything.

—WODEHOUSE, "GENESIS OF A NOVEL"

Unfortunately for posterity, Wodehouse used his wastebasket a great deal. He saved few of the letters he received (the only major exception being those William Townend sent him after his move to the United States, which he kept and reread). He also saw no reason to save the notes and drafts of his stories and books. Admittedly, the several sets of manuscript material that do survive are voluminous, and, given Wodehouse's prolificacy, he would have eventually been inundated by hundreds of reams of paper. His many moves made transporting such material difficult, and anyhow, he saw no reason to keep his drafts and manuscripts. The few that he gave away have commanded high auction prices, in part because of their scarcity, but Wodehouse never conceived that the stacks of scribbled paper could be worth anything.

Luckily, some materials have been preserved and a few were still in his office at his death. Moreover, many of his correspondents treasured the letters he sent them (of which he kept no copies). He sent huge numbers of letters, occasionally composing as many as twenty in a day before launching into his regular writing. As he answered his own fan mail all his life, many of these were short and standardized, but when he corresponded with his author friends, he often described his work at length. Thus, by looking at the notes and manuscripts that do survive, in combination with his letters, we get a fairly clear picture of how Wodehouse constructed his literary works.

There are striking features in his writing process. First, the apparently casual, effortless plots and style were the product of lengthy trial and error and of assiduous revision. Second, his projects typically began as a tiny germ of an idea, often derived from another author's work and usually consisting of one simple situation. Third, he worked with small, interchangeable units (whether situations, characters, or phrases), combining and recombining them at each stage of writing.

All these aspects of his compositional method suggest that for Wodehouse writing meant the initial creation of an intricate plot based on the manipulation of a limited repertory of types of characters and situations. This plot then became the thread along which discrete units of language—jokes, quotations, clichés, and so on—could be strung, like beads. His method was routinized in such a way as to allow him to depend on the combination and recombination of familiar elements in ways that make the reader aware of their absurdity.

Most of the surviving manuscripts come from relatively late in Wodehouse's career, beginning in the mid-1950s. Many notes have survived, however, from as early as the 1920s, for he kept files of plot ideas and consulted them in later decades. On the basis of such ideas, we can assume that for much of his life, Wodehouse's creative process began with a single idea, often involving no specific characters or locales. He proceeded to write out many pages of disconnected notes, playing with possible characters, situations, and motivations for working the basic idea up to a full narrative. He used these notes to write what he called the "scenario," a condensed sketch of the narrative that often ran about 30,000 words. He then typically produced about three drafts, revising each extensively. This approach fit in perfectly with Wodehouse's use of clichés and formulaic writing. The initial ideas were often conventional, and typically the last additions came from his repertory of quotations and pet phrases. Overall, the lengthy process transformed the simple basic ideas into strange and complex prose.

THE INITIAL IDEA

Wodehouse often claimed that getting the initial idea was the most difficult part for him, and he certainly worked hard at it. (He found the process even more difficult later in life.) Sometimes he would ask his friends for ideas, as in a 1955 letter to Townend: "Can you think up a plot involving Ukridge, Jeeves, etc.?"[1] Townend's letters do occasionally make suggestions, none of which, it seems, Wodehouse ever used. Wodehouse certainly considered a few, however, for pages from Townend's letters made their way into his file of plot ideas.

This remarkable file hints at how Wodehouse began his projects. Apparently in the 1920s and 1930s his imagination was at its peak, and he spent hours or even whole days making lists of plot ideas; many of these were numbered, dated, and occasionally cross-referenced.[2] Some sheets were held together by brads, paper clips, or pins, arranged into groups whose logic is not always apparent. He added plot germs to the file, though the collection contains fewer notes from each succeeding decade. As he used an idea, he marked it. The early notes contain the basic sources of novels or stories written years or even decades later. In a list headed "Jeeves Ideas," dated April 18, 1937, the following item appears: "14. Aunt Dahlia makes Bertie come down to Brinkley Manor at Christmas either (a) to produce children's play or (b) to play Santa Claus in costume."[3] Wodehouse has crossed out part (b) and noted "used." It figures in "Jeeves and the Greasy Bird" (1965).

Few of these ideas were ever developed. The April 18, 1937, list of

Jeeves ideas is incomplete, but the three surviving pages contain seventeen ideas, and only one other passage is checked off as having been used. It contains elements that may have gone into *The Code of the Woosters*:

> 9. Bertie does something which gets him in wrong with Aunt Agatha. A girl catches him and threatens to expose him unless he does something to help her.
>
> For instance, she has written a very uncomplimentary diary about the man to whom she has since become engaged, having changed her first impressions of him.
>
> Another girl has got hold of the diary and is threatening to give it to the man unless girl does something for her.
>
> Query—Is it another girl? Or butler? Or someone outside story? At any rate, what this second figure wants the girl to do is to steal something—e.g., Stanway Cameo idea—so that Bertie has to steal it.

If we assume the diary became Gussie Fink-Nottle's, the girl became Stiffy Byng, the cameo became a cow-creamer, and so on, we begin to recognize the situation—and such fiddling and substitution were the means by which Wodehouse worked out his plots.

There are hundreds of other ideas in the file, many related to the Jeeves/Wooster series. Here are a few unused items:

> 38. Jeeves story. Bertie wants to have his flat done over in very modern manner by girl decorator with whom he is in love. Jeeves objects. The story would be about how Jeeves cures him of his infatuation.[4] [ca. late 1930s]
>
> Jeeves story. Shy novelist, tormented by prim and domineering secretary. He yearns to be rid of her, but has not the nerve to sack her. Bertie tells him to kiss her. This will outrage and disgust her and she will swoop out of the room and leave.
>
> Novelist comes to Bertie and says he tried the dodge. And how it happened he doesn't quite know, but now they are engaged.
>
> How end? [no date]

Jeeves Story

Uncle Tom brings TV magnate to Brinkley. He sees Anatole and engages him for TV commercial. A. becomes ham and gives notice. How to prevent him leaving? [ca. 1955?]

Jeeves novel

Try this. Aunt Dahlia's son Pongo [sic] has got into trouble at his school. His headmaster (housemaster?) was at school with Bertie and she says B must go and stay at village pub and personate [sic] housemaster to let Bongo off. She says if B was at school with him, he must know all sorts of shocking secrets about him and can blackmail him.

↕

How get Aunt D. and Jeeves into story? [December 6, 1966]

If Wodehouse found an idea promising, he might go on to work it out for a page or more, though many such ideas were abandoned. He had a code, marking an *X* or writing "good" by certain passages and drawing horizontal lines between ideas, with arrows through the middles of the lines if two contiguous sections were for the same project (as in the last idea quoted above).

The Jeeves/Wooster series is exceptional in that ideas were often conceived from the start as belonging specifically to it. Most of the other ideas in the file do not involve specific characters; they simply outline situations. In 1951, Wodehouse described to Townend how he generated plot ideas:

> I find that the best way to get my type of story is to think of something very bizarre and then make it plausible. I remember in Full Moon I started with a picture in my mind of a man crawling along a ledge outside a house, seeing a man through the window and gesturing to him to let him in, and the man inside giving him a cold look and walking out of the room, leaving him on the ledge. I find that, given time, I can explain the weirdest situation.[5]

In the process of making bizarre events plausible, Wodehouse would draw upon reality for characters, events, or atmosphere—just as long as reality suited his plot.

For example, this 1925 letter to Townend indicates how Wodehouse could make a character's situation as the basis of a plot, *then* find out if that situation were realistically possible:

> He starts in the firm, and his job involves going down to the docks at all sorts of unearthly morning hours to interview shippers of incoming boats belonging to the firm.
>
> *Now, is there such a job?*
>
> It must be something that would irk a lazy man, because the effect on him when he chucks it is to make him stay in bed all day, which annoys the heroine and leads to a good situation.[6]

It is not clear that the actual nonexistence of such a job would have prevented Wodehouse from using the idea; in 1961 he wrote to his step-grandson, a lawyer, for advice on the situation of *Stiff Upper Lip, Jeeves*:

> I have just got out a magnificent Jeeves novel plot, and I want you to vet the final sequence. (No fee.)
>
> Sir Watkyn Bassett owns something valuable, a curio of some sort. Bertie is found in possession of it, and Sir W. is convinced that he has pinched it for his Uncle Tom, who is known to covet it. Sir W has Bertie arrested and taken to the village police station and intends to give him—in his capacity of Justice of the Peace—a stiff sentence. (What? Thirty days? Sixty days?)? But Sir W has long coveted Jeeves, and he consents not to press charge if J will leave B and come to him, which J agrees to do,—planning, of course, to hand in his notice in a week or so and return to Bertie.
>
> Now then, can a Justice of the Peace try a man for stealing something from him? (You can stretch a point here if it's not usually done, as no-one will know.) And if a complaintant withdraws a charge after an arrest has been made, does this release the criminal?
>
> It's one of those cases where if you tell me it's all wrong legally, I shall have to go ahead and do it just the same, but I'd rather have it right if possible.[7]

An example of Wodehouse using realistic detail for atmosphere occurred with "Bertie Changes His Mind"; in 1922 Wodehouse wrote to Leonora, then in an English girls' school:

> I say, I've got out the plot of a Jeeves story where Bertie visits a girls' school and is very shy and snootered by the girls and the headmistress. Can you give me any useful details? What would be likely to happen to a chap who was seeing over a school? Do you remember—was it at Ely?—the girls used to sing a song of welcome. Can you give me the words of the song and when it would be sung? And anything else of that sort that would be likely to rattle Bertie.[8]

We tend to think of Wodehouse as starting to write by departing from reality and moving toward a fantasy world, but such inquiries suggest that in some sense he began with an utterly fantastic idea, and, in working it out, tried to motivate it realistically here and there.

Often Wodehouse consciously recycled earlier ideas, both from other authors' works and from his own. In 1949 he wrote to Townend: "At the age of sixty-seven and a half I have just discovered how to write short stories. You read the magazines until you come on a story that has something in it, then you sit down and rewrite it, changing all the essentials." The Lord Emsworth story "Birth of a Salesman," he adds, was derived from a Gerald Kersh story in the *Post*.[9] Actually, Wodehouse had used variants of this method for decades. In 1937 he wrote to Townend:

> Your query about Marquand's plot touched a tender spot. I have long had my eye on the man myself. I find nowadays that the only way I can get plots is by reading somebody else's stuff and working from there, and Marquand is a man whose stories are very suggestive. I was reading a book of his the other day, called NO HERO, where the fatal paper is hidden in a man's flask, and the man, who has always been a ready drinker, suddenly decides to reform and so does not touch the flask. If I can't get something out of that, I'm not the man I was.
>
> I don't think there is any objection to basing one's stuff on

> somebody else's, providing you alter it enough. After all, all one wants is motives.[10]

In at least two cases where Wodehouse wanted to use extensive ideas from another author's work, he bought the rights to do so. Scott Meredith recalls that he negotiated the purchase, for about $2700, of the right to adapt George Kaufman's play *The Butter and Egg Man*, which became the basis for *Barmy in Wonderland*. The situation of the early portions of *French Leave* (1956) is adapted from Michel Perrin's *The Man Who Lost His Keys*; according to Guy Bolton, "I gave Plum this play in French. He *bought* English rights from owners and used idea in book."[11]

Wodehouse's idea file confirms that he consciously derived his ideas from other authors. Many of the notes refer to previous works. A few samples from unused Jeeves/Wooster ideas:

> Jeeves Story. Based on idea in Man With Red Hair that a great perilous experience opens eyes of man and girl and links them together. Lukewarm couple, man always on verge of proposing, but never able quite to get down to it. Bertie arranges some violent experience for them—e.g, shutting them up with a swan or something. Not that, of course, but something on those lines.
>
> This ought to go wrong, and Jeeves finds the right solution. [no date]

> Pinch that scene from Elizabeth Bowen's The Hotel, where man takes bath in private bathroom. Make it the solution of a Jeeves story.
>
> Bertie is entangled with girl at a hotel, and Jeeves gets him to take a bath in girl's mother's private bathroom.
>
> Scene, mother banging at door. Bertie tries to escape by climbing out of window, is discovered on tiles or gets into some woman's room and there is a row. All this leads to Bertie being thought looney and engagement broken off.
>
> Might work it into a story of Aunt Agatha wanting Bertie to marry a girl and taking him to hotel in South of France where girl and mother are staying. This would be better than

> having Bertie wanting to marry the girl. He would send for Jeeves and tell him of the difficulty he's in. [no date]
>
> 24. Idea for a Jeeves novel. Bertie has an old school chum and Oxford pal who is a police constable and wants to be promoted to the C. I. D. (C.p. Bobby in E. R. Punshon's 'Information Received'). His uncle will do something for him if he makes good.
>
> Bertie and Jeeves engineer a burglary at house on hero's beat in order to let him find the jewels later or something. Something goes wrong, there is a real burglary, and B. is suspected. (I want to get a scene like the one in Ben Travers' "Hyde Side Up.")[12] [April 18, 1937]

The last of these (one element of which may have made its way into *Joy in the Morning*) cites two previous works, suggesting how Wodehouse made his own work original by combining disparate elements. The first idea's mention of a swan also suggests that he got new ideas by recalling situations in his own earlier work (in this case "Jeeves and the Impending Doom") and changing them. In a set of random notes for a "Jeeves Novel" dated July 14, 1937, he advises himself to "Try 'Girl on the Boat' formula" (from his 1922 novel). His ideas could also be deliberate twists on clichés and conventions, as in this unused Jeeves/Wooster idea:

> 21. Jeeves story. Idea of widow with small son.—hero loves her—problem for Bertie and Jeeves to solve is to conciliate son so that he will give his consent to the match. (Like Father's Consent in the oldfashioned [sic] novel.)[13]

Wodehouse used one other type of note. Several books in his library (mostly mysteries) have notes for his own projects written on the flyleaves. For example, a copy of Leo Bruce's *Death by the Lake* (1971) contains a sketch of the opening of *Aunts Aren't Gentlemen*. Whether Wodehouse got ideas from these books or just happened to have ideas while reading them, the act of reading apparently stimulated his imagination.

PRELIMINARY NOTES

Once he had settled on the basic situation, Wodehouse would write up voluminous notes, trying many variations and possibilities. Again, most of this material was jettisoned once he found the right combination. Wodehouse described the process to Townend as he was writing *Pigs Have Wings* in 1951:

> I have suddenly started to get what looks like being a quite good Blandings Castle plot. It is still in the chaotic state and when I read the notes I have jotted down, I think I must be going cuckoo. But this always happens with me. I find the only way I can get a plot is to shove down everything that comes into my mind. Then gradually it becomes coherent. I always find my best way is to think up some crazy situation and manipulate the characters to fit it and make it plausible.[14]

Indeed, in reading the notes from this early stage of plotting that do survive, one is struck by their seemingly chaotic nature; most of them are unbound and disorganized. For example, a single loose, undated (probably 1967) page of notes for *Much Obliged, Jeeves* works on the basic idea of someone stealing the Junior Ganymede Club Book (opposite). Here Wodehouse tries four ways to develop this idea, two of which he marks "good"—yet none of which bears any resemblance to the final plot. One project might consume dozens or even hundreds of such pages, from which a few ideas make their way into the book.

Sometimes, in casting about for ideas, Wodehouse changed the characters and situations so much that it is difficult to tell if certain notes ended up as part of a finished book. One set of pages dated from January 25 to February 23, 1948, involves a project that kept flipping back and forth between being a Blandings and a Jeeves/Wooster plot. After Wodehouse had spent a month trying to work out a plot, he apparently abandoned the project. One minor idea tucked in among the rest, of Bertie accused of stealing a necklace while staying at a country house, probably became the basis for *Jeeves and the Feudal Spirit.* Other little motifs may also have been salvaged from

For *Jeeves* novel

Don't forget the idea of members of Junior Ganymede stealing the club book.

Possible solution – Bertie is engaged to girl he dislikes & J. shows her the book & she, being starchy girl, chucks him.

↕

Good

Or suppose Bertie & burglar pal have to burgle the Ganymede Club to get book. (But why?). ¶ A good burst wd be burglar getting book & keeping it to blackmail.

↕

Good

¶ Does Aunt Dahlia suddenly learn that Seppings has contributed stuff abt her to the book? This looks good. (She must have some big reason why it wd be fatal for her past to be revealed). (Or shd it be Uncle Tom?)

2nd. Bertie has got engd to a girl – finds out she is a barrister – goes to court & hears her cross-exam'd a witness – is appalled – feels that he can have no secrets from her.

The notes left read:

For *Jeeves* novel

Don't forget the idea of member of Junior Ganymede stealing the club book.

Possible solution—Bertie is engd to girl he dislikes & J. shows her the book & she, being starchy girl, chucks him.

Good Or suppose Bertie & burglar pal have to burgle the Ganymede Club to get book. (But why?). A good twist wd be burglar getting book & keeping it to blackmail.

Does Aunt Dahlia suddenly learn that Seppings has contributed stuff abt her to the book?

Good This looks good. (She must have some big reason why it wd be fatal for her past to be revealed/or shd it be Uncle Tom?

Bertie has got engd to a girl—finds out she is a barrister—goes to court & hears her cross-examine a witness—is appalled—feels that he can have no secrets from her.

this set of notes and emerged, unrecognizable, as part of other finished works.

A considerable portion of the preliminary notes for *Jeeves in the Offing* survive, and they demonstrate what a lengthy, convoluted process Wodehouse went through before he reached anything close to the book's final plot. The earliest extant notes are dated November 15, 1956. After two pages of handwritten ideas, separated, as usual, by lines, there come two typed pages labeled "*Jeeves Novel. Lay-out of story.*"[15] This bears little resemblance to the novel as we know it. The plot has Aunt Dahlia and Uncle Tom away in America, with Aunt Agatha and Lord Worplesdon staying at Brinkley Court. An American millionaire whom Agatha wants Bertie to butter up is staying there, too, and complications arise over the theft of the familiar silver cow-creamer. The American millionaire and the cow-creamer carried over, but virtually nothing else did. The lay-out pages end:

> *Problems*
> Who is Girl B?
> How do she and American get together?
> How is cow-creamer restored to Amer's aunt?

At the top of the lay-out, Wodehouse has added in pencil: "Suppose Bertie reads in paper of his engt to girl whom he has never met? Lover has taken it for granted that B. won't mind. (A bit like Crystal Clear—Does it matter?)" In notes dated November 27, 1956, Wodehouse returned to this idea:

> Note: I ought to get some solid reason why B. agrees to pretend to be engaged to girl, as he wd presumably dislike her.
> *WORK ON THIS*
> Could B. be on verge of getting engd.—against his will—to Honoria Glossop and this will get him out of it?

Wodehouse worked on this project on and off over the next few years, but it was not until January 11, 1958, that he finally solved this problem by deciding to use Bobbie Wickham as the pretend fiancée who announces her engagement to Bertie in the paper.

Another idea that survived into the novel crops up very early in this preliminary note-making process. On November 16, 1956 (the second day for which notes survive), Wodehouse writes to himself: "I have a note in my Jeeves notes that Sir R. Glossop has come to house as butler to watch someone. Man wd never allow him to watch him directly. Glossop wd be suspected of robbery. This might work into something." It did, but the process of figuring out whom Glossop was to watch went on and on. As late as January 18, 1958, he still knew only that the person was supposed to be a kleptomaniac. In the end, he switched to the premise that Glossop was there to determine the sanity of a rich woman's prospective fiancé.

Wodehouse dropped the project, and then, after a long gap, stretching from late 1956 to early 1958, resumed work on it. On January 10, 1958, he briefly tried out the idea of turning the project into a Blandings novel. He also kept trying out an idea he was clearly keen to use: "If I cd get someone landing B with the racetrack cat, that wd be terrific" (January 22, 1958). Years later, he finally was able to use the racetrack cat as one of the main bases for *Aunts Aren't Gentlemen.*

Overall, the preliminary stages of note-making indicate that Wodehouse did not start with a general outline of a plot and then hone and expand it into a well-crafted whole. Instead, he kept casting about, dropping elements that would later return, changing characters, keeping several mutually exclusive premises as possibilities. It would not be an exaggeration, I think, to suggest that for each large- or small-scale idea that appeared in the final book, Wodehouse had tried out dozens of others.

SITUATIONS AND CHARACTERS

As this description of the preliminary planning suggests, Wodehouse often began with situations rather than characters. He then tried "casting" his plot with different series characters. Most often he tried his plots as Jeeves/Wooster situations. One set of undated notes on a story about a novelist includes this:

> It could be a Jeeves story making Rosie M. Banks the author of book and Bingo coming to Bertie.
>
> ---
>
> If so, Bingo has got to get money to pay bookie or someone and R. and H. have offered him a large sum if he will personate Rosie.

From here the notes go back to discussing the story in the abstract, without the Jeeves/Wooster characters.

Wodehouse tried several times to combine the Blandings and Jeeves/Wooster series. The preliminary notes for *Service with a Smile* revolve around the idea that someone has shot a fox and that it has to be buried secretly: "Try it as a Jeeves story. Lord E lands B with the fox and B and J bury it (B says like thing he learned at school abt burial, Sir John Moore). Possibly get B into trouble while out at night." The notes indicate that Wodehouse spent three days working on this idea before going back to a straight Blandings plot.[16] In 1974 he tried the same thing for a few paragraphs in the notes for "Novel A" *(Sunset at Blandings)*, quickly concluding, "I don't believe it's a Jeeves story."

More rarely he went the other way, considering switching a Jeeves/Wooster project into another series. The earliest notes for *Much Obliged, Jeeves* indicate that it was initially conceived in late 1966 for the Jeeves/Wooster series:

> *Jeeves Novel*
>
> Dec 10, 1966
>
> Idea for a Jeeves novel. The club book at the Junior Ganymede is stolen. By whom? Some crook butler who wants to use it for blackmail. [illegible word] Start with scene when he calls on Bertie—Jeeves is away on holiday—and tells him Aunt A. will be informed of B's eleven pages if B. does not undertake some dreadful task. What task.

Wodehouse has marked this "good"; he played with various ideas involving the Club Book on and off until November 9, 1967. Then four pages of notes dated November 12–13, 1967, explore the same situation as an "Uncle Fred Novel," beginning:

> Try making that idea of the Ganymede Club book being stolen an U. Fred story.
>
> Might start with UF lunching at G Club with Albert Peasemarch, who tells him abt the club book.

At some point over the next four years he worked up the project as *Much Obliged, Jeeves,* but the rest of the surviving notes are undated.

Just as Wodehouse shuffled ideas around to find the ideal combination, he treated characters as interchangeable markers, to be put into plots as necessary. They were in effect like a set of actors, being cast into existing roles in the plot. Consider, for example, the case of G. D'Arcy "Stilton" Cheesewright, Bertie's menacingly jealous and muscular old schoolmate. The set of functions Stilton was to perform in *Joy in the Morning* was partially worked out before Wodehouse began to consider who the character would be. In 1940, Wodehouse described to Townend how he had cannibalized an unpublished story for an idea for the novel:

> I wrote four short stories at the beginning of the year, and have now discovered that one of them will have to be chucked away because I need the plot for a novel. Does that ever happen to you? It's agony, as the short story was really good. But it contains a solution for a Jeeves novel, so I am trying to work out a plot. Listen, is it possible for a hard-up young peer to become a *country* policeman? A London one, yes, but this must be country. Could such a man start in as a village cop, with the idea of later on, if in luck, getting into Scotland Yard? I wish you would buttonhole the next policeman who passes your door and ask him if it would be possible for him to soar to the heights. (My chap has got to be a policeman, because

> Bertie pinches his uniform in order to go to a fancy dress dance, at which it is vital for him to be present and he has no other costume).[17]

The premise of a country constable aspiring to get into Scotland Yard remained, but the "hard-up young peer" became Stilton. He thus provided the mechanism for allowing Bertie to steal a constable's outfit and also, through his jealousy over Bertie's supposed love for Florence Craye, created an extra menace.

Surprisingly, Stilton also played a central role in *The Mating Season* well into the project. The following synopsis, which Wodehouse sent to his step-granddaughter in early 1946, shows that many elements of the novel were already in place:

> I am working very hard trying to plan out a story about Bertie Wooster and Jeeves which I began to work at in 1942 and couldn't get on with because I couldn't think what could happen. Yesterday and this morning it suddenly began to come out, and now I really think it is going to be funny. Bertie has a friend called Stilton Cheesewright—at least, his name is really D'Arcy Cheesewright, but everybody calls him Stilton—and they are both going to stay at a house in the country with some people they have never met. Well, the night before they are supposed to go Stilton (who is rather quick-tempered) has a fight with someone in the street and is arrested by the police and the magistrate says he will have to go to prison for two weeks. And if he does not go to the house for this visit of his his family will find out that he is in prison and will be very angry with him, so Bertie asks Jeeves what is to be done, and Jeeves says the only thing to do is for Bertie to go to the house pretending to be Stilton. So Bertie goes, and the first thing he finds out is that the man who owns the house is a great enemy of Stilton's, though they have never met. (This sounds odd, but it is all explained in the story.) This makes things very awkward for Bertie, because he can't say he isn't Stilton. Meanwhile, the magistrate thinks it over and decides that he was too hard on Stilton, so he says Stilton can pay a fine instead of going to prison. So Stilton comes to the house be-

> cause he is going to marry a girl and she will expect to get letters from him every day written from the house, and he can't go as himself because Bertie is pretending to be him, so he comes there pretending to be Bertie. So everybody thinks Bertie is Stilton and Stilton is Bertie and all sorts of funny things happen. I haven't got the middle of the story yet, but I have thought out the end of it, which is always the most important part, and I believe it is going to be good.[18]

Happily, Wodehouse realized that Gussie Fink-Nottle would be far funnier in this role, and he reserved Stilton for a return in *Jeeves and the Feudal Spirit.* Wodehouse had small groups of characters who played similar functions, and he substituted one for another to gain variety from book to book, without disturbing the essentially formulaic quality of his plotting.

Just how interchangeable his characters were during the planning phase of writing is evident if we turn back to the rough notes for *Jeeves in the Offing.*[19] On December 20, 1956, about one month into his work on the project, Wodehouse treats his characters purely as slots into which any stock figure could be placed:

> Lay-out
> (1) X wants to marry Y, gets B. to say he is engd. to Y. Formidable mother.
> (2) something happens to queer X with Y and Y continues be engd to B.
> (3) Z, another man, is in love with Y. She wants to marry him, but somehow mother is obstacle.
> (4) Jeeves somehow works it that Bertie gets in bad with Mother and at same time Mother gets matey with Z.
> *THIS IS SOMETHING TO WORK ON.* Z might have a girl A. Then X wd. pair off with A and Z with Y.

Another note (November 18, 1956) gives further evidence that Wodehouse thought of his characters as stock roles: "The Menace wd threaten to have B arrested so as to discredit the other fellow."

The process of "casting" a story could be quite prolonged. On a page of notes for *Jeeves in the Offing* dated August 26, 1958 (nearly two years after the project was started), Wodehouse wrote:

> What characters have I got?
> Owner of house
> Mother of girl
> Girl
> Her lover
> The American big pot [Wodehouse's term for a VIP]
> His son
> Sir R. Glossop
> Bertie
> Jeeves

Pencilled notes nearby include "(Who is the kleptomaniac, or rather the supposed kleptomaniac? The son)." As of August 27 he had a more specific list:

> CHARACTERS
> Aunt Dahlia
> Uncle Tom
> Uncle Tom's Sister
> Her daughter
> American millionaire (J. Birdsey Coker)
> His son (Judson Coker)
> Edwin the Boy Scout (who acts as detective)
> Lover of U. T.'s sister's daughter
> 2nd girl (who?) for whom he falls after quarrelling with
> Girl
> Bertie
> Jeeves
> (Another kid ('Old Stinker') to play Watson to Edwin?)

Readers familiar with *Jeeves in the Offing* will recognize that some of these characters, including Tom's sister and Edwin, are not in the book.

THE SCENARIO

Wodehouse's letters and interviews frequently refer to the "scenario" that he created for each project. His "scenario" was an extensive but condensed sketch of the plot; it allowed him to write quickly once he started an actual draft. He seems to have developed this method in 1923, while writing *Bill the Conqueror*:

> I wrote an elaborate scenario for the first third of my novel yesterday. I've got a new system now, as it worked splendidly with Bill the Conqueror. That is to write a 30,000 word scenario before starting a novel. By this means you avoid those ghastly moments when you suddenly come on a hole in the plot and are tied up for three days while you invent a situation. I found that the knowledge that I had a clear path ahead of me helped my grip on the thing.
>
> Also, writing a scenario this length gives you ideas for dialogue scenes and you can jam them down in skeleton and there they are, ready for you to come to them.[20]

Two descriptions of the scenario that Wodehouse gave late in his life suggest, however, that it was an evolving set of notes. Herbert Warren Wind summarized what Wodehouse told him about the process of writing the scenario: "Putting his thoughts down on paper helps him clarify his thinking, so when he is developing a scenario he jots down daily the ideas that are going through his mind about the section of the plot he is currently concerned with." A description of his writing methods, which Wodehouse gave to Donald Bensen in 1971, may also relate to the scenario:

> WODEHOUSE: I don't actually compose in long-hand. I lie back in a long chair and make notes, you know, bits of dialogue and then another bit of description. You see, I don't try to make it continuous. Then I work at the typewriter.
>
> BENSEN: Your proper first draft is typescript.
>
> WODEHOUSE: Yes. I find one system that works very well with me is to sit at the typewriter and have a pad on my desk, you see, on which I write out the next bit of the story, maybe a

> bit of dialogue or description, by hand, and then transfer it to the machine. But I make several drafts. The stuff I do on the typewriter isn't the final version. I mess it about a lot with ink, and put in bits and alter adjectives and things, and then make a fair copy of it. The great thing is, I like working on the typewriter. It rather inspires me.[21]

The scenario may, then, have been a set of notes, with dialogue, partially handwritten and partially typed, which Wodehouse altered as he went along. It also may not have followed the order of the final plot, so that to anyone but himself it might look like rough notes.

Few of the surviving sets of manuscripts and notes I have examined contain a specifically labeled "scenario." There are, for example, a few typescript pages among the notes for "Jeeves and the Greasy Bird" so designated.[22] Even these, however, do not constitute a single, complete, condensed version of the action. Rather, they are partial synopses containing many important elements that were later dropped from the story. Hence these pages may not be typical of Wodehouse's use of his scenarios, and they may not be the only scenarios written for this project.

There are actually two scenarios extant for "Jeeves and the Greasy Bird." The earlier (November 28, 1965) begins with the situation very different from that of the completed story. Bertie is about to leave for the Drones Club, instead of having just returned from visiting Sir Roderick Glossop. The motif of Jeeves wanting to catch a tarpon is present, but when Aunt Dahlia calls, it is to ask Bertie to hire a conjuror for her Christmas party. This assignment provides the reason why Bertie visits Jas Waterbury's theatrical agency; the notion of him being tricked into an engagement with Waterbury's niece and thus being threatened with a breach-of-promise suit is not used. Bertie then goes to visit Glossop, who tells him that he cannot marry Lady Chufnell until Honoria is engaged, and Honoria dislikes the one man who loves her, Blair Eggleston, a patient in Glossop's clinic. The scenario ends abruptly with the note "This ends Act One." Aside from the premise that Bertie must help Sir Roderick by getting Honoria engaged to Blair, little of this material was kept.

The second scenario, written only six days later (December 4, 1965), contains some remarkable changes. The story now opens with Bertie and Jeeves in New York. Aunt Dahlia phones him from England to come for Christmas and play Santa Claus. She also asks him to visit Wilfred Cream (the playboy character referred to but never seen in *Jeeves in the Offing*), who is a patient at Sir Roderick's clinic in Chufnell Regis. Much of the story then concerns Bertie learning that Wilfred has reformed upon falling in love with Honoria, and he must help get her engaged to Wilfred so that Sir Roderick can marry Lady Chufnell. Again this scenario stops short, with a note, "The story now proceeds as in original version." This note suggests that Wodehouse rewrote portions of his scenarios as he proceeded and that there was no single, enduring scenario as such. Certainly the scenario(s) for "Jeeves and the Greasy Bird" were not enough to prevent enormous changes well into the writing process. Up to a fairly late point in one draft, Roderick Spode was supposed to be prominent in the story, and it was he who ended up playing Santa Claus!

One page of the *Much Obliged, Jeeves* material appears to be a sort of combination synopsis and sketch for bits of dialogue and description. It relates to the scene in chapter 8 when Bertie goes campaigning for Ginger Winship and has the bad luck to call unwittingly on the other candidate, Mrs. McCorkadale. The page begins with a typed synopsis describing the final action exactly, except that the individual elements appear out of order:

> B, expecting a male household, on meeting woman has to swallow his story, which was a bit too jovial.
>
> B to maid. 'Can I see the householder?'
>
> The maid turns out to be the one in AD's employment on page—of the Jeeves book where the black cat is. p.79 in JIn Offing.
>
> B asks her what sort of man boss is. She says female and he realizes he will have to cut story.
>
> It might have been difficult to get the conv going, but fortunately Ginger had told me that his lot, if they won the larger

> portion of the suffrages of the many-headed were going to cut taxes etc
>
> She was what I wd call a grim woman, not as grim as aunt Agatha, which was hardly to be expected, but certainly the equal—or even t superior, of the woman who used to sit and knit at foot of guilln.

Beneath this, Wodehouse has written in ink a series of phrases and sentences for use at various points in the scene:

> —and bring the pound back to form
>
> and I saw no reason to suppose wouldn't feel the same.
>
> I began, therefore, by asking her if she had a vote, and she said Yes, she had a vote, and I said 'I strongly advise you to cast yours for Harold Winship.'
>
> If Mr Winship gets in, which he won't he will be an ordinary humble back-bencher.
>
> It was a line of talk which Jeeves had roughed out for my use and I had committed to memory.
>
> Not a ripple appeared on the stern and rockbound coast of her map. She looked like Aunt Agatha listening to me when a boy trying to explain away a window broken by a cricket bat.
>
> the man who with his hand on the helm of the ship of state, will steer England to prosperity and happiness.

All of these items, some of them embroidered clichés, appear in the final version, though some were revised or expanded.

The illustration (overleaf) shows a similar page for the next scene, where Bertie meets Bingley in the street. The typewritten portion gives three versions of a passage, the last of which is close to the one in the book. Wodehouse goes on to sketch in a bit of dialogue, which is all used in the final version, though in rearranged and expanded form.

If we can assume that such bits of synopsis combined with sketches of prose represent at least part of the "scenario" phase of the project, then the scenario seems to represent the transition between the plotting and drafting phases—not simply the end of the plotting.

DRAFTS AND REVISIONS

As we might expect from his enormous output, Wodehouse wrote quickly once the planning process was over. In 1920 he apparently adopted an approach of depending heavily on revision:

> (1) I now write stories at terrific speed. I've started a habit of rushing them through and then working over them very carefully, instead of trying to get the first draft exactly right, and have just finished the rough draft of an 8000 word story in two days. It nearly slew me. As a rule, I find a week long enough for a short story, if I have the plot well thought out.
> 2. On a novel I generally do eight pages a day, i.e., about 2500 words.[23]

Such steady, quick writing depended on extensive planning, as Wodehouse's 1945 comments concerning Trollope indicate:

> Of course I read Trollope's *Autobiography* and found it interesting. But I still don't understand his methods of work. Did he sit down each morning and write exactly 1500 words, without knowing when he sat down how the story was going to develop, or had he a careful scenario on paper? I can't believe that an intricate story like *Popenjoy* [i.e., *Is He Popenjoy?*] could have been written without minute planning. Of course, if he did plan the whole thing out first, there is nothing so very bizarre in the idea of writing so many hundred words of it each day. After all, it is more or less what one does oneself. One sits down to work each morning, no matter whether one feels bright or lethargic, and before one gets up a certain amount of stuff, generally around 1500 words, has emerged. But to sit down before a blank sheet of paper without an idea of how the story is to proceed and just start writing, seems to me impossible.[24]

[illegible], [illegible]

Having been informedby Jeeves that this blot on the species resided in MS, I was not surprised to see him. but I certainly wasn't pleased. The last thing ~~[illegible]~~ [illegible]

Having been informed by Jeeves that this blot on the species resided in MS, I had been expecting to run into him sooner or later

Having been informed by Jeeves that this blot on the species hung out in Market Snodsbury and expecting in consequence that I would run into him sooner or later, I was not surprised to see him, but I certainly wasn't pleased. The last thing I wanted in the delicate state to which the McCorkadale had reduced me was to converse with a man who set cottages on fire and chased employers hither and thither with ~~a~~ carving ~~knife.~~ knives.

He was as perky as ever. One noticed no diminution of the [illegible].

He was still as [illegible] as he had been at the [illegible].

'And what are you doing in these parts, cocky?' he enquired, having first slapped me on the back.

'I'm staying with my aunt, Mrs T. She has a house near here.'

'I know it. Nice place.'

— You might have th^t that a knives had never come between us.

Having been informedby Jeeves that this blot on the species resided in MS, I was not surprised to see him. but I certainly wasn't pleased. The last thing

Having been informed by Jeeves that this blot on the species resided in MS, I had been expecting to run into him sooner or later

Having been informed by Jeeves that this blot on the species hung out in Market Snodsbury and expecting in consequence that I would run into him sooner or later, I was not surprised to see him, but I certainly wasn't pleased. The last thing I wanted in the delicate state to which the McCorkadale had reduced me was to converse with a man who set cottages on fire and chased employers hither and thither with carving ~~knife~~ knives.

The hand-written insertions in the illustration at left read:

Redfaced old girl, isn't she?

Judging by his

knives.

He was as perky as ever. One noticed no limitation of the ch. [?]

He was still as ch. [?] as he had been at the J. Gan.

'And what are you doing in these parts, cocky?' he enquired having first slapped me on the back.

'I'm staying with my aunt, Mrs T. She has a house near here.'

'I know it. Nice place.'

—You might have tht that c knives had never come between us.

Still, he did gradually slow down as he got older. Wind summarized Wodehouse's writing methods toward the end of his life:

> His method of composition remained virtually unchanged through the years. He did his first draft in long-hand, in pencil. Then he sat down at the Royal and did a moderate amount of revising and polishing when he typed it. His average output on a good working day was about a thousand words in his last twenty years, but when he was younger, it was closer to two thousand five hundred.[25]

Aunts Aren't Gentlemen, perhaps the only Jeeves/Wooster work for which virtually all the notes and drafts survive, gives some sense of Wodehouse's elaborate process of drafting and revising. In writing it, Wodehouse prepared extensive notes, then a sixty-one-page set of longhand writing marked "Rough Notes and rough writing." The latter is done in units set off by horizontal lines; some are only a sentence or two, while others run for more than a page. Wodehouse has put various marks, primarily Xs and letters, by some, probably indicating material to develop or move. One page ends with a note to, "Add stuff above." These notes and sketches of prose may have formed the "scenario." Next comes a 170-page draft, again in longhand, under the title *Red Spots in the Morning*. This draft is similar to the final book in stretches, but there are distinct differences. It begins with a paragraph Wodehouse cut in the next draft, presumably because he had changed the book's title: "I give the spots star billing because if it hadn't been for them, what my biographers will refer to as the Maiden Eggesford Horror would never have got itself under way. (air-borne?)" Bertie at this early stage sings " 'Swannee' by the late George Gershwin" in his bath, though Wodehouse has noted "the toreador song from the opera Carmen" (his final choice) in the margin.

The first typed draft of *Aunts Aren't Gentlemen* is closer to the final version, but it is still very brief. Chapter 1 of the novel is short, but this draft is less than a third as long, running only a page and a half, double-spaced. The opening is:

> I noted the spots first while I was in my bath, singing, if I remember rightly, the Toreador song from the opera Carmen, and I viewed them with concern.
>
> "Jeeves," I said at the breakfast table, "I've got spots on my chest."
>
> "Indeed, sir?"
>
> "Pink."
>
> "Indeed, sir?"
>
> "I don't like them."
>
> "A very understandable prejudice, sir."
>
> "It can't be measles, because I've had measles, and you can't get them twice. Isn't there a rule to that effect in the rule book?"
>
> "I believe that view is generally supported by the medical faculty, sir."

In ink, Wodehouse has crossed off the final "sir" and added "Might I ask if they itch, sir?," but Bertie's response, Jeeves's advice that he not scratch, and the subsequent comic exchange about Barbara Frietchie and "the poet Nash" are not yet present. This draft suggests that Wodehouse initially wrote to get down the basic action and dialogue, then put in additional humorous lines and quotations later, along with general polishing. Of the three quotations in chapter 1 of *Aunts Aren't Gentlemen,* the draft contains only the one from "the poet Herrick" near the end.

The third draft of the book is typed and very close to the final version. Here the changes in ink are mostly brief. For example, Jeeves's comment about Barbara Frietchie, "A lady prominent in the revolt of our North American colonies, sir," is changed to its final, and more accurate, version, "A lady of some prominence in the American war between the States, sir." A number of revisions involve substituting equivalent phrases from Wodehouse's repertory of clichés, slang, and quotations. After Orlo Potter jumps into Bertie's car, for example, Wodehouse originally had: "He was plainly all of a doodah, and some fellows when all of a doodah enjoy telling. . . ." This has been changed to "He was still panting like a hart, and some fellows when panting like harts enjoy telling. . . ." Shortly after this, ". . . what I have heard Jeeves call the green-eyed monster that doth mock the meat it feeds on was operating on all twelve cylinders" becomes ". . . that doth mock the meat it feeds on was beginning to feel the rush of life beneath its keel." In chapter 14, "If you want to know how this proposition affected me, I can put it in a nutshell by saying that the scales fell from my eyes," is changed to "by saying that I read him like a book." There would appear to be little to choose between the two phrasings of each of these passages, but perhaps Wodehouse tried to rotate his standard lines. The "scales fell from the eyes" phrase was used earlier in *Aunts Aren't Gentlemen* (Chap. 4), and so it was presumably cut here to avoid repetition.

Other revisions make the prose more dynamic:

> "This seemed to soothe him. He went on brooding, but now not so much like a murderer getting . . ." ("a murderer" becomes "Jack the Ripper"; Chap. 8)
>
> "any twig trodden on by her [in the evening of her life] would go off . . ." (phrase in brackets added; Chap. 11)
>
> "I gave him a look, lack-lustre in every respect." ("in every respect" becomes "to the last drop"; Chap. 11)

And, for some reason, one delightful simile got watered down. From "just like my Aunt Agatha, before whose glare, as is well known, strong men curl up like carbon paper" became ". . . curl up like rabbits."

There was a final typed version that was sent off to the respective agents. Few such final versions survive; it seems that none does for *Aunts Aren't Gentlemen*. The copy of *Plum Pie* sent to Herbert Jenkins is available, however, and it reveals that even the final version contains minor changes by Wodehouse. "Jeeves and the Greasy Bird" has about one change every page or two. A few examples:

> " 'If your allusion is to the American poet John Howard Payne, sir, he compared it to its advantage with pleasures and palaces. He [called it sweet and] said there was no place like it.' " (phrase in brackets added)

> " 'Should she learn of my official status, I do not like to envisage the outcome. If I may venture on a pleasantry . . .' " (becomes ". . . the outcome, though if I may venture . . .)

These changes make Jeeves's speech a bit more elaborate. The happiest last-minute change comes at the end. Originally it ran: " 'Heaven help the tarpon that tries to pit its feeble cunning against you, Jeeves,' I said. 'It will be a one-sided contest.' " The last sentence became " 'Its efforts will be bootless.' "

Another of the very late drafts survives for *Jeeves in the Offing.*[26] It contains similar small changes. In the sentence, "His blood pressure was high [, his eye rolled in what they call a fine frenzy,] and he was death-where-is-thy-sting-ing like nobody's business," the clause in brackets was inserted. A bit of dialogue is also expanded:

> "Have you seen it?"
> "Actually no." ["It's been lying what the French call *perdu*."] (Chap. 8)

Other changes substituted one phrase or word for another.

These examples are all from relatively late works, and we might wonder whether he had to revise more as he got older. *Aunts Aren't Gentlemen* was his last completed book, and, though it is the shortest of the Jeeves/Wooster novels, Wodehouse still had trouble getting it to its final length; in 1973 he wrote to Tom Sharpe: "I have seen a way to lengthen my Jeeves novel by at least 20 pages so now it may come out the right length."[27] But there are indications that even at the peak of his abilities Wodehouse had to write and revise a great deal before he completed a version that satisfied him. Compare the following passages from letters to Townend:

> I have spent the summer writing and rewriting the first 30,000 words of *Summer Lightning,* and must have done—all told—about 100,000 words. It is one of those stories which one starts without getting the plot properly fixed and keeps going off the rails. I think all is well now, but I am shelving it to do some short stories. [1928]

> I have written sixty-four pages of *Thank You, Jeeves* in seventeen days, and would have done more but I went off the rails and had to rewrite three times. That is the curse of my type of story. Unless I get the construction absolutely smooth, it bores the reader. In this story, for instance, I had Bertie meet the heroine in London, scene, then again in the country, another scene. I found I had to boil all this down to one meeting, as it was talky. [1932]

> *Right Ho, Jeeves* has come out splendidly. I have almost finished typing it out again. Amazing how that improves a book. I've cut out a lot of dead wood and even so I have added ten pages. I find that when the labour of the first draft is off one's mind one is able to concentrate on small improvements. [1933][28]

The third quotation indicates that *Right Ho, Jeeves* went through at least two typed drafts, and that the process of revising generally made the books longer.

Many of the additions involved adding humorous items. When Wodehouse was writing *Much Obliged, Jeeves* in early 1971, Peter Schwed inquired: "So does your letter of January 27 imply that you'll finish adding the laugh lines and get the manuscript to me very quickly indeed?"[29] The illustration (overleaf) shows how that process of "adding the laugh lines" to *Much Obliged, Jeeves* went. It shows the first page of what is probably the first typed draft, with fairly extensive revisions. Some of the changes are:

> "The skies are blue, the sun is shining, [the dickey birds are singing,] and I [feel like a million dollars]." (The portions in brackets were cut and Wodehouse writes in "am sitting on top of the world with a rainbow round my shoulder." Ultimately he would cut the first two phrases and substitute "You might say I'm sitting . . .")

> "I feel full to the brim of Vitamin B." (added to Bertie's speech, which is then identical to the final version)

> A note after "Very true, sir" refers to a Shakespeare sonnet, number 33, the first eight lines of which Jeeves quotes in the

book, and Bertie's reply, "Exactly! I couldn't have put it better myself. One always has to budget for a change in the weather," has been added.

REFERENCE TOOLS

In his autobiography, *Over Seventy,* Wodehouse recalled that in 1909, after two of his stories were sold to *Cosmopolitan* and *Collier's,* he moved to Greenwich Village. He "settled in with a secondhand typewriter, paper, pencils, envelopes and Bartlett's book of *Familiar Quotations,* that indispensable adjunct to literary success."[30] That copy of Bartlett's (9th edition, 1891) was indeed important to him; it was in his library at his death, battered, but in a new library binding. Many of his stock phrases are listed in this Bartlett's. His library also contains other reference books of quotations: *The Viking Book of Aphorisms, The Dictionary of Humorous Quotations,* and the *Oxford Book of Quotations.* The latter was a present from his step-granddaughter in 1957. He wrote to her: "Thanks most awfully for the books and especially for the Oxford Book of Quotations, which was a wonderful present and will be invaluable." Wodehouse seems to have used it; asked if he used reference books to find his quotations, he replied: "Well, yes. But I've generally thought of the reference, then I use the *Oxford Book of Quotations* to verify it.[31]

It is likely that Wodehouse often relied on his memory for his quotations. As one critic has pointed out, Wodehouse would have been exposed at Dulwich to "most of the standard English and American readings and quotations ('memory passages') of which so large a part of the literary discipline of turn-of-the-century school boys in both England and America consisted."[32] One of Wodehouse's favorite quotations is from Longfellow's "The Building of the Ship":

> And see! she stirs!
> She starts—she moves—she seems to feel
> The thrill of life along her keel.

CHAPTER ONE

As I ~~parked myself~~ slid into my chair at the breakfast table that morning and started to ~~dig into~~ deal with the toothsome eggs and bacon which Jeeves had given of his plenty, I was conscious of a strange exaltation ~~, or, if you prefer it, exuberance~~. ~~I took a quick glance at the world and liked the look of it. Not a flaw in the set-up, it seemed to me.~~ Here I was, back in the old familiar headquarters, and the thought that I had seen the last of Totleigh Towers, of Sir Watkyn Bassett, of his daughter Madeline and above all of ~~Roderick~~ the blighter Spode, or Lord Sidcup, as he now calls himself, was like ~~rare and refreshing fruit~~ a shot in the arm.

"Jeeves," I said, "I am happy today."

"I am very glad to hear it, sir."

"The skies are blue, the sun is shining, ~~the dickey birds are singing,~~ and I ~~feel like a million dollars~~ am sitting on top of the world with a rainbow round my shoulder."

"A most satisfactory state of affairs, sir."

"What's that word I've heard you use, - begins with eu?"

"Euphoria, sir?"

"That's the one. I've seldom had a sharper attack of euphoria. I feel full to the brim of Vitamin B. Mind you, I don't know how long it will last. Too often it is when one is feeling fizziest that disaster steps in ~~with the sleeve across the windpipe~~ and does its stuff."

"Very true, sir."

"Still, the thing to do is to keep on being happy while you can."

"Precisely, sir. Carpe diem, the Roman poet Horatius Flaccus advised."

"~~Oh, did he?~~"

The hand-written insertions in the illustrations at left read:

slid into my chair

deal with

if I've got the word right.

Here I was, back in the old familiar headquarters, and

the blighter

a shot in the arm.

am sitting on top of the world with a rainbow round my shoulder.''

I feel full to the brim of Vitamin B.

and does its stuff.''

[?] from Sonnet. a change in the weather.

''Exactly! I couldn't have put it better myself. One always has to budget for

Wodehouse seems to have quoted it from memory, as he consistently gets it slightly wrong. In *Right Ho, Jeeves* he renders it as:

> She starts. She moves. She seems to feel
> The stir of life along her keel. (Chap. 9)

Or, in *Joy in the Morning,* "He moved, he stirred, he seemed to feel the rush of life along his keel" (Chap. 29). However Wodehouse twisted this passage around, he consistently missed the word "thrill" in the original. (Possibly the changes were intentional, but it is difficult to imagine what purpose they would serve. Indeed, the original version is a trifle funnier.)

Despite such small slips, his memory was good. In 1960 he told a friend about how he had first been inspired to become a writer when he read a serial, "Acton's Feud," in *The Captain*:

> It was so different from any other school story I had read, and it made me feel that this was the stuff and that I could do something along those lines myself. "Shannon, the old international, had brought down a strong team . . ." What a perfect opening for a school story.

The actual opening sentence of "Acton's Feud" is "Shannon, the old Blue, had brought down a rattling eleven—two Internationals among them—to give the school the first of its annual 'Socker' matches."[33] Given that Wodehouse did not have a copy of the serial and hence had not read it in several decades, his version is surprisingly close to this. (He was delighted when Citrine sent him a copy of the serial shortly thereafter.)

He also relied on his memory to keep track of his own works. Asked in 1971, while he was working on *Pearls, Girls and Monty Bodkin,* if he had a reference file to help keep his series consistent, he replied:

> No, just memory. I have to occasionally reread some of the earlier books—you know, so that I don't contradict myself. This one I'm doing now, Llewellyn is rather a different character than in the first book, he's rather a genial sort of character. But I don't know that it matters.[34]

Occasionally he made mistakes or simply changed things, but, as he rightly said, it did not particularly matter.

After his departure from England in 1939, Wodehouse could no longer base his English stories on firsthand experience. Many critics treat his late works as though they continue to deal with pre-World War II England, but he was concerned to keep them accurate and up to date. He got news from his family and friends in England and subscribed to several English Sunday papers and *Punch*. He also consulted his editors and agents on specific points. Scott Meredith recalls that Wodehouse would refer research questions to him; for a while Meredith had an office in England and at other times kept a subagent there, so that he could send the questions along to be answered. Several times Wodehouse consulted Hilary Rubenstein on technical matters of law, insurance, and the like. Christopher Maclehose remembers a phone call from Wodehouse asking if there was still a nightclub in Berkeley Square. Wodehouse's son-in-law, Peter Cazalet, trained race horses and was able to supply information on questions of betting.[35] Such realistic touches helped Wodehouse to make his "bizarre" ideas plausible within his fantasy world.

Wodehouse's writing methods reveal how he was able to render clichéd elements original. He often began with an idea based on a previous author's work or on his own work or with an idea so simple that few authors would consider it promising enough to develop into a plot; this idea he called the "motive," and he saw his art as the combination and reworking of motives. The working out of the plot often involved piling up repeated or familiar devices, rendered strange through recombination. The final polishing stages included stuffing the prose with quotations and stock phrases. As Wodehouse put it to Townend in 1935: "I now have got a new system for writing short stories. I take a Saturday Evening Post story and say 'Now, how can

I write exactly the same story but entirely differently?' "[36] All authors work with existing traditions, but many strive to foreground their original elements. Wodehouse foregrounded the fact that he was working with existing traditions, and that emphasis on convention makes his work "entirely different."

3

THE WORLD'S FIRST CONSULTING VALET: GENRE TRANSFORMATIONS IN THE SERIES

I suppose if the young lovers I've known in my time were placed end to end—difficult to manage, of course, but what I mean is just suppose they were—they would reach half-way down Piccadilly. —JOY IN THE MORNING

Whatever Wodehouse's originality consisted of, it did not result from his invention of genres. During his early career, from 1900 to 1914, he explored a variety of existing genres, all of them primarily associated with the popular magazines. Wodehouse stuck closely to the originals, though he wrote with a lighter touch. In inventing his two main series in 1915, the Blandings and Jeeves/Wooster sagas, he was still deriving genre and narrative formulas from existing works but now at such a high level of abstraction that the influences are not always apparent. He then reworked and recombined these formulas into new ones of his own. We have seen how both Wodehouse's publishing circumstances and his writing methods encouraged the creation of large-scale narrative formulas based on recombination. The dense texture of the series resulted from his development of the Jeeves-Bertie relationship and of his extraordinarily skillful manipulation of language and narrational tone.

Although Wodehouse worked out his most important series by recombining elements of existing genres and even of specific stories, he was nevertheless an original and important author. The Russian Formalist critics suggest that all innovation in literary history, even of the most revolutionary and original sort, derives from the reworking of existing literary devices and functions. Viktor Shklovsky stated the case simply in his 1925 *Theory of Prose*: "I imagine the tradition of a writer as his dependence on a general supply of literary norms, just as the tradition of an inventor consists of the sum of technical possibilities of his time."[1] In discussing Lermontov, Boris Eikhenbaum declared:

> The creation of new artistic forms is not an act of invention, but one of discovery, because these forms exist latently in the forms of preceding periods. To Lermontov fell the task of discovering that poetic style which had to appear to provide a way out of the poetic impass created after the 20s and which already existed potentially among some poets of the Pushkin epoch.[2]

Wodehouse carried out this process of discovery and reinvention in an extreme fashion, self-consciously and with the idea of making the combination of existing clichés the essence of his craft.

With the invention of the Jeeves/Wooster series, Wodehouse went beyond his early simple exploration of genre to add his own distinctive dimension to his originals. After his early concentration on the school story (from 1900 to 1909, ending with the publication of *Mike*), each of Wodehouse's novels explores a different genre common in popular magazines and books of the day. It seems safe to assume that his goal was to attain regular publication in magazines like *Saturday Evening Post* in the United States, where he was living during much of this time; his work was already appearing regularly in the most prestigious

British fiction magazine, *The Strand.* Many years later Wodehouse recalled this era and his first *Post* serial, *Something New (Something Fresh* in England), the initial Blandings book:

> When this book was first published—fifty-three years ago—writers in America, where I had been living since 1909, were divided into two sharply defined classes—the Swells who contributed regularly to the Saturday Evening Post and the Cannail or Dregs who thought themselves lucky if they landed an occasional story with *Munsey's* or the *Popular* or one of the other pulp magazines. I had been a chartered member of the latter section for five years when I typed the first words of *Something Fresh.*[3]

Each of Wodehouse's books during this period explores a different contemporary genre. Patrick Brantlinger has pointed out that *The Swoop* (published just before *Mike* in 1909, in England only) is a parody of a specific subgenre of the war fantasy novel—the British invasion fantasy. Several such fantasies were written between 1880 and 1914, after the original, Sir George Chesney's *The Battle of Dorking,* appeared in *Blackwood's Magazine* in 1871. Other examples were T. A. Guthrie's *The Seizure of the Channel Tunnel* (1882), H. G. Lester's *The Taking of Dover* (1888), and the anonymous *The Sacking of London in the Great French War of 1901* (1901). For Brantlinger,

> The essence of the genre is captured in P. G. Wodehouse's 1909 parody *The Swoop . . . A Tale of the Great Invasion,* in which Britain is overwhelmed by simultaneous onslaughts of Germans, Russians, Chinese, Young Turks, the Swiss Navy, Moroccan brigands, cannibals in war canoes, the Prince of Monaco, and the Mad Mullah, until it is saved by a patriotic Boy Scout named Clarence Chugwater.[4]

The Swoop is the only parody among Wodehouse's book-length works, but his subsequent efforts are each light, semicomic versions of specific existing models. In each case, however, Wodehouse begins by adhering to the original formula, then twists the narrative into a pattern more familiar from his later work.

Such a tactic appears in the first of the post-school-story novels, *A Gentleman of Leisure* (1910, American title *The Intrusion of Jimmy*). It is loosely derived from the Raffles series, whose first book had appeared in 1899. Indeed, *A Gentleman of Leisure* begins in a men's club where the members are discussing "the latest better-than-'Raffles' play." The play's hero is a gentleman burglar: "In faultless evening dress, with a debonair smile on his face, he had broken open a safe, stolen bonds and jewellery to a large amount and escaped without a blush of shame via the window." The play is one of many hits recently on Broadway to use this idea, and one of the club members glumly remarks: "A few years ago they would have been scared to death of putting on a show with a criminal hero. Now, it seems to me, the public doesn't want anything else. Not that they know what they do want" (*A Gentleman of Leisure*, chap. 1). Wodehouse avoids turning Jimmy into an amoral Raffles figure, living on the proceeds of his thievery. Instead, Jimmy agrees on a bet to break into a mansion in imitation of the play's hero, but he becomes diverted on a romantic quest to help a young lady whom he follows to England. The rest of the book is an early example of the familiar Wodehouse country-house plot.

Wodehouse's next novel, *Psmith in the City*, was a sequel to *Mike*, following Mike and his pal Psmith through their first jobs in a banking firm in London. It drew extensively upon Wodehouse's own experiences in a bank, and it was only published in England. Still, the genre of young men in business was one of the most common in the *Post*, and it seems likely that a few years later he might have been able to sell something of the sort in the United States.

In 1911, Wodehouse published his sole venture into the Ruritanian romance with *The Prince and Betty*. This subgenre had begun in 1894 with British romance writer Anthony Hope's *The Prisoner of Zenda*; it was set in the mythical European country Ruritania, and Hope followed it with other novels of Ruritanian life. The genre was further popularized by the American writer George Barr McCutcheon; his *Graustark: The Story of a Love behind a Throne* (1901) was immensely successful, and there were several sequels.

The American version of *The Prince and Betty* is not a parody of these books, but it does have a more comic tone. As in *A Gentleman of Leisure*, Wodehouse carefully points out the original from which he is working. The plot involves a rich businessman, Mr. Scobell, who owns the gambling concession in the mythical Mediterranean republic of Mervo. He reinstates the island's hereditary prince in order to publicize his casino. When the hero, John Maude, arrives in Mervo, problems develop:

> Mr. Scobell eyed him doubtfully. His Highness did not appear to him to be treating the inaugural ceremony with that reserved dignity which we like to see in princes on these occasions. Mr. Scobell was a business man. He wanted his money's worth. His idea of a Prince of Mervo was something statuesquely aloof, something—he could not express it exactly—on the lines of the illustrations in the Zenda stories in the magazines—about eight feet high and shinily magnificent, something that would give the place a tone. That was what he had had in his mind when he sent for John. He did not want a cheerful young man in a soft hat and a flannel suit who looked as if at any moment he might burst into a college yell. (Chap. 5)

This passage is interesting for a number of reasons. It provides more evidence that Wodehouse probably read most of his main sources in their original magazine publications and thus scrupulously kept up with current genres. The passage also displays his characteristic consciousness of the slightly absurd quality of much popular genre writing of the late Victorian period, along with his ability to cite the originals affectionately while turning them to his own comic purposes. Still, at this stage of his career, Wodehouse was capable of a straight use of the clichés he would later lampoon. In the scene in which Betty rejects John's declaration of love, this passage occurs, with no humorous undercutting: "She broke off. John stood motionless, staring at the ground. For the first time in his easy-going life he knew shame. Even now he had not grasped to the full the purport of her words. The scales were falling from his eyes, but as yet he saw but dimly" (chap. 7). Even in this fairly conventional novel, however, Wodehouse abandons the formula partway through. After about a third of the book has been devoted to the Mervo situation, Betty flees to New York, and the plot concerns her employment as a secretary at a weekly paper there.[5]

Wodehouse next published *The Little Nugget* (1913 in the United Kingdom, 1914 in the United States), an uneasy blend of the crime story and comic romance, followed by a book of stories, *The Man Upstairs* (1914, United Kingdom only). Thereafter he wrote *Something Fresh* and began his association with the *Post*. From that point on, he alternated his various series with light romantic novels. The experimentation with other traditional magazine genres virtually disappears, with the only major exception being *The Coming of Bill* in 1919. There Wodehouse worked in a specific existing subgenre of the romance: the novel in which a couple marries, separates, and eventually reunites. A typical example of a "straight" version of this type would be E. M. Dell's *The Way of an Eagle* (1911); Dell was, incidentally, an exponent of the "burning kisses" school of prose, which Wodehouse later mocked. From 1915 on, however, Wodehouse seems to have found the combination of genres he had sought, and the changes in his work relate mainly to the perfecting of the personal formulas he had devised by then.

Why, in creating those formulas, Wodehouse turned to English subject matter is unclear. Perhaps he wanted to guarantee book publication of each title in both countries. From 1910 to 1914, most of his books published in the United States center on American protagonists, and he tends to move his characters back and forth across the Atlantic in the course of the narratives. The fact that his first *Post* publications centered on English characters presumably encouraged him to expand them into permanent series. The demands of the *Post* may have been responsible for the specific form the English characters took. In 1951, Wodehouse recalled the situation: "I started writing about Bertie Wooster and comic Earls because I was in America and couldn't write American stories and the only English characters the American public would read about were exaggerated dudes. It's as simple as that."[6]

A survey of the genres of stories published in the *Post* from the beginning of 1911 to the end of 1914 suggests that this claim is generally right, though it needs to be qualified. The *Post* at this period ran relatively few stories set in England or on the Continent, and the majority of those involved American characters traveling abroad. The magazine's main genres were westerns (by Owen Wister and others), romances (such as those of Fannie Hurst and Mary Roberts Rinehart), regionalist stories (for example, Harry Leon Wilson, Ring W. Lardner), adventure stories, set mainly at sea or in distant, exotic lands (especially by Jack London), ethnic stories (such as Montagu Glass's Potash and Perlmutter series), mysteries (notably by G. K. Chesterton and E. Phillips Oppenheim), and many business-related stories. Cub-reporter stories were common (probably mainly because much magazine fiction was done freelance by journalists), to the point where Irvin S. Cobb could publish "Another of Those Cub Reporter Stories" in the May 17, 1913, issue. Genres that were rarely represented in the pages of the *Post* were costume pieces, fantasy or science fiction, war and spy stories (though this changed in late 1914), and sophisticated fiction set in Europe. Wodehouse seems to have wanted to make urbane English comedy viable as the basis for a series.

Serious stories set in England were not quite so absent from the *Post* as Wodehouse suggests. Mysteries such as those of Chesterton and Oppenheim were set in England. The occasional romance story, such as Anthony Hope's "From the Collection of the Duke" (July 26, 1913) could have a completely English cast and setting, and the number of such stories increased from 1913 on. Still, there are some instances of caricatural young Britishers of the "exaggerated dude" variety in *Post* stories. Morley Roberts' "Gloomy Fanny," a two-part story in the May 13 and May 20, 1911, issues is perhaps closest to a prototype for the Jeeves/Wooster series, though it still bears relatively little resemblance to Wodehouse's work. In "Gloomy Fanny," a young, indolent clubman, Lord Fanshawe, is disappointed in love; to liven him up his friends bet him he cannot spend a week in the East End of London and earn his own living. The first part of the story has some dialogue that could almost take place among Bertie's friends at the Drones Club. One chum remarks that Fanny has threatened to give up polo:

> "That's serious," said Ned Burke. "We must buck him up."
> "Get him to do something," said Russell.
> "Yes, somethin' reckless," said Ponsonby.

> "What kind of reckless?" the others asked eagerly.
> "Oh, just somethin' bally reckless, I don't know what," said Ponsonby.
> "Let's think," said Tommy Burke.
> A pained expression crept over his youthful, happy countenance, and the rest knew he was trying to think.

Still, the story quickly changes into one of social commentary on class barriers as Fanny takes a job with a Whitechapel greengrocer and falls in love with the man's daughter, whom he must leave to her working-class boyfriend at the end.

Another British dude figure appears in one of the stories in Charles E. Van Loan's "Buck Parvin and the Movies" series, "The International Cup" (July 12, 1913). Here a rich young English polo player is rejected by his beloved, comes to the United States, and runs out of money. He applies for a job playing polo, which turns out to be for a film. The director's first interview with Kenneth Clifford Devenham suggests the comic stereotype at which Wodehouse may have been aiming:

> Jimmy Montague had a wonderfully quick eye for detail, as every successful director must have. Even as his thumbnail grated inquiringly over the engraved surface of the card, his trained eye appraised the visitor from the top of his sleek, blond head to the soles of his heavy shoes. "What a type!" he thought. "Oh, what a comedy type!"

Devenham's friend Buck Parvin, the cowboy movie extra, nicknames him Lord Algy, and one of the films they make together is *My Lord the Tenderfoot.* Though neither of these stories involves characters as exaggerated as Bertie Wooster, they suggest why Wodehouse would infer that a British dude might be of interest to the *Post.*

Certainly writing regularly for the *Post* would encourage an author to build a series. One historian of the magazine has suggested that familiarity and repetition were as important to its success as were its stylishness, humor, and entertainment value. The use of series characters was particularly common:

> By 1911, half a dozen new writers had appeared in the *Post*, all bringing characters who would become part of the contemporary popular culture: Irvin S. Cobb's Judge Priest, Peter Kyne's Cappy Ricks, George R. Chester's Get-Rich-Quick Wallingford, Montgomery Glass's Potash and Perlmutter, Mary Roberts Rinehart's Tish, and G. K. Chesterton's Father Brown. Over the next years, they would be joined by Octavus Roy Cohen's Florian Slappery, Arthur Train's Mr. Tutt, Ring Lardner's The Busher, and William Hazlett Upson's Earthworm Tractor salesman, Alexander W. Botts.
>
> The idea of a series built around a recurring character was not, of course, new; Conan Doyle's Sherlock Holmes offers one striking earlier example. But in the pages of the *Post* this type of story flourished, virtually creating a sub-genre in short fiction.[7]

Clearly, the *Post* was the ideal publishing venue for Wodehouse.

It seems evident that up to 1915, by exploring various genres, Wodehouse was seeking to create one or more series which could provide the basis for the sort of quick, formulaic writing suited to the popular magazine market. In *Performing Flea* Wodehouse recalled, "My own experience is that you can't—unless you are extraordinarily inventive—write a series bang off. I started writing in 1902, and every day I said to myself, 'I must get a character for a series.' "[8] The obvious problem for a writer in creating a series is to establish a formula that lends itself to repetition with sufficient variation to keep the reader coming back. In Wodehouse's case, the process of devising such a formula depended on achieving a balance of elements derived from existing genres, transformed into something new. I shall briefly sketch out the bare bones of the Jeeves/Wooster series' formulas, then go on to suggest their sources in contemporary genres.

The Jeeves/Wooster formula, with few exceptions, remains remarkably stable over sixty years, and it involves surprisingly few basic ways of getting Bertie into trouble and delaying Jeeves's solution. In many cases, a pal of Bertie's arrives with a problem: He needs money from a relative; his romance seems hopeless as a result of his parent figure's disapproval; his romance seems hopeless because he has a rival; he is successfully but inappropriately in love (a situation not recognized by the pal as a problem); or he is married or engaged but is in danger of alienating his beloved or has already. In the latter case, the alienation has come about either because the pal has fallen inappropriately in love with someone else or he has gambled unwisely. Instead of, or alongside, this sort of problem, Bertie may have a task or obligation imposed on him. The most common of these is marriage: in the early period of the series, Aunt Agatha will insist on this, while later on it is more likely that a former fiancée will agree retroactively to marry Bertie. In a few cases Bertie goes temporarily insane and wants to get married. A second common problem that confronts Bertie involves theft, often imposed on him as an obligation by Aunt Dahlia.

As a variant of these patterns, Bertie is often mistakenly accused by a rival of wanting to get married or by an irate owner of having committed theft. Sometimes when a pal gets into trouble, his engagement is threatened, and since his fiancée has at some point been engaged to Bertie, she agrees again to marry him. Given this small number of possibilities for creating problems, Wodehouse uses even fewer types of delaying tactics: Jeeves and Bertie argue over an article of clothing, or Jeeves is temporarily stumped, or Jeeves is on vacation.

Based on this simple outline, we can examine how the series originated in specific genre convention of the early years of the century.

THE COMIC ROMANCE

One notable aspect of the series is that, though virtually all the stories involve engagements and romances, there are remarkably few weddings. Indeed, from fairly early in the series, the same young couples keep returning, continuing their engagements or switching partners. The emphasis on courtship places the series squarely in the romance genre, yet the basic conventions of that genre are usually reversed. Ordinarily, romances involve a protagonist who either wants to marry someone other than the one a parent or guardian figure has chosen or wants to marry someone who resists the idea or takes a dislike to someone he or she gradually comes to love.

An example of a light-romantic *Post* story set in England that uses the first premise is Richard Dehan's "Susanna and Her Elders" (May 23, 1914), where an earl uses reverse psychology on his rebellious, artistically minded daughter in order to induce her to marry a rich but unattractive duke. He introduces the duke to her as a poor artist, hiring a handsome young artist to do the actual painting while impersonating the duke. Susanna's instincts triumph, however, and she falls for the real artist, resulting in a happy ending. With a few minor twists, one can easily imagine this story's plot furnishing the basis for Bertie's engagement to an intellectual girl and Jeeves's solution using mistaken identities and "the psychology of the individual."

In Wodehouse's series, Bertie's long-range goal is to avoid marriage, and though his friends often successfully become engaged, they seldom walk down the aisle.

Bertie's perpetual flight from marriage proved ideal for a magazine writer who wanted a lasting series. Indeed, many turn-of-the-century romance writers wrote sequels to their most successful books, but these were often limited by the fact that the heroine had become engaged in the first book. Three-book series tracing her fortunes in youth, marriage, and old age were not uncommon in this period, but such a formula had obvious limitations. Wodehouse's approach permitted a stable repetition of situations over the series' sixty-year span.

The nonmarriage romance also permitted Wodehouse to create two central, equally important continuing characters. While in an ordinary romance Jeeves would play the standard "tricky servant" role, helping the young lovers and fading into the background at the end, here he could perpetually prevent his master's marriage and thus preserve his continuing involvement in Bertie's life.

Despite the fact that the Jeeves/Wooster series bears certain distinct similarities to the romance genre, Wodehouse considerably changed those aspects that he borrowed. Indeed, there was not an established tradition of strongly comic romance fiction in the popular magazines of the day.[9] Nevertheless, there are some romances of the pre-1915 era where a light tone predominates. "Susanna and Her Elders" provides one example; another comes in Mary Roberts Rinehart's 1909 *When a Man Marries*, the plot of which bears some superficial resemblances to the standard Jeeves/Wooster narrative. It is a mystery story with a romance involving the heroine, and it contains comedy as well as intrigue. Specific elements of the plot also resemble Wodehousian devices. At the beginning, the heroine and a group of friends gather for a dinner and bridge party at the home of a pleasant young man—an artist—on the anniversary of the date upon which his wife divorced him. Unexpectedly the young man's aunt, who supports him and who disapproves of divorce, arrives for a visit. As he has not informed her that he has divorced, the heroine agrees to pretend to be his wife. Unfortunately the Japanese butler is taken off to the hospital in the course of the evening, apparently suffering from smallpox. The other servants immediately leave, but the guests are all quarantined for weeks, during which a number of jewel thefts take place in the house. Needless to say, a young man to whom the heroine is attracted is the prime suspect. In the end, the butler turns out only to have had chicken pox, the thief turns out to be someone other than the hero, and the heroine is united with the man she loves. *When a Man Marries* mixes romance and mystery in a straightforward way, and the only resemblances to Wodehouse's work are the light tone and the device of having the protagonist help a friend who is dependent on a disapproving aunt for his livelihood.

On the whole, the comic aspects of Wodehouse's romance formulas come more directly from the stage, and specifically from musical comedy and romantic farce. In his usual self-conscious fashion, he best summed up the point himself; "I believe there are two ways of writing novels. One is mine, making the thing a sort of musical comedy without music, and ignoring real life altogether; the other is going right down deep into life and not caring a damn."[10] Here Wodehouse seems to be referring more to the unrealistic quality of his subject matter and localized devices rather than the overall structure of his plots. Indeed, Guy Bolton and P. G. Wodehouse are credited by most historians of musical comedy as having introduced relatively tight plot construction into the genre.[11] Before their collaboration with Jerome Kern on the "Princess musicals" beginning in the mid-teens, plays of this sort were usually built around a loose series of absurd events that could motivate the introduction of songs, dances, and comic turns.

The general situations and characters of some of these earlier musicals are somewhat Wodehousian, however. A 1909 musical, *Our Miss Gibbs,* by two of the period's most prominent English composers of this genre, Ivan Caryll and Lionel Monckton, provides a good example. The plot involves a series of mismatched lovers: Mary Gibbs, the much-admired manager of a flower department in a London store; an earl's son who loves her and passes himself off as a bank clerk; his fiancée, who in turn loves a young society man, Hughie, who has apprenticed himself to a crook in order to become a gentleman burglar. Hughie steals the Ascot Gold Cup and hides it in a suitcase which is then switched with an identical suitcase carried by the heroine's cousin. The cousin, accused of the crime, disguises himself as a marathon runner, and the rest of the absurd action involves attempts to prevent his arrest and match up the various characters with the people they really love.[12] (Incidentally, in 1918 Bolton and Wodehouse wrote the book for an Ivan Caryll musical, *The Girl behind the Gun,* better known under its 1919 London title, *Kissing Time.*)

Similarly, the action in Wodehouse's narratives often revolves around tiffs between the various engaged couples of the plot, and the premises for their disagreements are deliberately made to seem ludicrous. For example, in *Right Ho, Jeeves,* Tuppy's refusal to believe Angela's story that she was nearly inhaled by a shark while aquaplaning at Cannes, plus Angela's retaliatory statement that Tuppy is fat, combine to keep these two at loggerheads through most of the action. The very absurdity of the entanglements in these plots illustrates how dependent they are upon conventional romantic literature.

In terms of structure, Wodehouse's plots also owe a great deal to a related genre, the sophisticated stage farce. This genre stresses carefully constructed plots essentially derived from nineteenth-century French-style comedy by Scribe, Labiche, Feydeau, and others. Like the musical, the modern stage comedy downplays psychological exploration, realism, social comment, and the like, and depends instead on light, superficial premises: mistaken identity, unwarranted jealousy, theft, chases in and out of bedrooms, couples switching partners. Often such comedies involve a primary, more "serious" couple and a secondary, more comic or frivolous one, with disapproving parents providing barriers to happiness.

As always, Wodehouse recognizes the conventionality of his models and points it up. In *The Mating Season*, he multiplies the number of sundered couples, including five in all. One character, new to the Jeeves/Wooster series, is Catsmeat Potter Pirbright, an actor who specializes in exactly this sort of comedy:

> He is the fellow managers pick first when they have a society comedy to present and want someone for "Freddie," the light-hearted friend of the hero carrying the second love interest. If at such a show you see a willowy figure come bounding on with a tennis racket, shouting "Hullo, girls" shortly after the kick-off, don't bother to look at the programme. That'll be Catsmeat. (Chap. 2)

As we shall see in chapter 6, Catsmeat plays the same role off the stage as well, and he is typical of the many young men who fall in and out of love in the series.

In general, Wodehouse stressed the playlike quality of his prose narratives by including frequent references to the stage and by structuring his dialogue so that it somewhat resembles a script. His descriptions sometimes use theatrical terminology, as in *Joy in the Morning*. Bertie rushes into Lord Worplesdon's study, which "proved to be what they call on the stage a 'rich interior,' liberally equipped with desks, chairs, tables, carpets and all the usual fixings." Later in the same scene Worplesdon sends his butler to fetch Jeeves: "During the stage wait, which was not of long duration, the old relative filled in with some *ad lib* stuff about Boko, mostly about how much he disliked his face" (chap. 22). Descriptions of characters' gestures or statements may characterize them as theatrical conventions. In *Jeeves and the Feudal Spirit*, Florence Craye is upset when her fiancé unexpectedly knocks on her bedroom door while Bertie is with her: "Florence clapped a hand to her throat, a thing I didn't know anybody ever did off the stage" (chap. 13). When Madeline Bassett thinks Gussie has knocked Spode out, Bertie describes her reaction: " 'I hate you, I hate you!' cried Madeline, a thing I didn't know anybody ever said except in the second act of a musical comedy" (*Stiff Upper Lip, Jeeves*, chap. 15).

Such moments would not in themselves be enough to give a theatrical flavor to Wodehouse's prose, but they serve primarily to point up a distinctive rhythm in the dialogue and action. Overall, Wodehouse downplays extensive description of setting, of atmosphere, and of characters' appearances. Lengthy stretches of his writing consist of dialogue, with Bertie's comic comments filling in with clichés and slang. Sometimes the dialogue is even rendered in script format, as in the first chapter of *Right Ho, Jeeves*:

> As I recall, the dialogue ran something as follows:
> SELF: Well, Jeeves, here we are, what?
> JEEVES: Yes, sir.
> SELF: I mean to say, home again.

This banter keeps up for twelves lines, until Bertie describes his reaction to the dialogue. This rhythm of *répliques* is reinforced by the slapstick rushing about that typically occupies the later sections of the narratives, especially the novels. Often Bertie will be beseiged in his bedroom in a country house, visited by a series of characters who are chasing each other and appeal to him for help, or who are threatening for some imagined misdeed on his part. The entrances and departures of these characters often mark the chapter breaks, as do moments like Jeeves's discovery of the stolen policeman's helmet in Bertie's suitcase at the end of chapter 12 in *The Code of the Woosters*.

Wodehouse's characters, too, are the amusing but superficial types of the stage comedy. In *Performing Flea*, Wodehouse claimed: "In writing a novel, I always imagine I am writing for a cast of actors. Some actors are natural minor actors and some are natural major ones. It is a matter of personality. Same in a book."[13] One vital consequence of this approach is that he could forestall indefinitely any actual marriage among his major characters without the reader feeling any sympathy for them. Until very late in the series, the only major pal who ever actually gets married is Bingo Little. These characters fall in love easily, drop their engagements without a pang, and pick them up again, only to stray once more at their next appearances in the series. Thus Wodehouse's particular blend of romantic conventions, derived from the existing clichés of the prose and stage literature of his day, permitted him to sustain his series over a long stretch of time.

Beyond simply creating an ongoing formula, however, Wodehouse added considerably to the comedy and emphasized the conventional nature of the series by combining these romance elements with others from another genre, the detective story, specifically the Holmes/Watson series. He extracted certain important traits of that series: the unreliable narrator who has a somewhat rebellious and uneasy relationship with the smarter character; the comic "marriage" implicit in the Holmes/Watson relationship; and some of the formulaic conventions of the Doyle stories' time-schemes. But he drops the mystery elements, replacing them with the conventions of romance we have just examined.

THE JEEVES/WOOSTER SERIES AND THE HOLMESIAN DETECTIVE STORY

In the Jeeves/Wooster series, Jeeves is a close parallel to Holmes, and Bertie resembles Watson in several ways. Jeeves is the problem solver, Bertie the admiring onlooker who records the pair's adventures in what he consistently calls the Wooster "archives." Rather than having the two be social equals sharing a flat, as in the original series, Wodehouse gains additional humor by making Bertie the master, Jeeves the servant—then making it clear that Jeeves is really the one in charge. Bertie's inability to understand completely Jeeves's thoughts and actions creates an aura of mystery around the valet similar to that which surrounds Holmes.

There is no doubt that Wodehouse long knew and loved Doyle's work; indeed, it is difficult to imagine such an avid schoolboy reader in the 1890s not reading the Holmes stories as they appeared in *The Strand*. Doyle experts have located numerous references to his oeuvre in Wodehouse's writings. Andrew Malec notes evidence of Wodehouse's early interest in Doyle in the form of five recently discovered early pieces that refer to or parody Doyle: two articles in the March and April 1902 issues of *Sandow's Magazine of Physical Culture and British Sport,* and three more in 1903 issues of *Punch.*[14] The latest references occur in *Aunts Aren't Gentlemen* (1974).

As Barrie Hayne points out, the original Holmes/Watson series itself contains considerable humor. Much of this humor obviously results from Holmes frequently pointing up Watson's slow reasoning. Just as importantly, however, humor arises from the innately domestic relationship between Holmes and Watson:

> That the "alliance" of Holmes and Watson is psychically a marriage needs no insistence here, since it has been taken so long for granted, and reared into the kind of comedy that passes for Baker Street Irregularity by no less a personage than Rex Stout, in the famous "Watson Was a Woman," nearly fifty years ago. But it is worth noting that from the marital nature of their alliance arises much of the comedy of the Sherlock Holmes stories, and especially the badinage that goes on between two people who clearly care about one another, but who sometimes feel the irritations of familiarity. . . . One surely does not need to verify the comic qualities of marital tension.[15]

Hayne takes Holmes to be the husband and Watson the wife, which seems valid. The relations are reversed in the Jeeves/Wooster series, however, with the narrator figure, Bertie, clearly being thc husband. This is partly due to class differences, with Jeeves's having duties as a "domestic," and partly due to the constant emphasis on separation through Bertie's engagements. Jeeves becomes the faithful wife and builder of the home, Bertie the potentially errant husband. As we shall see in the next chapter, these roles shape enormously the pair's respective narrative functions.[16]

What Wodehouse has apparently done, probably self-consciously, is to recognize that this domestic quality of the Holmes/Watson series has considerable comic potential. He concentrates on the domestic aspects while jettisoning the mystery plots. Again, in turning to the romance formula, he realized that the task of *not* getting Bertie married was ideal. It conforms to the domesticity of the Doyle stories, and it allows the Jeeves/Wooster series to go on indefinitely.

Since Wodehouse's own approach to writing was to depend upon, even heighten, the formulaic and the clichéd, it is not surprising that he seized upon a set of conventions from a series which is itself very formulaic. As Viktor Shklovsky points out in his analysis of *The Adventures of Sherlock Holmes*, the stories often begin with the device of having Watson list a number of cases, from which he chooses one to relate to us. Two of the stories in this volume begin with Holmes and Watson observing an approaching client from their window, while Holmes makes inferences about the person's identity and errand ("A Case of Identity" and "The Adventure of the Beryl Coronet"); three of them involve Holmes making deductions about his clients by examining their hands ("The Speckled Band," "A Case of Identity," and "The Red-headed League").[17] Hayne points out that the Holmes series three times employs the device of having a man lured away from a locale in order that a crime may be committed there. He also suggests that the series verges at times on self-parody, especially in the stories after the apparent death of Holmes at Reichenbach Falls—the parodic element coming partly in the increasingly baroque references to cases not recounted.[18]

Among the devices of the Holmes/Watson series that Wodehouse adopted was the typical time structure. Often Bertie's friends and relatives come to lay their problems before him as he is still in bed or at breakfast—as often happens with Holmes. (Doyle's decision to have Holmes receive clients in his home rather than in a separate office played a large role in linking the domestic routine to the cases.) In both series, the case may take days or weeks to solve, but the final resolution often happens in the evening. Holmes and Watson might end a story by going off for supper and a box at the opera, while Bertie ends his by receiving a nightcap from Jeeves, but the devices function in the same way. Again, Wodehouse seized upon a "domestic" aspect of the Holmes/Watson narratives and adapted it for comic purposes.

The domestic cycle that governs so many of the narratives relates to another aspect of the specifically British detective story. As a number of commentators have pointed out, comedy is important in a particular subgenre. According to Earl F. Bargainnier:

> One method of solving the uneasy relationship [between crime and comedy] is most evident in British classical detective fiction and is indicated by the epithet "cosy." This cosiness prevents a clash between crime and comic action. It owes a great deal to the novels of P. G. Wodehouse and the early ones of Evelyn Waugh, especially as to characterization. One can be comfortable at houseparties with silly-ass young men and bubble-headed, though titled, damsels. Murder becomes simply a lark: a game hardly more threatening than croquet on the manor lawn.[19]

H. R. F. Keating suggests that, while other authors have occasionally mixed comedy and crime, it is most characteristic of British detective writers:

> It arises, I suspect, from the prevalence among British practitioners of the crime novel designed to establish a feeling of cosiness rather than of the crime novel designed to establish an atmosphere of unease. Agatha Christie, most British of writers, is, of course, in most of her output the archetype of the cosy crime novelist.[20]

Interestingly, Christie and Wodehouse admired each other greatly, corresponding and dedicating books to each other. And certainly Wodehouse would have an equal claim as the "most British of writers," but his cosiness arises from an even less threatening world.

The "cosy' brand of British crime fiction has been linked to the "What fun!" school of detection, named for a verbal motif in A. A. Milne's *The Red House Mystery* (1922).[21] There a murder takes place at a country house, and a pleasant young wanderer who happens to have been coming to visit a friend at the house decides to become an amateur detective and investigate, with the help of the friend. It is the latter who frequently exclaims "What fun!" when some clue is found or discovery made.

Yet despite the fact that the notion of cosiness and the "What fun!" approach are generally dated to the post–World War I era of British detective fiction, there is no doubt that the basic elements are there in the Holmes/Watson series. Certainly the cosiness of the Turkish slipper, the gasogene, and Mrs. Hudson's homely meals do much to set up the domestic atmosphere that Wodehouse copies so directly.

Aside from the domestic element and temporal structure of the problem-solving plot, the main device Wodehouse borrows from Doyle is the by-then almost archetypal Watsonian unreliable narrator. Certainly long before Wodehouse invented the Jeeves/Wooster series, imitators had picked up the use of a friend of the brilliant detective-figure who relates the story from a limited perspective, relying on the detective for final revelations concerning how the crime was solved.

In some cases the appropriation of the Doyle formula was crude. Arthur Morrison's Martin Hewitt series, which appeared in *The Strand* from the mid-1890s (and thus alongside the Holmes/Watson stories themselves) was a pale imitation of the original. The Hewitt stories are purportedly narrated by his friend Brett, a journalist who lodges in the same apartment building. But Brett, aside from being a colorless figure, is seldom actually along on the investigation: "Such of the cases, however, as I personally saw nothing of I have put into narrative form from the particulars given me" ("The Lenton Croft Robberies," 1894). Hewitt has an office where most cases are brought to him, so that the domestic situation of the Holmes/Watson series is absent. To an even greater extent than in Doyle, clues are withheld from the reader, so that the revelation of the criminal's identity typically comes four-fifths of the way through, with the remainder reserved for a lengthy explanation by the detective.[22]

The Watsonian narrational principle could work for criminals as well. E. W. Hornung's Raffles series is a much more successful imitation of the Holmes/Watson series than are the Martin Hewitt stories. Here Raffles' schoolmate Bunny becomes his companion in crime and the first-person narrator of the series. As with Watson, Bunny is frequently kept in the dark; he also occasionally doubts Raffles' loyalty but always realizes in the end that Raffles has worked events to their mutual advantage. In a sense, Hornung has inverted the Holmes/Watson series in a simple but effective way, by making the forces for law and order into successful criminals. Wodehouse's twisting of the series to his own purposes created a more abstract approach, combining certain conventions with those of other genres.

By the mid-teens, when Wodehouse started the Jeeves/Wooster series, the narrator-friend was standard issue for detectives. An important crime series of the era, Arthur Reeves's Craig Kennedy stories (which appeared in *Cosmopolitan* and then in a uniform edition of books) featured an amateur scientific detective who was also a chemistry professor. The narrator was Walter Jameson, a reporter who shared Kennedy's apartment (equipped with an up-to-date laboratory beyond Holmes's wildest dreams) and detailed the efforts of various bizarre criminals, such as "The Clutching Hand," to defeat his friend. (Bertie Wooster's reading matter owes not a little to the Craig Kennedy type of detective literature.) The most prominent of the adventures, *The Exploits of Elaine* (1915) demonstrates the clumsiness of the first-person narrational device in the hands of an unskilled author. Jameson constantly has to move among events, skipping back temporally to fill in what was happening "meanwhile" somewhere else. Whenever Jameson cannot plausibly be present for an action, he has to claim that he learned about it later, from a passing streetsweeper or from the other characters. At one point, Elaine is kidnapped, and the narrator informs us "What had really happened, as we learned later from Elaine and others . . ."—thus letting us know ahead of time that Elaine survived the kidnapping and deflating the suspense of the entire episode!

The notion of the Watsonian narrator was widespread by this point, and it is good-naturedly acknowledged by Milne in *The Red House Mystery*. There, as outlined above, an amateur detective and his friend undertake to solve a murder at a country house. Chapter 8 is forthrightly entitled "Do You Follow me, Watson?" In it, Antony, the protagonist, and his pal Bill wander out into the grounds to discuss the case:

> "Are you prepared to be the perfect Watson?" he asked.
>
> "Watson?"
>
> "Do-you-follow-me-Watson; that one. Are you prepared to

> have quite obvious things explained to you, to ask futile questions, to give me chances to score off you, to make brilliant discoveries of your own two or three days after I have made them myself—all that kind of thing? Because it all helps."
>
> "My dear Tony," said Bill delightedly, "need you ask?" Antony said nothing, and Bill went on happily to himself, "I perceive from the strawberry mark on your shirt-front that you had strawberries for dessert. Holmes, you astonish me. Tut, tut, you know my methods. Where is the tobacco? The tobacco is in the Persian slipper. Can I leave my practice for a week? I can."

Here Milne illustrates, in a flood of verbiage, how clichéd and yet how current the Holmes/Watson stories were. (The last of them were still appearing during the 1920s.[23]) By then Wodehouse had already begun to take the Holmesian narrative structure as a clichéd and yet viable pattern for his own work.

That Wodehouse was aware both of the mechanics of Watsonian narration and of its potential for comedy is beyond doubt. Late in his life he contributed the foreword to John McAleer's 1977 biography of Rex Stout, in which he perceptively analyzed the first-person narrator in the Nero Wolfe series:

> But Stout's supreme triumph was Archie Goodwin.
>
> Telling a mystery story in the third person is seldom satisfactory. To play fair you have to let the reader see into the detective's thoughts, and that gives the game away. The alternative is to have him pick up small objects from the floor and put them carefully away in an envelope without revealing their significance, which is the lowest form of literary skulduggery. A Watson of some sort to tell the story is unavoidable, and the hundreds of Watsons who have appeared in print since Holmes's simply won't do. I decline to believe that when the prime minister sends for the detective to cry on his shoulder about some bounder having swiped the naval treaty and finds that he has brought a friend along, he just accepts the detective's statement that "This is Augustus So-and-So, who has been associated with me in many of my cases." What he would really do would be to ring the bell for the secretary of

> state and tell him to throw Mr. So-and-So out on his ear. "And I want to hear him bounce," he would add. Stout has avoided this trap. Archie is a Watson in the sense that he tells the story, but in no other way is there anything Watsonian about him. And he brings excellent comedy into the type of narrative where comedy seldom bats better than .100.[24]

Much of what Wodehouse says here could apply to Bertie Wooster as a narrational figure, with pure comedy resulting.

As always, Wodehouse did not want his readers to miss the fact that he was drawing upon an established formula. The Jeeves/Wooster series contains implicit and explicit references to the Holmes/Watson series, pointing up the parallel. In "Aunt Agatha Speaks Her Mind," Bertie describes his first meeting with Aline Hemmingway: "I don't pretend to be a Sherlock Holmes or anything of that order, but the moment I looked at her, I said to myself, 'The girl plays the organ in a village church!' " In fact Aline turns out to be part of a con team out to steal Aunt Agatha's necklace, so Bertie is wrong; Jeeves remains the Holmes figure in this pair. A more oblique reference comes in "Pearls Mean Tears," where Sidney Hemmingway (alias Soapy Sid) uses his supposed gambling debt to one "Colonel Musgrave" to con Bertie. Similarly, in "Indian Summer of an Uncle," Jeeves informs Bertie that Rhoda Platt lives at Wistaria Lodge in East Dulwich—presumably a reference to Doyle's "The Adventure of Wisteria Lodge."

The Holmes parallel becomes both more explicit and more dynamic in the early novels. In *Thank You, Jeeves*, Bertie boasts to Pauline and Chuffy that he will handle Stoker and, when he hears the latter approaching, remarks to them, " 'This, if I mistake not, Watson,' I said, 'is our client now' " (chap. 19). The device of comparing Bertie or Jeeves to Holmes becomes more central to *Right Ho, Jeeves*, where Bertie is in his rebellious phase and tries to solve the various problems himself without Jeeves's help. When Jeeves announces Gussie Fink-Nottle at an early hour, when Bertie has a hangover, Bertie notes, 'One can't give the raspberry to a client. I mean, you didn't find Sherlock Holmes refusing to see clients just because he had been out late the night before at Dr. Watson's birthday party" (chap. 5). Since

Jeeves is the real Holmes in the series, Bertie's comparison of himself to Holmes points up the degree of his presumption in this novel. Later he condescends to Jeeves in telling him that he has solved Tuppy and Angela's problem:

> "Indeed, sir. Might I inquire—"
> "You know my methods, Jeeves. Apply them." (Chap. 9)

Inevitably Bertie fails to solve the problems, and Jeeves outlines to Bertie a scheme for tricking the various characters out of the country house where they are all assembled by sounding a fire alarm; he suggests that this will cause the various men in the household to save their respective estranged fiancées, despite earlier quarrels. Bertie questions him:

> "Is that based on psychology?"
> "Yes, sir. Possibly you may recollect that it was an axiom of the late Sir Arthur Conan Doyle's fictional detective, Sherlock Holmes, that the instinct of everyone, upon an alarm of fire, is to save the object dearest to them." (Chap. 21)

Jeeves's scheme is in fact not based on this notion; he realizes that the couples will not be scared into reconciling, but he plans to solve all the problems by humiliating Bertie and uniting the other characters in their laughter at him. In this plan, Jeeves fares better than Holmes did in "A Scandal in Bohemia," where he was bested by The Woman.

The comparison of Jeeves to Holmes has become clearcut by *The Mating Season*. There Bertie suggests that Esmond Haddock consult Jeeves on his problem, and when the latter objects to bringing valets into the situation, Bertie declares:

> "No, one does not want to keep visiting valets out of this," I said firmly. "Not when they're Jeeves. If you didn't live all the year round in this rural morgue, you'd know that Jeeves isn't so much a valet as a Mayfair consultant. The highest in the land bring their problems to him. I shouldn't wonder if they didn't give him jewelled snuff-boxes." (Chap. 25)

(Holmes receives a gold snuff-box from the king in "A Scandal in Bohemia" and a ring from "the reigning family of Holland" in "A Case of Identity.") The comparison becomes even more explicit in "Jeeves and the Greasy Bird," where Bertie suggests that Sir Roderick Glossop consult Jeeves: "Jeeves is like Sherlock Holmes. The highest in the land come to him with their problems. For all I know, they may give him jewelled snuffboxes."

Jeeves continues to behave like Holmes, remarking to Bill in *Ring for Jeeves*, "The problem is undoubtedly one that presents certain points of interest, m'lord" (chap. 13). The most extended Holmes/Watson conversation between Jeeves and Bertie takes place in the series' last entry, *Aunts Aren't Gentlemen*, when Jeeves knows why Cook has accused Bertie of stealing his cat, even though Jeeves was not on the scene and has never met Cook:

> "I think I can explain, sir."
> It seemed incredible. I felt like Doctor Watson hearing Sherlock Holmes talking about the one hundred and forty-seven varieties of tobacco ash and the time it takes parsley to settle in the butter dish.
> "This is astounding, Jeeves," I said. "Professor Moriarty wouldn't have lasted a minute with you. You really mean the pieces of the jig-saw puzzle have come together and fallen into their place?"
> "Yes, sir."
> "You know all?"
> "Yes, sir."
> "Amazing!"
> "Elementary, sir. I found the habitués of the Goose and Grasshopper a ready source of information." (Chap. 5)

Thus it seems clear that Wodehouse hoped that this readers would recognize the similarities between his own series and Doyle's. Indeed, one could go further and conclude that the humor and complexity of the Jeeves/Wooster series is enhanced if the reader does see the connection.

It is worth noting that one of the most amusing stylistic devices of the Jeeves/Wooster series may have been derived from Doyle. As Holmes finishes examing the King of Bohemia's notepaper in "A Scandal in Bohemia," "His eyes sparkled, and he sent up a great blue triumphant cloud from his cigarette." A more straightforward rendering would be "He triumphantly sent up a great blue cloud from his cigarette." Here Doyle uses what Robert Hall has termed a "transferred epithet." In "A Scandal in Bohemia," where the prose style is not comic, the "triumphant blue cloud" has a faintly absurd quality. It seems just possible that Wodehouse derives his own oft-noted transferred epithets from this or similar passages. The device appears as early as "Jeeves takes Charge," where Bertie is drinking tea: "I sucked down a cheerful mouthful." It recurs many times, as in "Jeeves and the Greasy Bird": " 'I take it, Jeeves," I said as I started to pick at a moody fried egg, 'that Aunt Dahlia has told you all.'"[25] Wodehouse may have revered Doyle, but he also saw the comic possibilities in his hero's work.

Even though Wodehouse has transformed the original model of the Holmesian detective story by draining the mystery elements out and replacing them with comic ones, his affinity with the mystery also remains obvious in his own influence on later writers in that genre. Julian Symons' history of the detective story notes the similarity between Bertie's speech and that of Dorothy L. Sayers' Lord Peter Wimsey, and he speaks of the "Jeeves-like Bunter."[26] Elaine Bander cites Wodehouse as the originator of the "ass-about-town," Wimsey, and cites Bunter's reaction to hearing about the corpse in *Whose Body?* (1923): " 'Indeed, my lord? That's very gratifying!' "[27] In true Wodehousian fashion, Sayers herself points up the parallels by means of explicit references. Early in *Murder Must Advertise* (1933), a character describes Wimsey: " 'Tow-coloured, supercilious-looking blighter. . . . Cross between Ralph Lynn and Bertie Wooster' " (chap. 1).[28] Chapter 20 of *Strong Poison* (1930) contains the following bit of dialogue:

> "Oh, Bunter—here you are! Next time you hold Hannah's hand, will you ask her whether Mr. Boyes drank any water from his bedroom water-bottle before dinner?"
>
> "Pardon me, my lord, the possibility had already presented itself to my mind."

> "It had?"
>
> "Yes, my lord."
>
> "Do you ever overlook anything, Bunter?"
>
> "I endeavour to give satisfaction, my lord."
>
> "Well, then, don't talk like Jeeves. It irritates me. What about the water-bottle?"

Similarly, Wodehouse's comic country-house formula may have influenced Milne's *The Red House Mystery,* the first paragraph of which could pass for the opening of a Blandings novel:

> In the drowsy heat of the summer afternoon the Red House was taking its siesta. There was a lazy murmur of bees in the flower-borders, a gentle cooing of pigeons in the tops of the elms. From distant lawns came the whir of a mowing-machine, that most restful of all country sounds; making ease the sweeter in that it is taken while others are working.

The Red House Mystery, as we have seen, was a turning point in the "What fun!" school of British detective fiction. It brings out what had always been implicit in the genre: the fact that the murder was not a disturbing event for the reader but a pretext for a playful game of clever narration, plot surprises, eccentric characters, and witty dialogue. Wodehouse's comic variant of the "cosy" British detective story was not that far from its originals and could easily be converted back to provide eccentricity and comic overtones for the genre as it continued.

Wodehouse's particular method for combining elements from the detective story and the romance seems unique, but there have traditionally been links between the detective and romance genres. Doyle provided a romance and ultimately a marriage for Watson in *The Sign of the Four,* and for much of the rest of the series he had to wrestle with the problem of making his narrator-figure available to accompany the great detective. H. Douglas Thomson's classic 1931 study of the genre credits E. C. Bentley's 1913 *Trent's Last Case* as "the first successful introduction of the love element into the detective story."[29] Its other notable innovation is having the amateur-detective protagonist be wrong in his solution (not just once, but twice), primarily because he falls in love with the widow of the murdered man, and hence his struggle to remain objective throws his reasoning off balance. In simpler detective novels of the era, such as *The Exploits of Elaine* (1915), the romance between the detective and the heroine simply motivates his repeated desperate attempts to rescue her (and, in one isolated case in this novel, for her to rescue him).

Yet, as Jane S. Bakerman has pointed out, romance is common in stories where the protagonist is an amateur detective. With a few alterations, her description could easily fit the Jeeves/Wooster series:

> The most common crime story subplot is a romance (or two or three), and the detective's propensity for bearing patiently with lovers' sufferings, doubts, and confessions allows him to learn a great deal about various characters' true personalities. Since most amateur detectives are congenital advice-givers and born-again meddlers, few (apart from Wolfe and Greenfield) hesitate to guide love affairs, either directly or indirectly. Advice, after all, to heartbroken maiden, base seducer, or flawed social order is their stock in trade, and the detectives have earned the right to give it by their patience and by their insight into human nature.[30]

Jeeves may not be a detective, but his propensity for utilizing "the psychology of the individual" allows him to solve romantic problems, both to his own profit and in the interests of preserving his "marriage" to Bertie.

Since the romance genre inherently creates problems for an author's sustenance of a series, the introduction of romance into a detective series would most likely create problems—as the example of Watson's marriage shows. Wodehouse avoided Doyle's mistake with the premise that Bertie will not marry and by equating the romantic entanglements presented to Jeeves with Holmesian cases. The elements Wodehouse borrowed from Doyle helped him create the stable formula he needed for a series: the Holmes/Watson works went on for forty years with little change, while the Jeeves/Wooster series went for sixty. From this combination of the Holmesian detective story and the romance genre,

Wodehouse fashioned his own distinctive genre, a formula based on the formulaic.

As everyone who has read any of the stories or novels knows, however, the works themselves are far more complex than any outline of the formulas suggests. The remainder of this book is devoted to examining the specific structures and devices that transform Wodehouse's dependence on earlier genres and conventions into a complex and original set of narratives.

4

THE PSYCHOLOGY OF THE STEREOTYPIC INDIVIDUAL

Age cannot wither them, nor custom stale their infinite monotony, he seemed to be saying of his creations, and, of course, I agreed with him.

—MALCOLM MUGGERIDGE IN "Forever Wooster"

JEEVES AND BERTIE AS CONVENTIONAL CHARACTERS

Much of the power of the Jeeves/Wooster series comes from the juxtaposition of its two main characters. Yet the series does not concentrate on character psychology. There are certainly changes in the pair over the years: Bertie goes through a period of jealousy of and rebellion against Jeeves in the late 1920s stories and early 1930s novels, and the servant-master relationship gradually evolves into a closer, more equal partnership. On the whole, though, Jeeves and Bertie do not develop much during the series. These characters grow chiefly through the occasional addition of new facts about them—bits of information that come in when they are necessary to the plot or can provide a bit of humor. We learn in *The Code of the Woosters*, for example, that Jeeves belongs to the Junior

Ganymede Club, because the Club Book's information would be convenient for allowing Bertie to quell Roderick Spode; the book reappears frequently thereafter as a handy device for various plot purposes. In *Jeeves and the Feudal Spirit,* Jeeves reveals that he once studied jewelry under a cousin of his; this invention was one of the last things Wodehouse added to the novel, and it solved the problem of how Jeeves could recognize the two necklaces as being of cultured pearls. We learn in *Right Ho, Jeeves* that Bertie had won a prize for Scripture knowledge at school; thereafter this device permits many comic references to biblical stories.

I have suggested that Wodehouse's originality lies, paradoxically, in his systematic dependence on previous works and in his insistence on convention and cliché. Bertie, Jeeves, and the series' other characters have their origins in stock figures. Wodehouse acknowledged that Bertie stems from a type common in the popular theater and music hall of the early decades of the century: the stage "dude." This stereotypical figure was popularized by such actors as George Grossmith, with whom Wodehouse wrote several plays in the 1920s; Grossmith had his first big successes between 1901 and 1913 in London, when Wodehouse was becoming an author and moving into theatrical writing himself. (A British dude can be seen in the 1929 film *Bulldog Drummond,* in the person of Algy, the hero's sidekick.) Bertie's monocle, spats, and love of flashy clothes, his sketchy education, his schoolboy code, and many of his other traits came straight out of this comic stereotype.

Jeeves is as conventional in origin as his master. As several critics have pointed out, he belongs to a general literary tradition of clever servants, stretching back to the plays of Aristophanes (for example, Xanthias in *The Frogs*) and Plautus and extending through such figures as Sancho Panza and Sam Weller. Critics have combed Victorian and Edwardian literature for butlers and valets who might have provided more immediate sources for Jeeves. Phipps, in Wilde's *An Ideal Husband,* has been suggested,[1] but the part is a tiny one, and Jeeves is not as supercilious as Phipps. (Wodehouse did, however, borrow this conventional butler name for *The Old Reliable.*) *The Admirable Crichton* is widely assumed to be a major source,[2] but again there is virtually no resemblance between Crichton and Jeeves, beyond the fact that each is more competent than the people he serves.

There is, however, a more plausible model for Jeeves and one which also bears interestingly on Bertie's origins. Frances Donaldson mentions Harry Leon Wilson's *Ruggles of Red Gap* as a possible source, basing her inference on a remark Wodehouse made to an interviewer late in life. Donaldson is cautious in suggesting *Ruggles* as a source, since she sees "no evidence of direct plagiarism, but Harry Leon Wilson must be counted as an influence if nothing more."[3] There is, however, evidence that *Ruggles* (serialized in the *Post* in 1914, published in book form in 1915) was a direct inspiration for the Jeeves/Wooster series. In 1965, Wodehouse described the process:

> I read Ruggles when it first came out in the Saturday Evening Post in 1914, and it made a great impression on me and in a way may have been the motivating force behind the creation of Jeeves, for I remember liking the story very much but feeling that he had got the English valet all wrong.
>
> I felt that an English valet would never have been so docile about being handed over to an American in payment of a poker debt. I thought he had missed the chap's dignity. I think it was then that the idea of Jeeves came into my mind.[4]

Certainly the timing is right, since the first Jeeves/Wooster story appeared in 1915.

In chapter 2 we saw how Wodehouse would cannibalize plots and phrases from other writers' works, recombining them in various ways that transformed them thoroughly. Wilson influenced Wodehouse considerably. For example, echoes of the lengthy drunk scene in chapter 3 of *Ruggles* are evident in chapter 6 of *Barmy in Wonderland,* where Mervyn Potter drags Barmy to a series of nightculbs, gets drunk, then tells his fiancée that Barmy led him astray. The title "Jeeves and the Song of Songs" probably stems from Wilson's 1915 "Ma Pettingill and the Song of Songs," published in the *Post* three weeks before the first Jeeves/Wooster story, "Extricating Young Gussie," appeared there (August 28 and September 18, 1915, respectively). A set of notes for Jeeves/Wooster plots, dating from about 1930, contains one idea:

"Church bazaar—J. raises money by a gambling device—cp [sic] H. Leon Wilson's story."[5] This idea was never used, but traces of Wilson do show up in the series. For example, in *Ruggles*, the valet is horrified when his new employer comes home after a binge wearing a policeman's cap: "I concealed the constable's cap in one of his boxes, for I feared that he had not come by it honestly" (American first edition, p. 76). The end of chapter 12 of *The Code of the Woosters* involves a stolen policeman's helmet in a suitcase. In "Jeeves and the Hard-boiled Egg," the "Boost for Birdsburg" buttons that Jeeves judges "scarcely a judicious addition to a gentleman's evening costume," recall the garish "Keep Your Eye on Red Gap!" billboard of which Ruggles disapproves.

Of course, Wodehouse's use of Ruggles as an inspiration for Jeeves was basically a negative one. As his letter suggests, Jeeves is far more dignified and intelligent than Ruggles (though they share an obsession with tasteful clothing). Ruggles is naive and often misunderstands the motives of others. Indeed, it seems possible that Ruggles is in some ways a source for Bertie as well. Wodehouse has split off his traits of naiveté and obliviousness and given them to a second character who can be a foil to the dignified Jeeves. Moreover, Ruggles narrates his story in the first person, and, like Bertie, he is an unreliable narrator. Since he often misunderstands the other characters, we must infer more about them than he tells us. We grasp, for example, how the widow, Mrs. Judson, deliberately makes Ruggles jealous and goads him into declaring his love, while Ruggles finds her actions inexplicable and believes that his declaration results from his own impetuousness. This device of filtering narrative information through a character who knows less than does the reader is just what Wodehouse uses with Bertie, though Wodehouse handles the reader's knowledge in a subtler fashion than does Wilson.

These, then, are the comic conventions and sources upon which Wodehouse drew for the characters of Jeeves and Bertie. The originality of these characters emerged from a combination of their narrative and narrational functions, their relationship, and their unique uses of language and quotation.

JEEVES TAKES CHARGE OF THE INIMITABLE WOOSTER

> Jeeves is not the perfect gentleman's gentleman. Jeeves is Fate and Jeeves is Brain and Jeeves is the God out of the Machine. . . . Always ready to do his utmost for the Bingos and Claudes of his acquaintance, [Bertie] has an actual appetite for incident; with nothing to do, he does everything.
>
> —GILBERT SELDES (1934)

Perhaps the most noticeable aspect of the Jeeves/Bertie relationship is the systematic opposition of virtually all their traits. Jeeves is intelligent, pragmatic, amoral, educated, intellectual, and quiet; his pastimes include playing bridge at his club, fishing, gambling, sailing, swimming, and reading "an improving book" at bedtime. Bertie is, if not stupid, at least a bit slow; he is idealistic, moral, relatively uneducated (despite his Oxford degree), nonintellectual, and lively. His pastimes include golf, riding, tennis, darts, practical jokes and bread-and-sugar tossing at *his* club, and reading mysteries and thrillers. Jeeves is laconic, though he can launch into verbose, quotation-laden speeches; Bertie describes his face as expressionless, but there are actually many descriptions of tiny changes in Jeeves's face—though he seldom allows his companions to read his thoughts unless he wants them to. Bertie, on the other hand, is talkative and expressive; Jeeves and the other characters have no trouble interpreting his facial expressions. These systematic oppositions between the two reflect Jeeves's and Bertie's most basic narrative functions: Jeeves provides a force for closure, Bertie one for openness.

I am using these two terms in a straightforward way, as they are employed in literary theory. That is, narratives typically begin in a stable state; then some sort of conflict creates an unbalanced, "open" set of events; the resolution of the conflict restores stability to the narrative. That stability constitutes "closure." Not all narratives achieve closure, since it is possible to end without a resolution. Wodehouse's narratives, however, almost never take that approach.[6] Similarly, a narrative that begins in medias res places the reader immediately in an unstable, open situation. For example, at the beginning of "The Inferiority Complex of Old Sippy," Bertie is in the course of ticking Jeeves off for objecting to his new Chinese vase. Yet Bertie quickly fills us in on events that had disturbed their domestic equilibrium: his purchase of the vase and Jeeves's disapproval.

In the Jeeves/Wooster series, Bertie usually initiates the problem or problems and then acts as a force (however unwilling) to keep the narrative open. Most typically, a friend or aunt assigns Bertie a task; he then either asks Jeeves to accomplish it or tackles it himself and then, having failed, turns it over to Jeeves. Jeeves, on the other hand, acts largely as a force for closure; once he solves the problems, the narratives end, usually with an epilogue echoing the stable situation of the beginning. In keeping with the Holmesian formula, many of the narratives begin with Bertie waking in the morning or having breakfast, with the endings coming as he sips a nightcap or goes to bed. Between these images of narrative stability and closure come the various problems that disrupt this placidity. I shall look first at Jeeves's part in creating and maintaining that placid state of narrative closure, then go on to examine how Bertie and most other characters function to create and maintain openness.

JEEVES, THE MAYFAIR CONSULTANT

Given Jeeves's combination of brains and pragmatism, plus his many conflicts with Bertie, we might ponder why the relationship survives. In an early story, Bertie writes, "It beats me sometimes why a man of his genius is satisfied to hang around pressing my clothes and what not. If I had half Jeeves's brain I should have a stab at being Prime Minister or something" ("The Artistic Career of Corky"). A number of critics have echoed this puzzlement,[7] but the reasons for Jeeves's apparent lack of ambition seem apparent. Most basically Jeeves, as a force for closure in the narratives, is characterized as wanting a placid existence. He achieves this as Bertie's valet, despite the frequent disturbances caused by aunts, temporary fiancées, and beleaguered pals. In "Bertie Changes His Mind," Jeeves views with horror the idea of having Bertie's sister and nieces come to live with them: "The course of action outlined by Mr. Wooster meant the finish of our cosy bachelor existence"; he also says he "had no desire to sever a connexion so pleasant in every respect as his and mine had been." Given Jeeves's class origins, this cosy, pleasant life is relatively luxurious; on realistic grounds, there is every reason to think that he would consider himself lucky to be leading it.

Jeeves comes, after all, from a lower-middle-class background. His cousin is a jeweler, and Jeeves apparently once considered taking up that profession. In "The Rummy Affair of Old Biffy," we learn that Jeeves has a niece, Mabel, a model and aspiring actress whom Biffy describes as coming "of good, sturdy middle-class stock"; her father runs either a milk-walk or bootshop. Some of Jeeves's relatives are in service: his uncle Charlie is a butler in a country house, where Jeeves's cousin Queenie works as a maid. Another cousin, Egbert, is a country constable.

Given this background, Jeeves manages to achieve a remarkably independent existence by working for Bertie. We know that Jeeves has certain duties, such as answering the phone, taking care of Bertie's clothes and car, and doing the cooking and serving at table when Bertie eats at home. Beyond that, however, we find out little about how Jeeves earns his living. Bertie is invariably vague on this subject, and we must suspect that he does not check up on Jeeves much; his typical description of Jeeves's work would be "Jeeves was there, messing about at some professional task" (*The Code of the Woosters*, chap. 10) or "Jeeves was in my room when I got there, going about his gentleman's gentlemanly duties" (*Stiff Upper Lip, Jeeves*, chap. 7). Jeeves seems to have plenty of free time. In "The Rummy Affair of Old Biffy," he asks for the afternoon off and a ride to the British Empire Exposition, and Bertie grants both. In *Jeeves and the Feudal Spirit*, Bertie offers to lend Jeeves his car to go to London for a luncheon at his club (though Jeeves had planned to take the train); Jeeves departs "richly apparelled" in the two-seater (chap. 15, 16). Bertie is often deferential when he calls Jeeves in for help, as in "Jeeves and the Greasy Bird":

> "Oh, Jeeves," I said, "I hope I'm not interrupting you when you were curled up with Spinoza's Ethics or whatever it is,

> but I wonder if you could spare me a moment of your valuable time."
>
> "Certainly, sir."

Jeeves is on duty here, and this deference would hardly be the way an employer addresses his valet. Jeeves's job, then, is far from onerous. But why does he need free time?

Aside from the times when he is actually shown working, Jeeves's activities are those of an upper-middle-class or even upper-class man. While Bertie is a member of the Drones, Jeeves belongs to the Junior Ganymede, which Bertie describes as "a rather posh club" on Curzon Street (in the Mayfair area where Bertie lives; *Jeeves and the Feudal Spirit*, chap. 1). There Jeeves plays bridge, has occasional meals, and drinks brandy.[8] His pastimes all suggest that he aspires to the life-style, not of a gentleman's gentleman, but of a gentleman, period. He augments his income by betting quite successfully on horse races, and his knowledge of turf statistics is encyclopedic. In one of the most remarkable displays of Jeeves's independence, Bertie goes to Cannes for two months, leaving Jeeves in England because he had "intimated that he did not wish to miss Ascot"—this despite the fact that Bertie gets quite upset during Jeeves's absences for his annual two-week vacation. When asked how he did at Ascot, Jeeves replies that he has won "Quite a satisfactory sum, thank you, sir" (*Right Ho, Jeeves*, chap. 1).

Jeeves's class aspirations seem to impel him toward money. While acquisitiveness is not Jeeves's main motivation, he undeniably seizes upon chances to make a bit on the side. Not only does he receive frequent tips from Bertie in the short-story period, but Bertie's friends pay him for his help. At the end of "Pearls Mean Tears," Jeeves receives £20 from Bertie; his most successful operation, the transfer of Anatole and the maid to different households in "Clustering Round Young Bingo," nets him £95 in tips (and he has the satisfaction of banning soft silk evening shirts from Bertie's life). Such a sum would be large to a valet, whose annual salary would have been around £65-80 in the 1920s.[9] While the monetary rewards disappear in the novels, some of his bonuses there are quite lavish: a round-the-world cruise

(*The Code of the Woosters*) and trips to Florida ("Jeeves and the Greasy Bird") and New York (*Aunts Aren't Gentlemen*).

Perhaps Jeeves could have chosen another profession that would make more money, but hardly one where he would have the leisure time to enjoy his hobbies. In this context, it is notable that Jeeves is depicted as being in his mid-forties (according to the stage directions in *Come On, Jeeves*). He is about twenty years older than Bertie and aspires, in effect, to lead the sort of life-style that Bertie might settle into when he becomes middle-aged (if, that is, he ever grew older—see appendix B). Despite Jeeves's class origins, Wodehouse depicts him as being nearly Bertie's equal in his life-style, something other professions plausibly open to him would not permit.

Since he desires a placid, upper-class life, Jeeves has a great incentive to solve Bertie's problems quickly. Wodehouse makes his own task harder by giving Jeeves another trait: near infallability. In most cases Jeeves is right (the few exceptions are discussed in the chapters on narrative). But if Jeeves both desires a quiet life and can settle things swiftly, the narrative threatens to stop before it gets started. In other words, since the force for closure seems so very strong, how can the narrative be prolonged?

One crucial aspect of a narrative's dynamics is *delay*. Given that the number of events an author chooses to depict in a single narrative is arbitrary, he or she may use a few events, with delaying devices to stretch them out, or alternatively may jam many events in to fill out the plot. Like many authors, Wodehouse was working for specific publishing outlets and had to fit his narratives into certain lengths (a *Post* story or serial episode, for example, was 5,000 to 6,000 words); his method of starting from a single idea and gradually lengthening the narrative by adding material at each revision meant that he faced the problem of finding delaying material to expand the action.[10] Through much of his career, one of Wodehouse's main problems in writing was in making his stories and books long enough.

In Doyle's Sherlock Holmes series, the fact that the problem is a mystery permits Holmes to spend time gathering clues and then puffing away at his pipe as he fits them together into a solution. The problems handled by Jeeves are not mysteries, and he often comes up with a solution almost immediately. How then to keep him from closing off the narrative in the first scene? This question determined the functions of many of the series' characters and situations.

The central strategy that Wodehouse used for introducing delay was to create a careful balance of control between Bertie and Jeeves. At points of closure in the narrative, this balance between the two is maintained, but, as Bertie puts it, "When two men of iron will live in close association with one another, there are bound to be occasional clashes" (*The Code of the Woosters,* chap. 1). Of course, Bertie's will is far from being as strong as Jeeves's, but he can be just stubborn enough to keep the action open for the duration of the narrative.

The earliest instance of conflict between the pair is Jeeve's sartorial tyranny. In the first three stories ("Extricating Young Gussie"—where Jeeves scarcely appears—, "The Artistic Career of Corky,' and "The Aunt and the Sluggard"), he is characterized primarily by his obsession with tasteful clothing, but he does not clash with Bertie over a specific item. The familiar motif of Jeeves forcing Bertie to dispose of an offending object first appears in the fourth story, "Jeeves Takes Charge," where checked trousers act as the emblem of Jeeves's gaining control over Bertie. From that point on, Bertie's insistence on wearing such items as purple socks, vivid plus-fours, moustaches (twice), and a blue Alpine hat with a pink feather forms one of the most pervasive internal clichés of the series.

Such clashes formed one of Wodehouse's earliest means of preventing Jeeves's perfection from cutting short the action. Jeeves could help but will not. In the fifth story, "Jeeves and the Unbidden Guest," he holds a grudge against Bertie over a hat and tie for a remarkably long time—throughout the month-long visit of Lady Malvern to the United States. Gradually Bertie gets desperate and appeals to Jeeves:

> "Jeeves," I said, "haven't you any scheme up your sleeve for coping with this blighter?"
>
> "No, sir."
>
> And he shimmied off to his lair. Obstinate devil! So dashed absurd, don't you know. It wasn't as if there was anything

> wrong with that Broadway Special hat. But, just because he preferred the White House wonder, he left me flat.

This obstinacy on Jeeves's part endures throughout the series. By the later novels, though, he bides his time, realizing that whenever he ties up the last dangling problem, the moment of reward will bring Bertie's capitulation. This motif remains fresh despite its many reappearances—an indication of Wodehouse's skill at flaunting his repetitiveness and making the reader like it every time. At most, he varied the motif by making the offending object a vase or banjolele or by having the pair clash over a proposed vacation.

This whole motif might seem a bit trivial as a reason for Jeeves to withhold his help, especially when Bertie is often desperate to have him cooperate. But Jeeves is not simply a clever valet, loyally protecting Bertie. Rather, he is a thoroughly pragmatic, occasionally Machiavellian figure. On the surface, his devotion to "the feudal spirit" seems to parallel Bertie's "Code of the Woosters": noblesse oblige for Bertie, selfless service for Jeeves. Bertie often seems to believe that Jeeves really is content to play serf to his chevalier, but the lines about "the feudal spirit" come more often from his lips than from Jeeves's—and usually in situations where Bertie is lamenting the death of that spirit. One of the most revealing indications of Bertie's lack of understanding of Jeeves's pragmatic nature comes when Bertie states that his valet's motto is "Service" (*The Code of the Woosters,* chap. 12). Earlier, in "Bertie Changes His Mind"—the only story narrated by Jeeves—it was revealed that his motto is "Resource and Tact." Jeeves's pragmatism further explains why he often delays solving problems; he will not do so until it is to his advantage.

The contrast between Bertie's idealism and Jeeves's cynical pragmatism is vividly evident in the scene in *Much Obliged, Jeeves* when Bertie calls Jeeves in to help him persuade Aunt Dahlia to return a silver porringer she has stolen. Bertie has been shocked by the theft and appeals to Jeeves:

> "I hold that it was a breach of hospitality and the thing must be returned. Am I right?"

> "Well, sir . . ."
>
> "Go on, Jeeves," said the ancestor. "Say I'm a crook who ought to be drummed out of the Market Snodsbury Ladies Social and Cultural Garden Club."
>
> "Not at all, madam."
>
> "Then what were you going to say when you hesitated?"
>
> "Merely that in my opinion no useful end will be served by retaining the object." (Chap. 15)

He explains that the porringer's value is too low for it to be an effective bargaining weapon when Aunt Dahlia demands that its owner hand over a large sum of money to her future son-in-law. Dahlia, who was unmoved by Bertie's moral appeal, gives in to Jeeves's practical argument and agrees to return the porringer.

As this scene suggests, Jeeves's pragmatism is accompanied by a fundamental amorality. He frequently resorts to trickery and blackmail to solve the problems at hand and to get his way. In *Jeeves in the Offing*, he steals Aubrey Upjohn's speech for Bobbie Wickham to use as a blackmail tool against Upjohn. Defying the Junior Ganymede's rules, he also gives out information that permits Bertie and Aunt Dahlia to blackmail others (*The Code of the Woosters, Much Obliged, Jeeves*). Jeeves even occasionally resorts to violence: he knocks Sippy out with a putter to further the latter's romance with Gwendolyn Moon ("The Inferiority Complex of Old Sippy"); he puts Constable Dobbs temporarily out of commission with Thomas's cosh (*The Mating Season*); and he uses a Mickey Finn on the villainous Bingley (*Much Obliged, Jeeves*). Bertie is profoundly upset by the first two incidents:

> I had, as you will readily understand, much food for thought. The revelation of this deeper, coshing side to Jeeves's character had come as something of a shock to me. One found oneself wondering how far the thing would spread. He and I had had our differences in the past, failing to see eye to eye on such matters as purple socks and white dinner jackets, and it was inevitable, both of us being men of high spirit, that similar differences would arise in the future. It was a disquieting thought that in the heat of argument about, say, soft-bosomed shirts for evening wear he might forget the decencies of debate

> and elect to apply the closure by hauling off and socking me on the frontal bone with something solid. One could but trust that the feudal spirit would serve to keep the impulse in check. (*The Mating Season*, chap. 24)

Of course, Jeeves always keeps his impulses in check. Some would say he has no impulses, but we learn differently in "Bertie Changes His Mind": "I concealed my perturbation, but the effort to preserve my *sang-froid* tested my powers to the utmost." Certainly Jeeves never uses violence against Bertie, though he does—regretfully—get Aunt Dahlia to knock him out as part of the solution in "Jeeves Makes an Omelet." Jeeves says in "Bertie Changes His Mind" that he is "fond of Mr. Wooster," but that does not prevent him from getting Bertie into some sticky situations.

As a final indication of Jeeves's pragmatism, it is interesting to note that, although he is willing to go out of his way to help Bertie, he never once in the entire series does so if his efforts would require a real sacrifice on his part. Given a conflict between Bertie's goals and his own, he invariably takes the route of self-interest. (In *Ring for Jeeves* and the plays, he uncharacteristically offers to make sacrifices for his employers but is never actually required to do so.) Such behavior often creates considerable delay.

Wodehouse used another pattern for delaying Jeeves's solutions, one that was typically far simpler than Jeeves's sartorial tyranny and other clashes with Bertie. Once in a while Jeeves goes on vacation and hence is absent for the bulk of the narrative. This device results in a much simpler construction in two cases: "The Love That Purifies" and *Jeeves in the Offing*. These are the only cases where Jeeves is a deus ex machina in a strict sense, because Bertie calls him back from Herne Bay or Bognor Regis, and Jeeves solves the problem without having been involved in it. These two narratives do not involve any conflict between Jeeves and Bertie or any other complicating factor. ("The Pride of the Woosters Is Wounded" uses the same premise, but complicates it by balancing Jeeves's remark about Bertie being "mentally neglible" against the threat of Bertie's reengagement to Honoria Glossop.)

Other means of delaying Jeeves's solutions were provided by Bertie and the other characters, who constitute forces for openness in the narratives.

BERTIE AND THE STATELY HOMES OF E.

Bertie is the series' main force for getting the narratives going, though he seldom initiates the complicating actions voluntarily. Left to himself, he might very well be content in the "cosy bachelor establishment" with Jeeves, confining his livelier activities to the Drones.[11] Aside from his occasional desire to wear gaudy clothing and his competitions with fellow Drones in games and practical jokes, he has few ambitions that would generate a major narrative premise. In 1960 Wodehouse outlined the problem: "I'm very fond of my characters, but I suppose the Jeeves series must be approaching its end. You have to find some trouble for Bertie to get into, and it's hard for a man with a large private income to keep getting into trouble."[12] Happily for us, Bertie did keep getting into trouble, but he had a lot of help from friends, relatives, and enemies.

Wodehouse developed a small set of variants on ways that these characters could make demands on Bertie that he would be constrained to try and satisfy. One such constraint arises from the fact that Bertie is basically timid. He usually prefers the sneak down the drainpipe to the direct confrontation, and he sees pugnacious enemies as upwards of seven feet tall. Aunt Agatha holds such terrors for him that he never dreams of refusing to do her bidding (though he manages to get around her in a few cases, with Jeeves's aid). Aside from the men who threaten Bertie with physical violence, the main people he has to fear are those who want to change him, to make him give up his extended schoolboy existence under Jeeves's protection. In this sense, Bertie is indeed inclined to a stable existence but is forced out of it by the attempts of Aunt Agatha and others to develop him into a mature man: cultured, employed, and married.

Balancing Bertie's timidity are his generosity, idealism, and chivalry. These traits were there from the series' beginning, but they only came to be summed up as the Code of the Woosters in the book of the same name.[13] The Code arises from Bertie's immaturity, for it is basically a schoolboy notion of honor: "Well, of course, if a man you've been at private school, public school and Oxford with says he's relying on you, you have no option but to let yourself be relied on" (*The Mating Season*, chap. 2). Wodehouse built the notion of the Code up gradually. In the earliest stories, Bertie is in New York and helps his American pals. The old-school-chum motif comes in with Bingo Little in the 1921 story, "Jeeves Exerts the Old Cerebellum" and becomes pervasive thereafter. Bertie's Code also forces him to become engaged to various women against his will. 'If a girl thinks you're in love with her and says she will marry you, you can't very well voice a preference for being dead in a ditch. Not, I mean, if you want to regard yourself as a preux chevalier, as the expression is, which is always my aim" (*Much Obliged, Jeeves*, chap. 1).

Bertie, then, may have an "actual appetite for incident," as Gilbert Seldes wrote, but it is an appetite for helping others or avoiding changing his ways. He is not innately venturesome. The other characters are generally the ones who make him the means for creating narrative openness—they cause him to set a series of goals for himself and Jeeves to achieve before closure can finally be reached.

Indeed, virtually all of the other characters in the series, whether positive or negative, function to get Bertie into trouble. Some are very distinctive and memorable, of course, but all except the bit players can be placed into several categories: pals, uncles, aunts, male menaces, unpredictable females, fiancées, pesky children, and other servants. The last group is the only one made up mainly of characters who help Bertie, since they are often friends of Jeeves whom he uses as sources of information. The other categories are not entirely exclusive: Aunt Dahlia, for example, fits into both the "aunts" and "unpredictable females" categories. Still, these groupings simply describe narrative functions, and the characters become tokens to be shunted about as needed.

Bertie's pals are certainly distinguishable: most notably the newt-fancier, Gussie Fink-Nottle, but also the hopelessly clumsy Rev. H. P. "Stinker" Pinker, the susceptible Bingo Little, and many others. They virtually all exist, however, for one purpose: to place the responsibility for solving their problems on Bertie's shoulders. Bertie may be reluctant, but his generosity and the Code never allow him to resist for long, as in "Bingo and the Little Woman":

> [Bingo:] "We were at school together."
> "It wasn't my fault."
> "We've been pals for fifteen years."
> "I know. It's going to take me the rest of my life to live it down."
> "Bertie, old man," said Bingo, drawing his chair closer and starting to knead my shoulder-blade, "listen! Be reasonable."
> And of course, dash it, at the end of ten minutes I'd allowed the blighter to talk me round. It's always the story. Anyone can talk me round.

This premise of Bertie's eternal willingness to help a pal proved inexhaustible in its possibilities for generating narratives, and it recurs as one of the main internal clichés of the series.

There is relatively little to be said about the uncles in the series. They usually stay offstage, creating some sort of problem that an aunt can pass along for Bertie to solve: Tom's desire for the cow-creamer or his reluctance to pay for *Milady's Boudoir*, Uncle George's near-marriage to Rhoda Platt. They are basically elderly versions of the cousins or old pals, still behaving like children and hence generating basic problems for Jeeves and Bertie to solve.

Wodehouse did not repeat this same device in every story, however. Aunts—though far fewer in number than pals—were equally powerful as a means of precipitating Bertie into the gumbo. Wodehouse cleverly managed to invent two main aunts of opposite types—one menacing, one jovial—who are both adept at creating problems for Bertie.

Agatha is the more obvious troublemaker, being out to improve Bertie. "Improvement" may involve getting him a job (for example, as secretary to Cabinet Minister Filmer in "Jeeves and the Impending Doom"), or it may mean that he must marry the woman of her choice (mainly Honoria Glossop). Occasionally she demands Bertie's help in solving some family crisis, usually caused by a relative who is about to disgrace the family. Aunt Agatha's main villainy, suggested only a few times, is her dislike for Jeeves. Essentially she and he are rivals for control of Bertie, with Agatha wanting him to grow up and Jeeves protecting him from that fate—partly so that he can maintain his own control over Bertie.

Aunt Dahlia is the opposite of her sister, as Bertie and Jeeves agree:

> "She's the only decent aunt I've got. Jeeves, you will bear me out in this?"
> "Such has always been my impression, I must confess, sir."
> ("Clustering Round Young Bingo")

Dahlia and Jeeves get along well, in part because she never tries to change Bertie or marry him off. Indeed, she sympathizes when others try to do so, for she is content for him to remain the eternal schoolboy. Still, she gets him into trouble just as surely as does Agatha. As Frances Donaldson puts it, "She is a relentless blackmailer, completely unconcerned by the discomfort and indignity she causes him in order to attain some objective of her own. In the long run he suffers far more at her hands than he does at Aunt Agatha's."[14] Her amorality and pragmatism are comparable to Jeeves's, and perhaps she, too, prefers a childish Bertie because she can control him better that way. She calls upon Bertie to promote her own projects: stealing an antique cow-creamer for her collector husband, giving a speech at a local function that she is programming, entertaining guests she is buttering up, and so on. The premise that allows her to get away with all this (aside from both Bertie's and Jeeves's affection for her) is her superb chef, Anatole, the withholding of whose meals provides the ultimate threat for maneuvering Bertie to do her bidding. This threat is the functional equivalent of the pals' invocation of having been at school with Bertie: both force him into tangled problems that will keep the narrative open until Jeeves ends it.

Once the initial problem is launched, Wodehouse needs some way to prevent the nearly perfect mind of Jeeves from solving it right away. Plot complications are needed, and the fiancées, unpredictable females, male menaces, and pesky children provide these.

In some of the short stories, Bertie's infatuation with a young woman creates the main problem for Jeeves. Marriage for Bertie is out of the question (he is in most respects symbolically married to Jeeves), and Jeeves must avoid it at all costs. This device appears in "Jeeves and the Spot of Art," with Gwladys, and in "Jeeves and the Yule-tide Spirit" and "Jeeves and the Kid Clementina," both involving the charming but deadly Bobbie Wickham. Such infatuations are rare, since we are used to Bertie fleeing from marriage. Yet Wodehouse also has to characterize Bertie as having many short, intense attractions to women and as having proposed to many. The series has several passages like the following, from "The Great Sermon Handicap," concerning Cynthia Wickhammersley:

> There was a time when I had an idea that I was in love with Cynthia. However, it blew over. A dashed pretty and lively and attractive girl, mind you, but full of ideals and all that. I may be wronging her, but I have an idea that she's the sort of girl who would want a fellow to carve out a career and what not. I know I've heard her speak favourably of Napoleon. So what with one thing and another the jolly old frenzy sort of petered out, and now we're just pals.

We learn that Cynthia laughed at Bertie when he proposed to her.

There are many such women in Bertie's past. Most of his engagements in the novels are, after all, *re*engagements. The premise is that these women, as long as they remain single, can at any time agree retroactively to marry him. The Code means he must then accept them. Cynthia never pulls this trick, but his brief engagement to Pauline Stoker does come back to haunt him in *Thank You, Jeeves.* On the whole, the actual or threatened reengagements occur as plot twists in the course of the longer narratives of the novels—another internal cliché. Jeeves is helpless to prevent these reengagements, since they are not a matter of logic or psychology (at which he excels) but of the Code. Jeeves may have no code himself, but he always honors Bertie's—an indication, perhaps, of his affection for his employer. (Besides, if he did not, the narratives would collapse.)

The male equivalent of the fiancée is the menace. These men acquire some idée fixe concerning Bertie and then pursue him doggedly. Sir

Roderick Glossop assumes him to be loony, Stoker thinks he has seduced Pauline, Sir Watkyn Bassett and Roderick Spode take him for a thief, and Stilton Cheesewright believes he is out to steal Florence Craye. Stilton is a rare case of a pal who is also a menace; at the beginning of chapter 2 of *Jeeves and the Feudal Spirit*, Bertie says that he, like Glossop and Stoker, is one of those "blokes whose presence tends to make me ill at ease," adding, "Considering that he and I have known each other since, as you might say, we were so high, having been at private school, Eton and Oxford together, we ought, I suppose, to be like Damon and what's-his-name, but we aren't by any means." Like the fiancées, these characters' relations to Bertie are not based on logic, and Jeeves finds it difficult to cope with them on rational grounds. He usually quells them with some sort of blackmail, and since finding the right bit of damaging information takes time, closure can be further delayed. The older male menaces typically threaten some form of incarceration. (Glossop initially wants him in a padded cell, Stoker locks him in a stateroom, Bassett is a vindictive magistrate.) The younger ones are over seven feet tall, with short tempers and jealous imaginations. They all provide complications that delay the solutions of the more basic problems.

Of Wodehouse's delaying devices, one of the most distinctive is the unpredictable-female character. She is typically a young woman who for no rational reason expects Bertie to help her carry through a dangerous and silly scheme, either to help her get revenge on someone or to further her marriage plans. Such characters are useful in spinning out the action, since Jeeves cannot possibly anticipate their harebrained ideas when he initally plans his strategy; he must simply adjust his maneuvers to take their ideas into account as they crop up. These women are seldom fiancées, potential or actual, of Bertie (with the spectacular exception of Bobbie Wickham, who is as unpredictable as they come). Rather, they are old friends, the female equivalents of his schoolmates, and they assume they have a complete hold on him—one often accomplished through blackmail. Stiffy Byng, Corky Pirbright, and Nobby Hopwood all have similar outlooks on life. The one older character who fits into this pattern is Aunt Dahlia, whose amorality and sudden whims create numerous plot complications. She sends Bertie after a silver cow-creamer, while Stiffy expects him to guard a stolen policeman's helmet, but the impulses are parallel. The unpredictable female is, in effect, the equivalent of the Drone, with an addiction to practical jokes and petty resentments. The similarity among these various unpredictable females comes out in *The Code of the Woosters,* when Bertie has just failed to talk Stiffy out of her plan to have her fiancé steal a policeman's helmet:

> I gave it up. I could see plainly that it would be mere waste of time to try to argue her out of her girlish daydreams. She had the same type of mind, I perceived, as Roberta Wickham, who once persuaded me to go by night to the bedroom of a fellow guest at a country house and puncture his hot-water bottle with a darning-needle on the end of a stick. (Chap. 4)

This passage and the one above comparing Stilton Cheesewright to Glossop and Stoker show how Wodehouse was aware of the strong functional similarities among his characters and how he strove to reveal their repetitiousness and conventionality to readers.

Pesky children (and all children in the series are pesky to some degree) feature less prominently than do these other kinds of characters, but Wodehouse uses them to advantage as a means of introducing plot twists. For example, in his zest for doing good deeds, Bertie's cousin Edwin accidentally burns down the cottage Bertie and Jeeves were to stay in (*Joy in the Morning*); his cousin Thomas maroons Filmer on an island ("Jeeves and the Impending Doom"). With their obsessions and pranks, children function as variants of the pals and unpredictable females. The boys seem likely candidates for the Drones Club when they grow up (though Thomas will undoubtedly cross over into the male menace category); Clementina will probably follow in Bobbie Wickham's path.

Although Jeeves claims in "Fixing It for Freddie," "I have had little or no experience with children," he manipulates them effectively. He arranges Bertie's discomfiture before an audience of giggling schoolgirls ("Bertie Changes His Mind"), gets the producer's son to have Cyril Bassington-Bassington, a protégé of Aunt Agatha, thrown out of a play ("Startling Dressiness of a Lift Attendant"), and bribes Bertie's cousin Thomas to run away from school, thereby delaying Aunt Agatha's arrival in *The Mating Season*. Wodehouse seldom *had* to use children for such complications—so many of his adult characters could supply the necessary childish behavior. Children simply added variety.

Most of the other servants are minor figures upon whom Jeeves can draw for help in effecting his solutions. He has a vast acquaintance among valets and butlers and calls upon them for information and favors. For example, in *Thank You, Jeeves*, Jeeves arranges for his friend Benstead (Stoker's valet) to send the cable that causes Stoker to buy Chuffy's white elephant of a house. In a few cases, however, problems with romantic attachments among servants form part of the main action. In "Indian Summer of an Uncle," Jeeves's valet friend Smethurst is Uncle George's rival for Rhoda Platt's hand; Jeeves arranges for George to marry her aunt instead. Smethurst exists only as a name, a means of giving Jeeves some necessary information. Queenie's tiff with Constable Dobbs brings her more firmly into the action of *The Mating Season*; the book involves an absurd escalation of the number of sundered couples, and Queenie serves to swell their ranks.

Two servants perform unique functions. The French cook Anatole is initially a minor character in "Clustering Round Young Bingo," but once he enters Aunt Dahlia's employ, he becomes her main weapon for forcing Bertie to do her bidding. Anatole thus gives Dahlia as much power over Bertie as Agatha has, yet permits her to remain a likeable character. Moreover, a number of narratives involve someone trying to steal Anatole away from Dahlia, which Jeeves must prevent at all costs. In a sense, Anatole could be parallel to Jeeves: the perfect servant, in the employ of a sympathetic character, whose loss is a constant threat. Yet Wodehouse avoids making Anatole into a strongly individualized character. He appears onstage only once, in *Right Ho, Jeeves*; his ranting monologue against Gussie Fink-Nottle is a stylistic tour-de-force of fractured English, but it also distances him as a French comic stereotype. Overall, Anatole remains an offstage pawn, manipulated by others for their own ends; this distance prevents him from seeming equivalent to Jeeves.

Bingley is a different case altogether.[15] He really is equivalent to Jeeves, in the literal sense that he is Bertie's valet after Jeeves's resignation in *Thank You, Jeeves.* As a result, he becomes a threatening figure, getting drunk, chasing Bertie with a carving knife, and burning down his cottage. Bertie's rehiring of Jeeves, however, seems to banish Bingley for good. (He returns only once, in *Much Obliged, Jeeves,* but there he accomplishes the seemingly impossible: he proves that Jeeves can be wrong.) Whether intentionally or not, Wodehouse experimented briefly with a character who showed what Jeeves might be like if he were utterly unscrupulous. (After all, Jeeves has never stolen the Club Book, but he has used it for blackmail purposes.) It is undoubtedly going too far to say that without Bertie Jeeves would be just like the Bingley of *Much Obliged, Jeeves.* Nevertheless, Evelyne Gauthier makes the interesting point that, in general, it is "the touching innocence of Bertie which redeems stratagems which are quite dishonorable by giving them an altruistic and honorable goal."[16] Bingley's presence, brief as it is, helps point up this moral dimension of the Jeeves/Bertie relationship.

All these types of characters—the pals, aunts, uncles, menaces, unpredictable females, fiancées, pesky children, and other servants—show up at intervals through the entire series. There is a notable shift in the use of characters at one point in the series, however: at the move from the short stories to the novels. In order to create the longer form, Wodehouse needed complicating material and provided it by introducing more of these unpredictable characters. In order to bring all these characters together to bounce off each other, he turned definitively, with *Thank You, Jeeves,* to the country-house plot. Some of the short stories had centered around visits to the country. In "Without the Option," Bertie went to stay with a family near Cambridge, impersonating his pal Sippy (a plot device that later would be expanded in *The Mating Season*). This is the only story of the ten in *Carry On, Jeeves* that involves such a visit, however. Three stories of eighteen in *The Inimitable Jeeves* use the device. The last collection, *Very Good, Jeeves,* shows that Wodehouse was increasingly dependent on country houses to assemble groups of characters; five of the eleven stories use them. Only with the novels, however, did the device come to dominate his narratives. All eleven use it. In some cases, like *Thank You, Jeeves, Joy in the Morning,* and *Aunts Aren't Gentlemen,* the characters stay in different houses in the country or in a village, but the same function of bringing the characters together in a single rural locale is served.

The longer plots of the novels usually involve these characters gathering, with a set of goals already conceived. In *The Code of the Woosters,* Bertie and Aunt Dahlia visit Bassett to steal the cow-creamer (though Bertie also plans to help Gussie and possibly Stiffy), Jeeves wants his round-the-world cruise, Bassett and Spode want to prove Bertie a thief, Gussie wants to reconcile with Madeline, and so on.

With Jeeves on the scene, however, the old problem remains: with his brains, why can't he solve all these problems right away? Often he does come up with some solutions early on. Here the unpredictable characters come into play, doing ridiculous things on the spur of the moment, deliberately or accidentally. At the beginning of *The Code of the Woosters,* Gussie Fink-Nottle has already come to Jeeves, asking for help in giving a speech without being overcome by fear. Jeeves told Gussie to develop a contempt for his listeners, and this idea has enabled Gussie to give a successful speech at the Drones Club. In the short stories, this idea alone would have been enough for a major plot line. Here, however, it simply sets up the fact that Gussie then does something stupid that Jeeves could not have foreseen: he writes down his contemptuous thoughts in a notebook which he then loses while visiting a country house full of the very people he has disparaged. One problem thus becomes preventing Bassett—a prominent figure in the notebook and Gussie's prospective father-in-law—from reading it. But Stiffy Byng is also at the house, and she finds the book and uses it to blackmail Bertie into going along with *her* scheme . . . and so, as Bertie would say, the long day wore on. The gathering at the country house, itself a cliché of mammoth proportions, became the basic device for stringing out the novel-length narratives.

TWO MEN OF IRON WILL: JEEVES, BERTIE, AND NARRATIVE CONFLICT

> It is true, of course, that I have a will of iron, but it can be switched off if the circumstances seem to demand it. The strong man always knows when to yield and make concessions. I have frequently found myself doing so in my relation with Jeeves.
>
> —*Joy in the Morning*

The Jeeves/Bertie relationship works along two intricate and opposite sets of assumptions: one about the pair's mutual dependence and affection, the second about power and control. These assumptions function in the structuring of the narratives.

The first aspect of the relationship, the pair's mutual affection and dependence, helps create that "cosy bachelor establishment" which Jeeves protects. As we saw in chapter 3, the narratives are based not only on a comic inversion of the Holmesian detective story but also upon a second comic inversion of the conventions of the romance novel. In the more complex narratives, there is a threat, not only to Bertie and his pals or relatives but also to the Jeeves/Bertie relationship itself. This threat may be an internal conflict that keeps them apart or an external threat when a fiancée comes between them. Symbolically, the Jeeves/Bertie relationship functions as a marriage, and ultimately, of all the disasters that threaten Bertie, loss of Jeeves is the worst.

Here we can also see why Jeeves stays with Bertie, beyond any monetary considerations. In "Jeeves and the Hard-boiled Egg," Bertie worries over how his friends keep trying to lure Jeeves away:

> Young Reggie Foljambe to my certain knowledge offered him double what I was giving him, and Alistair Bingham-Reekes, who's got a valet who has been known to press his trousers sideways, used to look at him, when he came to see me, with a kind of glittering, hungry eye which disturbed me deucedly. Bally pirates.

Thus we know the relationship is not based simply on money and other benefits. One characteristic of Bertie apparently helps explain Jeeves's fondness for him: his generosity. In *Thank You, Jeeves,* Pauline Stoker reports that Jeeves had told her that Bertie is "mentally somewhat negligible, but he has a heart of gold" (chap. 7). The entire series contains only one other direct indication as to why Jeeves likes Bertie (see chap. 5). There are personal bonds between Jeeves and Bertie, and these provide the potential for considerable narrative conflict to upset their placid existence. We shall look at these bonds later in this chapter.

The question of why Bertie would want to keep Jeeves on raises no similar question, since the master is utterly dependent on the man, and again, the relationship is like a marriage. The premise that, for Bertie, keeping Jeeves and getting married are incompatible alternatives becomes explicit early on. In "Introducing Claude and Eustace," Bertie lunches with Aunt Agatha and his fiancée, Honoria Glossop; Honoria lays down the law as Bertie helps himself to fried potatoes:

> "Bertie," she said suddenly, as if she had just remembered it, "what is the name of that man of yours—your valet?"
>
> "Eh? Oh, Jeeves."
>
> "I think he's a bad influence for you," said Honoria. "When we are married, you must get rid of Jeeves."
>
> It was at this point that I jerked the spoon and sent six of the best and crispest sailing on to the sideboard, with Spenser gambolling after them like a dignified old retriever.
>
> "Get rid of Jeeves!" I gasped.
>
> "Yes. I don't like him."
>
> "*I* don't like him," said Aunt Agatha.

> "But I can't. I mean—why I couldn't carry on for a day without Jeeves."
>
> "You will have to," said Honoria. "I don't like him at all."
>
> "*I* don't like him at all," said Aunt Agatha. "I never did."
>
> Ghastly, what? I'd always had an idea that marriage was a bit of a wash-out, but I'd never dreamed that it demanded such frightful sacrifices from a fellow.

We infer that Aunt Agatha has put Honoria up to this and that for Bertie, Honoria is simply a younger version of that dreaded relative. This conversation echoes implicitly through every discussion of Bertie's possible marriage for the rest of the series.

Jeeves indicates, too, that Bertie's marriage would mean his departure. At first, in "Bertie Changes His Mind," he seems to fear that the wife would make Bertie let him go: "My experience is that when the wife comes in at the front door the valet of bachelor days goes out at the back." By *Thank You, Jeeves,* he makes it clear that he would leave whether or not the wife wanted him to: "It has never been my policy to serve in the household of a married gentleman" (chap. 22). Thereafter, every potential wife for Bertie explicitly means the loss of Jeeves: hence perhaps Jeeves's increasing willingness—as he becomes closer to Bertie—to solve problems despite arguments with Bertie and without expecting a bonus.

Characteristically, Wodehouse makes this functional and symbolic marriage implicit in the Jeeves/Bertie relationship obvious by linking it frequently to clichéd imagery. Among the images he uses for that relationship (Jeeves as shepherd, Bertie as sheep; Jeeves as nanny, Bertie as child), one reveals the device explicitly. At the end of "Jeeves and the Unbidden Guest," Bertie reacts to Jeeves's solution:

> I felt most awfully braced. I felt as if the clouds had rolled away and all was as it used to be. I felt like one of those chappies in the novels who calls off the fight with his wife in the last chapter and decides to forgive and forget. I wanted to do all sorts of other things to show Jeeves that I appreciated him.

Note that Bertie does not feel simply like a husband but like a husband in a novel. This passage could describe the endings of many of the narratives.

There are many other, less direct indications that the pair's relationship is like a marriage. It is instructive, for example, to notice how often Bertie links Jeeves with the idea of "home." His relationship with Jeeves is also the only major one Bertie has formed as an adult; all the other characters are old pals, relatives, or casual friends who show up only for one story. Perhaps most significantly (and subtly), Jeeves seems to be the one character who can put up with Bertie on a full-time basis. (As we have seen, Barrie Haynes has found the same sort of relationship at work in Doyle, though he, probably rightly, identifies the narrating figure, Watson, as the long-suffering wife and Holmes as the eccentric husband.) Time and again Bertie remarks how a short dose of his company is enough for his friends and relatives. In *Right Ho, Jeeves*, shortly after the quarrels over the white mess jacket and the correct tactics for solving Gussie's problem, Bertie receives a telegram from Aunt Dahlia urgently summoning him to her country house. Bertie is puzzled, given that he has just returned from a two-month vacation at Cannes with her:

> "But why, Jeeves? Dash it all, she's just had nearly two months of me."
>
> "Yes, sir."
>
> "And many people consider the medium dose for an adult two days."
>
> "Yes, sir. I appreciate the point you raise. Nevertheless, Mrs. Travers appears very insistent." (Chap. 3)

Here Jeeves is more annoyed with Bertie than at almost any other point in the series, and his reply, "I appreciate the point you raise," carries an irony that Bertie misses. Yet the passage does point up the fact that Jeeves, of all the characters, manages to put up with and even enjoy Bertie's continuing society.

This "marriage," then, constitutes the stable situation that is threatened by outside forces. Had Wodehouse left it at that, the narratives would have been less intricate and dynamic; Jeeves and Bertie would join to fight off the threats from real marriage partners, with comic results. But he also created a relationship with internal conflicts and tensions. Both Jeeves and Bertie realize that they participate in an uneasy balance of power and control, though they seldom explicitly mention this.

The turning point occurs in "Jeeves Takes Charge," the fourth story. Up to this point, Wodehouse had not told how Bertie came to hire Jeeves, but apparently as the series developed he felt it necessary to backtrack and define the relationship. Here Bertie is engaged to Florence Craye (it being the first of many narratives in which Jeeves gets Bertie out of an engagement). In order to stay engaged to Florence, Bertie must prevent the delivery of his uncle's scandalous memoirs to the publisher, and he orders Jeeves to hide them. Instead, Jeeves sends them to the publisher, Bertie fires him, and Jeeves tells him that he is well out of the engagement. Next morning, Bertie realizes that Jeeves was right and hires him back, but he hesitates before giving in over their conflict regarding Bertie's beloved checked suit. Initially Bertie defied Jeeves over the suit, recognizing exactly what was at stake:

> I'd seen so many cases of fellows who had become perfect slaves to their valets. I remember poor old Aubrey Fothergill telling me—with absolute tears in his eyes, poor chap!—one night at the club, that he had been compelled to give up a favourite pair of brown shoes simply because Meekyn, his man, disapproved of them. You have to keep these fellows in their place, don't you know. You have to work the good old iron-hand-in-the-velvet-glove wheeze. If you give them a what's-it's-name, they take a thingummy.

Yet Bertie realizes at the end that there are advantages in such a relationship; he weighs the pros and cons before giving in:

> I hesitated a bit. I had a feeling that I was passing into this chappie's clutches, and that if I gave in now I should become just like poor old Aubrey Fothergill, unable to call my soul

> my own. On the other hand, this was obviously a cove of rare intelligence, and it would be a comfort in a lot of ways to have him doing the thinking for me. I made up my mind.
>
> "All right, Jeeves," I said. "You know! Give the bally thing away to somebody!"
>
> He looked down at me like a father gazing tenderly at the wayward child.
>
> "Thank you, sir. I gave it to the under-gardener last night. A little more tea, sir?"

Note the perfect balance of Jeeves's final line as he flaunts his own presumption in having given away the suit before receiving permission (he does not have to tell Bertie this), then immediately switches into his deferential-servant mode. Thus the bargain is consciously made: Bertie will surrender a good portion of his power to Jeeves, and Jeeves will in turn help him out of any difficulties that require mental exertion.

But this exchange occurs at the *end* of a story. Bertie is willing to reward Jeeves by discarding the suit because Jeeves has earned the sacrifice. Bertie is less willing to stick by this implicit bargain at the *beginnings* of narratives, where he often defies Jeeves. The series becomes a perpetual tug between two states: the placid life which Jeeves desires and the periodic impluses Bertie feels to assert himself.

This relationship goes through different stages, and these changes govern the dynamics of the narratives at each period of Wodehouse's career. In the earliest stories, before "Jeeves Takes Charge," there is no tension between the two, and Jeeves is a less-developed character than Bertie. In the stories originally published during the teens, Bertie has a humble view of his own mental abilities and defers to Jeeves. For example, of his friendship with Bicky in "Jeeves and the Hard-boiled Egg," Bertie says: "He was a frightful chump, so we naturally drifted together."

By the middle-period short stories, however, Bertie is a bit jealous of Jeeves and tries to solve some problems on his own. This twist proved a fertile device for creating narrative conflict. By the later stories and early novels, Bertie is in a rebellious stage. Early signs of this appear in "The Pride of the Woosters Is Wounded," where Bertie is upset by overhearing Jeeves call him mentally negligible. Later, Bertie outlines a scheme to Bingo:

> "You didn't think that out by yourself, Bertie?" said young Bingo in a hushed sort of voice.
> "Yes, I did. Jeeves isn't the only fellow with ideas."

This motif of Jeeves not being the only one with brains returns throughout the series, but it occurs most frequently in the period 1925–34. Bertie postively boasts about his own mental abilities in "Fixing It for Freddie":

> I doubt if the idea that occurred to me at this juncture would have occurred to a single one of the dozen of the largest-brained blokes in history. Napoleon may have got it, but I'll bet Darwin and Shakespeare and Thomas Hardy couldn't have thought of it in a thousand years.

From this point on, Bertie ticks Jeeves off quite frequently—though he had opined in "The Pride of the Woosters Is Wounded" that "I doubt whether it's humanly possible to tick Jeeves off." Bertie defies Jeeves over such matters as going to Harrogate with Uncle George ("Clustering Round Young Bingo") and Jeeves's dislike of Bertie's Chinese vase ("The Inferiority Complex of Old Sippy"). Bertie now becomes resentful when relatives and friends tell him to ask Jeeves for help; when Aunt Dahlia reveals that Tuppy Glossop has thrown Angela over, she continues:

> "So place the facts before Jeeves and tell him to take action the moment you get down there."
> I am always a little piqued, if you know what I mean, at this assumption on the relative's part that Jeeves is so dashed essential on these occasions. My manner, therefore, as I replied, was a bit on the crisp side.
> "Jeeves's services will not be required," I said. "I can handle this business." ("The Ordeal of Young Tuppy")

Bertie's rebellion against and desire to compete with Jeeves continue into the novels.

A minor motif enters the series in *Thank You, Jeeves,* one that seems to add more motivation for Bertie's jealousy of Jeeves. Not only do Bertie's friends and relatives keep pointing out how much more intelligent Jeeves is than Bertie, but it turns out that Jeeves is also better looking than his employer. We know already that Bertie is not particularly handsome. In "Episode of the Dog McIntosh," Bertie learns that Blumenfeld, Jr., is coming to lunch, and he threatens that if the boy tells him he has a face like a fish, Bertie may hit him:

> "Perhaps the young gentleman will not notice that you have a face like a fish," Jeeves suggested.
>
> "Ah! There's that, of course."

In the original magazine version, Jeeves's line was ". . . will not say that you have a face like a fish." The change makes this line into Jeeves's first and only criticism of Bertie's looks (when clean-shaven, that is) and also makes it clear that Bertie does have a fishlike face. Later, in *The Mating Season,* there is more evidence of Bertie's homeliness, when Catsmeat tells him, to his horror, that he closely resembles Gussie, who Bertie considers looks "like something on a slab."

Jeeves, on the other hand, is apparently handsome, as we learn in *Thank You, Jeeves.* Bertie describes him at their first encounter at Chuffnell Regis: "There, standing in an attitude of respectful courtliness, with the sunshine playing upon his finely-chiselled features, was Jeeves" (chap. 4). Jeeves's good-looks also sharpens the contrast between the two when Bertie gets into blackface; he uses the same term when Jeeves inadvertently betrays amusement at Bertie's appearance in the boot polish: "I noted a soft smile playing over the finely-chiselled face and resented same" (chap. 13).

This phrase becomes a standard motif in the series for describing Jeeves. It is again linked with Bertie's resentment of Jeeves in *Right Ho, Jeeves,* when Bertie smuggles the mess jacket to Brinkley Court. Jeeves tells Bertie that he has "inadvertently" forgotten to pack the jacket, but Bertie triumphantly reveals that the jacket is downstairs in a paper parcel:

> The information that his low maneuvres had been rendered null and void and that the thing was on the strength after all, must have been the nastiest of jars, but there was no play of expression on his finely chiselled to indicate it. There very seldom is on Jeeves' f-c. (chap. 9)

After Jeeves tames Bertie at the end of *Right Ho, Jeeves,* Bertie becomes less critical of Jeeves, and the jealousy motif largely disappears. His description of Jeeves in *The Mating Season* uses the same term but is positively adulatory: "a godlike man in a bowler hat with grave, finely-chiselled features and a head that stuck out at the back, indicating great brain power" (chap. 23).

In the first two novels, however, the motif makes it all the more plausible that Bertie should resent his valet. In *Thank You, Jeeves* he allows Jeeves to quit, and in *Right Ho, Jeeves* his rebellion peaks. There Bertie concludes early on that Jeeves has lost his intelligence, and he belittles his valet and tries to take his place as the one who can set all things right. In the end, Jeeves not only solves all the problems that Bertie has left in a tangle, but he exacts a terrible revenge on Bertie (the eighteen-mile nocturnal bike ride). Thereafter Bertie becomes more docile, exhibiting only occasional signs of jealousy. Bertie's rebellion was a strong device for creating conflict, enabling Wodehouse to devise some of his best-constructed plots.

The novels and stories after *Right Ho, Jeeves* place Jeeves and Bertie in a relationship of increasing equality. The monetary bonuses disappear, and Jeeves's rewards involve activities like travel, in which they both participate. Whereas Bertie casually offers Jeeves a drink at the end of "The Ordeal of Young Tuppy" because Tuppy has left it behind, the two sit down together over drinks in later narratives: in a pub, in *The Mating Season* and at the Junior Ganymede in *Much Obliged, Jeeves.* Overall, the novels written after Bertie's rebellious behavior ends are slightly weaker in their underlying conflicts and less perfectly plotted, but they compensate through a gain in the emotional depth of the Jeeves/Bertie relationship.

AN UNRELIABLE NARRATOR AND HIS VALET

> Give Bertram Wooster a good, clear story to unfold, and he can narrate it well.
>
> —*The Code of the Woosters*

Bertie is a superb narrator, of course, but the stories he tells are not always as clear as he may think. One of the series' most complex aspects is the way Wodehouse created a narrator who misses part of what goes on around him. The reader must search for subtle clues in Bertie's presentation in order to infer additional events he has failed to notice and report. Jeeves is as important a character as Bertie, despite his apparently smaller role and less comic behavior and language, partly because he adds ambiguity and depth to the narratives.

As I have suggested, Bertie's narration is based in part on the Holmes series. In Doyle's stories, Watson tags along without understanding Holmes's methods; hence we get the lengthy explanations by Holmes at the end. With the Jeeves/Wooster series, it is as if Watson were a bumbling detective who keeps taking cases, only to have them solved by his clever valet, Holmes. Wodehouse, however, develops Doyle's model in ways that make the Jeeves/Wooster series more complex than the Holmes stories. For one thing, the relationship between Jeeves and Bertie is far from an easy one; the frequent conflicts between the two mean that Jeeves is seldom wholly on Bertie's side, and Bertie is not always simply the admiring chronicler of Jeeves's feats.[17]

Like Watson, Bertie understands part of what is going on as the narrative progresses, and Jeeves, like Holmes, fills him in at the end by reciting what has happened. But unlike Holmes, Jeeves does not always tell all. He reveals information to Bertie slowly and often in a scrambled order calculated to create a specific effect on his naive employer. Consider his juggling of events at the end of "The Inferiority

Complex of Old Sippy." Jeeves has called Sippy to the flat, knocked him unconscious, called Gwendolyn Moon to the scene, and witnessed the couple's declaration of love for each other; at some point early on, he also broke Bertie's pet vase. In telling Bertie this he pursues his usual tactic of parcelling out information fact by fact, pausing to let Bertie react in puzzlement and amazement. Bertie also has to ask a question or make a comment to elicit each item of information, since Jeeves seldom volunteers anything (unless it is to his advantage to do so). Here Jeeves first tells Bertie of the engagement, then fills him in on earlier events, in this order: Jeeves telephoned Sippy, Jeeves telephoned Gwendolyn, Sippy had an accident, Jeeves caused the "accident" by striking Sippy with a putter, Jeeves told Sippy the vase hit him, and Jeeves broke the vase to make this plausible. Thus he delays the revelation of one of the middle events—the breaking of the vase—until last, after he has revealed the success of his scheme to bring the couple together. Presumably he hopes this tactic will moderate Bertie's wrath at the loss of the vase (the breaking of which constitutes Jeeves's reward, which he had taken without permission).

At other points Jeeves uses the gradual revelation of his past actions to impress Bertie with his cleverness. His summaries are typically punctuated by such comments from Bertie as "I gaped at the man" or "The scales fell from my eyes." At the end of *Stiff Upper Lip, Jeeves,* Jeeves tells Bertie that he induced Bassett to drop the theft charge by agreeing to enter Bassett's employ. Bertie, aghast, asks, "You're leaving me?" Jeeves says he will do so only temporarily, and Bertie has to ask, "Temporarily?" before Jeeves finally explains that he will soon find an excuse to quit and return to Bertie. Brilliant though some of his plans are, Jeeves makes them even more impressive to Bertie through careful manipulation of information.

Bertie's limited knowledge gives rise to an even more complex device: Wodehouse suggests that a considerable portion of the valet's life is outside Bertie's ken and that even when actively engaged with Bertie's problems, Jeeves does things about which he never tells Bertie. These latter cases sometimes involve instances when Jeeves deliberately pushes Bertie deeper into the soup, either to teach him a lesson or to gain a reward.

We learn at various points that Jeeves in general leads an offstage life to which Bertie is not privy. Almost invariably, Bertie is surprised when he happens to learn something about Jeeves's offstage activities. For example, in "Jeeves Exerts the Old Cerebellum," Bingo tells Bertie that he bought tickets to a charity dance from Jeeves. Bertie responds:

> "Jeeves I didn't know he went in for that sort of thing."
> "Well, I suppose he has to relax a bit every now and then. Anyway, he was there, swinging a dashed efficient shoe."

This same story gives us our only glimpse into Jeeves's love life, when Bertie is surprised to learn that Jeeves is involved with two women. Incidentally, even though we never learn about Jeeves's relations with any other women thereafter, this story establishes early on that: (a) if he had any, Bertie probably would not find out about them and hence could not tell us; and (b) Jeeves, unlike Bertie, is adept at getting out of engagements (or "understandings")—not being constrained by any scruples, let alone a Code. Bertie is also surprised at other points to discover: that Jeeves is a member of the Junior Ganymede Club (*The Code of the Woosters*), that he has done political campaigning in the past (*Much Obliged, Jeeves*), that he has an uncle in service (*The Mating Season*), and that he has a first name, Reginald (*Much Obliged, Jeeves*).[18] In general, Bertie shows little curiosity about Jeeves's past and activities—which is one reason Jeeves can operate so independently.

The pay-off to Bertie's ignorance about Jeeves's doings comes in those stories where Jeeves keeps some of his actions and motives secret from Bertie, withholding them even in the final summing up. To take a relatively simple case, at the end of "Clustering Round Young Bingo," Jeeves outlines how he solved the various servant problems and what tips he has received from the grateful householders. He also mentions getting money from Uncle George, whom he had persuaded Bertie to join, reluctantly, during George's cure at Harrogate:

> "Don't tell me that Uncle George gave you something, too! What on earth for?"
> "Well, really, sir, I do not quite understand myself. But I

> received a cheque for ten pounds from him. He seemed to be under the impression that I had been in some way responsible for your joining him at Harrogate, sir."

Of course, Jeeves *had* been responsible, in a direct way. He had initially pressed Bertie quite hard to go, and when Bertie refused, he had maneuvered Bertie into a situation where he had to leave town for awhile and was finally persuaded to go to Harrogate. It is clear in retrospect that George either offered Jeeves the ten pounds to persuade Bertie or that Jeeves at least strongly anticipated a reward on the basis of something George had said. Yet Jeeves cannot tell Bertie this, so he equivocates in the above speech, in a way which Bertie cannot interpret, but the reader can: note the hesitation of the beginning ("Well, really, sir" being a stock Jeevesian phrase indicating that he is a bit nervous concerning what he is about to tell Bertie) and the hedging ("I do not *quite* understand . . ."). He half admits the reason but in terms that suggest George was mistaken in thinking that Jeeves got Bertie to Harrogate. The reader may strongly suspect that George bribed Jeeves, but Bertie does not: "I gaped at the fellow." Indeed, Bertie offers Jeeves another five pounds, adding, "And I don't know why I'm giving it to you." "No, sir," Jeeves replies, pocketing the fiver without bothering to explain further. ("No, sir" here does not imply "I don't know either"; it means "That's right, you don't know.")

"Clustering Round Young Bingo" is the earliest story in which this sort of clue as to Jeeves's offstage activities is dropped so subtly, and it also marks a considerable increase in narrative complexity within the series. In the earliest stories, Jeeves is not such a devious, powerful character, and there is no room for such manipulation. Revelations about him usually come directly, as when Bertie chances to overhear Jeeves call him mentally negligible in "The Pride of the Woosters Is Wounded."

A turning point both for Jeeves's character and for the manipulation of narration came with "Bertie Changes His Mind." This 1922 story is the only item in the series narrated by Jeeves. Given that his writing style is stodgy and some unpleasant aspects of his character are introduced, most critics have dismissed it as a minor work or even as a mistake on Wodehouse's part.[19] Such dismissal misses the point. Not only are Jeeves's pompous style and heavy-handed irony funny in themselves, but the story was vital in allowing Wodehouse to build up Jeeves's character considerably, making him, for the rest of the series, into a character we would understand better than would Bertie.

One of the many fascinating aspects of "Bertie Changes His Mind" is how the story reveals the degree to which Jeeves deceives Bertie. To realize how different their degrees of knowledge are, one need only imagine how the same events would come across if Bertie had narrated the story. There is no summing up at the end. Bertie never realizes that Jeeves took him into the girls' school deliberately to induce him to give up the idea of inviting his sister and nieces to live with him, that Jeeves asked Miss Tomlinson to arrange the lecture, or that Jeeves faked the car's breakdown to prevent Bertie from escaping. From the start Jeeves has cynically manipulated events. Although Wodehouse never used Jeeves as narrator again, he apparently expected readers to remember this one instance and to assume Jeeves capable of similar secret manipulations of events.[20]

Once we become suspicious of Jeeves, there are many things we can infer that he may have done in the later stories and novels. For example, in "Jeeves and the Kid Clementina," Bertie carries through Bobbie Wickham's crazy scheme for smuggling her AWOL cousin back into her girls' school; he ends up in a tree in the school grounds, confronted by a policeman. The only information we receive about how the cop got there is when he says, "We had a telephone call at the station saying there was somebody in Miss Mapleton's garden." Tracing back through the time scheme, we realize that Bertie parted from Jeeves and Clementina, saying that he would give Jeeves ten minutes' start before carrying out his part of the scheme. We must assume that Jeeves either used that time to call the police himself or got someone else, like Miss Mapleton, to do it. His motive in doing this is partly to convince Miss Mapleton that there *are* burglars about and hence that Bertie is a hero and partly to scare Bertie so thoroughly that he will realize what dangers Bobbie had sent him into; Jeeves of course knows that he will be able to rescue Bertie from the police. His plan succeeds, and Bertie praises him, giving up all ideas of a vacation in Antibes with Bobbie. At the end, Bertie asks for the usual summing up: "I say, tell me all. I am fogged." Jeeves does, with one key omission.

This instance is fairly clear-cut, but a more ambiguous case occurs in "Jeeves and the Yule-tide Spirit." At the end, Jeeves reveals to Bertie that Sir Roderick Glossop's hot-water bottle was punctured a second time during the night, by Tuppy—who had thought he was playing the joke on Bertie. Bobbie Wickham, Jeeves explains, had treacherously put both Bertie and Tuppy up to the same scheme. This revelation makes Bertie realize the folly of his infatuation with Bobbie, and he and Jeeves take off for Monte Carlo (where Jeeves had wanted to be all along). We, however, might ponder various possible offstage events: perhaps Jeeves suggested to Bobbie that she urge Tuppy to perpetrate the joke; perhaps Jeeves himself told Tuppy and blames it on Bobbie; perhaps Jeeves punctured the hot-water bottle himself and blamed the others; perhaps the whole thing is a lie to get Bertie out the back door and onto the Blue Train. There is no specific suggestion that Jeeves did any of these things or that he is not telling Bertie the truth. But again, if Bertie had been narrating "Bertie Changes His Mind," we would have no idea that Jeeves told Miss Tomlinson that Bertie would appreciate being asked to give a speech. After that early story, we should always consider the events as they might look from Jeeves's point-of-view. They might often be very different indeed.

In *Thank You, Jeeves,* or instance, we must infer—for Jeeves never tells Bertie and Bertie never tells us—that Jeeves is scheming almost from the beginning to return to Bertie's employ and get rid of his banjolele. The first hint we get is when Jeeves comes out to the grounds of Chuffnell Hall to summon Pauline to see her father; after Pauline's departure, Jeeves stays with Bertie, though he has no apparent reason to do so. He does not initiate the conversation but gives Bertie a chance to place the problem of Chuffy's undeclared love for Pauline before him. We can infer by this point that Jeeves may have taken the job with Chuffy because he knew he would be near Bertie and could take advantage of any chance to get back into Bertie's employ. The big question then becomes, to what degree does Jeeves help *create* any of the problems he eventually solves. One can hardly imagine that the poetic justice Jeeves wreaks is accidental: with boot polish, he manages in the end to turn Bertie into a pseudo-Negro minstrel, the thing Bertie had aspired to be in taking up the banjolele. We might even suspect that Jeeves had a hand in determining that Brinkley (Bingley) would be sent to Bertie as his successor—one who he knew would prove unacceptable. Might it be Jeeves who arranges that Stoker, not Chuffy, is the one who sees Bertie kiss Pauline? Jeeves tells Bertie that he did not encourage Pauline to swim away from the yacht and show up in Bertie's cottage—but can we believe him? Of course, we can never determine one way or another, since Bertie does not know.

As Edward L. Galligan has pointed out, this use of Bertie as an unreliable narrator is quite virtuosic in relation to Wodehouse's polished plot construction:

> For the writer of a loosely ordered novel, the choice of first-person point of view may be a form of self-indulgence, but for a writer of a very tightly plotted novel the necessity of having the narrator present in every important scene can be a considerable inconvenience, especially if, like Wodehouse, the writer refuses to cheat by having other characters strain to give the narrator detailed accounts of scenes which he missed. It makes matters more difficult if the narrator is incapable of analyzing motives and purposes: Bertie has enough trouble perceiving what anyone, himself included, is doing without trying to grasp why he is doing it.[21]

The challenges of such writing were enormous, yet Wodehouse makes the result seem effortless, to the point where it is easy to miss noticing this complex and subtle device.

In one of the most-quoted passages from *Performing Flea,* Wodehouse wrote: "By the way, it's not all jam writing a story in the first person. The reader can know nothing except what Bertie tells him, and Bertie can only know a limited amount himself."[22] He realized, however, that the struggle was worth it; in 1951 he was writing a novel and considering whether to make it a Jeeves/Wooster story. (It eventually became *Barmy in Wonderland.*) He wrote to Townend; "If

I tell this one in the first person, I lose most of Kaufman's first act but gain enormously in every other way. I can get so much more out of a story if it is told by Bertie."[23] He could indeed, and the results present a perpetual and delightful challenge to the reader. Through Bertie's eyes we see the clichéd activities of the series' characters both as conventional and as novel.

5

PERFECTING THE FORMULA: THE SHORT STORIES

My trouble is that every time I get a good idea I find it's something I wrote in 1930 or thereabouts.

—WODEHOUSE TO LORD CITRINE, SEPTEMBER 1, 1964

Wodehouse depended upon repetitive narrative formulas, and he was also very prolific. These factors mean, first, that he needed to have powerful methods of plotting to sustain repetition without boring loyal readers and, second, that he needed a repertory of devices to allow variation on such insistently recurring patterns. Given Wodehouse's general formula of combining a Holmesian detective-story structure with an inverted romance plot, we can then examine the specific narrative formulas he used to flesh out these borrowed genre conventions.

By analyzing the short stories according to the periodization given in the introduction, we shall see that some of Wodehouse's early experiments introduced formulas he later jettisoned. The early-period stories, for example, usually portray Jeeves as only slightly clever, making mistakes he then must rectify with his final solution. The joke is that Bertie, who is very stupid, finds Jeeves's solutions brilliant. Only in the middle period does Wodehouse develop the omniscient Jeeves that we now consider a sine qua non of the series.

The middle period contains anomalous elements that would later be eliminated, such as Jeeves's Don Juan-ish behavior in the early stories in *The Inimitable Jeeves*. Still, many elements crucial to the rest of the series were also introduced in this period, and we can trace this process systematically. By the late-period stories of *Very Good, Jeeves*, Wodehouse's plotting was well-nigh perfect.

Throughout, his main strategy was to use Bertie as a force to create an open plot line through conflict, with Jeeves providing closure. Also, because of Jeeves's abilities as a problem-solver (except in the early stories) Wodehouse had to concentrate on strategies to delay his bringing the narrative to a premature end. In one way or another, all characters, settings, and events in the series can be examined as strategies for creating narratives based around this simple dynamic of a balance between Bertie and Jeeves, openness and closure, problem and solution.

Plotting based around a problem-solution construction is common in popular literature. Genres like detective fiction, thrillers, farces, and science fiction depend on presenting characters with some trouble or challenge against which they struggle for the bulk of the narrative. Such genres are minimally dependent on factors like psychological conflict, social comment, naturalism, and other sorts of conventions associated more with high literature. In part because of this dependence on a problem-solution model, mechanical perfection of plotting was a central issue for Wodehouse.

We can trace, for example, how Wodehouse eliminated coincidence from his plots as much as possible. Coincidence is acceptable in some genres, such as the melodrama, but in the types of stories he was writing—especially with their origins in the detective story—coincidence is typically considered less artful and less demanding than better-motivated plotting. Most importantly, the series posits that Jeeves controls events so he can solve all problems. Major coincidences would imply, however, that he does not depend on intelligence and deviousness so much as luck. Coincidence also makes it easy to fool the reader (for example, by keeping back the fact that the menace's valet happens to be Jeeves's friend who happens to have overheard something). To make events seem less simple, then, such coincidences must be hidden, and this camouflaging process can be clumsy. We saw in chapter 2 that Wodehouse expended much effort in plotting his narratives intricately, with thorough motivation.

While working to eliminate coincidence, Wodehouse also moved from fairly simple plots in which Jeeves has one or two goals to plots where he juggles a whole series of Bertie's goals and often one or two of his own as well. In analyzing Wodehouse's narrative strategies, I am assuming that the most well-plotted stories and novels are those which avoid coincidence and contain several interwoven problems and which thoroughly motivate their causal chains to avoid inconsistencies or pointless gaps. The more complex narratives may, however, contain deliberate, systematic gaps, since these elements lead us to infer things that happen outside Bertie's ken (primarily Jeeves's offstage activities). A combination of these elements engages the reader's understanding on a number of levels and helps defamiliarize the clichéd, traditional plot devices that Wodehouse uses as his material. Delightful though all the stories are, the process of watching the enormous strides which Wodehouse took during the first decade of the series toward such complexity can be fascinating.

AN ISOLATED CASE: BERTIE WITHOUT JEEVES (1915)

Though Jeeves is barely present in "Extricating Young Gussie," the story contains certain aspects of the series in a surprisingly complete form. Jeeves's typical functions are already here, but they are fulfilled by Aunt Julia, who will not figure in the later stories.

Some familiar elements of the series are recognizable immediately. The first scene takes place in Bertie's home as he is rudely awakened by a visitor—Aunt Agatha. Although there will be some adjustments concerning her name, marital status, and offspring, she possesses her small set of vital characteristics. "She sprang it on me before breakfast. There in seven words you have a complete character sketch of my Aunt Agatha"; "she held me with her glittering eye. I have never met anyone who can give a better imitation of the Ancient Mariner." These descriptions do not differ significantly from Bertie's later characterizations of Agatha: she is always out to run Bertie's life and Bertie speaks of her in exaggerated terms ("kills rats with her bare teeth," "wears barbed wire next to the skin"). Her basic functions are to introduce conflict into Bertie's life and to provide enough of a threat that he will go against his own interests to placate her.

Bertie also gains several of his primary traits here: he is never at his best in the early morning, drinks heavily (though his drunkenness is later deemphasized), and fritters away his time at golf, bridge, and nightclubs. He will become a far more complex character, but the most basic narrative pattern associated with him is established here: he is presented with a problem, realizes himself to be inadequate to it, and passes it along to another character for solution.

This is, however, the only story in which that other character is not Jeeves. Jeeves barely exists here, although the few traits he displays will be permanent ones. He functions to introduce the disturbing agent into Bertie's bedroom, as in so many later narratives. His phlegmatic attitude appears in the second of his two lines:

> "Jeeves," I said, "we start for America on Saturday."
> "Very good, sir," he said, "which suit will you wear?"

Beyond this, Jeeves appears only in his standard tea-bearing role and as a conventional servant, getting baggage through customs.

Yet even without Jeeves as a central figure, the plot establishes the pattern that became familiar in the later stories, if in a simpler way. Aunt Agatha gives Bertie an assignment which he tries to carry out: get cousin Gussie out of vaudeville and away from his low-born fiancée. Bertie proves helpless and upon arriving in New York totters off to get tipsy. He encounters Gussie by accident and tags along with him as Gussie gets a job in vaudeville. At this point, the basic conflict is completed: one relative (Aunt Agatha) objects to her nephew marrying a vaudevillian, while another (Joe Danby) objects to his daughter marrying anything but. Bertie already realizes that he has failed: "It was clear to me by now that Aunt Agatha had picked the wrong man for this job of disentangling Gussie from the clutches of the American vaudeville profession. What I needed was reinforcements." In later narratives the "reinforcements" would be Jeeves. Here Bertie calls upon his Aunt Julia, Gussie's mother.

Indeed, as described by Bertie, she resembles Jeeves: "the most dignified person I know," "Aunt Julia's manner seems to suggest that I am more to be pitied than censured," and "she exudes dignity." Bertie takes Julia to see Gussie's act, then Ray's, and proposes to take her to see Ray's father: "When I've put you in touch with him I rather fancy my share of the business is concluded, and it's up to you." As Jeeves will soon do, Julia takes charge.

Yet during the visit to Joe Danby, Aunt Julia loses her "Jeeves" functions almost visibly. She "had shed her *grand-dame* manner completely and was blushing and smiling." It turns out that Joe is her old vaudeville partner; they decide to marry and revive their act. The character called upon to solve the problem turns out to be the one with the relationship that will make that solution possible. Julia thus combines two roles that will be split across various characters in later Jeeves/Wooster narratives. "Indian Summer of an Uncle," for example, has a similar structure: Aunt Agatha enlists Bertie's help to prevent his Uncle George from marrying a waitress. In that case Jeeves arranges that Uncle George will marry his old flame, the waitress' aunt. In "Extricating Young Gussie," the participants, including Aunt Julia, are all involved in the action. But in "Indian Summer of an Uncle," Jeeves stands aside as an objective, godlike manipulator. Thus the later stories gain complexity by separating two functions (solver and solution), embodied by Aunt Julia here.

Despite its simplicity, "Extricating Young Gussie" clears up its problem neatly. Aunt Julia turns the initial conflict on its head. While Agatha felt Gussie was marrying beneath his class, Julia argues that Ray, an experienced vaudevillian, is marrying below *her*self by accepting a beginner like Gussie. Julia goes back into vaudeville, disappearing from the series, and Bertie is left to placate Aunt Agatha. And, as often happens, he avoids her wrath by staying at a distance, cabling her not to come to New York. He anticipates he will have to remain there himself for "about ten years." Aunt Agatha has already become so powerful a villain that there is no way of actually defeating her. Even Jeeves, though he often manipulates her to his own advantage in controlling Bertie, never defeats her. Except for the two times Bertie finds occasion ("Pearls Mean Tears") or courage (*The Mating Season*) to defy Agatha, the plots involving her tend to end in flight (down the rain pipe, to Monte Carlo, to New York). Jeeves almost never confronts Agatha directly—the one major exception, as we shall see, being in the story that is so similar to this one, "Indian Summer of an Uncle."

THE EARLY PERIOD (1916–1917)

The solution in "Extricating Young Gussie" depends on an enormous coincidence; the woman Gussie loves happens to be the daughter of his mother's old vaudeville partner. Hence despite her impressive demeanor, Julia's solution does not spring from any cleverness on her part. Oddly enough, the same is true of the early narratives featuring Jeeves. In these five stories, published in the space of just over a year, Jeeves relies heavily on coincidence. Some of the schemes he suggests to Bertie and his friends are simple, seeming clever only in contrast to the stupidity of the young men. Most surprisingly, four of the five stories contain a double delay, with Jeeves proposing a plan that fails, then having to find another, successful solution.

All four stories center on a young man under the thumb of an oppressive relative. He goes against the relative's wishes, risks getting into trouble, and is finally able, with Jeeves's help, either to keep in the good graces of the relative or to strike out on his own. The pattern is remarkably similar:

—"The Artistic Career of Corky." Corky's uncle, Alexander Worple, is his principal source of income; Corky's engagement to Muriel threatens to alienate Worple; Jeeves eventually suggests the means for Corky to become a successful cartoonist and make his own living.

—"The Aunt and the Sluggard." Rocky, a lazy country dweller who hates New York City, is dependent on an allowance from his aunt, Miss Rockmetteller. She decides she wants him to send her letters describing nightlife in New York, which inspire her to visit there and do the rounds with Rocky. He hates this, but Jeeves arranges for the aunt to undergo a religious conversion and condemn the sinful life of the big city.

—"Jeeves and the Unbidden Guest." Lady Malvern, a friend of Aunt Agatha, leaves her repressed son Motty with Bertie while she gathers material for a book on America. Motty begins leading a drunken, boisterous existence, and Bertie fears this will bring down Aunt Agatha's rage upon him. Jeeves persuades Lady Malvern that Motty acted to help her with her book, and the danger is averted.

—"Jeeves and the Hard-boiled Egg." Bertie's pal Bicky is financially dependent on his uncle, the Duke of Chiswick, who wants him to work as a rancher; Bicky hates the country, so he pretends to his uncle that he has become successful in New York. Jeeves enables Bicky to blackmail the duke into giving him a well-paid job as his secretary.

"Jeeves Takes Charge" is an exception to this pattern, in that it involves, for the first time, Bertie being engaged and Jeeves's getting him out of the alliance. Florence Craye demands that Bertie destroy the manuscript of the scurrilous memoirs written by his Uncle Willoughby because it mentions her father. Bertie assigns its destruction to Jeeves, who instead sends it to be published, causing Florence to break off the engagement.[1]

In this early period, Wodehouse already has a set of characters whose functions are similar and who are nearly interchangeable units. In "The Aunt and the Sluggard," Bertie compares Miss Rockmetteller to Aunt Agatha. Lady Malvern in "Jeeves and the Unbidden Guest" is a friend of Agatha's and has somewhat the same effect on Bertie: "She made me feel as if I were ten years old and had been brought into the drawing-room in my Sunday clothes to say how-d'you-do." This tactic of creating sets of similar characters was basic to Wodehouse's method of constructing narratives, but at this stage his formula was still narrow. Aside from Bertie and Jeeves, there is virtually nothing but young men, aunts, and uncles.

With the exception of "Jeeves Takes Charge," each of these stories involves Jeeves's coming up with an initial solution that fails. In "The Artistic Career of Corky" he suggests that Corky's fiancée, Muriel, ingratiate herself with his uncle without letting on that she knows Corky; the result is that Worple marries her himself. It is hard to imagine Jeeves making such a miscalculation in the middle or late stories. He does solve Corky's financial problem, suggesting that Corky use his failed portrait of Worple and Muriel's baby as the basis for a comic strip. Yet, while Corky may become self-supporting, he has lost Muriel through Jeeves's initial suggestion.

Jeeves's plan to help Rocky fool his aunt in "The Aunt and the Sluggard" leads to less serious consequences, but it backfires all the same. Jeeves agrees to go out on the town himself in New York and to provide Rocky with material for his letters to Miss Rockmetteller. The resulting letters, however, are so effective that Miss Rockmetteller is inspired to come to New York, and she takes Rocky on the very nightclub circuit that he had sought to avoid. Bertie also suffers in that Rocky has to pretend to be the proprietor of Bertie's flat, hosting his aunt there while Bertie moves to a hotel. Eventually Jeeves tricks Miss Rockmetteller into attending a religious meeting at which she is converted; she denounces New York as sinful and orders Rocky to move to the country.

In "Jeeves and the Unbidden Guest," Motty's drunken revels drive Bertie out of his apartment; he flees to visit Rocky, leaving Jeeves to cope with Motty's dissipation. He does so by provoking Motty to hit a policeman and so end up in jail, away from the temptations of the great city. At first Bertie approves of this solution, but, in another example of extreme coincidence, Lady Malvern happens to visit that same prison while gathering material for her book. She sees Motty and accuses Bertie of having led him astray. Jeeves comes up with a solution on the spur of the moment, convincing her that Motty went to prison voluntarily to help her with her research. Bertie is thus saved from getting in trouble with Aunt Agatha. As in all the early stories, however, there is little sense that Jeeves controls events; he merely seizes upon fortuitous opportunities.

"Jeeves and the Hard-boiled Egg" emphasizes Jeeves's inadequate initial solution even more, since here he proposes two schemes in a row that fail. Moreover, both are particularly weak. Since Bicky has lied to his uncle, saying that he has successful business dealings in New York, Jeeves proposes that Bertie lend Bicky his expensive flat during the duke's visit. They laud Jeeves's proposal, but it has one glaring drawback. Once the duke sees how well Bicky is apparently doing, he will presumably cancel Bicky's allowance—as in fact he does. Jeeves attempts to compensate for his first failure through a scheme for Bicky to make money by selling chances to shake hands with the duke to a group of yokels from Birdsburg. During the session, however, the Birdsburgers mention that they have paid to meet the duke, and the latter angrily calls the whole thing off. Jeeves undoes his second failure by hinting to Bicky that he might sell the story of the handshaking session to the tabloids; the duke, terrified of such publicity, gives Bicky a cushy post as his secretary. Jeeves resorts to blackmail here for the first time, perhaps as a result of his double failure. The fact that Jeeves comes up with two unsuccessful schemes also suggests why "Jeeves and the Hard-boiled Egg" was the last of the stories in this period. Wodehouse could hardly develop this repetitious formula further. It was more than a year before the next story appeared.

Given this constricting pattern, we can see "Jeeves Takes Charge" as offering some rich possibilities that were later developed to expand the formula of the early stories. Here Jeeves does not offer a solution that initially fails. He is more in control, removing the memoirs manuscript from Bertie's drawer so that Uncle Willoughby will not find it. He then disregards Bertie's instructions to destroy the volume, managing to persuade him that marriage to Florence would be trying.

This is also the story where Bertie surrenders control of his life to Jeeves, thus creating rich possibilities for placidity and tension. Even within the early period, with its relatively simple narrative pattern, the introduction of tension between Jeeves and Bertie provides a source of narrative conflict and delay. The next story, "Jeeves and the Unbidden Guest," begins with Bertie's first attempt to stand up to Jeeves. He mentions that Jeeves has "jolly well oppressed me" over clothes, having "made me give up one of my new suits." The latter is clearly the checked suit given away by Jeeves in "Jeeves Takes Charge." Now Jeeves gets downright stubborn over the "Broadway Special" hat and pink tie Bertie fancies.

In the first two stories in which he figures prominently, Jeeves disapproved of Bertie's taste in clothes, but no conflict between the two resulted, and the narrative progression was not affected. "The Artistic Career of Corky" ends with Jeeves telling Bertie to wear a different suit than the one Bertie has picked out, but there had been no earlier reference to this suit; in "The Aunt and the Sluggard" Bertie humbly gives in to Jeeves over a tie, and Jeeves mentions that Bertie has only two dinner jackets "for practical purposes," since he "cannot wear the third." There is no sense in either story, however, that Jeeves would withhold his aid over such disagreements. After "Jeeves Takes Charge," conflicts over Bertie's appearance become a major way of motivating Jeeves's initial refusal to help Bertie.

Jeeves's reward in the early stories are also simple. Since Jeeves and Bertie's relationship is still undeveloped at this point, Jeeves has scant personal involvement in the plots. With the exception of "Jeeves Takes Charge," there is no external threat to their household. Hence Jeeves solves problems in return for money or a sacrifice by Bertie. Indeed, he usually gets both.

Despite their formulaic quality, these early stories hint at some narrative devices that later become more important. "The Aunt and the Sluggard" in particular contains elements that anticipate the 1920s stories. It is the only early story to suggest the marriagelike ties between Bertie and Jeeves. Bertie becomes forlorn when forced to go to a hotel while Jeeves stays behind:

> I looked round the place. The moment of parting had come. I felt sad. The whole thing reminded one of one of those melodramas where they drive chappies out of the old homestead into the snow.
>
> "Goody-bye, Jeeves," I said.
>
> "Good-bye, sir."
>
> And I staggered out.

And when Jeeves brings more clothes to the hotel, Bertie describes his entrance: "It was all so home-like when he floated noiselessly into the room that I nearly broke down." As so frequently happens, Bertie compares himself to a character in a clichéd literary situation.

"The Aunt and the Sluggard" also gives the first indication of Jeeves's offstage existence. Bertie is astonished to discover that Jeeves spends his evenings off in ritzy nightclubs and later sees him at the Midnight Revels: "He was sitting at a table on the edge of the dancing floor, doing himself remarkably well with a fat cigar. His face wore an expression of austere benevolence, and he was making notes in a small book." This hardly squares with Bertie's usual depiction of the restrained Jeeves, but it does indicate Jeeves's aspirations to a middle-class or even upper-class life-style.

Finally, in one of the subtlest devices in the early stories, Wodehouse has Miss Rockmetteller describe the effects of Jeeves's final scheme. Here Jeeves explains little to Bertie at the end, and we are left to infer his tactics by what she says. She describes Jeeves as stupid and as having mistakenly taken her to the revivalist meeting; we realize that Jeeves steered her there deliberately. She mentions that she was in the middle of a row and hesitated to disturb others by leaving; we suspect that Jeeves got her such a seat to trap her there. In later narratives Wodehouse becomes adept at suggesting Jeeves's activities.

Despite the simplicity of the early stories and their dependence on coincidence, they are not uninteresting. Much of Bertie's verbal style is already developed, and the contrast between his slang and Jeeves's formal diction contributes greatly to the humor.

THE MIDDLE-PERIOD STORIES (1918–1925)

While the early stories were largely dominated by single formula, the middle ones show Wodehouse experimenting with a variety of narrative devices and characters in order to broaden the series' possibilities. In some cases such experiments produced anomalous plots and inconsistent character traits that are later dropped.

The middle-period stories eliminate the pattern of Jeeves's proposing one solution which fails and a second (or third) which clears up the problems caused by the first. Gradually he becomes more intelligent until he reaches virtual omniscience, and as he gains complexity as a character, Bertie expands correspondingly. The plots become more varied and intricate, though many still depend on coincidence for Jeeves's solution.

Traces of these changes are apparent in "Letter/Startling,"[2] which acts as a transition between the early and middle stories. It concerns Bertie's efforts to get Cyril Bassington-Bassington out of a part in a Broadway play. Jeeves eventually gets the producer's son to have Cyril fired. For the first time Jeeves neither makes an initial mistake (as in the four early stories) nor goes deliberately against Bertie's will (as in "Jeeves Takes Charge"). Instead, he bides his time and seizes upon a chance to set everything right. This, in crude form, is the pattern of many of the middle-period stories. In "Letter/Startling," Jeeves also has his own goal: getting rid of the purple socks. He refuses for a while to help Bertie, then effects his solution and claims his reward. Thus the casual line connected with the solution has been changed radically, but the problem itself still resembles those of the early stories, depending on a young man who risks getting in bad with his family. His family are friends of Aunt Agatha, who will become angry with Bertie if he fails to protect the young man.

NEW CHARACTERS AND FORMULAS

In these stories, Wodehouse plays further with new characters and plot formulas. In the next story, "Cerebellum/No Wedding," Bingo Little enters the series. At first glance he is like the dippy young men Bertie has helped earlier, yet he is an old pal instead of a new American chum or a British pest. Thus he has more potential as a series character, being a lot like Bertie—except for his extreme susceptibility. As long as his infatuations are thwarted, he can return, adding the stability, combined with variety, that the series needed.

Bertie's sense of obligation to help Bingo is motivated at Bingo's second appearance, in "Comrade/Bingo":

> I don't know why, ever since I first knew him at school, I should have felt a rummy feeling of responsibility for young

> Bingo. I mean to say, he's not my son (thank goodness) or my brother or anything like that. He's got absolutely no claim on me at all, and yet a large-sized chunk of my existence seems to be spent in fussing over him like a bally old hen and hauling him out of the soup. I suppose it must be some rare beauty in my nature or something.

Here we see Wodehouse striving for a way of explaining why Bertie should go to such lengths to help Bingo. The "rare beauty" in his nature would gradually crystallize into the Code.

By Bingo's third appearance, in "The Great Sermon Handicap," the pattern of his thwarted romances is clear. Wodehouse seems to have realized that the series could be sustained better by using a number of characters who do not get what they want or who are at least delayed considerably in getting it. None of the pills or pals that Jeeves and Bertie helped in the early stories had reappeared. By thwarting his characters' desires, Wodehouse could keep them around longer. Here the premise is simple: Bingo falls hopelessly in love, over and over, only to lose out to a rival or to fail to get the allowance that would make marriage possible. Aunt Dahlia's later perpetual problems in financing *Milady's Boudoir* or the delays in the marriages of Gussie and Madeline, Tuppy and Angela, etc., are more sophisticated examples of this device. The use of continuing situations and characters, though it fosters more apparent repetition than in the early stories, actually provides variety—partly because Wodehouse becomes adept at inventing situations and partly because he keeps adding recurring characters.

"Cerebellum/No Wedding" also turns the repetitiousness of the pals' appeals for help to good use by setting up Jeeves's Holmes-like consulting practice. This is the first story where a pal (Bingo) comes to Bertie appealing specifically for Jeeves's help. (Previously they asked Bertie for help, and he suggested turning to Jeeves.) Bingo opines that Bertie is too stupid to be of assistance, while Jeeves is "by way of being the brains of the family." Jeeves's reputation among Bertie's friends sets up a greater variety of narrative possibilities that continues across the entire series. They can consult Jeeves without Bertie finding out until after the fact (as with Gussie in *Right Ho, Jeeves*) or can simply confide in Jeeves, giving him information he needs to solve the problem (as with Chuffy in *Thank You, Jeeves*). Jeeves's fame also makes possible events like Chuffy's scooping him up immediately when he quits.

Aunts and uncles are still prominent in this period, but they gain additional functions. In the early stories, Agatha called upon Bertie to defend family or friends from disgrace. Now she interferes more directly in his life, trying to pressure him into marriage. The notion of Bertie being forced to marry is itself a new motif, since his one previous engagement—to Florence—had been voluntary. Agatha's threat is also extended to Jeeves in the middle-period stories. Previously Jeeves had saved Bertie from her wrath but had never been its victim himself. In "Claude/Sir Roderick," she comes right out and says she dislikes him. She presumably realizes that he controls Bertie and fosters him in the life-style she deplores. There is also an implication that her hatred has a element of class bias about it. In telling Bertie about Sir Roderick, "she paused, for Spencer had come in with the coffee. When he had gone she went on." This seemingly trivial detail suggests that Agatha would never discuss family matters before the servants, let alone confide in one. Her final confrontation with Jeeves in "Indian Summer of an Uncle" makes her elitism explicit.[3]

Bertie gains another aunt during this period. Dahlia figures in only one story, "Clustering Round Young Bingo," but there she appears complete with her husband, Tom, her magazine, *Milady's Boudoir*, and, by the end, her superlative chef, Anatole. I have discussed their general functions in chapter 4, and we shall see much more of them, but at this juncture they inject a large dose of domesticity into the series. Bertie's family expands signficantly, and *Milady's Boudoir* also creates the first problem involving Bingo since his marriage. Perhaps Wodehouse decided that more stability would benefit the series, and certainly the new domestic elements proved most effective in this and later plots. The formulas based on Bertie helping old pals or cousins and on being threatened by Aunt Agatha were not dropped, yet this new surge of domesticity makes for variety and creates a more permanent set of motivating characters. Claude and Eustace, funny as they are, could only get into trouble in certain ways. They were basically intensified versions of Bertie and Bingo—so they served their purpose twice and disappeared.

With "Clustering Round Young Bingo," Wodehouse sets up two major households—the Traverses and the Littles—which parallel Jeeves and Bertie's domestic establishment. Previously most of the problems were those of bachelors: getting the right woman, escaping the wrong one, avoiding the wrath of relatives, winning bets. This is not to say that domestic life is innately funnier, but now Wodehouse doubled his possibilities. He could use the conventional problems of marriage *and* of bachelorhood. The momentous nature of this change is signaled by the heavy emphasis on marriage and romance: not only with the two new households but also in the subject of Mrs. Little's maudlin article ("How I Keep the Love of My Husband-Baby") and in Jeeves's manipulation of the romantic relations of the various servants.

CHANGES IN JEEVES AND BERTIE

In the early stories Bertie's character was considerably more developed than was Jeeves's. In the middle period, Wodehouse concentrated on making Jeeves more personally involved in the problems and suggesting what he did when offstage.

The first attempt at doing both takes a startling form: Jeeves becomes a sort of Don Juan figure. "Cerebellum/No Wedding," written after a three-and-a-half-year gap in the series, presents Jeeves as acting for purely personal reasons: he is juggling his romantic entanglements with two women. Wodehouse's experiment was not wholly successful, probably because it offered limited possibilities. The threat posed by Jeeves's potential marriage would not seem to generate much narrative conflict. Bertie depends on Jeeves so much that he would presumably hire his valet's bride as a maid or cook, and things would go on as before. But the threat that Bertie will marry someone who either would get rid of Jeeves (for example, Honoria Glossop) or whom Jeeves could not control as he does Bertie (Bobbie Wickham) could provide a more powerful premise for generating narratives. Moreover, since Bertie is innately funny and weak, such repeated engagements are perpetually amusing, while the notion of Jeeves flitting from one broken "understanding" to another would make him an unpleasant seducer figure. Indeed, Wodehouse seems to have realized that Jeeves came across a bit that way here. Subsequent stories emphasize that Bingo bounces back and falls in love again, while one of Jeeves's fiancées, Miss Watson, marries a man who becomes a peer. (We never learn about the unfortunate Mabel, but we must assume that her taste in ties would quickly sour Jeeves on her.)

Another obvious way that Wodehouse made Jeeves more personally involved in the action was to use his gambling to make him a sort of chum to Bertie and his friends. A trio of stories, from "The Great Sermon Handicap" to "The Metropolitan Touch," have Jeeves either joining an informal betting syndicate with them or buying the book on Bingo's chances of getting married. This tactic presented difficulties as well, since Jeeves becomes so self-serving that he must occasionally work against the others, especially Bingo. (For example, the feeble suggestions he makes concerning Bingo's courtship in "The Metropolitan Touch" almost imply that Jeeves makes Bingo fail so that he can profit on the betting.) Most of the stories of the middle period after "The Metropolitan Touch" are concerned with balancing Jeeves's desire to help Bertie against his ability to serve his own interests.

Jeeves's offstage activities are worth emphasizing, since the tactic of suggesting his actions outside Bertie's ken is a central way of adding complexity to the narratives and of involving the reader in what seem at first to be straightforward comic stories. During this central period Wodehouse worked out some basic ways for suggesting that Jeeves is up to far more than Bertie can report to us.

Early on, there is little suggestion that Jeeves has been manipulating events extensively without Bertie knowing about it. In "Claude/Sir Roderick" we have no idea whether he has done anything to help Bertie, aside from letting the three aspiring "Seekers" leave their cats, fish, and hat in the apartment. Similarly, in "Agatha/Pearls" we have little basis for understanding why Jeeves acts as he does. The story involves two con artists who trick Bertie into loaning them money by offering as collateral a pearl necklace they have stolen from Aunt Agatha. Jeeves immediately recognizes Sidney as a notorious jewel thief and extortionist yet does not tell Bertie, merely extracting the necklace from Sid's pocket. Jeeves's deftness saves Bertie thousands, since he will not have to replace the necklace, but the failure to expose Sid on the spot costs Bertie the hundred pounds he "loans" Sid. Bertie overlooks this, so delighted is he at being able to lord it over Aunt Agatha by returning her pearls. But he could have done that if Jeeves had unmasked Sid. We might possibly infer the following motive: Jeeves assumed that Sid would victimize Bertie and let him do it in order to get Bertie into a panic, whereupon he could save Bertie and thereby get him to give up the scarlet cummerbund. Still, Jeeves could hardly anticipate that Agatha's pearls would be the means for Sid's scheme, so he could not know that Bertie would be particularly grateful for their return. Such a chain of inference would probably only occur to someone who has read some of the late, complex stories, where Jeeves manipulates events from an early stage. At this point in the series, it seems reasonable to assume that Jeeves simply withholds his help from Bertie because he is in a snit over the cummerbund, then seizes upon the lucky chance that he recognizes Sid and that the pearls happen to be Agatha's. Any uncertainty we may experience concerning Jeeves's motives and actions here is, I think, due to Wodehouse's uncertain plotting rather than to any systematic ambiguities.

"Bertie Changes His Mind," the story that reveals how extensively Jeeves manipulates events behind Bertie's back, was published less than half-way through this middle period. Yet surprisingly, Wodehouse did not immediately follow up on the narrative possibilities it offered. The fifth story after that point, "Clustering Round Young Bingo," does, however, as we saw in chapter 4, invite us to think back over events and realize that Uncle George must have offered Jeeves money to get Bertie to go to Harrogate with him. Such retrospective hints, however, are not common until the late stories.

Since Bertie was a more developed character than Jeeves in the early stories, he undergoes fewer sudden changes. There are no startling experiments with his character comparable to the brief use of Jeeves as a Don Juan figure. Still, Bertie gains in complexity during this middle period. The changes occur largely as a response to Jeeves's more radical alterations. Indeed, Bertie must become more complex to stay balanced against his valet.

In general, Bertie ceases to be the brainless, drunken dude of the early stories. The magazine versions of those stories frequently refer to his constant drinking: "I was so darned sorry for poor old Corky that I hadn't the heart to touch my breakfast. [I told Jeeves to drink it himself.] I was bowled over. Absolutely. It was the limit" ("The Artistic Career of Corky"). This version was retained in *My Man Jeeves*, but the sentence in brackets was cut for *Carry On, Jeeves*. Although much is made in the later stories and novels of Bertie's hangovers, it is clear that he usually drinks only at certain points in his domestic routine and that his festive nights out come on special occasions like Boat Race Night. At breakfast he drinks tea.

Bertie also gains in intelligence in the middle period stories. His development is particularly apparent in "The Rummy Affair of Old Biffy," where Biffy is such an absent-minded chump that Bertie wonders how he can get along in the world. When Jeeves refuses to help Biffy, Bertie borrows a tactic Jeeves used in "Claude/Sir Roderick," telling Biffy to act insane during a luncheon with his prospective father-in-law, Sir Roderick. When Biffy fails to carry through the simple scheme, Bertie gives up on him. Here, instead of being on the same level with his pal, Bertie occupies a middle ground. No other character is quite as dim as Biffy, but the story does serve to signal the change in Bertie. In a sense, Bertie must become more intelligent if he is to convey Jeeves's increasing genius to us; he must be better able to comprehend Jeeves's actions and to talk to Jeeves in a semi-intelligent way.

The two arguments the pair has over Jeeves's refusal to help Biffy are interesting in this regard. In a brief scene in the kitchen, Jeeves declines to act, without revealing that he believes Biffy has jilted Jeeves's niece, Mabel. Bertie defiantly declares that he will solve the problem himself. Later, in the car on the way to Wembley, Bertie fills Jeeves in on Biffy's romance with Mabel, and Jeeves realizes that he has misjudged Biffy. These conversations show Jeeves and Bertie in a different relationship than in the early stories. In the first scene, they are really at odds, while the second has an intimacy, an informality, and a complexity that depend on Bertie not being quite so funny as he has been. He is funny at most times, of course, and these two scenes have touches of humor, but he can be serious. Jeeves is also less the comically dignified stage valet. They have developed a more equal relationship, one capable of generating nuanced situations.

Perhaps the main sign of Bertie's growing complexity is his ability to defy Jeeves. The early period sets up the potential for tension in "Jeeves Takes Charge," when Jeeves first displays the iron hand in the velvet glove. Subsequently Bertie defies Jeeves over items of clothing but does not question Jeeves's solutions or consider taking over from him to help his friends. During the middle period, however, Wodehouse experiments increasingly with ways of bringing the two into conflict.

At first the situations are fairly simple, as in "Letter/Startling," where Jeeves will not help get Cyril out of the play because he is upset over Bertie's purple socks. In later stories, by making Bertie more defiant, Wodehouse motivates the conflicts and, hence, Jeeves's delays in offering assistance more effectively. "Pride/Hero's" is the first story where Bertie conceives a grudge against Jeeves (upon overhearing the "mentally negligible" remark). He is so upset that he refuses to ask for help, even though he faces marriage to Honoria. This grudge proved an effective delaying device, for Wodehouse was able to sustain the longest narrative in the series to that point: it extends over two magazine stories (split into chapters 5 to 8 of *The Inimitable Jeeves*). Bertie flaunts his defiance to Jeeves:

> "Jeeves," I said. "I'm in a bit of a difficulty."
>
> "I'm sorry to hear that, sir."
>
> "Yes, quite a bad hole. In fact, you might almost say on the brink of a precipice, and aced by an awful doom."
>
> "If I could be of any assistance, sir—"
>
> "Oh, no. No, no. Thanks very much, but no, no. I won't trouble you. I've no doubt I shall be able to get out of it all right by myself."
>
> "Very good, sir."

> So that was that. I'm bound to say I'd have welcomed a bit more curiosity from the fellow; but that is Jeeves all over. Cloaks his emotions, if you know what I mean.

This sort of conversation becomes more and more common in the stories, climaxing in the lengthy feud in *Right Ho, Jeeves.*

Bertie's defiance increasingly surfaces. In "The Delayed Exit of Claude and Eustace," he gloats because he wrongly thinks that the problem has worked itself out without Jeeves's intervention. He is delighted to hear that Claude and Eustace have departed but is also still annoyed with Jeeves:

> Had circumstances been other than what they were, I would at this juncture have unbent considerably towards Jeeves. Frisked around him a bit and whooped to a certain extent, and what not. But those spats still formed a barrier, and I regret to say that I took the opportunity of rather rubbing it in a bit on the man. I mean, he'd been so dashed aloof and unsympathetic, though perfectly aware that the young master was in the soup and that it was up to him to rally round that I couldn't help pointing out how the happy ending had been snaffled without any help from him.
>
> "So that's that, Jeeves," I said. "The episode is concluded. I knew things would sort themselves out if one gave them time and didn't get rattled. Many chaps in my place would have got rattled, Jeeves."
>
> "Yes, sir."
>
> "Gone rushing about, I mean, asking people for help and advice and so forth."
>
> "Very possibly, sir."
>
> "But not me, Jeeves."
>
> "No, sir."
>
> I left him to brood on it.

Again Jeeves does not react, being well aware that Bertie will soon learn that he in fact caused the twins' departure. Then Bertie will be all the more remorseful for having gloated and hence all the more prepared to give up the plaid spats.

Wodehouse continued to add elements to this formula for creating conflict between the two. In "The Rummy Affair of Old Biffy," their conversations become quite tense at moments. By this point Bertie is capable of getting angry at Jeeves, of standing up to him, of determining to take his place as problem solver, and of boasting about it to Jeeves. He also expresses annoyance when Biffy has no faith in him and wants Jeeves to solve his problem. This story is anomalous, in that Jeeves and Bertie's conflict results from a misunderstanding on Jeeves's part. Perhaps Wodehouse wanted to try using a subject of contention less trivial than the usual garish clothes: the apparent jilting of Jeeves's niece. This kind of serious situation proved unnecessary, however, and later on some of the most complex conflicts arise over trivial objects like white dinner jackets.

Another motif of Bertie's rebellion appears in "Without the Option," though in this case the dispute is a brief, mild one. Jeeves suggests the scheme of Bertie impersonating Sippy in a visit to a country house. Bertie not only initially rejects the idea but for the first time sarcastically impugns Jeeves's intelligence and even his sanity: " 'Jeeves,' I said sternly, 'pull yourself together. This is mere babble from the sickbed,' " " 'the scheme is a loony one,' " and " 'surely you can see for yourself that this is pure banana oil. It is not like you to come into the presence of a sick man and gibber.' " In more intense form, such an attitude helps structure the early novels.

MULTIPLE GOALS AND COINCIDENCES

During this middle period there is a sporadic move toward more complex plots. The clashes between Jeeves and Bertie over clothes often give Jeeves a goal of his own, beyond the problem Bertie asks him to solve. This double goal remains simple, in that the solution of Bertie's problem automatically brings the jettisoning of the item of apparel as a reward. Jeeves's goals can be more intricate, however. "Cerebellum/No Wedding" involves a tricky balancing act: Jeeves wants to thwart Bingo's marriage to Mabel by getting his allowance cut off and he wants out of his understanding with Miss Watson, old Mr. Little's cook; he also keeps Bertie and Bingo thinking that he is working to help Bingo. He accomplishes his goals by influencing Bingo's uncle to marry his cook, with the result that he cuts off Bingo's allowance and

Jeeves is left without a rival for Mabel. His double success on his own behalf results, however, from an uncharacteristic decision not to accomplish the task Bertie sets him.

"The Delayed Exit of Claude and Eustace" is more complex and more characteristic of the series as a whole. Here Jeeves's role is subtle and his actions ambiguous, largely as a result of his implied offstage actions. He has three problems: to get Claude and Eustace to go to South Africa, to help Bertie avoid going to Harrogate with the ailing Uncle George, and to force Bertie to get rid of his plaid spats. We are led to wonder whether Jeeves tries to solve the problem of getting rid of Claude and Eustace because: (1) they are pests causing him extra work; or (2) he expects a monetary reward from the woman they are both courting, Marion Wardour; or (3) he wants to please Bertie and thus pressure him to dispose of the spats. The reason could be any or all of these—though if it is all three, Jeeves displays more foresight here than in any other story before the later period. Beyond this, how does he find out that George would benefit from his pick-me-ups (the administration of which allows George to cancel the Harrogate visit)? The most probable implication is that Jeeves used his frequent tactic of eavesdropping, overhearing Aunt Agatha tell Bertie of George's drunkenness and bad nerves. Yet there is no mention of Jeeves's eavesdropping in the story, and the reader must be alert to notice that this is virtually the only way Jeeves could get this information. Perhaps Wodehouse is depending too much on our ability to infer things about Jeeves based on the revelations in "Bertie Changes His Mind" (where Jeeves discourses on the advantages of eavesdropping). He still has not worked out his full repertory of cues for signaling us as to Jeeves's offstage activities.

"Clustering Round Young Bingo" presents Jeeves with more problems than does any other middle-period story. Not only does he confront five separate problems, but he solves them with a few deft manipulations of the relatively large cast of characters: he gets a new housemaid for the Littles, acquires Anatole for the Traverses, prevents Mrs. Little's maudlin article about Bingo from being published, gets Bertie to go to Harrogate with Uncle George, and forces him to accept the banishment of the silk evening shirts. Simply by moving one housemaid from the Travers household to the Little establishment, he sets off a chain reaction that solves the two servant problems and gets Mrs. Little to withdraw her article. Moreover, because Bertie has botched his attempt to steal the article for Bingo, Jeeves persuades Bertie to go to Harrogate, thus earning a reward from Uncle George. While Bertie is gone, Jeeves takes his reward by sending back the shirts—an act which Bertie has no choice but to accept.

This is the first story in which Jeeves has gained his full set of Machiavellian traits. He correctly anticipates the consequences of all actions, he realizes that he must back down in his initial argument with Bertie, he knows when to wait and when to act, and he judges accurately how much information to withhold from Bertie. As a set of plot possibilities, he is essentially complete here. After this, his major new trait will be his enhanced erudition, primarily added for comic effect.

Despite the complexity of "Clustering Round Young Bingo," however, Jeeves's solutions of three of its problems still depend on a major coincidence. As he tells Bertie, " 'I was baffled for a while, I must confess, sir. Then I was materially assisted by a fortunate discovery.' " (That discovery involves an extra servant who had not previously been mentioned.) In this respect, it resembles a number of other stories that depend heavily on coincidence. In "Letter/Startling" Jeeves runs into a valet friend, now employed by the producer of the play in which Cyril has a part; that friend tells him how the producer's son influences all his decisions, and Jeeves uses the kid to get Cyril fired. "The Great Sermon Handicap" works to Jeeves's advantage only because a butler pal tells him that Reverend Bates will preach an uncharacteristically lengthy sermon; thus Jeeves can place the only winning bet in the handicap. The heroine of "The Rummy Affair of Old Biffy" turns out, remarkably, to be Jeeves's niece. Jeeves's chancy scheme of getting Toodles to reconcile Freddie and Elizabeth in "Fixing It for Freddie" initially backfires, and a happy ending results only because Elizabeth finds the idea amusing. Jeeves's control is more complete in the late stories, most of which are models of complex structuring without coincidence.

THE LATE STORIES (1926–1930)

Although only ten months elapsed between "Without the Option" and "The Inferiority Complex of Old Sippy," Wodehouse's manipulation of narrative abruptly becomes far more adept. Coincidences and causal gaps are all but absent in the late period, and the old formulas are honed to permit considerable recombination and variation. Few new characters are added, and, aside from Jeeves's accretion of erudition, Bertie and Jeeves undergo few changes. There is little experimentation of the type common in the middle period.

NEW CHARACTERS, OLD FORMULAS

Only two major, continuing characters make their first appearances in this set of eleven stories, but they both provide strong new narrative possibilities.

Tuppy Glossop is the only one of Bertie's pals whom we meet here, and he provides new twists on the old pattern. For one thing, when we first hear about him, Bertie is planning to get back at him for the incident of the looped-back ring in the Drones swimming-bath. Hence Tuppy is not in the usual situation of coming to Bertie for help; rather, Bertie's goal is revenge. Moreover, in two later stories ("Jeeves and the Song of Songs" and "The Ordeal of Young Tuppy") he is more or less engaged to Bertie's cousin Angela and in danger of straying to another woman. In each case Aunt Dahlia solicits Bertie's help. Tuppy's links to Dahlia would also prove useful when she takes over as the main aunt in the novels, for then her prospective son-in-law provides problems she refers to Jeeves. Thus Tuppy is the only pal to figure in both the short stories and the novels. Among the late stories, the only other pals who appear are Sippy (once) and Bingo (twice).

Another old idea is revived to yield a more spectacular new character: Bobbie Wickham. Bertie has been engaged of his own accord once, in "Jeeves Takes Charge," but Wodehouse dropped that possibility from the middle-period stories. There Aunt Agatha tries to force fiancées upon Bertie. When he faces marriage to Honoria, things are relatively simple, since Bertie approves Jeeves's efforts to turn the threat aside. Bobbie is a greater menace in that Bertie is attracted to her and resents Jeeves's plotting to prevent the match. The pair's most heated argument in the entire series comes in "Jeeves and the Yuletide Spirit," when Bertie tells Jeeves he loves Bobbie and Jeeves tries to convince him he is making a mistake. Though Bobbie seems to like Jeeves and never threatens to fire him, as Honoria had, Jeeves clearly views her as a far stronger threat than any of the other potential brides. When she comes to lunch in the "Episode of the Dog McIntosh," Jeeves observes Bobbie embracing Bertie:

> I saw Jeeves pause at the door and shoot me the sort of grave, warning look a wise old father might pass out to the effervescent son on seeing him going fairly strong with the local vamp. I nodded back, as much as to say "Chilled steel!" and he oozed out.

Here Bertie gives no sign of wanting to resume his romance with Bobbie, but he comes nearer to succumbing in "Jeeves and the Kid Clementina" by agreeing to a trip to Antibes with Bobbie. There Jeeves's reaction to Bertie's meeting with Bobbie is stronger:

> His voice was chilly and seemed to suggest that, whatever brought Bobbie Wickham to Bingley-on-Sea, it could not, in his opinion, be anything good. He dropped back into the offing, registering alarm and despondency. . . . Jeeves was behind me, and I couldn't see him, but at these words I felt his eye slap warningly against the back of my neck. . . . The man's tone was cold and soupy: and, scanning his face, I observed on it an "If-you-would-only-be-guided-by-me" expression which annoyed me intensely. There are moments when Jeeves looks just like an aunt.

No other character can so disturb Jeeves's aplomb. The reason, we can infer, is that Jeeves sees in her the worst impulses that characterize Bertie. She encourages Bertie's worst immature traits—those which disrupt the calm routine of Jeeves and Bertie's cozy bachelor establishment. While Honoria and Florence want to "improve" Bertie and Madeline is so sentimental as to have nothing in common with him,

Bobbie appeals to a side of Bertie which Jeeves has managed to confine to the Drones Club. She is essentially a practical joker and lives by principles acquired in her school days, as her plan in this story shows. This sort of thing appeals to Bertie, a practical joker himself, but if he married Bobbie, that part of his life would invade his home.

Only one other story involves Bertie's attempt to woo a woman he finds attractive: "The Spot of Art," with Gwladys Pendlebury. Compared to Bobbie, Gwladys is a bland character. We do not see much of her directly and know only that she is an artist (given our faith in Jeeves's judgment, not a good one) and drives a red sports car. While Bobbie might well want to marry Bertie, it is not clear whether Gwladys is particularly attracted to him; she has another boyfriend to whom she soon gets engaged. She contributes to the story's action mainly through the havoc she indirectly wreaks on Bertie's life. Gwladys serves an important function in the series, however, since for the first time we realize that Jeeves would not sanction *any* marriage for Bertie. He opposed Honoria because she wanted him fired and Florence and Bobbie because they were obviously wrong for Bertie. Here Jeeves does not express any opinion about Gwladys. This story makes the implicit point that Jeeves will keep Bertie a bachelor if possible and will quit otherwise—something he does not state explicitly until the end of *Thank You, Jeeves*. Aunt Dahlia makes the point clear in this story, remarking to Bertie: " 'You don't suppose for a moment that Jeeves will sanction this match.' " She dislikes Gwladys, but we must suspect that Jeeves needs no such reason to work against the marriage.

A few other motifs appear here that Wodehouse would use from time to time. Most importantly, Jeeves is revealed to love travel and the sea. There had been earlier hints of this, when he vacationed at the seaside in "Pride/Hero's" and wanted to go to Monte Carlo in "Jeeves and the Yule-tide Spirit" (where it was not clear whether his love of gambling or of travel was the reason for his picking that spot). In "The Spot of Art" Bertie suggests that Jeeves has a special fondness for sea travel:

> From the moment I had accepted the invitation, there had been a nautical glitter in his eye, and I'm not sure I hadn't

> heard him trolling Chanties in the kitchen. I think some ancestor of his must have been one of Nelson's tars or something, for he has always had the urge of the salt sea in his blood. I have noticed him on liners, when we were going to America, striding the deck with a sailorly roll and giving the distinct impression of being just about to heave the main-brace or splice the binnacle.

This urge, combined with Jeeve's love of fishing and New York nightlife, provides a major variant on the clothes motivation for putting the pair at odds.

It is also characteristic of the late period that Jeeves could be rewarded with travel, not money. And in several stories there is no reward. This change suggests that Jeeve's relationship to Bertie gives him a personal stake in the problem at hand, even when there is no threat of Bertie's getting married. In general, Jeeves comes to seem more Bertie's friend and equal.

Aunt Agatha makes her last direct appearance in "Indian Summer of an Uncle." To some extent her departure may have been due to Wodehouse's realization that she could be more effective as an indirect threat.[4] There is, however, another aspect to her disappearance. Wodehouse brings her to her most dramatically possible onstage incarnation when she confronts Jeeves in this story. We have seen how Agatha's character was fully formed in the first story—before Jeeves even existed as such. Here he refuses to be cowed by Agatha, offering his solution over her protests.[5] Perhaps after such a tense confrontation, Agatha could function solely as a malevolent force hovering over the series. Even in this story, Jeeves can only thwart, not defeat, her. Appropriately enough, at the end Bertie and Jeeves prepare to leg it "off over the horizon to where men are men." Hereafter, it is Agatha who lurks just "over the horizon" of the narratives.

By the late stories, Wodehouse has a small set of devices for generating action: Aunt Agatha, Aunt Dahlia, old pals (of whom there are only three: Sippy, Bingo, and Tuppy), and women whom Bertie wants to marry (only two: Bobbie and Gwladys). All eleven stories involve one or more of these elements:

"The Inferiority Complex of Old Sippy"—old pal
"Jeeves and the Impending Doom"—Aunt Agatha, old pal (Bingo)
"Jeeves and the Yule-tide Spirit"—Aunt Agatha, old pal (Tuppy), prospective fiancée (Bobbie)
"Jeeves and the Song of Songs"—Aunt Dahlia, old pal (Tuppy)
"Episode of the Dog McIntosh"—Aunt Agatha, prospective fiancée (Bobbie)
"The Spot of Art"—Aunt Dahlia, prospective fiancée (Gwladys)
"Jeeves and the Kid Clementina"—prospective fiancée (Bobbie), Aunt Agatha
"The Love That Purifies"—Aunt Dahlia
"Jeeves and the Old School Chum"—old pal (Bingo)
"Indian Summer of an Uncle"—Aunt Agatha
"The Ordeal of Young Tuppy"—Aunt Dahlia, old pal

In general, the combination stories tend to link Aunt Agatha and Bobbie, emphasizing the threat to Bertie. Aunt Dahlia is aligned more closely with the pals, especially Tuppy; most such stories involve Bertie and Jeeves helping someone as their main task. Similarly, when Agatha provides the sole central conflict, it is as a threat, while Dahlia's story, "The Love That Purifies," involves Bertie doing a favor. In the novels, however, Dahlia would prove quite capable of being a threat, however genial.

MULTIPLE GOALS

We have seen how Wodehouse complicated the series by giving Jeeves several problems to solve and that in the middle period this trend was most evident in "Clustering Round Young Bingo." Such juggling acts are common in the late period. Typically at least one goal will be Jeeves's own, or Jeeves will deliberately work against a goal Bertie sets him.

In "The Inferiority Complex of Old Sippy," for example, Jeeves has to bring about Sippy's engagement to Gwendolyn Moon, to embolden Sippy to reject an article by his intimidating old headmaster, Waterbury, and to get rid of the vase—the latter against Bertie's wishes. In the event Jeeves deftly uses the solution to the vase problem to solve the engagement problem, which in turn leads Sippy to reject the article. Jeeves's ability not only to solve multiple problems but to link them marks Wodehouse's mastery of his narrative formulas.

In the next story, "Jeeves and the Impending Doom," Jeeves works against Bertie's stated goals rather than having one of his own. Bertie says that he must obey Aunt Agatha by ingratiating himself with Filmer and also that he and Jeeves must keep Bingo in Aunt Agatha's good graces so that he will not lose his tutoring job. Jeeves discovers, however, that Agatha wants to get Bertie a job with Filmer and thus goes against Bertie's orders, giving Filmer the false impression that Bertie had marooned him on an island with an irate swan. Bertie in fact has done his utmost to help Filmer, while Bingo has failed to prevent his charge, Thomas, from doing the marooning. In implicating Bertie, Jeeves saves Bingo's job, and Bertie agrees in the end that Jeeves was right, since he does not want to work for Filmer. But there is an implicit third goal—to keep Agatha mollified. This of course fails. Once more Jeeves and Bertie resort to flight.

"Jeeves and the Yule-tide Spirit" is arguably the most complex of the stories. It is the only one to combine three major motifs: the Aunt Agatha menace, the Bobbie Wickham threat, and the old pal motif. Moreover, here the old-pal motif introduces the twist of Bertie being out to harm rather than help Tuppy. It is also the first double marriage threat: if Bertie placates Sir Roderick, as Aunt Agatha desires, he will end up reengaged to Honoria. If he wins Bobbie, he will be engaged to that charming but unacceptable young lady. Bertie's early phone conversation with Aunt Agatha is crucial, since he hangs up before she can explain why she wants Sir Roderick to realize that Bertie is not insane. Thus he goes through the story without grasping the implication that he could end up engaged to Honoria. The light dawns only when Jeeves points this out at the end.

Here, for the first time, all three goals toward which Jeeves works run contrary to Bertie's intentions. Bertie tells Jeeves that they will not go to Monte Carlo as planned and that they will strive to make Bertie attractive to Bobbie. He does not tell Jeeves that he wants to ingratiate himself with Sir Roderick, but he does make a little progress with the latter, until Jeeves apparently undercuts his efforts. Jeeves's motives are obvious, at least by the end: he wants to go to Monte Carlo and to keep Bertie from falling into either marriage trap. In order to go to Monte Carlo, he contrives to get Bertie out of the Honoria alliance in such a way that Bertie is terrified of the repercussions with Aunt Agatha and agrees that flight is the only solution. Jeeves has deliberately kept the original train reservations—though he tells Bertie that this was an oversight. Here Jeeves not only must solve the three problems, but he must also make Bertie accept three outcomes that go against his initial desires. To top it all off, one of Bertie's original goals, revenge on Tuppy, is not accomplished. Jeeves never approved of it, partly because it was the initial reason Bertie gave him for canceling the Monte Carlo jaunt. Instead, Jeeves makes Bertie's revenge plot his means for achieving his own goals. Here and elsewhere, in keeping with the increasing use of the device of Bertie's rebelliousness, Jeeves becomes expert at turning Bertie's own goals against him in clearing up the other problems.

"Episode of the Dog McIntosh" pulls another, though simpler, variation on the triple goal. Here things begin fairly straightforwardly, with Bertie wanting to help Bobbie get her mother's play produced by Blumenfeld. There are also hints that Jeeves intends to scotch any possibility of Bertie again becoming infatuated with Bobbie. The explicit goal is accomplished quickly through Jeeves's expedient of having Bertie absent himself from the luncheon for Bobbie and the Blumenfelds. This move also solves Jeeves's implicit problem, since after lunch Bobbie gives Aunt Agatha's dog McIntosh to the pair and Bertie becomes thoroughly annoyed with her and concerned only with retrieving the dog in order to avoid Agatha's wrath. Jeeves must then contrive a way to get McIntosh back without causing Blumenfeld to cancel the play's production. He does so by having Bertie take McIntosh back, telling Blumenfeld that Bertie is insane, and giving Blumenfeld a second terrier he thinks is McIntosh. Here Jeeves solves successive problems, but the new ones result from Bobbie's unpredictable move of giving away Agatha's dog rather than from any miscalculation on Jeeves's part. This structural ploy proved capable of greater expansion in the novels, where unpredictable females frequently cause Jeeves's best-laid plans to go agley.

By midway through the late period, the pattern of Jeeves's multiple goals is established, and Wodehouse calls our attention to it in "The Spot of Art." Again Jeeves and Bertie work at cross purposes, and again the cancellation of a vacation desired by Jeeves is at stake. Bertie bows out of a yacht cruise with Aunt Dahlia because he is infatuated with Gwladys. Moreover, Gwladys has painted a portrait of Bertie that he admires and Jeeves detests. Bertie breaks the news to Aunt Dahlia that he will not be going on the cruise, explaining about Gwladys. She disapproves but is not worried:

> "Well, I'm prepared to make a small bet with you, Bertie. Jeeves will stop this romance."
> "What absolute rot!"
> "And if he doesn't like that portrait, he will get rid of it."
> "I never heard such dashed nonsense in my life."
> "And, finally, you wretched pie-faced wambler, he will present you on board my yacht at the appointed hour. I don't know how he will do it, but you will be there, all complete with yachting-cap and spare pair of socks."
> "Let us change the subject, Aunt Dahlia," I said coldly.

This dialogue neatly lays out Jeeves's initial goals. He also has successive goals set up as the action progresses, as Gwladys's boyfriend Pim is ensconced in the flat with a broken leg and Pim's brother-in-law, Mr. Slingsby, conceives the idea that Bertie is out to seduce his wife. Bertie leaves Jeeves to deal with these, and Jeeves does so without resorting to coincidence—and probably without telling Bertie what he has really been up to. As usual, Jeeves not only accomplishes his goal but also leads Bertie to accept the outcome—in this case, happily. Indeed, the end of this story lingers over their delight at the prospect of the trip:

> "Yo-ho-ho, Jeeves!" I said, giving the trousers a bit of a hitch.
> "Yes, sir."
> "In fact, I will go further. Yo-ho-ho and a bottle of rum."
> "Very good, sir. I will bring it immediately."

Jeeves's uncharacteristic joke emphasizes the fact that the story ends with another case of a mutual reward—the cruise. This is, by the way, the only case in which Bertie is finally persuaded that the object he admires—the portrait—is in bad taste.

Although the complexity of the problems confronting Jeeves has increased, his dependence on luck and coincidence has nearly disappeared. "The Inferiority Complex of Old Sippy" starts the late period off with a model narrative in which Jeeves manipulates events from the start. Its plot is the first that does not depend on any luck or coincidence. Jeeves hears the problem, makes his plan, and executes it, and though he says that Sippy's being knocked out by the vase was a "nasty accident," he has actually left nothing to chance. Bertie's own scheme is to plant a bag of flour that will fall on Waterbury and render him a foolish figure whom Sippy could defy. This plan depends on luck instead of deception; Bertie not only fails but also walks into his own booby trap.

Throughout the late story period, narratives in which Jeeves depends on accident are exceptional. In the simplest story, "The Love That Purifies," Jeeves can set up animosities among the three boys involved in the Good Conduct contest because each happens to be in love with a different movie actress. "Jeeves and the Song of Songs" is more typical in that it avoids coincidence and even foregrounds this fact. Dahlia asks for help when Tuppy, who has been courting her daughter Angela (introduced here), has taken up with a singer, Cora Bellinger. Jeeves devises a scheme for alienating Cora from Tuppy by making the latter sing "Sonny Boy" at an amateur concert—having first arranged for Bertie to sing the same song just before him. Tuppy is booed, but Cora has car trouble and arrives too late to observe his failure. Here Jeeves's idea would work except for an *un*lucky coincidence. He stays at the concert after Bertie departs, clearly already planning to turn this misfortune to his advantage. Later he reports that Cora also sang "Sonny Boy" and was hooted off the stage. The story emphasizes that the happy outcome does *not*, as Bertie initially thinks, result from luck:

> "But, Jeeves, what a coincidence!"
>
> "Not altogether, sir. I ventured to take the liberty of ac-

> costing Miss Bellinger on her arrival at the hall and recalling myself to her recollection. I then said that Mr Glossop had asked me to request her that as a particular favour to him—the song being a favourite of his—she would sing "Sonny Boy." And when she found that you and Mr Glossop had also sung the song immediately before her, I rather fancy that she supposed that she had been the victim of a practical pleasantry by Mr Glossop.

From this point on, coincidence is usually a device for throwing stumbling blocks in Jeeves's way and hence of delaying his solution; his ability to overcome unforeseeable problems becomes part of his virtuosic handling of the situation.

JEEVES'S OFFSTAGE MANIPULATIONS

In the later stories Wodehouse developed a systematic set of cues for suggesting that Jeeves has hidden motives and acts outside Bertie's ken. We can infer events which *may* have taken place but which we can never be sure really did. This is not to suggest Jeeves is a real person or that we could ever determine what "really" occurred within a series of fictional events. But since all fictional events are represented to us through explicit or implicit means, consistently ambiguous cues invite us to speculate on possible events. Such speculation can provide an author with a powerful means of creating narrative connections.

By the period of the late stories we should be prepared to take much of what Jeeves says to have a hidden meaning, especially if his statement is enigmatic and is not explained later in the narrative. In "The Inferiority Complex of Old Sippy," for example, Jeeves shows up five minutes late with Bertie's tea—a unique bit of negligence. Bertie remarks on this, and Jeeves explains he was dusting Bertie's new vase. Bertie naively takes this as a sign that Jeeves is "learning to love the vase." We know better, but we might wonder what Jeeves was actually doing in the sittingroom. In retrospect, we can assume that he was looking over the terrain, planning Sippy's "accident" with the vase. (Bertie's failure to bring off the flour gag results in part from his ignorance of the terrain: "It was a case of the sunken road, after all," referring to Napoleon's defeat at Waterloo.) Everything emphasizes this strange five-minute delay, yet there is no reference back to it. That fact alone should lead us to conclude that Jeeves was up to something. One effect of this scene is to point up how early Jeeves conceives his plan—and hence how he succeeds without luck or coincidence.

Similarly, in the story's last scene, there is no apparent reason why Jeeves should have come along with Sippy. He could have waited at the flat for Bertie. (Having decided to come, he presumably lets Sippy go up to the office alone in order to give him a chance to reject Waterbury's essay.) Presumably he wants to tell Bertie the story of the vase before Bertie actually sees its fragments. In that way his convoluted explanation could confuse and impress Bertie as much as possible before he revealed the last bit of information—that the vase is broken. His actions and motives are not obvious, but they are possible to infer.

"Jeeves and the Impending Doom" (the second of the perfectly plotted late stories to be published) works a change on this pattern, in that Jeeves learns more than Bertie knows in order to plan his tactics. Early on Bertie tells Jeeves that Aunt Agatha wants him to impress Filmer " 'for some dark and furtive reason which she will not explain.' " At the end Jeeves tells him: " 'I have ascertained that Mrs Gregson's motive in inviting you to this house was that she might present you to Mr Filmer with a view to your becoming his private secretary.' " He learned this, he explains, from the butler, who " 'chanced to overhear Mrs Gregson in conversation with Mr Filmer on the matter.' " Without telling Bertie, Jeeves has made inquiries offstage. (Incidentally, the fact that the butler "chanced to overhear" the dialogue does not count as a coincidence: in the series, servants invariably eavesdrop as often as they can.) How much of the subsequent action Jeeves controls is unclear. Presumably once he finds out this information, he awaits a chance to discredit Bertie with Filmer. His "informal conversation" with Thomas is a key moment in his manipulation of events. He may actually encourage Thomas in his intention to imitate Captain Flint by marooning Filmer on the island; indeed, Jeeves may plant the idea in Thomas's mind and simply attribute it to *Treasure Island* in reporting it to Bertie. Later, in telling Bertie of Thomas's plan to maroon Filmer, Jeeves behaves unconcernedly and distracts Bertie from the issue by calling his attention to his badly knotted tie (not "the perfect butterfly effect").

Whether or not Jeeves has manipulated events to this extent, he certainly performs one action in this story that Bertie fails to grasp and we can only appreciate in retrospect. At the end Jeeves faces the task of explaining why he told Filmer that Bertie had marooned him on the island: " 'I had scarcely left you when the solution of the affair presented itself to me. It was a remark of Mr Filmer's that gave me the idea.' " This is a subtle reference, and Jeeves is lucky that Bertie does not recall *which* remark it was. After being rescued by Bertie and Jeeves from the swan-infested island, Filmer assumed that Thomas had been the culprit: " 'He has a grudge against me. And it is the sort of thing only a boy, or one who is practically an imbecile, would have thought of doing.' " "Practically an imbecile" presumably gave Jeeves the idea to blame his "mentally negligible" employer.

We have already examined a particularly complex example of Jeeves's possible offstage activities in "Jeeves and the Yule-tide Spirit," where Jeeves may have been responsible, in a variety of possible ways, for the second hot-water bottle being pierced. Given the complicated nature of this story, it is interesting to note that Wodehouse takes care to be more precise about the time scheme than in most of the earlier stories. The third scene takes place at breakfast at Lady Wickham's country house; it consists of the intense argument in which Bertie reveals his love for Bobbie over Jeeves's objections. The next scene portrays dinner on the same day. There is no depiction of lunchtime, yet we later learn that it was just before lunch that Sir Roderick told Jeeves to inform Bertie that he had switched rooms with Tuppy. Also, that afternoon Bertie took a walk with Bobbie during which she suggested the hot-water-bottle prank to him. We know from Jeeves's final explanation to Bertie that during this elided period he found out about the switch in rooms and decided not to tell Bertie; we might also infer that he suggested the hot-water-bottle scheme to Bobbie, requesting that she pass it along to Bertie and Tuppy. Alternatively, he may have asked her to tell Bertie and then told Tuppy the same scheme himself or heard her tell Bertie the scheme and told it to Tuppy or. . . .

These possibilities imply an almost incredible deviousness and degree of foresight on Jeeves's part. Yet if we reject them all, what must we assume? Jeeves would have found out about the switch of rooms, and Bobbie would just coincidentally have given Bertie a scheme involving sneaking into Tuppy's bedroom. If we believe that, then Jeeves's only contribution to the whole plot would be a pointless decision not to tell Bertie that the two Glossops had traded rooms. I think that, given what we know of Jeeves by this late in the series, we *must* assume that Jeeves had something to do with setting up the hot-water-bottle business. We can never determine his specific actions, but the uncertainty encourages us to think back over an unusually complex plot. Note also that just before Jeeves suggests to Bertie that they flee to Monte Carlo, there is a pause and Bertie remarks, "He regarded me with a fathomless eye." Jeeves's actions are often fathomless for us as well, but to appreciate the full complexity of the stories, we must strive to trace them beyond Bertie's straightforward accounts.

Some of the plots in this period stress Jeeves's foresight, since it is this trait that allows him to manipulate events. In "Jeeves and the Song of Songs," Bertie arrives at the concert, and Jeeves describes how his plan requires Tuppy to sing "Sonny Boy" right after Bertie does. When Bertie objects that Tuppy will hear him sing the song and refuse to go on, Jeeves says he has sent Tuppy to a pub, the Jug and Bottle, to fortify himself for the coming performance. Further, he suggests that Bertie go to a different pub, the Goat and Grapes, for similar sustenance. Clearly Jeeves has anticipated Bertie's objection and has scouted out the local pubs in order to be able to send Tuppy and Bertie to separate ones. This might in turn suggest that he has found out that two other singers will render "Sonny Boy" before Bertie does and gets rid of Bertie in order to conceal this fact from him. The implications are that three people singing "Sonny Boy" before Tuppy does will be more effective for Jeeves's scheme but that Bertie would hardly go on if he knew he was third in line.

Similarly, in the "Episode of the Dog McIntosh" there is only one point in the time scheme when Jeeves could have bought the second terrier: while Bertie is at the Savoy retrieving McIntosh. Thus we must assume that he has foreseen all the consequences of the Savoy venture: that Bobbie will have to blame Bertie for the theft (Jeeves in fact tells her to do so), that Blumenfeld will come to the flat, that Jeeves will convince him that Bertie is dangerously insane, and that Jeeves will placate Blumenfeld by handing over the second terrier. If we trace events back, there can be no other reason why Jeeves would buy the second dog so early in the plot.

Some suggestions of Jeeves's offstage activities are indirect indeed. The very lack of coincidence in this period can be used in complex ways to suggest possible offstage manipulations by Jeeves. In "The Spot of Art," for example, Jeeves wants Bertie to go on the cruise with Aunt Dahlia, and she bets Bertie early on that Jeeves "will present you on board my yacht at the appointed hour." Jeeves in fact fails to do so, strictly speaking, but he does convince Bertie that the cruise is a good idea. When Bertie points out that the yacht had departed weeks ago, Jeeves tells him that Antole fell ill and the cruise was postponed. We must suspect, from what we know of Jeeves and Dahlia, that the pair is capable of having contrived the delay. Indeed, the combination of her early bet and the unwonted coincidence make it very likely. Other somewhat coincidental events in this story might also have been contrived by Jeeves. He tells Bertie that the doctor has ordered Pim, who has a broken leg, to stay in the flat. It seems implausible that a doctor would not be able to arrange to convey him elsewhere, since it is emphasized that he has only a mild fracture; thus we may wonder whether Jeeves has offered to let Pim stay. He could easily have colluded with Pim to conceal this fact from Bertie, and indeed Pim is quite insistent that Bertie not call in another doctor for a second opinion. Jeeves's motive would be to keep Bertie's rival on the scene with a view to alienating Gwladys and Bertie; Pim presumably would be delighted to cooperate. Admittedly, Jeeves could not predict that Pim would tell his sister, Mrs. Slingsby, that Bertie was the one who ran him down, thus setting up a possible lawsuit against Bertie. Still, when Pim later suggests that Bertie send roses to Mrs. Slingsby, Jeeves's touch may be again at work. Jeeves has had ample time to chat with Pim, learn that he has a jealous brother-in-law, and suggest the flowers to him, pointing out that Bertie's sending them would materially assist Pim in his wooing of Gwladys.

This may seem farfetched, since there are absolutely no overt cues that Jeeves has done any of this. Note, however, the depiction of Mr. Slingsby's arrival at the flat. Bertie has just returned from the Drones Club and is awaiting Mrs. Slingsby. Jeeves announces Mr. Slingsby, who accuses Bertie of trying to seduce his wife. Bertie is puzzled and then, as he grasps the implication, startled. At this point Mrs. Slingsby enters. She has been at the flat since before Bertie returned, but Jeeves did not mention this upon Bertie's arrival. When Jeeves announced Mr. Slingsby, he could have chosen to tell Bertie and Mr. Slingsby that Mrs. Slingsby was there visiting her brother—thus keeping Bertie abreast of events and cooling Mr. Slingsby's jealous rage at once. Why does he not do so?

Suppose Jeeves had listened outside the door the night before when Bertie talked to Pim and agreed to send the roses. Moreover, Bertie says, "I wouldn't leave the thing to Jeeves. It was essentially a mission that required the personal touch." Actually, there is no reason why Jeeves could not handle this errand, but the line motivates Bertie's absence when Mrs. Slingsby comes to the flat. It is even possible that Jeeves arranged to have Mrs. Slingsby drop by the flat at that point and that he had learned from Pim that Mr. Slingsby was expected back from Paris at about that same time. (Certainly Mrs. Slingsby expresses no surprise at her husband's presence.) Jeeves could then anticipate that Mr. Slingsby would see the roses before his wife did. This set of possible actions is extremely indirect, but we might be led to assume them by the fact that, without them, Jeeves plays only a slight role in this story.

Aside from adding complexity to the narratives and encouraging us to read and reread the stories more closely, Jeeves's offstage maneuvers have other effects. They create a vague sense of his omnipotence, since we seldom know exactly what he has done, and we might speculate that he has been up to all sorts of things. Moreover, by withholding information, Wodehouse gets comic effects of surprise by the sudden final revelation that what had seemed to be coincidences or inexplicable events were actually arranged by Jeeves. Indeed, we quickly learn that whenever Bertie is baffled by the outcome of some line of action and attributes it to luck, we can suspect that Jeeves was behind it. In order to see the humor in the fact that Jeeves tricks and manipulates

Bertie so extensively, we must ourselves understand more about Jeeves's actions than Bertie does. For this reason Wodehouse's stories of this period lead us, rather in the fashion of detective stories, to reconstruct events beyond those the narrator makes obvious to us.

CONFLICT AND EQUALITY

Bertie's rebellion against Jeeves intensifies during this late period and carries over into the first two novels. At the same time, however, the pair increasingly deal with each other as equals rather than as employer and servant. As always, the result is an increased possibility for narrative conflict.

For the first time, "The Inferiority Complex of Old Sippy" has Jeeves trying to stop Bertie from carrying through a scheme. Bertie wants to set a booby trap to cover Waterbury with flour, which will cause Sippy to lose his awe of his old headmaster and reject his article. Jeeves's reaction is " 'Really, sir, I would scarcely advocate—' ". He then suggests getting Gwendolen to admit her love as a result of Sippy being injured. Bertie scoffs, saying it could be years before Sippy suffered an injury. Jeeves admits, " 'There is that to be considered, sir,' " but he has already considered it and lined up the vase and putter. Bertie expresses a new skepticism: " 'It is not the old form, Jeeves. You are losing your grip.' " Overall this story depends on Bertie scolding Jeeves repeatedly and then suffering for it in a poetically just fashion. In the final scene, the flour he had set up for Waterbury falls on his own head—paralleling the falling vase that Jeeves tells Sippy had knocked him out.

In general, Bertie's rebelliousness is a powerful device. It allows Jeeves to get upset with Bertie but to suppress his resentment as he acts offstage. Rather than simply withholding help over a piece of clothing, Jeeves can receive Bertie's dressing-down, then add a bit of revenge to the solution he spins for the main set of problems. He thus demonstrates his control over his employer, since in such narratives Bertie must both be grateful for the solutions and contrite for doubting Jeeves.

"Jeeves and the Yule-tide Spirit" is a central instance of Bertie's rebellion, since for the first time he and Jeeves are seriously at odds from nearly the beginning to the conclusion. We have seen cases where Bertie rejected Jeeves's ideas because he thought, briefly, that Jeeves was losing his grip. Now the idea is introduced that Bertie thinks Jeeves may be past his prime. This idea comes as a reaction to the fact that Jeeves answers a phone call from Aunt Agatha and turns it immediately over to Bertie:

> You know, every now and then I can't help feeling that Jeeves is losing his grip. In his prime it would have been with him the work of a moment to have told Aunt Agatha that I was not at home. I gave him one of those reproachful glances and took the machine.

Of course, Jeeves has already taken offense at being told that the Monte Carlo trip is off, and he deliberately subjects Bertie to Agatha's phone call. Overall, as Bertie becomes more rebellious, Jeeves becomes more devious.

The argument following Bertie's revelation of his love for Bobbie is particularly tense. It begins with Jeeves using a string of neutral stock phrases as Bertie describes Bobbie; he then tries briefly to convince Bertie that Bobbie is unsuitable. " 'Well, sir—' " always signals Jeeves's fear that what he is about to say will displease Bertie—as it does. Soon Bertie unreasonably demands both that Jeeves state his objections to Bobbie and that he keep his opinions of her to himself. Jeeves is driven to snap at Bertie for the first and only time in their relationship:

> "Jeeves," I said coldly, "if you have anything to say against the lady, it had better not be said in my presence."
> "Very good, sir."
> "Or anywhere else, for that matter. What is your kick against Miss Wickham?"
> "Oh, really, sir!"

Jeeves does not employ exclamation points for nothing, and we need not be surprised when he arranges a humiliating fate for Bertie in this case.

As we have seen, Bobbie Wickham creates strong tensions between Bertie and Jeeves. In "Jeeves and the Kid Clementina" Bertie becomes downright pompous in describing Jeeves after the latter objects both to the plus-fours and to the Antibes trip:

> The trouble with Jeeves is that he tends occasionally to get above himself. Just because he has surged round and—I admit it freely—done the young master a bit of good in one or two crises, he has a nasty way of conveying his impression that he looks on Bertram Wooster as a sort of idiot child. . . .

Bertie also has the effrontery to use Bobbie against Jeeves. After she outlines her scheme for smuggling Clementina into her school, Bertie pretends to Jeeves that that scheme is his own. Jeeves was earlier set up as "in the background" of the scene in which Bobbie gave Bertie his instructions, so we can infer he overheard that the idea is hers rather than Bertie's. Thus he not only disapproves of the scheme but also knows that Bertie is deceiving him. Moreover, Bertie condescends to Jeeves as he describes the plan: " 'I have had one of my ideas. It may interest you to hear how my brain worked. . . . Your share in the proceedings, you will notice, is simplicity itself—mere routine-work—and should not tax you unduly.' " Small wonder that Jeeves calls in the police as a way of putting Bertie in his place.

Such tensions are smoothed over temporarily in "The Ordeal of Young Tuppy," where Bertie and Jeeves work together on the problem. Bertie tells Jeeves that they must save Tuppy, who has been inveigled, at the risk of life and limb, into a local football match. Jeeves replies with an unprecedented question: " 'What course do you advocate, sir?' " He is not being sarcastic here, and the two come up with a plan, writing a telegram, which is worded by Jeeves but based on Bertie's idea. Bertie forgets to deliver the telegram, and Jeeves must effect a second solution by telephoning Miss Dalgleish. Still, the telegram figures in the last scene, recalling Tuppy to his love for Angela, and, again backed up by a phone call from Jeeves, it achieves the happy ending. The collaborative nature of this solution is emphasized when Bertie figures out Jeeves's offstage activities unaided:

I gave him the eye.

"Was it you, Jeeves, who phoned to Miss What's-her-bally-name about the alleged water-spaniel?"

"Yes, sir."

"I thought as much."

"Yes, sir?"

"Yes, Jeeves, the moment Mr Glossop told me that a Mysterious Voice had phoned on the subject of Irish water-spaniels, I thought as much. I recognized your touch. I read your motives like an open book. You knew she would come buzzing up."

Bertie is able to reconstruct Jeeves's offstage activities in a way usually reserved for the reader. Indeed, this passage is also an excellent indication of Bertie's gain in intelligence since the series' beginning and of how the two have come to treat each other as friends and equals. They celebrate by having a drink together for the first time. Bertie's rebellion is far from over here—indeed, his next act will be to drive Jeeves to quit—but he understands Jeeves better than he ever has. With these and all the other elements perfected, the pair was ready for the move to longer narratives.

TWO LATE STORIES

Before going on to examine the novels, however, we need to look briefly at the two late short stories in the Jeeves/Wooster series. Both were written after Wodehouse's postwar crisis and his experimentations with Jeeves without Bertie. After *Come On, Jeeves* and *Ring for Jeeves,* Wodehouse brought Bertie back in *Jeeves and the Feudal Spirit* (1953), but after this point there was no new entry in the series until 1959, with "Jeeves Makes an Omelet," quickly followed by *Jeeves in the Offing* in 1960. This six-year gap was even longer than the lag between the completion of *The Mating Season* in 1947 and the writing of *Come On, Jeeves* and *Ring for Jeeves* in 1952. Apparently after reviving the old formulas with considerable success in *Jeeves and the Feudal Spirit,* Wodehouse's inspiration for story ideas for the series was running low. In 1956 he wrote to a friend: "What I would like to do next is another Jeeves story, but it's so difficult to think of any jam I can get Bertie into other than getting engaged to the wrong girl, and I have used that so often."[6] Although Wodehouse used the reengagement device in the rest of the novels, he dropped it for "Jeeves Makes an Omelet." It is not clear why Wodehouse returned to the short-story form for the series after nearly thirty years; perhaps he wanted one Jeeves/Wooster story for the anthology *A Few Quick Ones*. The result is a slight plot, the simplest since the early stories.

"Jeeves Makes an Omelet" begins with a diatribe against aunts, setting up the fact that Aunt Dahlia will be the main source of the narrative conflict. Wodehouse came to depend more and more on the arbitrary-aunt device, which gave him an easy way to generate plots. Three plots in a row—this story, *Jeeves in the Offing*, and *Stiff Upper Lip, Jeeves*—begin with Bertie in a cheerful state, interrupted by a call from Aunt Dahlia. This device is a simpler way of getting narratives going than having a scene of calm broken by a quarrel between Bertie and Jeeves and *then* the arrival of a friend or aunt who poses a problem. (*Stiff Upper Lip, Jeeves* does introduce the Alpine hat *after* the main action has begun, but it serves as a motif, not as a way of keeping Jeeves and Bertie at odds.) This increasing dependence on Aunt Dahlia in the late period tends to push Jeeves into the background for longer stretches of the action, making him more of a deus ex machina and also forcing him to depend more on luck and coincidence late in the plot.

In "Jeeves Makes an Omelet," Wodehouse creates, for the first time since the early stories a narrative involving only one problem for Jeeves and Bertie. Aunt Dahlia wants a serial for *Milady's Boudoir*, and Bertie must help her influence its author, Cornelia Fothergill to lower the price.[7] She has a plan that involves Bertie stealing and destroying a ghastly painting by Cornelia's father-in-law, Edward Fothergill, and this goal forms the sole line of action. There is no conflict with Jeeves, no potential marriage for Bertie, and no other premise to substitute for these standard sources of action. A single unpredictable event complicates the action, when Bertie mistakenly burns the wrong painting. The element of Cornelia's father-in-law, Edward, wanting his painting back seems to add a twist, but it is actually the coincidental factor that aids Jeeves in solving the problem by staging a theft of both paintings. Yet even without this bit of luck, Jeeves presumably could rescue Bertie by burning Edward's painting and staging the break-in in the same way.

The thinness of the plot is evident in the casual introduction of the oft-used threat of Aunt Dahlia's withholding Anatole's cooking. She does not mention Anatole during her initial phone conversation with Bertie, yet both Bertie and Jeeves simply assume that if Bertie refuses to go along with her scheme, she will ban him from her table. The story would have been stronger had Jeeves, who also enjoys Anatole's cooking, forced Bertie to carry out Aunt Dahlia's demands to prevent both of them losing access to that superb chef's concoctions. Unfortunately, Wodehouse never exploited the possible links between Jeeves and Anatole. As it is, Jeeves seems unusally imperceptive here; he fails to follow Bertie's line of thought in the second scene and does not realize that Bertie has stolen the wrong painting until it has been cut up and burned. In devising his solution, he depends on two coincidences: Edward's desire to get his painting back and the recent series of art thefts in the neighborhood.

"Jeeves and the Greasy Bird" is nearly long enough to be a novella, but it has a relatively simple plot. Bertie decides to make the shy Blair Eggleston jealous enough to propose to Honoria by courting her himself, but of course this ends with Honoria saying she will marry Bertie. Bertie gets into this fix because he has conceived this plan and carried it through without consulting Jeeves. Once it backfires, Jeeves suggests that Bertie find someone to pretend to be his fiancée. Again Bertie carries out this scheme without Jeeves's aid, and he botches it by going to an unscrupulous theatrical agent to hire a fake fiancée. The agent tricks Bertie into stating before a witness that he is engaged to the agent's niece and then blackmails Bertie with the threat of a breach-of-promise suit.

Jeeves does not participate extensively in the action of the story. Although he is annoyed that Bertie has refused to take a trip to Florida, he does not seem to plot to push Bertie deeper into trouble. He could hardly anticipate that Bertie would go to Jas Waterbury to hire an actress to play his fiancée and so could not have devised a solution in advance. During Waterbury and Trixie's visit to the flat, Bertie is left defenseless by the fact that Jeeves has a day off. In this case, however, Jeeves does not depend on coincidence for his solution. Together he and Aunt Dahlia stage the scene in which they convince Waterbury that Bertie is bankrupt; Jeeves then suggests that Sir Roderick should play Santa Claus at Market Snodsbury—a role Aunt Dahlia originally intended for Bertie. Jeeves, of course, gets his Florida vacation and presumably will catch his tarpon.

These two late stories are pleasant, but they do not have the complexity of the late-period short stories. Wodehouse had jettisoned several key formulas of that period, when he moved into novels, and he does not revive them here. In a sense, he tried to pick out one or two typical motifs from the novels' formalas as the basis for these stories. Yet, just as the novels are not stretched-out short stories, so the stories could not be thin novels. These late stories were presumably written in response to Wodehouse's increasing success in placing his fiction with magazines as his postwar problems declined. Despite their delightful features, however, they demonstrate that Wodehouse had, at least as far as the Jeeves/Wooster series went, abandoned the short form and calculated his characters and situations for novels.

6 WHERE EVERY PROSPECT PLEASES . . . THE NOVELS

Priestley, however, was the worst of all, because he analysed me, blast him, and called attention to the thing I try to hush up—viz. that I have only got one plot and produce it once a year with variations. I wish to goodness novelists wouldn't review novels.

—P. G. Wodehouse to Denis Mackail, October 1932

THE NOVELISTIC FORM

Critics generally agree that Wodehouse's most consistently excellent work came in the period from the mid-1920s to the mid-1940s. For the Jeeves/Wooster series, this would include the late-period short stories and the novels from *Thank You, Jeeves* to *The Mating Season* (see appendix A). His postwar problems led him to experiment in a variety of ways, including writing plays; he also turned briefly to autobiographical writing with *Bring on the Girls* and *Performing Flea*. With *Pigs Have Wings*, he created the first postwar Blandings novel and later reintroduced Bertie in *Jeeves and the Feudal Spirit*. By this point Wodehouse was in his early seventies, and many of his subsequent writings are not quite on the high level of the earlier decades. During the next twenty years he occasionally produced a story or novel that was close to the old standard—most notably *Jeeves and the Feudal Spirit* (1954), *Ice in the Bedroom* (1961), *A Pelican at Blandings* (1969), and *Much Obliged, Jeeves* (1971).

For the Jeeves/Wooster series, these judgments apply primarily to narrative structures. In chapter 8, we shall see how Wodehouse systematically added complexity to the series' style, largely by accumulating and varying phrases and quotations. His prose remains lively in this period, as a passage like the description of Stinker Pinker that opens chapter 3 of *Stiff Upper Lip, Jeeves* demonstrates. Throughout his career, however, Wodehouse found plotting more difficult than writing drafts. In 1946, he described the ease of writing:

> I find I can't do anything in the writing line these days, except letters. I don't seem to get any ideas for a story. I've got a Jeeves novel mapped out but I'd like to get something else going so that I can be brooding on it in my spare time. The actual writing of a story always gives me a guilty feeling as if I were wasting my time. The only thing that matters is thinking the stuff out.[1]

The process of devising plots became increasingly troublesome for Wodehouse in his old age, though the continued brilliance of his prose helps counterbalance a certain sparseness and occasional awkwardness in the action's mechanics.

By definition, the novel and the short story differ in length. But this difference is not a superficial one; the novel is not merely a stretched out story. In the modern, post-Poe story, the brief form typically encourages the use of a small cast of characters and a limited set of actions aiming toward a sense of unity; the action tends to build steadily toward a high point at the end, with only a short epilogue section or a surprise ending where the climax is not followed by an epilogue. Similarly, the atmospheric or psychological short story à la Chekhov focuses on creating a unified impression through a few characters, while downplaying plot mechanics. In contrast, a novel seldom tries to keep building up the same set of actions steadily across hundreds of pages; its action will usually consist of a series of rising and falling moments. These may come successively, as in the episodic novel; more typically, the modern novel weaves several actions together simultaneously, using various delaying and deflecting devices.

Wodehouse's lists of ideas for the Jeeves/Wooster series indicate his awareness of this basic difference, for they almost inevitably specify whether a given idea is intended for a story or a novel, with labels like "Jeeves story," "Jeeves novel," or "Idea for a Jeeves novel." Some ideas for individual scenes or devices were even conceived for one form or the other: "Solution for a Jeeves novel. B. gets entangled with girl and Jeeves arranges that B. shall make an ass of himself in public, like Gussie at prizegiving—this leads to comic scene and girl chucks B."[2] A list of numbered ideas describes number 23 as "Motive for a Jeeves story" and number 24 as a "Sequence for a Jeeves novel."[3] Even at this early creative stage, when the note consisted of only a sentence or a few phrases and when Wodehouse had no idea whether he would develop it, he evidently thought that different types of devices would sustain different prose forms.

The novel's longer form led Wodehouse to change his tactics for constructing Jeeves/Wooster plots. Every major aspect of the narrative form would demand adjustments: in creating problems that would sustain an entire novel, in delaying the solutions to these problems across the length of the narrative, and in achieving closure in all the plot lines.

NEW FORUMLAS

> "I feel that my next novel ought not to have a country house setting, and I can't see how I can get a rapid action plot except in same. Also I must give the idea of someone stealing something a rest for at least one book. But what else there is to write about, I can't imagine."[4]

I have suggested that for Wodehouse one of the main problems was to delay Jeeves's solution of the problems at hand. The novel format exacerbated that problem. One tactic Wodehouse used involved simply introducing more characters who could place their troubles before Bertie and Jeeves; these troubles would be introduced gradually (an expansion of the structure of "The Spot of Art"). As a result Jeeves and Bertie typically have more goals in the novels than in the stories, and these goals are often more short-term. Still, given that the types of characters and troubles used in the stories were extremely limited, Wodehouse could hardly just multiply them. In fact the series' cast changed considerably between the stories and novels, with only a few characters besides Jeeves and Bertie carrying over. The new characters' traits reflect new sets of functions in the longer narratives. Most prominently, many of the newcomers behave in unpredictable ways and thereby create new twists and problems that even Jeeves cannot be expected to foresee.

As in the short stories, these new characters and methods for creating plot problems and delays are extremely formulaic. Perhaps to an even greater extent than in the stories, the novels emphasize repetitiousness and convention. One reason for this might be the fact that the stories were short and came out in quick succession, so that their similarities would be more readily apparent. They were also reprinted in groups as books, thus encouraging people to read several within a short span. The novels came out at longer intervals, and hence Wodehouse may have felt the need to emphasize their similarities in order to make readers notice them.

Moreover, the longer form of the novel gave Wodehouse more space to spin out Bertie's conversations and narration in digressions inessential to the plot's action. In some of these passages, Bertie harks back to incidents from earlier stories and novels, comparing them to events in the novel at hand. For example, he often mentions Jeeves's past triumphs. In *Right Ho, Jeeves,* he alludes to three earlier stories:

> Mind you, after what had passed between us in the matter of that white mess jacket with the brass buttons, I was not prepared absolutely to hand over to the man. I would, of course, merely take him into consultation. But, recalling some of his earlier triumphs—the Sipperley Case, the Episode of My Aunt Agatha and the Dog McIntosh, and the smoothly handled Affair of Uncle George and The Barmaid's Niece were a few that sprang to my mind—I felt justified at least in offering him the

> opportunity of coming to the aid of the young master in his hour of peril. (Chap. 21)

Here Bertie gives the events titles suggestive of detective stories, particularly emphasizing the series' play with conventions from Doyle (for example, "The Problem of Thor Bridge," "The Reigate Puzzle," and "The Episode of the Barrel," a chapter in *The Sign of Four*). After Jeeves saves Bertie from a speeding taxi in *Much Obliged, Jeeves,* Bertie praises him: "It's amazing how you always turn up at the crucial moment, like the United States Marines. I remember how you did when A. B. Filmer and I were having our altercation with that swan, and there were other occasions too numerous to mention" (chap. 4). Here Bertie compares Jeeves's feats to a cliché in literature and film, the last-minute rescue, and his comparison points up the fact that the series itself habitually employs it. (By the way, the episode of Filmer and the swan occurred thirty-five years earlier, in "Jeeves and the Impending Doom.")

Another tactic Wodehouse uses for emphasizing the formulaic quality of his narratives is to call attention to the characters similarities, mostly falling into such categories as the male menace and the unpredictable female. Rather than disguising the fact that these characters are often nearly interchangeable, Wodehouse flaunts it. For example, he gives characters within each type similar names. Bertie's main female relatives have names that virtually rhyme: Agatha, Dahlia, Angela, Julia. His uncles have simple names: Tom, George, Henry, Clive. In contrast to this, the pals usually have elaborate names, with amusing nicknames: Claude Cattermole Pirbright ("Catsmeat"), George Webster Fittleworth ("Boko"), Reginald Herring ("Kipper"). The same goes for the unpredictable females: Zenobia Hopwood ("Nobby"), Stephanie Byng ("Stiffy"), Cora Pirbright ("Corky"). It is as if Wodehouse set out to prevent all but dedicated readers from keeping these characters straight. The confusion should make us notice their similar narrative functions.

Wodehouse also turns that inevitable problem of the literary series—repetitive exposition—to his advantage, using it to stress the parallels between the various books. Meir Sternberg has discussed the tactics used by "novelists celebrated for their progressive creation of some private, full-fledged fictive world" such as Trollope, Balzac, Faulkner, and Christie (in the Hercule Poirot series). According to Sternberg, such authors typically do not depend on the reader's memory of earlier works in the series but "take the necessary precautions to render each of their works as expositionally autonomous as possible." He cites a passage from Trollope:

> In the second chapter of Trollope's *Barchester Towers*, for instance, the narration informs the reader that "it is hardly necessary that [he] should here give to the public a lengthened biography of Mr. Harding up to the period of the commencement of this tale. The public cannot have forgotten how ill that sensitive gentleman bore the attack that was made on him in the columns of *The Jupiter*, with reference to the income which he received as Warden to Hiram's Hospital, in the city of Barchester. Nor can it yet be forgotten that a lawsuit was instituted against him," and so on. Although Trollope ostensibly professes to assume that Mr. Harding's ordeal, formerly narrated in *The Warden*, must by now be a matter of common knowledge, he in fact cunningly recapitulates the occurences expositionally relevant to *Barchester Towers*.[5]

What Wodehouse does with Bertie's narration must be at least equally cunning. Rather than ostensibly avoiding exposition while actually giving it, Bertie points up the fact that he has to cope with giving exposition across a series of narratives; by the late novels, he frets at length over the problem.

This device first appears in simple form in the stories. In "Without the Option," Bertie compares Heloise Pringle to Honoria Glossop, remarking "I think I may have told you before about this Glossop scourge," before briefly summarizing chapters 5 through 8 of *The Inimitable Jeeves*. In "Jeeves and the Yule-tide Spirit," his self-conscious narration becomes more comic. There Bertie prefaces his description of Sir Roderick Glossop, "Stop me if I've told you this before: but in case you don't know, let me just mention the facts in the matter of this Glossop."

The novels gave Wodehouse room to expand such devices. The opening of *Right Ho, Jeeves,* where Bertie ponders how to begin his narrative, is the first major instance, though the passage does not emphasize repetition from earlier works. In *The Code of the Woosters,* the problem of returning motifs and exposition comes to the fore at the first mention of Gussie Fink-Nottle:

> A thing I never know, when I'm starting out to tell a story about a chap I've told a story about before, is how much explanation to bung in at the outset. It's a problem you've got to look at from every angle. I mean to say, in the present case, if I take it for granted that my public knows all about Gussie Fink-Nottle and just breeze ahead, those publicans who weren't hanging on my lips the first time are apt to be fogged. Whereas, if before kicking off I give about eight volumes of the man's life and history, other bimbos, who were so hanging, will stifle yawns and murmur "Old stuff. Get on with it."
>
> I suppose the only thing to do is to put the salient facts as briefly as possible in the possession of the first gang, waving an apologetic hand at the second gang the while, to indicate that they had better let their attention wander for a minute or two and that I will be with them shortly. (Chap. 1)

This leads into two-thirds of a page of information on Gussie and his engagement to Madeline (introduced in the previous novel, *Right Ho, Jeeves*). The joke here is partly that Bertie claims he will "put the salient facts as briefly as possible," while this lead-in is nearly as long as the expositional passage itself. There is also his absurd pretense that regular readers skip the expositional material, while new ones read it. Yet this elaborate comic treatment of exposition probably makes such moments more delightful to the habitual reader than to the novice.

Perhaps no other tactic in Wodehouse's work so succinctly demonstrates how he brings mundane, repetitious literary conventions to our attention and defamiliarizes them through absurd overemphasis. Most of the novels use comic expository passages, but two examples should suffice to show how self-consciously Wodehouse exploits this device. Upon the first mention of Gussie Fink-Nottle in *The Mating Season,* Bertie addresses the reader:

> I wonder, by the way, if you recall this Augustus, on whose activities I have had occasion to touch once or twice before now? Throw the mind back. Goofy to the gills, face like a fish, horn-rimmed spectacles, drank orange juice, collected newts, engaged to England's premier pill, a girl called Madeline Bassett. . . . Ah, you've got him? Fine. (Chap. 1)

The most elaborate instance in the series comes in *Much Obliged, Jeeves,* which begins with a cheerful scene at breakfast:

> Well, all right so far. Off to a nice start. But now we come to something which gives me pause. In recording the latest instalment of the Bertram Wooster Story, a task at which I am about to have a pop, I don't see how I can avoid delving into the past a good deal, touching on events which took place in previous instalments, and explaining who's who and what happened when and where and why, and this will make it heavy going for those who have been with me from the start. "Old hat," they will cry or, if French, "Deja Vu."
>
> On the other hand, I must consider the new customers. I can't just leave the poor perishers to puzzle things out for themselves. If I did, the exchanges in the present case would run somewhat as follows:
>
> SELF: The relief I felt at having escaped from Totleigh Towers was stupendous.
>
> NEW C: What's Totleigh Towers?
>
> SELF: For one thing it had looked odds on that I should have to marry Madeline.
>
> NEW C: Who's Madeline?
>
> SELF: Gussie Fink-Nottle, you see, had eloped with the cook.
>
> NEW C: Who's Gussie Fink-Nottle?
>
> SELF: But most fortunately Spode was in the offing and scooped her up, saving me from the scaffold.
>
> NEW C: Who's Spode?
>
> You see. Hopeless. Confusion would be rife, as one might put it. The only way out that I can think of is to ask the old gang to let their attention wander for a bit—there are heaps of things they can be doing; washing the car, solving the crossword puzzle, taking the dog for a run,—while I place the facts before the newcomers. (Chap. 1)

Thus Bertie's comic exposition points up the series' narrative repetitiousness. It also creates humor by seeming to acknowledge that the convention of exposition across a series is usually mundane—and in the process making it anything but mundane.

Despite such insistence on the series' repetitiousness, the novels could not be structured in the same way as the stories. With his orientation toward plots centered on problems and solutions, Wodehouse needed new formulas that could sustain longer narratives. He found these in part by placing greater emphasis on unpredictable characters who introduce new problems at intervals. He also came to rely exclusively on the country-house setting, where everyone stays within one area, facilitating quick entrances and exits, with attendant surprises and plot twists.

We have seen how *Jeeves and the Feudal Spirit*'s plot originated with the simple idea of having Bertie accused of stealing a necklace while staying at a country house. In general, Bertie has three main ways of getting into trouble: reengagement to a former fiancée, a physical threat from a jealous man in love with that woman, and accusation of theft. Over the course of the series, Bertie is several times accused of theft and even brought into court; in "Without the Option" he is fined for stealing a policeman's helmet. Gradually such incidents, real or imagined, snowball, as magistrates and other menaces blow his minor police record out of proportion. By late in the series, he is widely assumed to be a kleptomaniac.

Wodehouse may have been so absorbed with this motif of having Bertie accused of theft because its incongruity with his naive honesty is amusing. In every novel from *The Code of the Woosters* to *Aunts Aren't Gentlemen*, he is suspected of a theft, and often this suspicion constitutes a major plot line: a cow-creamer and policeman's helmet (*The Code of the Woosters*); a photo and, through Gussie's impersonation of Bertie, a dog (*The Mating Season*); a necklace (though Jeeves bears the brunt of the suspicion, *Jeeves and the Feudal Spirit*); a camera and the same cow-creamer (*Jeeves in the Offing*); an amber statuette (*Stiff Upper Lip, Jeeves*); a porringer (*Much Obliged, Jeeves*); and a cat (*Aunts Aren't Gentlemen*). Twice Jeeves's solutions involve convincing others that Bertie really is a thief (*Jeeves in the Offing*) or a kleptomaniac (*Stiff*

Upper Lip, Jeeves), and Bertie pretends to be a kleptomaniac in *Much Obliged, Jeeves* in order to avoid marrying Florence.

The engagements, jealousies, and accusations of theft, combined with Bertie's desire to help his pals and Aunt Dahlia, form the basis for much of the novels' action, and the unpredictable characters throw in complications to delay the ending.

NEW CHARACTERS

Many of the major characters of the stories disappear in the novels, and several minor characters are brought back and elevated to a higher status. Other major characters carry over but gain important new traits that alter their narrative functions considerably.

Thank You, Jeeves uses a largely new supporting cast: Pauline Stoker and her father, Bertie's old schoolmate, Chuffy, and the new valet Brinkley. The only character whom we have met before, Sir Roderick Glossop, suddenly changes from a menace to a pal. Up to this point, he had been the only angry prospective father-in-law in Bertie's life. He did *not*, however, want Bertie to marry Honoria; the threat came not from upsetting him, which Bertie had to do to avoid this fate, but from the fact that by annoying Sir Roderick, Bertie irritated Aunt Agatha. But with Agatha herself absent, Sir Roderick is not a threat.

The mantle of main menace therefore passes to Stoker, who does want Bertie to marry Pauline, against both their wills. This is a more serious difficulty, and Bertie says that Stoker is the worst threat he has ever encountered: "Bless my soul, Jeeves, I can remember the time when I thought Sir Roderick Glossop a man-eater. And even my Aunt Agatha. They pale in comparison, Jeeves" (chap. 13). Stoker appears only in this novel, but his functions are split between Sir Watkyn Bassett and Roderick Spode, both introduced in *The Code of the Woosters* and destined to become the premiere menaces for the rest of the series.

The return of Sir Watkyn was an inspiration on Wodehouse's part. Rather than creating a new magistrate to be Madeline's father, he brings back the unnamed one who had a bit part in "Without the Option." There Bertie and Sippy stole a policeman's helmet, and now, by making that magistrate into Sir Watkyn, Wodehouse establishes that Basset thinks Bertie is a thief. Sir Watkyn is a more directly equivalent replacement for Sir Roderick than was Stoker in that he too dislikes the idea of Bertie marrying his daughter (or his niece, Stiffy). Spode, however, takes over Stoker's trait of trying to force Bertie into matrimony. Despite being in love with Madeline himself, in *Stiff Upper Lip, Jeeves* and *Much Obliged, Jeeves*, he believes that she loves Bertie and insists that the latter make her happy. Both Sir Watkyn and Spode are also physical threats, the one able to lock Bertie up and the other with a violent temper and a physique like a gorilla's. Such threats were relatively rare in the stories—even Sir Roderick never seriously threatened to commit Bertie when he thought him mad—but they become common in the novels.

Such substitutions of functionally similar characters are a familiar aspect of Wodehouse's narratives by now. But what of the transformation of Aunt Agatha into an offstage threat? We have seen that many of the novels' characters need to be unpredictable in order to slow down and complicate the plots. Agatha is completely predictable (as was Sir Roderick before *Thank You, Jeeves*), and she was more suited to creating the intense, short-term problems of the stories than to sustaining a lengthy set of plot twists. Moreover, Agatha knew Bertie all too well, while the menaces of the novels minsunderstand him and hence consistently misjudge his actions. Rather than retain Agatha as a major source of problems, Wodehouse ingeniously substituted Dahlia for her. Dahlia's geniality makes this an unlikely move, yet she too gets Bertie into seemingly hopeless situations.

Dahlia does not figure in *Thank You, Jeeves*, and in *Right Ho, Jeeves* she plays her familiar role of getting Bertie to help pals and relatives. In *The Code of the Woosters*, however, she leaps into the unpredictable female category by ordering Bertie to steal the cow-creamer. While Agatha's oppression of Bertie stemmed from her narrow notions of correct behavior and family honor (from which her predictability resulted), Dahlia is revealed to have little sense of morality. Theft and blackmail will figure more prominently from now on. Thus, despite their opposed character traits, Dahlia's most basic functions in creating narrative dynamics are similar to Agatha's. Wodehouse makes this clear in *The Code of the Woosters*, when Bertie meditates on the universal villainy of aunts:

> It is no use telling me that there are bad aunts and good aunts. At the core, they are all alike. Sooner or later, out pops the cloven hoof. Consider this Dahlia, Jeeves. As sound an egg as ever cursed a foxhound for chasing a rabbit, I have always considered her. And she goes and hands me an assignment like this. (Chap. 2)

Her threat to withhold Anatole's cooking, first used here, gives her as much power over Bertie as Agatha had.

The potential-marriage threat becomes crucial in the novels, and a small set of Bertie's ex-fiancées accumulates. Madeline Basset first appears in *Right Ho, Jeeves*, and in *Joy in the Morning* Florence Craye (who was engaged to Bertie in "Jeeves Takes Charge") returns. They provide Wodehouse with two opposite types of potential fiancées to work with: the squashily sentimental Madeline and the intellectual Florence. He alternates them systematically until *Much Obliged, Jeeves*, where Bertie gets engaged to both. The only other threatened fiancées are Bobbie Wickham, brought back in *Jeeves in the Offing*, and a new character, Vanessa Cook, in *Aunts Aren't Gentlemen*. Both constitute less effective threats than do Madeline and Florence.

The unpredictable characters create important delaying forces in the novels. Most plots contain a young woman who likes practical jokes, an attitude that indicates her entire outlook on life. When in chapter 8 of *Thank You, Jeeves* Bertie and Pauline believe that her father is knocking at the door, she proposes that they pour water on him; Bertie is shocked:

> She had made the suggestion as if she considered it one of her best and brightest, and I suddenly realized what it meant to play host to a girl of her temperament and personality. All that I had ever heard or read about the reckless younger generation seemed to come back to me.

In *Joy in the Morning,* Jeeves says that Nobby Hopwood had called earlier and wanted to wake Bertie with a wet sponge. In *The Mating Season,* Corky Pirbright drives the infatuated Gussie to put frogs in Constable Dobbs's cottage.

The Code of the Woosters emphasizes Stiffy's unpredictability and her concomitant ability to generate plot twists. When she refuses to return Gussie's notebook, both Gussie and Bertie assume they know where she would hide it. Bertie takes his cue from a mystery novel's claim that women usually hide things on the tops of cupboards[6]; he insists on searching the one in Stiffy's room, where he and Jeeves are trapped by her dog Bartholemew. Needless to say, the notebook is not there, nor in Stiffy's stocking, where Gussie looks for it—thereby getting himself in worse trouble with Madeline. Bertie even compares Stiffy to Aunt Agatha: "Her voice took on the kind of metallic hardness which I have so often noticed in that of my Aunt Agatha during our get-togethers" (chap. 8). This passage points up the functional equivalence between Stiffy and Agatha; both create conflict and keep the narrative open, though in different ways.

Most of the pals in this period resemble those in the stories: amiable chumps who need help in making money or in straightening out their romances. With the growing string of Bertie's ex-fiancées, some old pals are more prone to jealousy, but that is the main change in the pattern. There is one major exception, however: Gussie Fink-Nottle. Gussie is as spectacularly unpredictable through sheer goofiness as ever Bobbie Wickham was through her vaunted *espièglerie.* We must realize this from the first, since Gussie's early actions in *Right Ho, Jeeves* lead to a failure of Jeeves's initial plan of sending him to propose to Madeline at a fancy-dress ball. His forgetfulness and incompetence cause him to miss the ball, though Bertie, in his rebellious phase, unfairly blames Jeeves. Later on, Bertie and Jeeves both lace Gussie's orange juice with gin, only to discover that this lifelong teetotaller has become roaring drunk on whiskey. Similarly, in *The Code of the Woosters,* before the action begins, Jeeves has advised Gussie to get through a speech by thinking about how he despises his auditors. But Gussie goes beyond Jeeves's advice by writing his contemptuous thoughts down and tops that off by losing the notebook. Gussie is such an enduring character partly because, unlike the other pals, he unwittingly foils Bertie and Jeeves's efforts to help him; the happy endings they arrange for him unravel by the next novel in which he figures. At his last appearance, in *Stiff Upper Lip, Jeeves,* he just as unpredictably solves his own problem by eloping with Emerald—once again saddling Bertie with Madeline as a fiancée.

By late in the series, Wodehouse had used most of the pals, menaces, and ex-fiancées more than once, and as of *Jeeves in the Offing* he began to alter the series' ingredients somewhat by gradually marrying off these characters. This novel eliminates Bobbie Wickham from Bertie's life for good. In *Stiff Upper Lip, Jeeves,* Stiffy and Stinker are finally in a position to marry, and the Gussie-Madeline romance, which figured in four novels, is resolved; Gussie, Sir Watkyn, and Totleigh Towers disappear forever. "Jeeves and the Greasy Bird" creates a fiancé for Honoria Glossop (who had not appeared in the series since the mid-1920s), and *Much Obliged, Jeeves* ends with Tuppy and Angela, as well as Madeline and Sidcup (né Spode), off to be married. After learning that Bertie is supposedly a kleptomaniac, Florence renounces him and remains single—presumably being too much the perfectionist ever to marry. Wodehouse was so thorough in arranging the characters' situations by *Much Obliged, Jeeves* that, when he wrote *Aunts Aren't Gentlemen* three years later, he had to invent a largely new cast. Most of these new players, however, fit snugly into the old molds: Cook, the male menace, recalls Bassett and Runkle; Vanessa pops up as another ex-fiancée of Bertie's; Orlo Potter bears a striking resemblance to Stilton Cheesewright, being a threatening, jealous old schoolmate; and Dahlia's coconspirator in catnapping, Angelica, fills the unpredicatable-female slot last occupied by Stiffy Byng.

Throughout these shifts in dramatis personae, certain motivations for action remain central, though here too Wodehouse changes them to suit the novelistic form. For example, though involuntary marriage remains a threat to Bertie, Aunt Agatha is no longer around to pressure him into it. Rather than transferring her function of forcing Bertie into engagements from her to another character, Wodehouse invented the Code. Bertie's code of honor, in effect, gives the series an element of predictability that it lost with the exit of Agatha: whenever the Code is invoked, Bertie is in danger of becoming reengaged.

The Code—though not yet by that name—is first linked to the idea of involuntary engagement in *Right Ho, Jeeves,* when Madeline mistakes Bertie's wooing on behalf of Gussie for his own proposal:

> My whole fate hung upon a woman's word. I mean to say, I couldn't back out. If a girl thinks a man is proposing to her and on that understanding books him up, he can't explain to her that she has got hold of entirely the wrong end of the stick and that he hadn't the smallest intention of suggesting anything of the kind. He must simply let it ride. (Chap. 10)

The Code provides a more flexible way of getting Bertie reengaged, and it is also more dangerous than Agatha. While Jeeves was able to thwart her attempts to marry Bertie off, even he cannot violate the Code and so must get each fiancée to give Bertie up. The Code illustrates how, with the multiplication of unpredictable characters, Wodehouse needed a persisting convention that could force Bertie into difficulties. As usual, that convention is based on cliché: notions of chivalry and loyalty as boiled down in British boys' stories and melodramatic romances.

In a few anomalous narratives, both Bertie and Jeeves undergo radical changes that make for plot premises quite different from those of standard country-house formula. The postwar plays *Spring Fever* and *Come On, Jeeves* and the novel *Ring for Jeeves* eliminate Bertie; in *Win with Wooster* and *Betting on Bertie,* Bertie is altered to make an effective stage character. These changes did not carry across the series, however, and we shall examine them separately in the next chapter.

THE RETURN OF COINCIDENCE

Because of its greater length and larger number of characters and goals, the novelistic form presented Wodehouse with greater problems for creating plots without coincidences or unmotivated casual gaps. Perhaps it is not surprising that he came to rely more on coincidence and luck for

Jeeves's solutions, particularly from *The Code of the Woosters* on when the number of short-term obstacles, and hence the number of small-scale solutions required, increased. Possibly the disappearance of the motif of Bertie's rebelliousness led to this slightly less rigorous plotting. Since Jeeves is not struggling for power over Bertie and thus withholding his aid, he must confront external problems more frequently and directly.

As one sign of this change, *Right Ho, Jeeves* is one of the few novels with no major menace. There the conflict between Jeeves and Bertie is enough to create a strong plot. After their feud is resolved, the two main male menaces of the novels are introduced: Bassett and Spode in *The Code of the Woosters*. This is also the novel in which we learn about Jeeves's membership in the Junior Ganymede and about the Club Book. According to the Club rules, every member must contribute an entry describing his employer. The Book is the main motivation for Jeeves's solutions to most of the problems: the blackmailing of Spode solves the helmet crisis, which in turn enables Bertie to blackmail Sir Watkyn into consenting to the two couples' engagements and ignoring the theft of the cow-creamer. The Book's information also induces Bertie to agree to the world cruise. The fact that the Book provides information so important to the plot is pure luck, of course—especially since we have never heard about Jeeves's club before. In later books, the Club Book seems less of a rabbit-out-of-the-hat device, though there, too, Jeeves's solutions involving the Book will depend on luck and opportunity rather than foresight. Even in *The Code of the Woosters*, the Book is introduced so early in the plot that by the end we may assign everything to Jeeves's skill. In fact, his only tactic consists of suggesting various forms of blackmail, based on the Book. In general, the Book fits in well with the increasing prominence of blackmail and other unethical means.

Joy in the Morning is carefully plotted, with Jeeves manipulating most of the solutions to the various problems. There is, however, one instance in which he depends upon luck. Early in the novel, Bertie writes a letter to Nobby Hopwood, suggesting that she help Stilton out of his engagement to Florence by pointing out all the latter's faults—which he details in the letter. Later, Bertie keeps trying to get Nobby to show it to Florence, so that she will give up the idea of becoming reengaged to him. Nobby in turn blackmails Bertie by threatening *not* to show the letter to Florence. Eventually Edwin, the Boy Scout, throws the letter away as part of a good deed. Jeeves cannot solve this problem, but luckily Stilton quits his job as a policeman and Florence reconciles with him—thus letting Bertie off the hook.

Jeeves's dependence on luck and coincidence is more striking in *The Mating Season*. That his Uncle Charlie happens to be the butler at Deverill Hall is not necessary to Jeeves's solutions (and indeed, as we shall see, he does not solve many of the problems). It simply enables him to provide expositional material about Esmond Haddock and his aunts. The fact that Charlie Silversmith knows Jeeves also motivates both the delay in Jeeves's arrival at the Hall and Catsmeat's presence there posing as Bertie's valet. Furthermore, *The Mating Season* depends on a miscalculation on Jeeves's part, one which is reminiscent of his initial solutions in the early stories. Jeeves is faced with the situation of Gussie having to visit Deverill Hall but being jailed for two weeks. The obvious solution would be to concoct a story about Gussie being ill or having to visit a sick relative. Instead Jeeves suggests that Bertie go to the Hall impersonating Gussie. But Jeeves surely must realize that Bertie is already scheduled to go to the Hall and appear at the village concert *in persona proper* and that he will get in trouble with Aunt Agatha if he fails to do so. Moreover, when Jeeves comes to the Hall as valet to "Bertie" (that is, Gussie), he tells Bertie that they came because Madeline would expect to get letters from Gussie, postmarked King's Deverill. He must have foreseen this earlier, or if he learns it from Gussie once the latter gets out of jail, he could arrange for Bertie to forward Gussie's letters to Madeline. Essentially Wodehouse switches premises on us about one third of the way through, and we must conclude that Jeeves's initial solution—sending Bertie to the Hall—did not solve much of anything. At the end, Jeeves has relatively little control over the outcomes of the various problems. Most notably, he could not foresee that his coshing Constable Dobbs would bring about his religious conversion and hence his reconciliation with the housemaid Queenie.

The role of luck is also obvious in *Jeeves in the Offing*, since Jeeves is idle and absent during so much of the action and does not manipulate events or plan ahead. His two simple solutions involve seizing on opportunities. First, he steals the speech that he happens to find among Upjohn's possessions, and second, he advises Glossop to reveal his identity to Mrs. Cream and tell her that he is investigating Bertie, who has stolen the cow-creamer. Bertie is annoyed over this second solution but is mollified when Jeeves points out that he has done Uncle Tom a good turn. Bertie's sudden sentimental attachment to Uncle Tom is an important motivating factor in getting Jeeves off the hook here and also distracts our attention from the relative simplicity and perfunctory presentation of Jeeves's solutions.

Again in *Stiff Upper Lip, Jeeves* Jeeves depends heavily on luck and opportunity for solutions. Given the coincidence that Stinker is a prop forward and that Plank not only needs a prop forward for his local football team but also has a vicarage to bestow, Jeeves makes the obvious move of bringing the two together. He solves the Madeline-engagement problem on the spur of the moment after he overhears Sidcup tell Madeline that Bertie is a thief; since Jeeves has the statuette, he simply shows it to her and claims that Bertie is a kleptomaniac.

In *Aunts Aren't Gentlemen*, Jeeves does not control events or even work to solve problems as they arise. For over half the book, he functions mainly to provide expository information. Not until chapter 14 does he solve anything; there he neutralizes Orlo as a menace by reminding him that he sold Bertie an insurance policy and will lose his job if he harms Bertie. After this, Jeeves has little to do, and Wodehouse has him go to visit his aunt. During his absence, the main plot premise is reversed: while Aunt Dahlia had insisted that Bertie help steal the stable cat and cause Cook's horse to lose a race, she now says the cat must be returned to Cook in order to prevent her honest friend Briscoe from scratching his horse from the rigged race.

The problems soon start sorting themselves out with little help from Jeeves. Orlo stands up to Cook and wins Vanessa back after her brief reengagement to Bertie. Jeeves frees Bertie after Cook and fellow menace Plank tie him up and gets rid of Plank by pretending to be Bertie's solicitor, but his solution to the cat problem seems to depend on pure coincidence. It turns out that the cat belongs to Jeeves's aunt, and thus he and Bertie can make any demand on Cook, who is desperate to keep it. Possibly Jeeves has concocted the idea of having his aunt claim to own the cat, but the book contains no hint of this. And even if Jeeves lies about the cat, it is coincidence enough that he happens to have an aunt in the same village where Aunt Dahlia rents Bertie a cottage.

Despite all these instances of good luck and coincidence, Jeeves often does use skill to solve problems. Moreover, the late stories and early novels had firmly established that Jeeves has the godlike traits that Bertie ascribes to him throughout the series. The later imperfections in his actions would not be enough to wipe out that impression, and most readers probably think of Jeeves as solving virtually everything.

One reason Jeeves ceases to solve all the problems is that, after *Right Ho, Jeeves,* Bertie works more closely with him. Wodehouse continued a trend, begun in the middle-period stories, of making Bertie more intelligent and more a partner to Jeeves. His flashes of cleverness, while rare, surpass anything he would have been capable of in the short stories. In *Joy in the Morning,* for example, he objects to one aspect of Jeeves's plan about the fancy-dress ball, suggesting that he and Boko should attend it. Jeeves expresses "cordial agreement" and modifies his plan. At the ball, Bertie influences Worplesdon on Boko's behalf. Worplesdon resists, but Bertie reminds him that Boko had once kicked the troublesome Edwin, and this half-convinces Worplesdon. It is one of Bertie's smartest moves.

In *Jeeves and the Feudal Spirit,* Bertie is in Florence's bedroom while Stilton, enraged with jealousy, lurks in the hallway; suddenly "something seemed to go off in my brain and it was as though I had swallowed a brimming dose of some invigorating tonic, the sort of pick-me-up that makes a bedridden invalid rise from his couch and dance the Carioca" (chap. 14). Bertie points out to Stilton that he cannot thrash Bertie, having drawn his name in the Drones Club Darts sweep. This solution is positively Jeevesian; indeed, as we have just seen, Jeeves uses something like it in *Aunts Aren't Gentlemen,* mentioning the insurance policy Orlo sold Bertie when the latter threatens to beat Bertie up.

Bertie displays unusual perspicacity in *Stiff Upper Lip, Jeeves* as well, advising Stiffy to get Bassett's promise of a vicarage for Stinker in writing. When in *Much Obliged, Jeeves* he is caught searching another guest's bedroom, he for once manages to concoct an excuse, telling Runkle that he has come to ask him to take some photographs of Brinkley Court. In *Aunts Aren't Gentlemen*, Plank hears meows coming from the kitchen, and Bertie claims that his valet is practicing his cat imitations—not a particularly clever ruse, but one which satisfies Plank. As Jeeves remarks to Pauline in *Thank You, Jeeves*, "Mr. Wooster is capable of acting very shrewdly on occasion" (chap. 18). With Bertie more able to act independently and less inclined to work against Jeeves, the pair become partners cooperating in finding solutions to problems in which they share an interest.

STRATEGIES FOR DELAY

One crucial task forcing the novelist who concentrates on plot action is to delay closure in a motivated way. Given a set of character types and a small number of formulaic ways for getting Bertie into trouble, Wodehouse perpetually had to face the problem of Jeeves's perfection as a problem-solver. Moreover, though the series depends on repetitive narrative patterns, the repetitions that create that delay could not be too exact or the defamiliarizing force of the humor would be lost. To create originality and variation, Wodehouse used several delaying tactics—some problematic, some dazzling in their possibilities for exaggerating or twisting literary conventions.

I shall examine these tactics in turn. A detailed analysis of each novel is beyond the scope of this book, but I have chosen a few for lengthier treatment. Some of the novels use atypical delaying devices: *Jeeves in the Offing* depends on Jeeves's absence; *The Mating Season* multiplies its romance plots to an absurd degree; *Much Obliged, Jeeves* uses a serious error by Jeeves. *Jeeves and the Feudal Spirit* displays the episodic introduction and solution of problems more typical of the series, and it will serve as a summary example of that tactic. Finally, the extremely strong structures of the two novels that depend on Bertie's rebelliousness, *Thank You, Jeeves* and *Right Ho, Jeeves,* warrant extended analysis.

JEEVES ON VACATION

The least common strategy for delaying closure was to have Jeeves go away, usually on vacation. This ploy appeared during the short-story period in "The Pride of the Woosters Is Wounded" and "The Love That Purifies." In such cases, Bertie gets into trouble and cannot appeal to the absent Jeeves; hence closure is automatically postponed. Wodehouse probably uses this tactic so seldom because it generates relatively simple plots; it also means that for considerable stretches of the action there are none of the dialogues between Jeeves and Bertie that provide part of the series' appeal.

Jeeves in the Offing revives this device, eliminating Jeeves for the bulk of the plot and bringing in another valet/butler figure: Sir Roderick Glossop, disguised as "Swordfish." Indeed, the whole plot depends both on the absence of major characters and on disguise and mistaken identity. Once Bertie gets to Brinkley Court, three characters depart for long stretches: Aunt Dahlia to tend her sick son, Bobbie Wickham to placate her mother, and Aubrey Upjohn to institute his libel suit. The plot is thin, since after bringing a group of characters together as usual, Wodehouse must disperse them to make the narrative work. The Dahlia plot line depends on her mistaking the respectable Wilbert Cream for his playboy brother Wilfred; as part of her scheme, she has Glossop substitute for her butler Seppings, who is, like Jeeves, on vacation. Wodehouse could have pushed the role-switching further, as with the sundered couples in *The Mating Season,* but he sticks to a few simple premises.

The books's raison d'etre seems to be to get Glossop into a comic disguise, complicated by the introduction of Bertie's old housemaster. This device could have worked brilliantly had Wodehouse contrived to throw Jeeves and "Swordfish" together. As it is, Jeeves's absence pervades the novel, with others trying to play his role. Glossop schemes for Bertie to win over Upjohn by rescuing him from the pond; Jeeves might have suggested such a plan in the early stories, but here it is treated as silly. Dahlia also substitutes for Jeeves. She recalls the incident (in *Joy in the Morning*) when Bertie was supposed to call his Uncle Percy names so that Boko could defend and thus ingratiate himself with Worplesdon. Dahlia proposes trying the same thing with Kipper and Upjohn. These proto-Jeevesian schemes show that the substitution of other characters for Jeeves dominates the novel; thus Jeeves himself has to be "in the offing." Such inadequate schemes help delay closure, and delays are vital, since the final solutions are so simple: the discovery of Wilbert's identity, the theft of Upjohn's speech, and the claim that Bertie is insane.

A few other novels involve Jeeves's absence for more limited stretches of time. In *The Mating Season* he returns to London for a lecture and, somewhat inexplicably, stays away from Deverill Hall for days, missing important developments there. He visits his aunt in *Aunts Aren't Gentlemen*, again being absent for a sizable portion of the action. Each of these departures creates delays, but perhaps the best uses of Jeeves's absences are in those books where they occur just before the action begins: his separation from Bertie when the latter is at Cannes in *Right Ho, Jeeves*, the vacation from which he returns as *Jeeves and the Feudal Spirit* opens, and his stint as butler at Brinkley Court preceeding the action of *Stiff Upper Lip, Jeeves*. In these cases, Jeeves's absences set up major plot lines and hence contribute actively to the structures of these novels.

EPISODIC PROBLEMS, GRADUAL SOLUTIONS

An obvious option for creating delay would be simply increasing the number of problems that Jeeves and Bertie must solve. In the late stories, Jeeves often dealt with three or four problems. The novels are about twelve times as long as the stories, but they do not gain in length by multiplying plot lines proportionately. Certainly there are more lines of action, but Jeeves usually has about half a dozen goals. Because this material must extend over such a long stretch of prose,

Wodehouse often uses the tactics of introducing problems successively and of having unpredictable characters and unlucky coincidences impede Jeeves's solutions.

Wodehouse did not introduce these tactics in the earliest novels. Because Bertie was still in his rebellious phase, conflicts between him and Jeeves could create strong delaying factors. In *Thank You, Jeeves* and *Right Ho, Jeeves,* Wodehouse was able to extend the short-story formula of quickly introducing a set of problems and goals that last throughout the narrative. Such complex plotting must have been difficult to plan and sustain, however, and in *The Code of the Woosters* he introduced strategies for breaking the action into more discrete units; this approach became more typical of the rest of the series.

The Code of the Woosters introduces its main lines of action quickly, then resolves them in a leisurely fashion. During Bertie's visit to Aunt Dahlia, they discuss Gussie and Madeline and how Bertie's safety depends on their marrying, Uncle Tom and his desire to add the cow-creamer to his collection, and Sir Watkyn Bassett and his treacherous attempt to hire Anatole. Jeeves's desire to go on a cruise had been set up in the first scene, but his disagreement with Bertie does not lead to a feud or to any narrative conflict. Bertie's encounter with Sir Watkyn provides the main complicating action that starts things going; he then discovers that Gussie and Madeline are at odds and goes to Totleigh Towers, with its panoply of unpredictable characters. By chapter 7, Jeeves begins to tackle the problems by providing Bertie with information on Spode from the Junior Ganymede Club Book. Although this does not solve any specific problem at this point, the Book ultimately permits all the problems to be dealt with. Thus Jeeves's solutions are devised over the second half of the book, and he must work out new ways to blackmail and trick the other characters as the action unfolds.

Thus the plot becomes somewhat episodic: Jeeves solves one problem, only to face unexpected new twists. In chapter 10, Bertie congratulates Jeeves on a job well done, and Jeeves prepares to pack for their departure. The happy ending seems set, since all lines of action appear to have been resolved. Yet the notebook, cow-creamer, and policeman's helmet (the book's three main objects of contention) will all reappear, as will their respective plot lines. The helmet is already in one of the suitcases Jeeves gets out at this point, though he does not find it until the end of chapter 12—just after the pair again prematurely conclude that all is well:

> "Even this sinister house can surely have no further shocks to offer."
> "I imagine not, sir."
> "No, this is the finish. Totleigh Towers has shot its bolt, and at long last we are sitting pretty. Gratifying, Jeeves."
> "Most gratifying, sir."

At this point Jeeves finds the helmet, and the intrigue continues for two more chapters. Even after the departure of Gussie with the cow-creamer, the sense of intense action does not diminish until Bertie's final triumph over Sir Watkyn, accomplished through the threat of a lawsuit, an idea that Jeeves has at the last minute. Indeed, the episodic quality of *The Code of the Woosters* and the best of the subsequent novels aids the creation of comic surprises.

With many plot twists Jeeves also has many short-range goals rather than a few long-range ones. At least three times in the book, he states that he cannot think of a solution to the immediate problem he and Bertie face. This change of narrative tactics makes Jeeves less the perfect offstage manipulator, but it must have offered Wodehouse far more flexibility in plotting.

The basic strategies of *Joy in the Morning* are similar to those of *The Code of the Woosters*. Again Jeeves conceives a plan, to go fishing at Steeple Bumpleigh, and although Bertie objects, no serious rift results. Here, however, Jeeves forces Bertie to allow him to achieve his goal early on, rather than gaining it as a reward at the end. When he describes his plan to have Worplesdon meet his business associate at Bertie's cottage, Bertie realizes Jeeves has tricked him:

> "Jeeves," I said, "you have done the dirty on me."
> "I am sorry, sir. It seemed the only solution of his lordship's problem." (Chap. 4)

This may be the only solution that would allow Jeeves to get his own way, but Worplesdon's simple problem could be solved in other ways. Jeeves's plan gains him little, as he goes fishing only once, but it lands Bertie in a disproportionately large amount of trouble. Jeeves must then extract Bertie to earn his reward retrospectively. The fact that the novel begins with the last scene and flashes back emphasizes this reversal.

The episodic quality of *The Code of the Woosters* becomes more pervasive, though less effective, in some of the late novels. In *Stiff Upper Lip, Jeeves,* time and again the problems at hand wind down, and a new complication or premise has to crank the action up. When Bertie reaches Totleigh Towers, he finds Madeline and Gussie already reconciled, and there is no ongoing threat comparable to Gussie's lost notebook in *The Code of the Woosters*. Later, after it turns out that Bassett had paid Plank a fair price for the statuette, Stiffy returns it to the locked case, and only much later, when Bassett refuses to give Stinker a vicarage, does she remove it again and give it to Bertie. Thus at the midway point, the rift between Gussie and Madeline is the only major threat facing Bertie. Stinker needs a vicarage, but Bassett seems inclined to give him one, and, since Gussie is still engaged to Madeline, Sidcup is not menacing him or Bertie.

The action speeds up again as a result of the school treat. There Bassett decides not to give Stinker the vicarage, and Gussie falls in love with Emerald. The actual problems requiring final solution are set up quite late: Madeline decides to marry Bertie after Gussie elopes (chap. 18), Bassett again declines to give Stinker a post (chap. 19), and Bertie again receives the statuette from Stiffy (chap. 21). As a result of all this disappearance and reappearance of problems, Bertie and Jeeves often concentrate on one line of action for a stretch, and thus, despite the many plot twists and turns, we do not have the sustained, dense sets of problems of the pre-1950 novels.

Jeeves and the Feudal Spirit is one of the best of the postwar novels, and it is typical of the use of episodic problems and solutions. From its beginning, we encounter familiar motifs. As in *Right Ho, Jeeves,* Bertie is bathing, and he and Jeeves are reunited after a separation (Bertie's vacation in the earlier book, Jeeves's here); Jeeves soon discovers something that Bertie has acquired in the interval (the white mess jacket, the moustache) and disapproves. Here, however, Bertie does not rebel against Jeeves, and hence Jeeves has less reason to withhold his aid. By this point, Jeeves simply bides his time when such disagreements arise, presumably realizing that he will get his way eventually. Thus feuds between the two do not provide delays. We are in a mellower phase of the series, and although *Jeeves and the Feudal Spirit* may seem simply to return to old formulas, it actually varies them by combining approaches from the first two novels with those of the next three. Now Wodehouse can have Bertie and Jeeves feuding over one specific item but cooperating in every other way. In the late novels, the quarrel/reward pattern returns as an amusing motif without being structurally crucial.

As in the pre-1950s novels, the plot lines are quickly introduced. By midway through chapter 2, we know that Dahlia wants to butter up the Trotters (hoping they will buy *Milady's Boudoir*), that Florence's novel *Spindrift* is being dramatized (by Percy, who will pawn the second necklace to finance the play and eventually become engaged to Florence), that Stilton wants Bertie to keep fit for the Drones darts tournament (linked to Stilton's jealousy over Florence), and that Jeeves hates Bertie's moustache. Yet by chapter 8, all four problems seem to be solved. Florence has reconciled with Stilton, who is out of Bertie's way, hiding while he grows a moustache. Percy has the money to produce *Spindrift*, and Jeeves is not sulking over Bertie's moustache. Thus the plot has wound down, and Dahlia's command for Bertie to help cheer up Percy reactivates it.

After Bertie gets to Brinkley, two crucial ingredients enter the plot: the pearl necklaces and Spode, now Lord Sidcup. Thus the Junior Ganymede Club Book returns as well, though it turns out that its information about Eulalie Soeurs that stymied Spode in *The Code of the Woosters* is outdated, and Jeeves can no longer blackmail him.

The Junior Ganymede Club itself also returns to prominence for the first time since *The Code of the Woosters*. Jeeves's return to London to deliver a speech at a Club luncheon puts him beyond reach when Sidcup arrives at Brinkley. That visit to town permits Jeeves to learn from the Club Book why Trotter does not want a knighthood, and it also allows Bertie to fetch the cosh, which figures prominently in the action. In the rest of the series, the Club Book provides information used for both exposition and blackmail. Most spectacularly, as we shall see, it creates the structural core of *Much Obliged, Jeeves.*

In this late period, Wodehouse increasingly used sudden reversals of plot premises to create delays by means of an episodic structure. Jeeves, Bertie, and Aunt Dahlia may find their assumptions radically changed without warning. In *Jeeves and the Feudal Spirit,* Sidcup turns out to be impervious to blackmail, since he has sold Eulalie Soeurs. When Jeeves learns that Trotter has refused a knighthood, Aunt Dahlia threatens to reveal this to his social-climbing wife; yet at the end of chapter 20, Mrs. Trotter unexpectedly decides that her husband should refuse a knighthood, so that plan is scotched. Now even apparently predictable, fixated characters can suddenly change completely.

Jeeves preserves his surface appearance of omniscience, but as in the other novels after *Right Ho, Jeeves,* his solutions depend partly on luck and coincidence. Here both he and Sidcup turn out to be experts on jewelry. Moreover, when Jeeves volunteers to return Mrs. Trotter's necklace, he presumably does not know that it is an imitation. He must notice this that evening, however, since he does not return it during dinner as planned; it is found in his room the next morning. He must have concocted the scheme of exposing the necklace as fake, but he has primarily seized upon coincidence. This is a rare bit of unexplained offstage action in this late period, and there is no hint as to whether Jeeves knew Percy had pawned his mother's pearl necklace; if so, Jeeves could predict the course of events in the climactic breakfast scene. Finally, Stilton fortuitously finds a new love and thus ceases to be a threat to Bertie and a rival to Percy.

Jeeves's revelation that the necklace is a fake resolves several of the main problems: Florence drops her engagement to Bertie in favor of Percy, Trotter defies his wife and buys *Milady's Boudoir,* Bertie does not have to confess to being a thief, and Jeeves gets his reward when Bertie offers to shave his moustache. Presumably Sidcup's valuation of Dahlia's necklace will be delayed until she can get the real one out of hock, so her problem also seems to be solved. Despite his dependence on luck, Jeeves solves the problems with one deft gesture, as he had in the late stories and early novels.

A SURGING SEA OF AUNTS

Wodehouse did not, then, depend simply upon the multiplication of narrative elements as a formula for creating satisfying novels. In the case of *The Mating Season*, however, he did increase the number of characters and plot lines, though it also draws upon plot devices specific to the novels—especially the unpredictable character. *The Mating Season* uses exaggeration not only to create delays but also to poke fun at romantic conventions that Wodehouse habitually inverted in his Jeeves/Wooster plots. As a result, it comes closer to being a parody than do any of the other novels.

As the novel opens, Bertie faces the prospect of visiting Deverill Hall, and Jeeves, whose Uncle Charlie is the butler there, fills him in on the set-up: Esmond Haddock lives there with his five aunts. Thus begins the distinctive dominant of this novel, the exaggeration and multiplication of Wodehouse's standard devices. Aunts and uncles, servants, and sundered couples all appear in unusual profusion. Not only are there the five Deverill aunts, but Aunt Agatha becomes a more active force; though we never see her, she threatens to arrive, and at the end Bertie goes to confront her. As to servants, Jeeves's uncle Charlie Silversmith and his cousin Queenie work at the Hall, and Catsmeat goes there posing as Bertie's valet. There are five sundered couples, though Jeeves and Bertie deal with only four. Repetition itself becomes a motif: the confusion between the two green-bearded men after the village concert, the domination of the concert itself by seven members of the Kegley-Bassington clan, and even Esmond Haddock's repetitious hunting song. The repetition is also cumulative from other books. For the third time in a row we have an irate country constable; Gussie and Madeline return for a third round of romantic woes.

All these quantitiative shifts create a qualitative one, as old devices are defamiliarized by the very absurdity of their repetition. Indeed, Wodehouse simply pushes his usual tactic of calling our attention to repetition a step further. He used this sort of reductio ad absurdum only once, and *The Mating Season* seems an appropriate end to an era of his career. (It was the last novel he wrote before his permanent move to the United States.)

The conventionality of the characters and their problems is made explicit through the introduction of Catsmeat Pirbright (previously a minor offstage Drone). Catsmeat is an actor, described as usually playing "Freddie, the light-hearted friend of the hero, carrying the second love interest" (chap. 2). He plays that same role here, since his engagement to Gertrude Winkworth is one of the sundered-couples problems. By definition, the first love interest of the series is how to prevent Bertie's marriage. The notion of a "secondary love interest" is set up early so that we are cued to notice the novel's plethora of romantic problems: five secondary love interests, as well as complications like Catsmeat's engagement to Queenie, Corky's flirtation with Gussie, and Esmond's dalliance with Gertrude.

Once Bertie gets to Deverill Hall, the exaggeration begins in earnest. Although there are only five aunts present, Bertie describes them thus: "As far as the eye could see, I found myself gazing on a surging sea of aunts. There were tall aunts, short aunts, stout aunts, thin aunts, and an aunt who was carrying on a conversation in a low voice to which nobody seemed to be paying the slightest attention" (chap. 5). After dinner, Esmond sings Bertie his repetitious hunting song, intended for the concert: "Hullo, hullo, hullo, hullo!/A-hunting we will go, pom, pom,/A-hunting we will go./To-day's the day, so come what may, a-hunting we will go." Bertie considers this all wrong: "Well, think it out for yourself. You start off 'A-hunting we will go, a-hunting we will go' and then, just as the audience is all keyed up for a punch line, you repeat that a-hunting you will go. There will be a sense of disappointment" (chap. 6). Bertie suggests some improvements ("Hullo, hullo, hullo, hullo! A-hunting we will go my lads, a-hunting we will go, pull up our socks and chase the fox and lay the blighter low"), but it seems doubtful that these are incorporated in the version Esmond sings at the concert (where he does four encores plus an extra rendition of the chorus). Esmond's song carries the dominant structure of repetition down into the details of *The Mating Season*.

Gradually four sundered couples accumulate in the vicinity of King's

Deverill. One of these shaky relationships affects Bertie particularly, since if Gussie alienates Madeline (who is visiting her friend Hilda in Wimbledon), she will presumably decide to marry Bertie. Gussie becomes infatuated with Corky and writes to Madeline breaking their engagement, so that Bertie must sneak into Hilda's house and retrieve the letter before Madeline reads it. He succeeds but also encounters Madeline, who jumps to the conclusion that the lovesick Bertie has come to steal a photograph of her. Touched, she tells Bertie that Hilda (an athletic Honoria Glossop type) has broken off her engagement because her fiancé hogged a game of mixed doubles. Thus we have a fifth sundered couple (who manage to get back together on their own).

During this scene, Wodehouse inserts a reference to the sort of popular literary romances he typically defamiliarizes, as Madeline tells Bertie the sad story of *Mervyn Keene, Clubman*. Mervyn was wrongly imprisoned, lost the woman he loved, and spent years in dissipation, trying to forget. Finally he stole into his beloved's house to take a rose from her dressing-room; she recognized him, but her husband mistook Mervyn for a burglar and shot him. This is basically the tragic version of what Wodehouse plays as farce. It is also the most extensive synopsis we ever get of a work by Rosie M. Banks, author of slushy women's novels; Bertie describes it as "the world's worst tripe" (chap. 17). This scene foregrounds the notion of sundered lovers as a literary cliché. It also points up the comic inversion of the traditional romance that underlies the structure of the Jeeves/Wooster series, with Bertie fleeing marriage: while Madeline considers them similar, it would be hard to find a character more unlike Mervyn Keene than Bertram Wilberforce Wooster. Directly after Madeline tells this story Hilda comes in, having received a groveling letter from her fiancé, whom she decides to forgive—the day after tomorrow. This cynical reconciliation forms the first undercutting of *Mervyn Keene, Clubman*.

At the end, Bertie emphasizes the absurd number of romantic entanglements by listing them. The eight numbered names under "Sundered Hearts" are identical to those under "Reunited Hearts": "It came out exactly square. Not a single lose end left over. With a not unmanly sigh, for if there is one thing that is the dish of the decent-minded man, it is seeing misunderstandings between loving hearts cleared up, especially in the springtime, I laid down the writing materials." This harks back to Bertie's first encounter with Catsmeat's fiancée, Gertrude: "I was musing on these two young hearts in springtime and speculating with a not unmanly touch of sentiment on their chances of spearing the happy ending" (chap. 5). While Mervyn Keene comes to an unhappy end, Wodehouse's characters do not, and here the happy endings multiply along with all the other devices. Most importantly, the first love interest, Bertie's prospective reengagement to Madeline, also ends happily, with him remaining single.

BERTIE GETS SQUELCHED

Bertie's jealousy of and rebellion against Jeeves create strong plot conflict and effective delay in both *Thank You, Jeeves* and *Right Ho, Jeeves.* Indeed, Bertie becomes so uppity that by the end of the second novel, Jeeves takes drastic steps to teach his employer a lesson, and Bertie becomes more tractable thereafter. The resulting narratives form a transition between the short stories and the other novels, with the excellence of their plots deriving partly from the fact that they achieve something of the unity and sustained action of the short story within the longer form. Both introduce problems quickly and sustain them throughout, rather than using the gradual and episodic problem-solution structure more typical of the other novels.

In *Thank You, Jeeves,* the main problems are introduced across the early chapters. Bertie's banjolele playing and Jeeves's consequent resignation create the first; then Bertie meets Chuffy, who needs to sell Chuffnell Hall. Shortly after arriving in the country Bertie learns that Chuffy loves Pauline but has picked up a complex from a character in a play he has seen and cannot propose. Bertie turns to Jeeves:

> "What would you advise, Jeeves?"
>
> "I fear I have nothing to suggest at the moment, sir."
>
> "Come, come, Jeeves."
>
> "No, sir. The difficulty being essentially a psychological one, I find myself somewhat baffled. As long as the image of Lord Wotwotleigh persists in his lordship's consciousness, I fear there is nothing to be done."
>
> "Of course there is. Why this strange weakness, Jeeves? It

> is not like you. Obviously the fellow must be shoved over the brink." (Chap. 5)

Bertie is right that it is not like Jeeves to be baffled. In the stories he coped easily with complexes. But here the action must be delayed, so that Bertie can try to make Chuffy jealous by kissing Pauline—a gesture which considerably complicates the action. In general, as we saw with *The Code of the Woosters*, Jeeves is more apt to declare himself at a loss in the novels than in the stories. Jeeves does object to Bertie's plan to kiss Pauline, so we can at least assume it is Bertie's fault that the situation worsens.

We might suspect, however, that Jeeves has deliberately led Bertie into trouble by arranging that Stoker rather than Chuffy sees the kiss. The only hint of this is when Bertie learns that Chuffy is jealous after hearing that Bertie had been engaged to Pauline. Bertie comments: "I began to perceive that in arranging that Stoker and not he should be the witness of the recent embrace the guardian angel of the Woosters had acted dashed shrewdly" (chap. 6). We know the identity of the somewhat diabolical guardian angel of this particular Wooster.

By the middle of chapter 6, two of the three goals seem to be accomplished. Stoker wants to buy the Hall, and Chuffy is engaged to Pauline. Up to here the structure has been like that of a story, with a money problem solved and a couple engaged. Were Bertie to give up the banjolele now, the plot would make a longish short story.

To get the action going again, Wodehouse inserts a two-hour gap during which Bertie wanders around. A great deal happens offstage, all reported by Jeeves. As the chapter title declares, "Complications Set In": the two little boys have a fight, Stoker backs out of buying the Hall, Chuffy gets jealous of Bertie, and Stoker confines Pauline to the yacht, believing that she loves Bertie. All the upcoming action is now set up, with Jeeves's goals being to induce Stoker to buy the Hall and to give his consent to the Chuffy-Pauline match and to get Bertie to give up the banjolele. Other problems crop up along the way, all of them resulting from unpredictable actions: Pauline's swim ashore leads to a quarrel with Chuffy and to Stoker's locking Bertie up on the yacht;

more pranks by the children leave Bertie with no butter to remove the boot polish from his face; and Brinkley's drunken violence destroys Bertie's cottage (and banjolele). All these new elements, however, are twists in the same plot lines. Unlike the later novels, no major new premises appear late in the plot and no problems are solved gradually.

Jeeves's role in creating these complications is unclear, since there are all sorts of opportunities for him to push Bertie deeper into the gumbo: arranging for Stoker to see the kiss, encouraging Pauline to visit Bertie's cottage, alerting Stoker to Pauline's presence there. When he delivers Stoker's dinner invitation to Bertie, Jeeves says he has assured Stoker that, contrary to Sir Roderick's claim, Bertie is sane. Bertie thanks Jeeves, taking the invitation to be an olive branch. Yet Jeeves knows that Stoker thinks Pauline and Bertie are in love, and he must realize that by vouching for Bertie's sanity, he makes it more likely that Stoker will arrange a shotgun wedding. Thus Jeeves may be trying to land Bertie in an engagement with Pauline, from which he can rescue him. Certainly Jeeves has performed one major action without telling Bertie: he sent a wire to his valet friend Benstead during that same two-hour gap, when many important complicating actions occurred. Thus Jeeves has anticipated that he will solve the two main problems—Stoker's purchase of the Hall and consent to Chuffy and Pauline's wedding—from relatively early on. Hence nothing would stop him from getting Bertie more deeply into trouble, knowing that the final solution would get him out of the engagement to Pauline. Bertie would in turn be more likely to give up the banjolele.

Thank You, Jeeves delays Jeeves's solutions effectively, since the pair's feud here is worse than in any of the stories. Bertie behaves so stubbornly as to accept Jeeves's resignation:

> The Wooster blood boiled over. Circumstances of recent years have so shaped themselves as to place this blighter in a position which you might describe as that of a domestic Mussolini: but, forgetting this and sticking simply to cold facts, what *is* Jeeves, after all? A valet. A salaried attendant. (Chap. 1)

Bertie does not maintain this attitude, later telling Pauline that he looks upon Jeeves as an uncle. Still, despite being stunned by Jeeves's departure, he refuses to give up the banjolele.

The argument over the banjolele suggests the differences between Wodehouse's tactics in the short stories and in the novels. In a short story with his premise, Jeeves would have let Bertie know that he hates the thing—never having been reticent about criticizing Bertie's possessions. Here, however, Wodehouse needs a stronger clash to separate Jeeves from Bertie; hence he uses a more obviously obnoxious object and has Jeeves hold off objecting to it. When Bertie compounds the problem by deciding to take a cottage, Jeeves suddenly complains and quits.

We have seen that the series' narratives are comic inversions of both the Holmes stories and the romance. *Thank You, Jeeves* in particular is constructed like a romance in which a married couple quarrels, separates, and eventually reunites. Despite the fact that the two are feuding, however, there is relatively little acrimony after the initial clash.

Their encounters in Chufnell Regis are friendly. In the first, Jeeves delivers a message to Pauline, finding her and Bertie near the Hall. Instead of going back inside, as would seem the logical thing to do, Jeeves stays; he does not speak but clearly wants to give Bertie a chance to initiate a conversation. Immediately the relationship moves toward its old footing:

> A rummy thing. It had been my intention after exchanging these few civilities, to nod carelessly and leave the fellow. But it's so dashed difficult to break the habit of years. I mean to say, here was I and here was Jeeves, and a problem had been put up to me of just the type concerning which I had always been wont to seek his advice and counsel, and now something seemed to keep me rooted to the spot. And instead of being aloof and distant and passing on with the slight inclination of the head which, as I say, I had been planning, I found myself irresistibly impelled to consult him just as if there had been no rift at all. (Chap. 5)

Thus Bertie and Jeeves can work together on the romantic problems of Chuffy and Pauline. When Jeeves delivers Stoker's invitation, Bertie is cool as a result of having heard that Jeeves called him "mentally negligible." He becomes friendlier as the scene goes on, however, and by the end the two linger wistfully over the fact that the banjolele still separates them:

> "Your views on the instrument are unchanged?"
> "Yes, sir."
> "Ah, well! A pity we could not see eye to eye on that matter."
> "Yes, sir."
> "Still, it can't be helped. No hard feelings."
> "No, sir."
> "Unfortunate, though."
> "Most unfortunate, sir." (Chap. 11)

Despite this friendliness, however, Bertie later displays another symptom of his conflict with Jeeves. When Jeeves begins to propose the plan of putting boot polish on Bertie's face, Bertie assumes that Jeeves's mind has snapped:

> "Leave me, Jeeves," I said. "You've been having a couple."
> And I'm not sure that what cut me like a knife, more even than any agony of my fearful predicament, was not the realization that my original suspicions had been correct and that, after all these years, that superb brain had at last come unstuck. For, though I had tactfully affected to set all this talk of burnt cork and boot polish down to mere squiffiness, in my heart I was convinced that the fellow had gone his onion. (Chap. 12)

As usual, Jeeves explains things in reverse, mentioning the boot polish before revealing that he plans a minstrel disguise. Once Bertie hears this, he is impressed by the scheme. He fails to learn from such episodes, however, and jumps to the same conclusion in *Right Ho, Jeeves*—where he takes far longer to realize his error.

The only flaw in the narrative structure of *Thank You, Jeeves* comes with one of Jeeves's solutions. The telegram he asks Benstead to send does not entirely solve the problems. Upon reading it, Stoker decides to apologize to Sir Roderick but says nothing about buying the Hall or blessing Pauline and Chuffy's union. He does so only after Jeeves mentions Sir Roderick's arrest—an event Jeeves could not have anticipated. His plan succeeds largely through a lucky coincidence. Otherwise, however, *Thank You, Jeeves* handles its complicated action skillfully, and the next novel contains a flawless causal chain.

The opening of *Right Ho, Jeeves* emphasizes the plot's unity by having Bertie discuss where he should start. He begins with a bit of dialogue from late in chapter 2, then cuts off:

> I don't know if you have had the same experience, but the snag I always come up against when I'm telling a story is this dashed difficult problem of where to begin it. It's a thing you don't want to go wrong over, because one false step and you're sunk. I mean, if you fool about too long at the start, trying to establish atmosphere, as they call it, and all that sort of rot, you fail to grip and the customers walk out on you.
>
> Get off the mark, on the other hand, like a scalded cat, and your public is at a loss. It simply raises its eyebrows, and can't make out what you're talking about.
>
> And in opening my report of the complex case of Gussie Fink-Nottle, Madeline Bassett, my Cousin Angela, my Aunt Dahlia, my Uncle Thomas, young Tuppy Glossop, and the cook, Anatole, with the above spot of dialogue, I see that I have made the second of these two floaters.
>
> I shall have to hark back a bit. And taking it all for all, and weighing this against that, I suppose the affair may be said to have had its inception, if inception is the word I want, with that visit of mine to Cannes. If I hadn't gone to Cannes, I shouldn't have met the Bassett or bought that white mess jacket, and Angela wouldn't have met her shark, and Aunt Dahlia wouldn't have played baccarat.
>
> Yes, most decidedly, Cannes was the *point d'appui*.

Right away there are references to all the major characters and hints as to three of the plot's seven major problems: the jacket starts a feud between Bertie and Jeeves, the shark causes Angela to break off her engagement with Tuppy, and Dahlia's gambling jeopardizes *Milday's*

Boudoir. The explanation of these problems, however, stretches over the first portion of the book. Gussie's inability to propose to Madeline comes up first, and Jeeves says he is working on that. Next he discovers the jacket, which causes what seems at first to be the standard chilliness between him and Bertie. So far the situation recalls the stories' set-ups, particularly that of "The Inferiority Complex of Old Sippy." Indeed, our attention is called to this similarity when Jeeves compares Gussie's problem to Sippy's, and Bertie says Gussie has a "newt complex." Soon, however, the two problems merge as Bertie concludes that Jeeves has lost his touch and takes on Gussie's case himself. Their feud creates a long delay before Jeeves acts to clear up any of the problems. It also causes him to conceive an implicit goal: to teach Bertie a lesson and regain control over him (with a spot of revenge as well).

Bertie thinks he has solved Gussie's problem by sending him to Brinkley Court. He also gets Gussie to take his place as prize-giver at the grammar school—the only goal he achieves in the book, though at the cost of getting engaged to Madeline. Bertie soon learns of the rift between Tuppy and Angela, and when he rushes to Brinkley to help, Aunt Dahila reveals that she lost the money for *Milady's Boudoir* at Cannes and must get more from her husband, Tom. By now, Bertie has three explicit goals, and Jeeves has two additional implicit ones. Bertie's attempts to solve his problems create new ones: Madeline concludes that he has proposed to her, Angela gets engaged to Gussie, Tuppy becomes violently jealous of Gussie, and Anatole threatens to quit, rendering Dahlia's task of getting money from Tom more difficult. These complications appear gradually, in chapters 11 to 20.

Bertie's rebellion is more intense in *Right Ho, Jeeves* than in *Thank You, Jeeves*, providing an unusually strong narrative conflict, plus an excellent motivation for Jeeves's delaying his solution. During the introduction of the problems and the twists caused by Bertie's blunders, Jeeves obeys Bertie and does not attempt his own solution. Amazingly, however, he works out the plan that will solve all these problems even before some of them arise—and hence there is considerable need for a strong delaying device. Jeeves proposes his fire-alarm scheme to Bertie in chapter 9, less than a third of the way into the book, and when Bertie scoffs, he simply waits for Bertie to get desperate enough to try it. Initially he says only that the ideas will reconcile Angela and Tuppy, but he presumably also intends it to help Aunt Dahlia and punish Bertie. Later Jeeves uses the same plan to solve the Madeline/Gussie and Anatole problems. The fact that this scheme solves all the problems (except the mess jacket) simultaneously is emphasized at Bertie's return from his eighteen-mile bike ride: "I had left Brinkley Court a stricken home, with hearts bleeding wherever you looked, and I had returned to find it a sort of earthly paradise." As he remarks to Jeeves, " 'The place is positively stiff with happy endings' " (chap. 23). The ending Jeeves arranges for Bertie is not so happy, however. Jeeves sticks to the letter of his promise not to ask Bertie to get rid of the jacket, but he disposes of it nonetheless. Bertie reluctantly gives in, and they are, just barely, reconciled.

Because he uses this single all-embracing solution, Jeeves is relatively inactive through much of the book. Thus his offstage activities are largely assumed; for the most part all we have to realize retrospectively at the end is that he has known everything all along. Still, the conflict with Bertie makes Jeeves withhold a few things which we might infer. We learn, for example, that the real point of his fire-alarm scheme is to get Bertie to bicycle to the house where the servants' dance is being held. Thus he must have planned from the start to execute the scheme on that specific night. The party is first mentioned on the second night of the pair's stay at Brinkley, the night before the party itself. *Right Ho, Jeeves*'s short time-scheme makes it plausible that Jeeves could anticipate all these factors. But to what degree did he manipulate events in order to time them to come to a head at the right moment? By the time Bertie consents to the fire-alarm scheme (around 9:00 p.m.), the servants have presumably departed to the dance and Jeeves therefore has already obtained the key from Seppings. It also seems likely that he is eavesdropping in the garden just before Bertie comes out after confronting his new fiancée, Madeline. Jeeves chooses the optimal moment to make himself available to help Bertie, though he claims he ran into Bertie by accident. We must also assume that he has planted the bicycle and the key. Similarly, he must have made sure that all the house's doors would be locked after everyone ran out in response to the fire alarm. This action is hinted at when Gussie tells Aunt Dahlia that the doors are locked:

> "What? Who shut them?"
> "I don't know."
> I advanced a theory.
> "The wind?"
> Aunt Dahlia's eye met mine.
> "Don't try me too high," she begged. "Not now, precious."
> And, indeed, even as I spoke, it did strike me that the night was pretty still. (Chap. 22)

After this novel, Jeeves's offstage actions are far simpler, since he has less reason to withhold information from Bertie.

The reverse side of Jeeves's delaying of his solutions is Bertie's stubbornness. When he asserts himself over the mess jacket, the plot seems off to a familiar sort of start. Then, however, Bertie hears that Jeeves is sending Gussie to the costume ball in a Mephistopheles costume to embolden him to propose to Madeline. Bertie concludes that Jeeves is losing his grip:

> Here was Jeeves making heavy weather about me wearing a perfectly ordinary white mess jacket, a garment not only *tout ce qui'il y a des chic,* but absolutely *de rigueur,* and in the same breath, as you might say, inciting Gussie Fink-Nottle to be a blot on the London scene in scarlet tights. Ironical, what? (Chap. 2)

This use of two items of clothing, one which Bertie loves and the other which he destests, starts the narrative conflict with a neat parallelism; note also that Bertie later decides that Gussie does need emboldening in order to propose—though his all-too-successful method is to slip gin into his pal's juice.

Bertie dismisses Jeeves's plan rudely: "I consider that of all the dashed silly, drivelling ideas I ever heard in my puff this is the most blithering and futile. It won't work. Not a chance." He orders Jeeves to leave Gussie's problem to him. Bertie also condescends to Jeeves shamelessly; after dispatching his disastrous telegram, "Lay off the sausages. Avoid the ham" (based on a plan that eventually drives Anatole to give notice), he tells Jeeves: "No doubt you realize now that it would pay you to study my methods" (chap. 6). Jeeves responds blandly, but the motif of his revenge comes up obliquely; when Bertie says he will make Gussie do the prize-giving at the grammar school, he mentions his own address to the girls' school in "Bertie Changes His Mind." There Jeeves taught Bertie a lesson by subjecting him to a traumatic experience; he uses the same tactic in this novel.

Bertie becomes more rebellious at Brinkley, insisting on handling the rift between Tuppy and Angela himself, over Dahlia's objections. The clash comes to its height as Bertie dresses for dinner and Jeeves outlines his fire-alarm scheme. Bertie is shocked: "Remembering some of the swift ones he had pulled in the past, I shrank with horror from the spectacle of his present ineptitude. Or is it ineptness? I mean this frightful disposition of his to stick straws in his hair and talk like a perfect ass" (chap. 9). Jeeves points out that Bertie's schemes have not always worked out—the first time that he has stated such an opinion so baldly: "There was a silence—rather a throbbing one—during which I put on my waistcoat in a marked manner." Bertie then describes his own scheme of advising Tuppy not to eat in order to show Angela he is pining. Jeeves points out, "I fear Miss Angela will merely attribute Mr Glossop's abstinence to indigestion, sir." Bertie is rattled but affects to pass it off.

Despite the deep rift between the pair, Wodehouse insists upon the "romance" formula by paralleling Jeeves and Bertie's quarrel to the lovers' tiffs. When Tuppy describes his estrangement from Angela, Bertie tries to talk him into apologizing, saying that Angela is probably heartbroken. When Tuppy replies that she does not look it, Bertie suggests, "Wearing the mask, no doubt. Jeeves does that when I assert my authority" (chap. 8).

Surprisingly, Jeeves makes the first conciliatory move by deciding, against his better judgment, to obey Bertie's order to lace Gussie's orange juice with gin. The reason for his action is not apparent, since if Bertie's plan works, Jeeves will have to admit that Bertie was right and he was wrong. Perhaps Jeeves is being fair-minded, despite his ruthlessness, and is simply willing to give Bertie's plan a try. More likely, however, Jeeves, recognizing that this is the worst rift he has ever had with Bertie, wants to get back in Bertie's good graces sufficiently for Bertie to try his fire-alarm scheme. If so, he succeeds, since from this point on the two collaborate more closely, with Bertie once more confiding in Jeeves—though it is some time before he despairs and agrees to try Jeeves's plan.

Inevitably, however, the moment comes when Bertie has gotten himself into such a tangle that, when he runs into Jeeves, he begins to capitulate: "I had formed the opinion that he had lost his grip and was no longer the force that he had been, but was it not possible, I asked myself, that I might be mistaken?" He decides to take Jeeves "into consultation" (chap. 21), then agrees to try the fire-alarm scheme, on condition that Jeeves not demand the mess jacket as a reward. Here Bertie tries to change the balance of power between them by inducing Jeeves to achieve Bertie's goals but not his own. Jeeves, however, being the force for narrative closure, will decide what problems are wrapped up and how to do it. Bertie cannot enforce his demand, as the reader is well aware. Jeeves must change his method of eliminating the offending garment, but he gets his way.

Bertie's rebellion here is so extreme that Jeeves squelches it once and for all, taking revenge in the process by basing his solution on an eighteen-mile bike ride Bertie must make at night without a lamp. When Bertie points out that he may have an accident, Jeeves inadvertently smiles, though he passes his amusement off as being occasioned by his recollection of a joke about two bicyclists being killed in an accident. This anecdote hints at Jeeves's reaction to the success of his revenge plot, though Bertie simply assumes that Jeeeves really finds the story amusing and accuses him of being morbid. (The fact that Jeeves comes up with this joke so quickly to explain his ill-timed smile—whether he remembers it or even makes it up on the spot—is one of the series' best indications of his intelligence.)

Before looking at Bertie's final capitulation to Jeeves, we should examine a pattern in the narrative which gives perhaps the subtlest sign of Bertie's rebelliousness. In *Right Ho, Jeeves,* Bertie uses the same sorts of schemes and depends upon the same sorts of coincidences that had characterized Jeeves's solutions in the earliest stories. Bertie in effect duels with Jeeves by trying to imitate Jeevesian solutions, but Jeeves invariably surpasses Bertie in the complexity of his schemes.

Jeeves bases his initial plan of sending Gussie to the costume ball on psychology: in a bright costume Gussie will have nerve enough to propose to Madeline. This scheme fails due to unforseen bad luck, as both Jeeves and Gussie tell Bertie. Bertie still, however, scoffs at Jeeves's incompetence. He manages to get Gussie together with Madeline, since it turns out that Madeline will be visiting Brinkley Court: " 'Gussie,' I said, smiling paternally, 'it was a lucky day for you when Bertram Wooster interested himself in your affairs. As I foresaw from the start, I can fix everything. This afternoon you shall go to Brinkley Court, an honoured guest' " (chap. 6). Bertie's methods are the opposite of Jeeves's: while he claims he "foresaw from the start" what would happen, he actually can help only through a lucky coincidence. Gussie tries to point this out, but Bertie attributes everything to his own genius:

> "What a bit of luck this Travers woman turning out to be your aunt."
>
> "I don't know what you mean, turning out to be my aunt. She has been my aunt all along."
>
> "I mean, how extraordinary that it should be your aunt that Madeline's going to stay with."
>
> "Not at all. She and my cousin Angela are close friends. At Cannes she was with us all the time."

The early portion of the plot depends on this extraordinary coincidence of Gussie's happening to be in love with the same woman Bertie met at Cannes. Wodehouse turns this coincidence into an advantage, not by hiding it but, as usual, by flaunting it.

At Brinkley, Tuppy tells Bertie how Angela had criticized him for being overweight and commented on how he puffed when climbing stairs. He then asks if he should sigh when he meets Angela. Bertie comments, "She would think you were puffing." Thus Bertie has some elementary foresight of a Jeevesian kind, yet in formulating his plan to have Tuppy refuse food, he overlooks a similar problem: that Angela will attribute Tuppy's abstinence to indigestion. Bertie puts this scheme for helping Tuppy and Angela in competition with Jeeves's, and on the face of it, the two solutions are similar, each being based on a clichéd notion of how people would react in a given situation. Indeed, both Jeeves and Bertie later extend their plans to cover a whole set of different characters and problems, with Bertie advising Tuppy, Gussie, and Dahlia to fast. His plan fails because it is again based on coincidence: there could be many reasons why they would refuse dinner. Moreover, when all three "happen" to refuse the same meal, Anatole gives notice, feeling that his culinary talents are not appreciated.

Jeeves's fire-alarm scheme, however, though seemingly based on a similar idea (that an alarm would cause Tuppy to rescue Angela and Gussie to rescue Madeline), is actually more complex than he lets on to Bertie. The real components of his scheme are based on *apparent* coincidence. He "happens" to find a bike Bertie can ride to fetch the key, and he later "happens" to find the key on the window sill. Jeeves's scheme really involves no coincidence at all. The same is true of the scorching of the mess jacket, which he passes off as an accident: "I was careless enough to leave the hot instrument upon it." Neither the reader nor Bertie believes him, but Bertie must knuckle under.

In the final scene, Bertie is so dazzled by the spate of solutions that he cannot even remonstrate with Jeeves about the bike ride. Jeeves is nominally respectful, but his greeting is actually the most insolent thing he ever says to Bertie:

> "Good evening, sir. I was informed that you had returned. I trust you had an enjoyable ride."
>
> At any other moment, a crack like that would have woken the fiend in Bertram Wooster. I barely noticed it. I was intent on getting to the bottom of this mystery.

Jeeves then reveals that he has ruined the mess jacket while ironing it, and Bertie, though experiencing a rush of "generous wrath," reluctantly surrenders: "there was nothing to be gained by g.w. now." Here

Jeeves reasserts the control he had initially gained in "Jeeves Takes Charge" (where he gave the checked suit away before Bertie told him to do so.) *Right Ho, Jeeves* is the last narrative in which Bertie challenges Jeeves's authority. From now on, he will be content to remain the Watson figure.

JEEVES MAKES A MISTAKE

One unlikely way of creating narrative delay would be to posit that Jeeves is capable of error. This tactic, used only once, proved effective in renewing the series' liveliness. After the relatively uninventive repetitions of the stories and novels of the late 1950s and 1960s, the departures from old formulas in *Much Obliged, Jeeves* are startling—especially given that Wodehouse wrote it at age eighty-nine, when he could have exploited his secure publishing situation by mining the old vein. Yet he apparently thought it might be his last book, at least in this series,[7] and he may have sought to make it distinctive by including a number of striking events: Jeeves's literally saving Bertie's life when he is nearly hit by a taxi, the series' only scene at the Junior Ganymede, the revelation of Jeeves's first name, and a plot constructed around Jeeves's first serious error in judgment.[8]

One reason why the originality and complexity of *Much Obliged, Jeeves* has not received much comment may be that the book contains less humor than do the other novels. Every scene has funny moments, and some scenes, like Jeeves's description of the political debate, are quite risible. The book's relative solemnity does not mean, however, that there are fewer interesting elements here than in earlier books. Rather, the action of *Much Obliged, Jeeves* is often more dramatic than funny, because Wodehouse uses Jeeves's first serious error of judgement to create a very strong central narrative conflict.

Much Obliged, Jeeves begins with the standard ploy of having Aunt Dahlia call Bertie at breakfast time, demanding his help for his old pal Ginger Winship, who is running for office. The plot resembles that of *Stiff Upper Lip, Jeeves*; again the pal begins by wanting to marry an ex-fiancée of Bertie's (Gussie and Madeline in the earlier novel, Ginger and Florence Craye here). Bertie tries to help but part-way through finds that the pal has found another love (Emerald Stoker, Magnolia

Glendennon); Bertie then faces reengagement to the rejected fiancée. He also has to help another pal financially so that he can get married (Stinker in *Stiff Upper Lip, Jeeves,* Tuppy in *Much Obliged, Jeeves*). The villians are also similar: L. P. Runkle, like Sir Watkyn Bassett, collects old silver. Moreover, Runkle's friendship with Sidcup creates a specific parallel with Bassett, and the scene in *Much Obliged, Jeeves,* where Runkle assumes Bertie is stealing his camera echoes the episode in the antique shop in *The Code of the Woosters,* where Bassett and Spode think Bertie is escaping with the cow-creamer. Once again Wodehouse flaunts the repetition by having Bertie state that the camera incident "reminded me of my first encounter with Sir Watkyn Bassett" (chap. 5). Later, Sidcup becomes jealous upon seeing Bertie take a gnat out of Madeline's eye, recalling the misunderstanding in *The Code of the Woosters* when Madeline got upset upon seeing Gussie taking a fly out of Stiffy's.

These elements give a different impression in *Much Obliged, Jeeves,* however, due to the daring idea of having the Club Book stolen. Because the Book has featured prominently in the series and because membership in the Junior Ganymede means so much to Jeeves, this theft is far more striking than that of the amber statuette in *Stiff Upper Lip, Jeeves,* an object which is not of much intrinsic interest.

In the opening scene, Bertie and Jeeves quarrel over the Club Book, for which Jeeves has just composed seven new pages on Bertie's misadventures in *Stiff Upper Lip, Jeeves.* Bertie suggests that a "man of ill-will" might steal the Book for blackmail purposes, and he even mentions Bingley as a possible thief. For a change, his opinions are accurate, while Jeeves errs in denying that such a thing could happen. Thus, though their argument seems to follow the standard opening that simply creates some chilliness between the pair, it actually sets up a systematic reversal of roles that will continue to the end.

Bertie emphasizes the situation's uniqueness when, after hearing of the theft of the Book, he asks Aunt Dahlia to break the news to Jeeves:

> Halfway there a thought occurred to me. I said:
> "How about Jeeves?"
> "What about him?"

> "We ought to spare his feelings as far as possible. I repeatedly warned him that the club book was high-level explosive and ought not to be in existence. What if it fell into the wrong hands, I said, and he said it couldn't possibly fall into the wrong hands. And now it has fallen into about the wrongest hands it could have fallen into. I haven't the heart to say 'I told you so' and watch him writhe with shame and confusion. You see, up till now Jeeves has always been right. His agony on finding that he has at last made a floater will be frightful. I shouldn't wonder if he might not swoon. I can't face him. You'll have to tell him."
>
> "Yes, I'll do it."
>
> "Try to break it gently." (Chap. 10)

This speech also suggests how far the Jeeves/Bertie relationship has come since Bertie's rebellious phase, when he gloated over Jeeve's supposed errors. Now he gets upset and imagines an impossibly exaggerated reaction from Jeeves. (In the event, Jeeves does not swoon, of course, but his uncharacteristically strong response is to declare himself "shocked and astounded" [chap. 11]. He wastes no time, however, in retrieving the Book.)

The scene leading up to the theft of the Book is one of the most dramatic—and least funny—in the series. A taxi nearly runs Bertie down outside the Junior Ganymede, and Jeeves, who has been lunching there (and presumably inserting his new material into the Book), pulls him to safety. Though Jeeves has aided Bertie in many important ways, this is the only time he literally saves his life, and that act helps to balance the fact that Jeeves is seriously mistaken about the theft of the Club Book. Ultimately he retrieves the Book, and the ending involves a unique reversal, as Jeeves rewards Bertie by destroying his eighteen pages. (He has even done so before Bertie asks him to, just as he has often taken his own reward before receiving permission.) Yet Jeeves never really defeats Bingley, and in the last scene he and Bertie deplore the fact that Bingley will still profit by the election through his bets on Mrs. McCorkadale.

Why does Wodehouse let Bingley, as villainous a figure as he ever created, escape punishment? The answer lies in the destruction of

Jeeves's contribution to the Book. Even if Bingley were put out of the way, there could be other blackmailers lurking about ready to steal the Book and threaten to reveal Bertie's misadventures to Aunt Agatha—just what Bertie fears in his initial quarrel with Jeeves. To make that threat vivid to the reader, I think, Wodehouse left Bingley (the only thief and blackmailer we know of in the Junior Ganymede) on the loose. Jeeves's decision to break the Club's rules by tampering with the Book (and thus to face expulsion) must be strongly motivated.

The one respect in which Bertie's prediction fails is that Bingley uses the Book not to blackmail him but to profit on the election. In the scene at the Junior Ganymede, Jeeves says that Ginger's valet has contributed eleven pages on him—exactly what Bertie has had himself up to that same day. Thus we must assume that there is plenty of lively material to prejudice Ginger's chances in the election. The fact that Ginger, not Bertie, becomes Bingley's target is crucial in the light of Jeeves's error. That error is not nearly as crucial as it seems, for even had Jeeves never been a member of the Club, the theft of the Book could occur (and another valet in Bertie's employ could have contributed). While Jeeves errs in his confidence concerning the Books's safety and presumably could have prevented its theft had he foreseen it, he does not actually cause the central problem.

For the first time, the Club Book is the source of a central problem as well as of an important solution. In the Book Jeeves finds the information needed to blackmail Runkle into giving Tuppy the money he needs to marry Angela. Moreover, the damaging entry on Runkle was written by his former valet, Bingley. Thus Jeeves reverses his mistake by turning the villains' tactics against them. Since Jeeves uses the Book's blackmail potential to extort money from Runkle (for Tuppy's benefit), his final willingness to renounce the Book and, implicitly, the Junior Ganymede seems important. As we have seen, Jeeves often uses amoral means, but here he seems willing to give up his access to blackmail information, reaffirming his permanent domestic situation with Bertie.

That is, of course, the implication of his destruction of Bertie's pages: they are unnecessary, since the post as Bertie's valet will never be open and hence no one will have to consult that entry. Conversely, if

Jeeves is expelled, he will not suffer from being cut off from the Book, since he will never need to check on prospective employers. (The American version ends with a passage, suggested by Peter Schwed, which makes this more explicit.) Again, these implications may reflect the fact that Wodehouse assumed *Much Obliged, Jeeves* would be the last Jeeves/Wooster novel and wanted to reaffirm the pair's relationship as well as to tie up the last dangling engagements. By the way, we might suspect at the end that the resourceful Jeeves will avoid getting expelled from the Club: he can always blame the Books's mutilation on Bingley.

Though Jeeves errs concerning the Club Book, he works more actively to solve problems than in any of the narratives since *Jeeves and the Feudal Spirit,* and he depends less on luck. The main piece of luck is Ginger's decision to try to lose the election. This switch would solve the problem of the Book's theft, even if Bingley still had it in his possession. Indeed, Jeeves's retrieval of the Book prolongs the election problem, since his refusal to make the entry on Ginger public means that Ginger may involuntarily win. Still, Jeeves does prevent that outcome.

Of the four major problems, Jeeves solves three. Bertie lays these problems out early in chapter 16 in list form:

> *a.* How am I to get out of marrying Madeline Bassett?
> *b.* How am I to restore the porringer to L. P. Runkle before the constabulary come piling on the back of my neck?
> *c.* How is the ancestor to extract that money from Runkle?
> *d.* How is Ginger to marry Magnolia Glendennon while betrothed to Florence?

This summary ignores the fact that if Ginger marries Magnolia, Florence will presumably agree to marry Bertie—a premise set up during Bertie and Jeeves's stroll to the Junior Ganymede. So far all Jeeves has done is to retrieve the Book and talk Dahlia out of using the porringer to extort money from Runkle. He ultimately solves problems (b) and (c) by giving her information from the Book to blackmail Runkle. Jeeves solves (d) by making the obvious suggestion that Ginger lose the debate and hence the election and Florence's love. It is not clear how Jeeves intended to get Bertie out of marrying Florence, but luckily they remain engaged for a record brief period—less than a page, until Runkle tells Florence that Bertie is a thief. Sidcup solves (a) by deciding to retain his title and not to run for the House of Commons. It is possible, however, that Jeeves throws or arranges for someone to throw the potato that hits Sidcup and causes him to change his mind. There is no direct hint at Jeeves's intervention, but Dahlia's response to this news places undue emphasis on how neatly things have worked out, and Bertie describes it in terms which hint that his "guardian angel" may have been Jeeves:

> A look almost of awe came into the ancestor's face.
> "How right you were," she said, "when you told me once that you had faith in your star. I've lost count of the number of times you've been definitely headed for the altar with apparently no hope of evading the firing squad, and every time something has happened which enabled you to writhe out of it. It's uncanny."
> She would, I think, have gone deeper into the matter, for already she had begun to pay a marked tribute to my guardian angel, who, she said, plainly knew his job from soup to nuts, but at this moment Seppings appeared and asked her if she would have a word with Jeeves, and she went out to have it. (Chap. 16)

It is tempting to think that some of the old complexity lent by Jeeves's offstage manipulations reappears in this scene. At any rate, *Much Obliged, Jeeves* is hardly a tired book, despite the fact that it was published to celebrate its author's ninetieth birthday and seems to have been designed to close off a series that had already been going for fifty-five years.

7

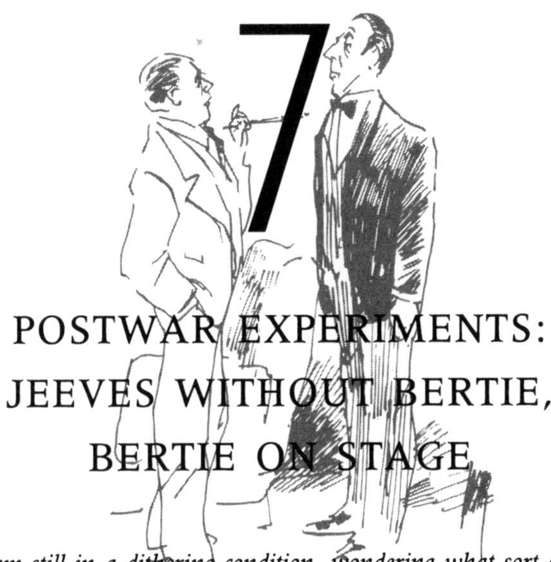

POSTWAR EXPERIMENTS: JEEVES WITHOUT BERTIE, BERTIE ON STAGE

I am still in a dithering condition, wondering what sort of a novel to write next. I wonder if I can still go on dishing out earls and butlers

—WODEHOUSE TO HESKETH PEARSON, DECEMBER, 25, 1950

A NEW CONTEXT FOR JEEVES

Though most modern readers think of Bertie Wooster as at least as important as Jeeves, for most of Wodehouse's career Jeeves was his most famous and lucrative character. While many of the short stories, especially in the middle period, did not have Jeeves's name in their titles, the four collections did. When *Cosmopolitan* started a series of late-period stories in September of 1929, it announced: "Beginning a group of stories which bring back *Jeeves*—butler, guide and mentor to Bertie Wooster." "Jeeves" appears in larger type than either Bertie's or Wodehouse's names, though in smaller print than the title. By the next issue (October), the announcement prints the valet's name in larger type than even the story's title, "The Borrowed Dog." From that point on, Jeeves's name was usually part of the title (for example, "Jeeves and the Love That Purifies"), and Wodehouse added it to some of the earlier stories in their book reprints. In early 1934, an executive of Little, Brown told Wodehouse that the company expected *Thank You, Jeeves* to outsell *Heavy Weather*: "We shall be much disappointed if the sale is not considerably larger than that of the other book. The fact that this is the first novel about your best-liked character should help."[1] That character was clearly Jeeves, not Bertie, since later that year Little, Brown brought out *Brinkley Court* (American title of *Right Ho, Jeeves*) with the blurb "Another Novel about Jeeves" on the cover.

Wodehouse recognized Jeeves's popularity. In 1926, when he incorporated in the United States in an attempt to avoid personal income tax, he called the company "Jeeves Dramatics, Inc."; a similar firm in England bore the name "Jeeves, Ltd."[2] Wodehouse also made money off Jeeves during the 1930s through the sale of motion-picture rights to 20th Century-Fox. In 1935, Fox bought the film rights to *Thank You, Jeeves*, plus a one-year option on the earlier Jeeves books; the deal also included the right for the company's staff writers to do other scripts using Jeeves.[3] *Thank you, Jeeves* appeared in 1936, starring Arthur Treacher as Jeeves and David Niven as Bertie; the plot was nothing like that of the original book. The film was a mild success, mainly on the basis of Treacher's performance, and Fox made another film, *Step Lively, Jeeves* (1937). This time Bertie did not appear, and the scriptwriters wrote an original plot not even nominally based on any Wodehouse work. This film was, to my knowledge, the first time that Jeeves appeared without Bertie, and perhaps this precedent prepared the way for Wodehouse to try a similar ploy in placing Jeeves in a plausible postwar situation.

After the war, Wodehouse evidently continued to think of Jeeves as his most lucrative character. In 1955 he wrote (implausibly) to his step-grandson that Sax Rohmer's character Fu Manchu had been sold to a film company for four million dollars: "Isn't it amazing! I could hardly believe it, but apparently it's true. You never know what's going to happen in this writing game. I wish someone would offer me even a measly two million for Jeeves."[4] No one did, but the BBC's mid-1960s "World of Wooster" television series boosted Wodehouse's income and convinced him that Bertie could also be a viable stage and screen character.

The interval after the war, when he used Jeeves without Bertie, produced relatively minor works in the series, but it should not be dismissed altogether. If we imagine Jeeves and Phipps, that slightly disguised version of Jeeves, as being nonseries characters, the books and plays of this period become more interesting. They are comparable to Wodehouse's many nonseries comic novels. Moreover, they reveal a great deal about his attempts to cope with his postwar situation.

Throughout his career Wodehouse set his narratives in the kinds of locales with which he was intimately familiar: boys' schools, London, British country houses, Greenwich Village, the New York theatrical world, ocean liners, and French resort towns. When he needed a plausible postwar setting in which people could still afford butlers, he turned to Beverly Hills and the Hollywood filmmaking community. Both the "Jeeves version" of *Spring Fever* and *The Old Reliable* take place there. Jacob Glutz, a producer at the Medulla-Oblongata-Glutz studio, figures in both; he is probably modeled on Louis B. Mayer, Wodehouse's boss at MGM in the 1930s. The former owner of the house which forms the setting for both, Mexican film star Carmen Flores, may have been based on Lupe Velez, who committed suicide in 1944 after affairs with Gary Cooper and others; the idea of her scandalous diary was most likely derived from the one kept by Mary Astor.

The third paragraph of *The Old Reliable* establishes that an English butler is a status symbol in this land of wealth:

> This was a butler, an unmistakably English butler, tall, decorous and dignified.... Everything in Mrs. Cork's domain spoke eloquently of wealth and luxury, but nothing more eloquently than the presence on the premises of this Phipps. In Beverly Hills, as a general thing, the householder employs a "couple," who prove totally incompetent and leave the following week, to be succeeded by another couple, equally subhuman. A Filipino butler indicates a certain modest degree of stepping out. An English butler means magnificence. Nobody can go higher than that.

Such butlers are scarce, however, as Bill points out to Phipps: "You could get a job anywhere. Walk into any house in Beverly Hills, and they'll lay down the red carpet for you" (chap. 1). As a result, they do well for themselves; we discover that Phipps has a car: "It is a very impoverished butler in Beverly Hills who does not own his own natty little roadster" (chap. 21). By the end of both the play and the novel, Phipps has a movie contract to do butler roles, so he presumably makes even more money.

Yet even in the Beverly Hills setting, remote as it is from Wodehouse's British country houses, there is a hint of nostalgia for the old subject matter. In *Spring Fever*, Phipps/Jeeves is the only English character, but *The Old Reliable* introduces a minor comic figure, Lord Topham, as Joe's rival for Kay. Topham is described upon his first appearance: "A long, lean young man, who appeared to have giraffe blood in him, came in carrying a bag of golf clubs. Phipps greeted him with respectful devotion" (chap. 4). Topham represents the British upper class, acting as a sort of token substitute for Bertie—a passing nod to the feudal spirit, which has apparently become a thing of the past.

Guy Bolton helped revive the feudal spirit by providing Wodehouse with the idea of an impoverished peer turning bookie. The result was *Come On, Jeeves*, in which Wodehouse adjusted his traditional subject matter to the postwar situation in England. Once again we have a country house, Rowcester Abbey, but it is no idyllic, sunny estate like Blandings; instead, its owner, Bill, wants to unload it on a rich American woman. (The emphasis on its dampness and leaky roof leads to one of the few Wodehouse novels where the weather is rainy and gloomy.)

The play begins with the entrance of Lord and Lady Carmoyle, or Rory and Monica. He is, as the stage directions state, "the sort of man who, twenty years ago, was one of the Drones Club Boys but has now, perforce, bowed to the inevitable. He is a shopwalker at Harrods." He and Monica immediately mention Bill's troubles in sustaining ancestral home, and Rory comments: "Why doesn't Bill get a job like the rest of the poverty-ridden peerage? Nowadays the House of the Lords is practically empty, except on evenings and bank holidays." Rory is an excellent comic creation, perhaps the best element in both the play and *Ring for Jeeves*; the reference to the Drones Club suggests that, beyond trying to find a plausible situation for Jeeves, Wodehouse may have been seeking a postwar replacement for the Drones type as well. Indeed, in *Ring for Jeeves*, Bill Rowcester is a member of the Drones, but he is beset by larger financial worries than had plagued the young men of the 1930s stories—whose main problem was usually how to touch Oofy Prosser for a tenner.

The postwar worries of the rich might even affect Bertie someday. In the play, Jeeves explains that he is working for Bill because Bertie has gone off to a school "designed to teach the aristocracy to fend for itself. Mr. Wooster, while at present financially sound, feels that it is prudent to build for the future." He is therefore studying shoe cleaning, sock darning, bed making, and elementary cooking. Upon hearing this, Rory remarks, "Well, I'm blowed. One doesn't realize how far the social revolution had gone" (act 1). At the end of *Come On, Jeeves*, Jeeves announces that Bertie has been expelled from the school: "In his letter he says that, should the revolution come, he will have no course but to emigrate." This line may suggest that Wodehouse was leaving open the option of moving the Jeeves/Wooster series to America and placing the pair in a plausible postwar situation there. By the time he finished *Ring for Jeeves*, however, Wodehouse was once more in a stable publishing situation, at Simon and Schuster, and he may have felt more confident about resuming the old formula; there Jeeves simply says of Bertie's expulsion that "the scandal has affected him deeply. I feel that my place is at his side" (chap. 22).

Why has Jeeves taken a job with such an impecunious peer? The implication is that most of the upper class is now impoverished, and he did not have much choice. Indeed, Jeeves states as much in explaining to Captain Biggar that Bill is broke:

> "I fear that your long residence in the East has rendered you not quite abreast of the changed conditions prevailing in your native land. Socialistic legislation has sadly depleted the resources of England's hereditary aristocracy. We are living now in what is known as the Welfare State, which means—

> broadly—that everybody is completely destitute." (*Ring for Jeeves*, Chap. 11)

This speech is the most explicit statement in Wodehouse's fiction of his view of the postwar situation in England. Although it is an over-simplified version of that situation—and we must remember that Wodehouse never visited England after 1939—it is also clearly a subject that bothered him considerably.

Wodehouse identified the prewar serving class closely with his own writing, and its disappearance was one of the main features of postwar society that worried him. As his various essays on servants written after the war indicate, he felt that the new breed of servants was a pale shadow of the butlers, cooks, and others that he remembered from his youth. He portrays a pair of young, slovenly servants in *Ring for Jeeves*: Colonel Wyvern's pimply sixteen-year-old butler Bulstrode and his insolent, incompetent fifteen-year-old cook. Wyvern broods on Bulstrode after scolding him for his various deficiencies:

> In the golden age before the social revolution, he was thinking, a gaping, pimpled tripper over rugs like this Bulstrode would have been a lowly hall-boy, if that. It revolted a Tory of the old school's finer feelings to have to regard such a blot on the Southmoltonshire scene in the sacred light of a butler. (Chap. 16)

Wyvern goes on to compare this stripling to Jeeves, "a butler in the fine old tradition of his youth."

Wyvern's opinions imply that Jeeves is an anachronism in the post-"social revolution" world. How then did Wodehouse attempt to fit his most famous character into this new society? Early in *Ring for Jeeves*, Rory (now a floorwalker at "Harrige's") characterizes his brother-in-law, Bill, as lacking drive, "the sort of drive you see so much of at Harrige's. The will to win, I suppose you might call it. Napoleon had it. I have it, Bill hasn't" (chap. 2). This opinion is not without foundation, since Bill tends to lapse into despair at each new adverse event. He requires someone to push him into action, and that someone is usually Jeeves. Initially Monica and Rory make much of the fact that

Bill seems able to afford a staff of servants, but given the fact that Jeeves succeeds in solving both Bill's financial and romantic difficulties, it turns out that he is not a drain on his employer's funds but an actual moneymaker. This is the first time in the series that Jeeves has to supply his employer with the basic necessities in this way, but he proves as adept at this as in the other problems he has tackled.

It is also interesting that at one point, when things are looking particularly bleak, Jeeves offers to work without payment. Bill has just said he will have to pay his gambling debt to Captain Biggar by monthly installments and cut back on his budget. He tells Jeeves:

> "You'll have to go, you know, to start with. I can't possibly pay your salary."
>
> "I should be delighted to serve your lordship without emolument."
>
> "That's dashed good of you, Jeeves, and I appreciate it. About as nifty a display of the feudal spirit as I ever struck. But how," added Bill keenly, "could I keep you in fish?" (Chap. 11)

This exchange occurs in the only book that acknowledges, implicitly, that Jeeves and Bertie's relationship essentially rests on the fact that Bertie is wealthy. By going off without Jeeves to a school for men who no longer have servants, Bertie implies that, should he lose his fortune, he will also lose Jeeves, no matter how much they both might regret the loss. Possibly this novel's emphasis on the feudal spirit stems from Wodehouse's realization, based on postwar events, of the fragility of the situation he had constructed for his two favorite characters. Jeeves repeatedly speaks of his feudal desire to serve Bill, even if it means giving up his salary and possibly going to jail.

This willingness to go against his own interests in serving his employers is not typical of Jeeves's character in any of the narratives with Bertie—including those after *Ring for Jeeves*. Yet, despite the fact that Jeeves acts so generously to a man he serves only briefly, his whole situation in *Ring for Jeeves* creates, in a strange way, an implicit declaration that his bond to Bertie is deeper than his weekly pay envelope. Because Jeeves makes his offer to work without pay to someone other than Bertie, Wodehouse is implying that he would make the same offer to Bertie, should circumstances make it necessary. In an indirect way, Jeeves's offer, along with Bertie's refusal to allow himself to be taught how to get along without Jeeves, adds up to a reaffirmation of their marriagelike relationship comparable to that at the end of *Thank You, Jeeves.* (In both books, Jeeves quits and goes back to work for Bertie at the point when his new employer becomes engaged.) Whether or not Wodehouse intended it, *Ring for Jeeves* has as one of its main effects an acknowledgment of the postwar situation in England and also a demonstration that the Jeeves-Bertie relationship can survive it. They belong together, he seems to be saying, and no social revolution is going to keep them apart. The novels from this point on follow the old prewar formulas. Fortunately for his readers, Wodehouse realized that he needed no apology or justification for "dishing out earls and butlers."

PHIPPS: A PSEUDO-JEEVES

During the period when Wodehouse experimented with postwar subject matter, he tried out new characters and plot premises. In an apparent attempt to create a Jeeves-like character outside the Jeeves/Wooster series, he invented Phipps, in both the play version of *Spring Fever* and in *The Old Reliable*. While the play is only tangentially part of the series and the novel is not part of it at all, it is interesting to look at Phipps in both of these works to see in what directions Wodehouse seemed to feel his narratives should go at that point in his career.

The character Phipps in *The Old Reliable* bears some resemblance to Jeeves, both physically and mentally. He is tall and dignified, is able to quote serious literature (though not to the extent that Jeeves does), and achieves his goals—even though the protagonist works against him. Similarly, Phipps in *Spring Fever* is close enough to Jeeves that Wodehouse contemplated making him into Jeeves at the request of a potential producer. Still, there are many differences that set both of the Phipps characters apart from Jeeves. These differences add up to make these butlers more overtly funny than Jeeves himself is.

In general, I suspect Phipps may have been Wodehouse's attempt to develop a Jeeves-like character with a greater comic range. Over the course of the Jeeves/Wooster series, Jeeves had become such a dignified, godlike figure that there were many things he simply could not be made to do. For example, Wodehouse came to regret the following passage in *Joy in the Morning*: "The only occasion on which I have ever seen Jeeves really rattled was when he met Boko for the first time. He winced visibly and tottered off to the kitchen, no doubt to pull himself together with cooking sherry" (chap. 6). In 1966, Wodehouse responded to a fan who had apparently objected to this passage:

> How right you are about Jeeves and the cooking sherry, and what a lesson to all of us not to bung in a thing which is out of character just because it sounds funny. Of course Jeeves would never have lowered himself to drink cooking sherry. Bertie's best would have been none too good for him.[5]

All the same, a dignified butler who *could* drink cooking sherry (or crème de menthe) would be a useful addition to Wodehouse's cast, and Phipps is such a butler.

Early in *Spring Fever*, we learn that Phipps (revealed at the end of the play to be "Jeeves," working under a pseudonym) wants to be in the movies. He seems at first to achieve this goal when Glutz lets him make a screen test for a butler role, but it turns out that the producer has misled him, only wanting the footage in order to teach a real actor how to play a butler. Thus Phipps's desire for a genuine contract becomes one of the three main goals in the plot. The other two are: first, to get Mike and Kay (equivalent to Joe and Kay in *The Old Reliable*) engaged, and second, to make Smedley and Jane (the latter becomes Bill in *The Old Reliable*) financially independent so they can stop working for the imperious ex-silent film star, Adela. (In the play, neither Smedley nor Jane is related to Adela.) The plot, as in *The Old Reliable*, hinges on the scandalous diary of Carmen Flores, for which

Glutz and other studio executives previously involved with Flores will pay a great deal.

Although Phipps's main goal is to get into the movies, he also betrays an interest in the diary, and we jump to the conclusion that he wants it for selfish motives. At the end, Phipps/Jeeves uses the diary to blackmail Glutz into arranging that all the characters, except Adela, get what they want. Thus, like the Jeeves of the series proper, Phipps solves all the problems with one simple action. Still, through most of the plot, we are unaware that he has this altruistic plan; by putting "Jeeves" in an unfamiliar environment among new characters, Wodehouse can make his motives ambiguous—aided by the fact that we do not find out that he is "really" Jeeves until the end.

The Phipps of *Spring Fever* also has several attributes that strongly distinguish him from Jeeves. He is married, has been in prison as a safecracker, and preaches leftist politics. Still, his criminality is only an exaggeration of Jeeves's own lax moral code. Phipps, both here and in *The Old Reliable,* in a sense combines traits of both Jeeves and Brinkley (the valet in *Thank You, Jeeves*): his drunkenness and political slogans are similar to those of the latter character, but he is also Machiavellian and competent in a Jeeves-like way. Jane comments on this balance when she asks Phipps how he came to be a safecracker: "I mean here you are the world's most perfect butler, and here you are a champion safe-opener . . . which came first, the chicken or the egg?" (act 2, scene 1). (In *The Old Reliable,* Bill asks Phipps a similar question.)

On the other hand, throughout the play Phipps reveals traits reminiscent of Jeeves. For example, he has an effective pick-me-up for hangovers and is an expert on horse racing. He uses blackmail to solve all the problems, and the other characters lavish praise on him at the end in terms similar to those usually reserved for Jeeves. Nevertheless, he does other things that Jeeves would be unlikely to do. He is less repressed than Jeeves, saying that he will not give back the racy diary at least until he finishes reading it, and he also gets drunk.

In the "Jeeves version" draft of *Spring Fever* that survives, we learn at the very end that Phipps is Jeeves because his lawyer insists that he sign his real name on his contract with Glutz. The stage directions specify that when the lawyer reads out the names Jeeves, "Phipps, standing with a new and commanding dignity, nods his head in assent" (act 2, scene 2). So Phipps, as originally conceived before the producer had Wodehouse make him into Jeeves, was presumably a less dignified version of Jeeves. How Wodehouse would have gone about fitting Jeeves into the play is anybody's guess, of course, since subsequent drafts of the play turned the character back into plain Phipps. Those drafts provided the basis for *The Old Reliable*, where Phipps is again a less lofty Jeeves figure.

Aside from the problems with postwar subject matter, it seems possible that after a string of Jeeves/Wooster masterpieces, from *Thank You, Jeeves* to *The Mating Season*, Wodehouse may have considered Jeeves's character constricting. In *The Mating Season* he seems to be stretching Jeeves's traits a bit: having him drink beer in a pub and cosh a constable. Perhaps Wodehouse wanted to do comic, even slapstick things with Jeeves that were just not possible with such a staid character. Phipps is, in effect, a Jeeves who can unbend occasionally. Upon his first entrance he is described as "an unmistakably English butler, tall, decorous and dignified." He seems to be a universal confidant, as Jeeves is. Smedley, upset over his situation in Adela's household, reacts to Phipps's entrance: "There swept over him an urge to take this kindly butler into his confidence, concealing nothing"(chap. 1). Yet Phipps is not as godlike and aloof as is Jeeves.

The confrontation between Phipps and Bill (Wilhelmina) Shannon sets up a narrative opposition different from those of the Jeeves/Wooster series. Bill, the protagonist, is the sister of ex-silent-film queen Adela, whose memoirs she is ghost writing. Wodehouse immediately establishes the idea that Phipps and Bill like and respect each other, but for the bulk of the narrative they work against each other as well. Here is a rare case when Wodehouse sets up two strong, clever characters in opposition; Bill is, however, ultimately the smarter of the two, since Phipps has to exploit the weaker characters, Smedley in particular, in order to get his way.

As part of this balance between two major, opposed characters, Phipps is more immoral than Jeeves. The premise for his final success is set up in chapter 7, when Smedley remarks that Carmen Flores's valuable diary is written in Spanish. At the end, Phipps tricks Smedley into handing over the diary by claiming it is in English; he then escapes with it. Aside from the villainess, Adela, Phipps is the only immoral character in *The Old Reliable*, and in some ways this trait makes him similar to Jeeves—though Jeeves often uses his questionable tactics to help others. Unlike the situation in the play *Spring Fever*, Phipps wants the diary for himself, and he ultimately gets it, not using it to solve the other characters' problems. Given that the diary is worth $50,000 and that Phipps steals it, *The Old Reliable* is a rare case in Wodehouse's work where a character gets away with a major crime. Jeeves has of course committed minor crimes, and we might see Phipps as an instance of Wodehouse exaggerating this unscrupulous aspect of Jeeves's character to create a major comic criminal.

Phipps is less gullible in *The Old Reliable* than in *Spring Fever*, and hence he is closer to being like Jeeves here than he had been in the play. He is not tricked into a fake screen test by Glutz. Instead he gains a legitimate contract with the film company, and he uses it to try to get out of his agreement to burgle Adela's safe. As he enters to tell Bill and the others of the contract, the description again recalls Jeeves: "Dressed in what appeared to be his Sunday best, his gaze calm and steady, he seemed so competent, so reliable, so obviously capable of conducting to a successful conclusion any task to which he set the hand holding the bowler hat without which no English butler stirs abroad" (chap. 10). Yet Phipps's differences from Jeeves make him comic in ways that Jeeves could never be. As in the play, Phipps is evidently of working-class origins and beliefs. Upon hearing that Smedley has found the valuable diary that Phipps had been seeking, the latter drops his dignified manner and exclaims "Oh, my Gawd!" It also turns out that Phipps has a weak head for drink, which is why he had originally been caught as a safe-cracker. Bill exploits this trait by tricking Phipps into imbibing a strong concoction. There follows a lengthy and very funny drunk scene, exploiting the contrast between Phipps's former dignity and his uninhibited behavior while blotto. During this scene Phipps behaves disrepectfully to the other characters, reveals his socialist views, and is induced to burgle the safe. Wodehouse would never have written such a scene for Jeeves, of course, but he exploits the premise to the hilt here. I suspect that the ending of *The Old Reliable* reflects Wodehouse's desire for the amoral Jeeves to get away, just once, with a crime, and he arranges for this to happen through a surrogate. The character of Jeeves—though he is not actually present—allows the plot of *The Old Reliable* to exist.

The novel's ending, with Phipps driving off with a movie contract and a valuable diary in hand, would seem to set up the possibility for additional novels involving this character. He could go into the Hollywood studios, which Wodehouse knew so well, or off in any direction with the $50,000 realized from the diary. Guy Bolton, however, provided Wodehouse with an idea that permitted the return of Jeeves *in persona proper.*

JEEVES WITHOUT BERTIE

As we have seen many times in the course of this book, Bertie is the source of most of the series' overt humor; Jeeves is an amusing character, but usually only in his interactions with Bertie. How, then, could Wodehouse deal with Jeeves on his own? So far I have seldom mentioned *Ring for Jeeves* and its source, *Come On, Jeeves,* for they draw upon few of Wodehouse's standard characters and narrative patterns.[6] Perhaps this atypicality has led many readers and critics to dismiss *Ring for Jeeves* as peripheral to the Jeeves/Wooster series. Yet *Ring for Jeeves* is arguably comparable in quality to Wodehouse's nonseries works. If a butler other than Jeeves had been featured, this novel would have gained a better reputation. (Indeed, at one point, Bolton and Wodehouse planned to use a butler named Ponsonby.[7]) Aside from its innate interest, *Ring for Jeeves* (along with *Come On, Jeeves*) reveals how Wodehouse could deal with Jeeves's character if he were separated from Bertie and placed in a plausible postwar situation. Here Jeeves reveals quite a different set of traits.

Left on his own, Jeeves must become one comic character among many. In act 1 of *Come On, Jeeves* the protagonist's brother-in-law, Rory, introduces a series of comic riddles around the name "Bigger":

RORY: Perhaps Jeeves can answer. Jeeves knows everything.
JEEVES: What is the point, m'lord, on which you are seeking information?
RORY: Which is bigger, Jeeves, Mr. Bigger or Master Bigger?
JEEVES: Master Bigger, because he's a little Bigger.

The idea that Jeeves can answer riddles with a straight face, as if they were ordinary requests for information, becomes a motif in the play. At the end, Rory returns to this idea:

RORY: That reminds me—which is bigger, Captain Bigger or Mrs. Bigger? . . . I bet you don't know the answer to that one, Jeeves.
JEEVES (gravely): Mrs. Bigger, because she became Bigger.

Jeeves thus plays a part in overturning the usual vaudeville banter by being the straight man who delivers the comic line intended for the comic himself, in this case Rory.

Uncharacteristically, Jeeves also participates in physical slapstick in *Come On, Jeeves*. He suggests that he and Bill ambush Biggar (the captain's name is spelled Biggar, though the name used in the running gag is Bigger) and take his betting ticket as he enters in the dark; as a result, Bill accidentally jumps Jeeves and has him on the floor with a pillow over his face when the lights come on. Then the pair try to entangle Biggar in the curtains and end up catching Mrs. Spottsworth instead. In both cases Jeeves's schemes go wrong, and the failures result from Wodehouse's need to use Jeeves in a more comic fashion. Later, Jeeves dresses up as the ghost of Lady Agatha in order to steal the pendant for Bill. The idea of Jeeves dressing up as a ghost, female or not, would have been unacceptable in the stories or novels. (Indeed, this scene is dropped from *Ring for Jeeves*.) Again, his character had to be more flexible and comic for the stage.

Jeeves is more fallible and human in *Come On, Jeeves* than at any point since the middle-period short stories. He gets a tension headache upon receiving the letter from Bertie about his expulsion from school. He is also less prescient: when he takes Mrs. Spottsworth's pendant, he unthinkingly leaves his fingerprints on the case and has to wipe them off surreptitiously before the police inspect it. His lack of foresight also means that he participates less in solving the various problems in *Come On, Jeeves*. As in the earlier novels, like *The Code of the Woosters*, the motifs are introduced quickly: romance, gambling, the Abbey's dampness, and the necessity to sell the family estate. The main complication is Bill's obligation, as a bookie, to pay off a double win by Captain Biggar. When Bill and Jeeves first enter, they emphasize that Jeeves had advised Bill against the bet, and throughout Wodehouse stresses that Jeeves is not to blame for the problems that arise. Helping Bill pay the debt becomes Jeeves's major goal, and his means for doing so are quickly specified: to get Mrs. Spottsworth to buy the Abbey. Captain Biggar, however, having an inside tip on the Derby, demands the money right away, suggesting that Bill steal Mrs. Spottsworth's necklace for him to pawn. Jeeves rejects the idea, but Bill ignores him and agrees to the scheme. Thus in relation to the main initial problem and the attempted solution, Bill goes against Jeeves's advice.

In the romance plot line, however, Jeeves advises Bill badly. Bill is engaged to Jill, and he decides not to tell her of his troubles. Indeed, he asks Jeeves if he should reveal the truth to her, and Jeeves counsels him against doing so. This decision causes trouble subsequently, since Jill values honesty and breaks off the engagement because Bill lies to her. Eventually Jeeves reconciles Bill and Jill by telling her the truth about Bill's misfortunes as a bookie and persuading her that Bill did it all for love of her. Here Jeeves gives bad advice and makes up for it later, as he did in the early-period stories.

Overall, Jeeves solves only the problem of how to sell the Abbey to Mrs. Spottsworth but not the equally important problem of the missing pendant. He suggests to Mrs. Spottsworth that she buy the Abbey and ship it to be reconstructed in California—an idea which delights her and causes her to pay Bill the money he needs to settle his debt to Biggar and marry Jill. But Biggar still has the pendant that Bill and Jeeves had stolen, and only the lucky circumstances that Biggar returns and that Mrs. Spottsworth has fallen in love with him make for the complete happy ending. Thus there is no sense, as in many of the series' narratives, that Jeeves is in control all along or that he uses his wits to deal with each new twist in the action. Here he is far more a comic stage butler and less a superhuman figure.

Wodehouse attributed the bulk of the writing of *Come On, Jeeves* to Bolton,[8] though correspondence from the period suggests that the pair collaborated equally in writing it. Still, in adapting the play into the novel *Ring for Jeeves*, he tightened up its structure significantly. For one thing, in the first chapter he introduced the idea that Captain Biggar and Mrs. Spottsworth had known and been attracted to each other years earlier—thus motiviating their romance at Rowcester Abbey. Similarly, Wodehouse concocted an earlier flirtation between Bill and Mrs. Spottsworth, setting up both her inclination to buy the Abbey and Jill's jealousy over what she assumes had been a more serious alliance. Less centrally, but just as important in terms of Jeeves's character, now it is not Jeeves who inadvertently leaves fingerprints on the stolen pendant's case, but Bill himself—and Jeeves gets him out of this situation.

Yet even with its careful plotting, *Ring for Jeeves* is still like the nonseries novels. Jeeves, both as comic character and plot mechanism, is simpler than in the rest of the Jeeves/Wooster series. One major reason why Jeeves must be different emerges in chapter 3 of *Ring for Jeeves*, when we learn about his relationship to Jill. She is an anomaly in the Jeeves/Wooster series, even though she resembles many of the heroines of Wodehouse's non-Jeeves works. Nothing like her has ever confronted Jeeves before. She is normal, competent, and attractive—a plausible marriage partner whom Jeeves must help his employer to win. Above all, she is not like the unpredictable young women who have temporarily confounded Jeeves in earlier novels. Indeed, no such irrational force is introduced here. Biggar, Mrs. Spottsworth, and Jill, the sources of the main problems and goals of the novel, are all consistent and predictable.

In part to counter this lack of unpredictable characters, Jeeves's problems are introduced in a very episodic fashion. First he must persuade Biggar that Bill is not the bookie who ran out on him; then he must persuade Mrs. Spottsworth to buy the Abbey before the Derby ends. In the plot as a whole he does three main things: (1) he plans the theft of the pendant from Mrs. Spottsworth and helps Bill to carry it through, thus solving the Biggar threat; (2) he persuades Mrs. Spottsworth to buy the Abbey and ship it to the United States, solving the money problem; and (3) he regains Jill for Bill by telling her the truth about the bookie scheme. In all these cases, we have no indication when he decided on the plan; most likely he acts on inspirations of the moment. While nothing arises to delay Jeeves's solution, he takes a surprisingly long time to come up with these relatively simple ideas. Ordinarily he could have conceived the scheme for moving the Abbey to California early on. But again, Jeeves is simply not as smart in this book as in the rest of the series, mostly because he is not as pragmatic or unscrupulous. Instead, he is courteous, devoted, self-sacrificing—in a word, feudal. Indeed, he is nicer to Bill than to Bertie, even though Bill is not so clever or interesting as Bertie. Thus despite the fact that Jeeves is more overtly funny in *Ring for Jeeves*, this novel reinforces the idea that the main source of narrative and stylistic tension in the series is the delicate balance between Jeeves and Bertie.

Coincidence plays a strong role from the start, as Mrs. Spottsworth and Biggar happen to meet at a pub not far from the Abbey. At once the motif of his inability to propose to her, despite his love, is introduced. (His "conscience" consists of his memories of Tubby Frobisher and the Subhdor, back in Kuala Lumpar. This device delays the declaration of love between Biggar and Spottsworth, but it also serves as a Kiplingesque parody of Bertie's Code.) The early entrance of these characters means that Jeeves does not appear until well into the novel (chapter 4)[9]; thus the bases of two of the major plot lines are established before he has any way of knowing about them. This reinforces the similarity of *Ring for Jeeves* to the nonseries farce novels, with Jeeves acting as one character among many.

Indeed, as in the play, Jeeves has little foresight. Again he agrees that Bill should not reveal the situation to Jill, though he will himself tell Jill the truth later and thus reconcile the couple. When in chapter 8 Jeeves convinces Biggar (temporarily) that the absconding bookie used Bill's license plate number, Jeeves mistakenly agrees that the danger is largely over. As in the play, Jeeves comes up with some unsuccessful schemes for robbing Biggar of the betting ticket. Initially he and Bill decide to overpower Biggar by pulling down the curtains on him when he reenters via the French windows. After Jeeves proposes this idea, the narration remarks: "Bill was impressed, as who would not have been" (chap. 11). Here the third-person authorial voice cues the reader to assume that Jeeves is wise, even though the flimsy scheme he proposes fails almost immediately. Similarly, Jeeves does not object to the idea of placing a great deal of money on the horse Ballymore, even though there is no way that Biggar could " 'be certain beyond the peradventure of a doubt that Ballymore will win,' " as Jeeves puts it. Indeed, Ballymore ultimately comes in second, so it is really Biggar's decision not to place the bet that prevents Bill from ending up in worse trouble. It is only because Biggar realizes, as a result of what Mrs. Spottsworth tells him, that his Code is inadequate, that he is able to propose to her. Biggar's notion of a Far Eastern Code, based on clichéd and outdated Kipling imagery, is shattered; an impoverished British man can propose to a rich American heiress.

In short, without Bertie, Jeeves becomes one of Wodehouse's nonseries characters, and these plays and novels involving Jeeves and Phipps are entertaining in their own right. Still, it was the combination of Bertie and Jeeves that set the series apart from all Wodehouse's other works.

BERTIE GOES ON THE STAGE

In the mid-1960s, in the wake of the BBC's successful "World of Wooster" programs, Wodehouse and Bolton went back to *Come On, Jeeves* and rewrote it as *Win with Wooster*, inserting Bertie in place of Bill Rowcester. This play improves on its original. It combines traits of Bertie and Bill to create a character who is not exactly the "real" Bertie of the rest of the series. Wodehouse realized that his characters were fictitious creations, not real people; his correspondence shows that he felt the theater demanded different tactics and conventions than he used in his prose. Thus Wodehouse made Bertie get happily engaged at the end, presumably because the sort of play he was used to writing always turned out that way; he also had Bertie lose his fortune and inherit the rundown Wooster Abbey. Moreover, Wodehouse was unable to use Bertie's first-person narration to create humor, so he had to retain Jeeves's more overtly comic behavior from the original play. While familiar aspects of the series may be gone or altered, however, there is no need to dismiss the plays for requiring us to accept, temporarily, a new set of traits and situations. Bertie and Jeeves are simply different on the stage.

Both plays have to establish early on why Bertie is suddenly impoverished, living in a rundown country house, and working as a bookie. In *Win with Wooster*, his sister Monica (who, along with her husband, Rory, has been retained from *Come On, Jeeves*) says that Bertie's gambling debts have gotten him into trouble and that he has sworn off betting. Bertie had never been much of a gambler, but we must assume for the sake of the plot that he is one here. No motivation, however, is provided for the fact that Jeeves's turf expertise has not helped Bertie avoid this plight, yet his skill at picking winning horses becomes important in solving this problem. The musical version adapted from this play, *Betting on Bertie*, is a bit more effective in explaining Bertie's poverty: he has inherited the rundown Wooster Abbey from an uncle who left no money for taxes and upkeep.

Both versions contain a new character, Pongo Pilkington, who was not in *Come On, Jeeves*. He is another old pal of Bertie's and becomes his partner in the bookie business. Pongo does not need Bertie's help with a romantic problem, as had most of the pals in the series. Rather, he is a sidekick for Bertie, sharing his financial woes; he serves mainly to add humor and to distance Jeeves a bit from any blame for the failure of the bookie scheme and for Bertie's subsequent troubles.

Another major new character in these plays is Zenobia, who replaces Jill. She is again a veterinarian, but now she is Bigger's daughter. (The spelling of the captain's name was changed in the rewriting.) Bertie falls in love with her at first sight, reviving his old trait of becoming easily infatuated with women—a device common in the short-story period but which Wodehouse had not used since *Thank You, Jeeves*, with Pauline Stoker. In *Win with Wooster* Bertie proposes to Zenny after about five hours' acquaintance, and in *Betting On Bertie* he declares himself almost immediately. In both cases Jeeves realizes at once that Bertie loves Zenny and actively promotes the match. Like Jill in *Come On, Jeeves,* Zenny is an attractive, competent woman with none of the unpredictable traits of a character like Bobbie Wickham; hence the old premise that Jeeves would resist any marriage partner for Bertie is abandoned. Indeed, Zenny helps solve Bertie's problem by destroying the incriminating bookie outfit, going against her father's interests when she realizes she is in love with Bertie. Since Jeeves had carelessly left this outfit where it could be discovered, rather than destroying it as we might expect him to do, Zenny's action proves her capable of protecting Bertie in an almost Jeevesian way.

In *Win with Wooster,* as in *Come On, Jeeves,* Jeeves displays a mixture of carelessness and cleverness. He hides the bookie outfit, but Rory finds it and shows it to Bigger. When Bertie asks why he had not destroyed it, Jeeves replies that he had intended to do so the next morning. He again leaves his fingerprints on the pendant case in stealing it and has to wipe them off when the police arrive. His initial schemes for stealing the pendant from the rich divorcée, Mrs. Southworth, fail, and in general he has no overall plan, seizing on opportunity to solve problems. His ghost disguise secures the pendant for Bertie and Bigger; in the end he wins Zenny for Bertie by telling her the truth about the bookie scheme. He also persuades Mrs. Southworth to buy the Abbey by suggesting that she move it to California. These solutions are the same as in *Come On, Jeeves,* but here Jeeves pulls off one more feat that considerably enhances our impression of his intelligence: he sells Mrs. Southworth a portrait of Lady Agatha, whose ghost she believes she has seen. He then places the thousand pounds at twenty-to-one on the horse that wins the Derby, thus providing Bertie with another sizable sum at the end. There Jeeves reminds Bertie of the school that the latter has been attending, designed to teach him how to get along without servants. Bertie declares that the winnings will mean he will not have to take a refresher course—so presumably Jeeves will stay with Bertie even after the latter marries.

Surprisingly, this fairly neat set of solutions by Jeeves is almost entirely dropped in *Betting on Bertie,* where he is far less in control of events and ends by solving almost nothing. His scheme for stealing a pendant belonging to Brenda Beaumont (the equivalent of Mrs.

Southworth) works, but Jeeves is made to look silly in the process. He composes a serenade for Bertie to sing under Brenda's balcony, luring her out while Pongo sneaks in and gets the pendant; not only is the serenade itself atrocious, but Jeeves has to stand lookout and bark like a dog to signal when Pongo has accomplished his task. Moreover, although Bertie obtains the pendant through the serenade scheme, Zenny sees him beneath Brenda's window and becomes jealous; thus Jeeves actually creates a problem as well as solving one.

Even Jeeves's most successful ploys from *Win with Wooster* are jettisoned here. Brenda herself asks to buy the portrait, so that Jeeves's ability to place the thousand-pound bet for Bertie becomes luck rather than a deliberate move on his part. She also decides to buy the Abbey without prompting but expresses trepidation about using it, due to its dampness; only then does Jeeves suggest she ship it to California. Despite Jeeves's relative ineffectualness, however, the various happy endings are duly achieved, as befits a musical comedy.

Betting on Bertie was never produced, and a glance over the script suggests why. It was probably not so much a matter of changes in the characters or plot problems or even of the lyrics, some of which are quite good (particularly Jeeves's "Lament of a Gentleman's Gentleman," quoted in chapter 8). One of the most striking things about the play is how old-fashioned it is. Clearly Wodehouse and Bolton were sticking to conventions of the 1910s and 1920s, the height of their musical comedy careers. The change from the rich widower Mrs. Southworth in *Win with Wooster* to movie star Brenda Beaumont in *Betting on Bertie* seems to have been made primarily in order to introduce a chorus of school girls who are fans of hers. They enter at a few points, providing the sorts of dance numbers that the two collaborators may have assumed were still obligatory on the musical stage. Similarly, most numbers, except Jeeves's two solos, end with the characters doing a dancing exit of a type common, but certainly not essential, in the modern musical. The pair may have intentionally tried for a nostalgic appeal, since the stage directions specify that the musical is set in the late 1920s. A "campy" production might have been possible, but it seems unlikely that such a thing was what Wodehouse and Bolton had in mind.

In the context of the Jeeves/Wooster series as a whole, Wodehouse's experiments with Jeeves in the immediate postwar era and his treatment of Bertie on the stage might seem anomalous. Yet the challenges to his professional career after his move to America in 1947 make his tamperings with the established formulas of the series seem quite logical.

8

LE MOT JUSTE

Does it really much matter what Mr. Wodehouse writes about? —SATURDAY REVIEW, 16 OCTOBER, 1937

Most critics who defend Wodehouse as a great author do so on the basis of his style. There can be no doubt that the lengthy composition and revision processes yielded complex, virtuosic prose. Consider these excerpts from the Jeeves/Wooster series:

> [Bertie is trying to mollify an irate man who calls on him:]
> "Have a drink?" I said.
> "No!"
> "A cigarette?"
> "No!"
> "A chair?"
> "No!"
> I went into silence once more. These non-drinking, non-smoking, non-sitters are hard birds to handle. ("The Spot of Art")

> [Bertie accidentally encounters an ex-fiancée:]
> None of the embarrassment which was causing the Wooster toes to curl up inside their neat suede shoes like the tendrils of some tender plant seemed to be affecting this chunk of the dead past. (*Joy in the Morning*, Chap. 2)
>
> [Stiffy Byng is upset because her fiancé would not steal a policeman's helmet to prove his love for her:]
> Here, with a sniff like the tearing of a piece of calico, she buried the bean in the hands and broke into what are called uncontrollable sobs. (*The Code of the Woosters*, Chap. 8)

The third is a quintessentially Wodehousian sentence, creating humor by combining striking simile with slang term and a cliché which is signalled as such.

Wodehouse uses a great many original similes, metaphors, and other linguistic constructions, but, as these form perhaps the most obviously brilliant set of devices he uses, there is little point in examining them in detail here. It is worth noting, however, that the originality and perfection of Wodehouse's similes and their stylistic figures are not unconnected to his use of quotation and cliché. Philip M. Thody has commented:

> It is the appropriate use of quotations from the central tradition of English literature which is the first feature that defines P. G. Wodehouse as so quintessentially English a Writer, it is by no means the last, and perhaps not even the most important. For Wodehouse does much more than use quotations. As we have just seen in the description of the Aberdeen terrier [Bartholomew, in *The Code of the Woosters*, looking "from under his eyebrows like a Scottish elder rebuking sin from the pulpit"], he creates phrases perfect enough to become quotations themselves.[1]

Wodehouse's insistence upon clichés, repetition, and quotation, however, also creates a less obvious, but pervasive, set of devices in the Jeeves/Wooster series.

As I suggested in the introduction, Wodehouse's dominant principle of composition derives from this insistence on cliché, repetition, and quotation. Bertie not only uses clichés frequently, but he marks them *as* clichés by adding phrases like "as the fellow said" or "as the expression is." Wodehouse seldom leaves conventional material in its original form; instead he devised a wide repertory of devices for defamiliarizing the most outworn types of language. The result is almost invariably funny, mainly through incongruities between familiar language and the strange forms into which it is twisted.

In this context it is notable how few of the more conventional devices of British literary humor Wodehouse uses. We might expect Bertie, with his lack of learning, to employ malapropisms, yet there are hardly any in the entire series. The few that do crop up are not particularly funny: "my Aunt Agatha, for many years a widow, or derelict, as I believe it is called . . ." (*Joy in the Morning*, chap. 1). Wodehouse actually has to strain a bit to introduce this sort of misunderstanding, as when in *Joy in the Morning* Florence criticizes Stilton:

> "He is a mere uncouth Cossack."
>
> A cossack, I knew, was one of those things clergymen wear, and I wondered why she thought Stilton was like one. An inquiry into this would have been fraught with interest, but before I could institute it she had continued. (Chap. 18)

The characters seldom simply tell jokes. Bertie occasionally tries it, and his taste runs to the most banal sorts of Pat-and-Mike and earl-and-chorus-girl stories. Indeed, most frequently he simply refers to the joke without actually telling it. In these cases Wodehouse gets humor, not out of the fact that Bertie says funny things, but that he thinks such old chestnuts are funny. Bertie makes unconscious puns more often than deliberate jokes, as when in "Jeeves Takes Charge" he describes how his valet Meadowes was stealing his socks: "I was reluctantly compelled to hand the misguided blighter the mitten," and, "directly I found that he was a sock-sneaker I gave him the boot." In "The Love That Purifies," Bertie comments that during his vacation Jeeves "legs it off to some seaside resort for a couple of weeks, leaving me stranded." When he does try to make a joke, the result is so unfunny as to be funny; in *Much Obliged, Jeeves,* Ginger tries to discuss Florence with Bertie:

> "Bertie," he said at length.
> "Hullo?"
> "Bertie."
> "Yes."
> "Bertie."
> "Still here. Excuse me for asking, but have you any cracked gramophone record blood in you? Perhaps your mother was frightened by one." (Chap. 3)

Similarly, Jeeves seldom tells an actual joke. He can come up with only one to give Gussie for his grammar-school speech in *Right Ho, Jeeves,* and that is again a clichéd Pat-and-Mike item rendered funny by the fact that Gussie mangles it in the telling. One of Jeeves's rare jokes comes when he is playing a role, pretending to be a broker's man in order to convince Jas Waterbury that Bertie is bankrupt; he claims that Bertie is dependent on Aunt Dahlia, who would send him to Canada upon hearing of his debts: " 'Should she learn of my official status, I do not like to envisage the outcome, though if I may venture on a pleasantry, it would be a case of outgo rather than outcome for Mr. Wooster' " ("Jeeves and the Greasy Bird"). The pun is not funny in itself but is made so through Jeeves's restraint in telling it.

Instead of relying on conventional jokes, Wodehouse has created much of the series' humor through standing the familiar on its head. And though his prose sounds casual and spontaneous, he crafted it with great care. The late revision stages largely involved final decisions about what phrases to use, and this often meant the substitution of one cliché for another, sometimes to make the imagery livelier and sometimes to avoid the too-frequent repetition of the same phrase. One result was an extraordinarily systematic, careful introduction and development of verbal motifs. These appear, not only within a single work, but across the whole series.

Wodehouse also displays his obsession with writing in the Jeeves/Wooster series in a way that sets it apart from his other works. Of all Wodehouse's characters, Jeeves and Bertie are the most fascinated with language (except Psmith, of course). While the other works use the distinctive Wodehousian prose, the Jeeves/Wooster series permits its two central characters to linger over the conventions of language. Time and again the action pauses as Bertie asks Jeeves to supply a word or quotation he has forgotten or as they discuss which of two words is more appropriate. Bertie's and Jeeves's relations to language are, however, quite different and reflect their respective characters and narrative functions.

LEARNING FROM JEEVES

> "Oh, I'm not complaining," said Chuffy, looking rather like Saint Sebastian on receipt of about the fifteenth arrow. "You have a perfect right to love who you like."
>
> "Whom, old man," I couldn't help saying. Jeeves has made me rather a purist in these matters.
>
> —*THANK YOU, JEEVES* (Chap. 9)

As we have seen, within the overall dynamics of the narrative, Jeeves stands for closure. He desires a placid existence and protects Bertie from forces of change. He remains the mentor, Bertie the perpetual schoolboy. In keeping with this, Jeeves's command of language, especially in the novels, is essentially static. He behaves as if he has a mental file of memorized language and quotations, and his omniscience gives the impression of being timeless. Despite the fact that we know he frequently reads a newspaper or an improving book, we never sense that his quotations come from recent reading. Indeed, the one specific book that we see Jeeves reading during the series' action—Spinoza's *Ethics*—never gets quoted.[2]

Jeeves's mental card file allows him to quote accurately at length, as in the opening of *Much Obliged, Jeeves,* where he gives the first eight lines of Shakespeare's Sonnet 33 verbatim. In *Jeeves and the Feudal Spirit* he delivers a speech on diamonds he clearly had learned by rote when studying under his jeweler cousin. His range of knowledge is wide, concentrating on high British literature like Shakespeare, Pope, and Keats, but including popular songs (for example, "Home, Sweet Home") and current (fictitious) novelists like Florence Craye and Rosie M. Banks. He is fond of cliché as well and seems to regard the "correct" use of language rather as he does the correct kind of clothes: conservatively. He does not try to break Bertie of his habit of using slang, but he is ready with a word of praise when Bertie uses a cliché. In *The Mating Season*, upon discovering that people think he is Gussie and Gussie is he, Bertie remarks, "And ceaseless vigilance will be required if we are not to gum the game. We shall be walking on eggshells"—to which Jeeves responds, "A very trenchant figure, sir" (chap. 8). In *Stiff Upper Lip, Jeeves*, Bertie is puzzled about how to find Major Plank: " 'It'd be like looking for a needle in a haystack.' " Jeeves finds this " 'A very colourful image, sir' " (chap. 10). We might suspect that Jeeves is being ironic here, but he praises similar uses of cliché nine other times in the series. Moreover, he is himself fond of familiar quotations and clichés. For example, in *Jeeves and the Feudal Spirit*, when Bertie remarks that Stilton could easily beat him up, Jeeves agrees in a string of clichés: " 'Mr. Cheesewright's robustness would enable him to crush you like a fly. . . . He would obliterate you with single blow. He would break you in two with his bare hands. He would tear you limb from limb' " (chap. 16). We must assume that he wishes to foster Bertie's use of clichés (and he may even be appealing to Bertie's delight in clichés in order to get this point across more forcefully). Thus, just as Jeeves maintains the stability of the Wooster household, so he has a conservative, protective approach to quotation and cliché.

Bertie, on the other hand, works as the force for creating openness and conflict in the narratives. In keeping with this, his language is spontaneous; he does not think out the perfect way to express something but often tries to work out his language in the course of speaking or writing it. As he stumbles on, he creates bizarre juxtapositions. For example, he often has to search for the word he is after. This technique is pervasive (being used at least 160 times in the series), and it takes a number of forms. Bertie may use the correct word but qualify it because he is unsure of himself. When Jeeves enters at just the right moment in *Joy in the Morning*, "It was as if some sort of telepathy, if that's the word I want, had warned him that the young master had lost his grip and could do with twopennyworth of feudal assistance" (chap. 28). In many cases he has to call on Jeeves for the correct word or quotation; in describing a tiff between Madeline and Gussie, Bertie falters:

> "Hell's foundations are quivering. What do you call it when a couple of nations start off by being all palsy-walsy and then begin calling each other ticks and bounders?"
>
> "Relations have deteriorated would be the customary phrase, sir."
>
> "Well, relations have deteriorated between Miss Bassett and Gussie," (*Stiff Upper Lip, Jeeves,* Chap. 13)

A search for the correct term can foster repetition, as when Bertie criticizes Jeeves's scheme to send Gussie to a costume party as Mephistopheles in chapter 2 of *Right Ho, Jeeves*:

> "And this is not the first time this sort of thing has happened. To be quite candid, Jeeves, I have frequently noticed before now a tendency on your part to become—what's the word?"
>
> "I could not say, sir."
>
> "Eloquent? No, it's not eloquent. Elusive? No, it's not elusive. It's on the tip of my tongue. Begins with an 'e' and means being a jolly sight too clever."
>
> "Elaborate, sir?"
>
> "That's the exact word I was after. Too elaborate, Jeeves—that's what you are frequently prone to become."

But if Jeeves is not around, Bertie forges right ahead: "I quivered like a startled what-d'you-call-it" (*Jeeves in the Offing,* chap. 7). If he remembers later, he brings up the word, scrambling the prose:

> The conversation that followed was what you might call . . . I've forgotten the word, but it begins with a d. I mean, with Stinker within earshot Madeline and I couldn't get down to brass tacks, so we just chewed the fat . . . desultory, that's the

> word I wanted. We just chewed the fat in a desultory way. (*Stiff Upper Lip, Jeeves,* Chap. 5)

Such attempts to get the right word at any cost stem from Bertie's general fascination with language. This interest is signaled occasionally by his mention of parts of speech: " 'Moody' and 'discouraged' were about the two adjectives you would have selected to describe me as I left the summer-house" (*Right Ho, Jeeves,* chap. 19). Even when confronted by an angry Sir Roderick Glossop (whose hot-water bottle Bertie has just pierced), Bertie wants to get things straight:

> "Awful sorry about this," I said in a hearty sort of voice. "The fact is, I thought you were Tuppy."
>
> "Kindly refrain from inflicting your idiotic slang on me. What do you mean by the adjective 'tuppy'?"
>
> "It isn't so much an adjective, don't you know. More of a noun, I should think, if you examine it squarely. What I mean to say is, I thought you were your nephew." ("Jeeves and the Yule-tide Spirit")

In general, Bertie's language is elaborate and full of pauses, corrections, and backtracks. Moreover, it changes progressively across the series. If Jeeves's command of language is static and already learned, Bertie's develops right in front of us. The systematic changes created by Bertie's learning of language and quotations create one of the most original aspects of Wodehouse's treatment of familiar material.

Despite the common claim that the Jeeves/Wooster series remains constant, most critics notice a change in Bertie's use of language.[3] In 1974, Wodehouse commented, "You see, there is a development in him. He gets a bit brighter later on, a little shrewder. He learns a lot from Jeeves, especially in the matter of vocabulary. In the later stories, he drops some of the 'chappies' and the 'right hoes' and the old-fashioned slang."[4] Bertie's quotations change as well, as Richard Usborne suggests:

> The important thing, if you study Bertie, is not so much the width of his reading of bilge literature as the depth to which

> he absorbs the stuff. His little mind keeps a gooey sludge of words, phrases and concepts from what he has read, and it gives him a magpie vocabulary of synonyms and quotations.[5]

Much of Bertie's development comes from his contact with Jeeves, though he picks up language from other characters as well.

Yet Jeeves's erudition and influence on Bertie are introduced remarkably late in the series. This fact becomes apparent through an examination of the early stories in the order of their magazine publications (see appendix A). In the later stories and novels especially, Wodehouse systematically weaves in the multisyllabic phrases and quotations Bertie picks up from Jeeves. Across the series, the verbal complexity increases, and though the later books lose some of the intricate plotting of the early works, they make up for it with a dense mélange of slang, cliché, and quotation.

BERTIE'S EARLY VERBAL COMPLEXITY

Surprisingly, a survey of the early stories reveals that Jeeves neither uses foreign phrases nor provides words or quotations when Bertie is groping for them. Yet Bertie already uses these devices on his own. He is concerned about using the right words, and though he is a bit unsure of himself, he can come up with some fairly sophisticated terms:

> "I was speaking metaphorically," I explained, "if that's the word I want. I mean he got married." ("All's Well That Ends Well")
>
> "You know the trouble with you, Jeeves," I said, "is that you're too—what's the word I want?—too bally insular." ("Aunt Agatha Speaks Her Mind")

Jeeves does not begin to fill in regularly when Bertie searches for words until as late as "The Inferiority Complex of Old Sippy" (1926), the twenty-second story and the first entry in the more complex late short-story period:

> "The whole trouble being, Jeeves, that he has got one of those things that fellows do get—it's on the tip of my tongue."
> "An inferiority complex, sir?"
> "Exactly, an inferiority complex."

This new device considerably enriches Wodehouse's stylistic repertory. It provides the occasion for repetition within the dialogue, as in this case; it allows Jeeves to teach Bertie new words and concepts, or at least to remind him of ones he has forgotten. For example, the notion of Bertie's pals having complexes recurs after this story. At its next appearance Bertie seems not to recognize the word; in *Thank You, Jeeves,* Jeeves explains why Chuffy cannot propose to Pauline:

> "His lordship has a complex."
> "A what?"
> "A complex, sir. It seems that he once witnessed a musical comedy." (Chap. 5)

Jeeves says that Chuffy does not want to be like an impoverished peer in the musical who married a rich woman. Bertie apparently absorbs this, for he renders it back in the next novel, *Right Ho, Jeeves,* with a comic twist, in describing Gussie: " 'Mr. Fink-Nottle has a strong newt complex' " (chap. 1).

We will not remember that "newt complex" is Bertie's comic departure from the more conventional "inferiority complex" unless we read the series as a whole and remember such apparently minor details. Few readers probably noticed the hundreds of instances of this sort of repetition and variation, except in a general way. Yet such subtleties help considerably in explaining why one can reread these apparently repetitious and formulaic books with pleasure. The review of *The Mating Season* in the *Times Literary Supplement* expressed the general point:

> Just how funny it all is, an old and inveterate reader can hardly tell. For in reading and re-reading Mr. Wodehouse there comes a stage when the reader no longer waits breathlessly for what comes next or hunts up someone to share his

> laughter, but instead finds a new pleasure in seeing how exquisitely it is done.[6]

It is remarkable that an author aiming his material at the popular-magazine market could expect members of his public to read and reread so carefully—yet some apparently did. R. D. B. French has noted that by the 1930s Wodehouse had a wide audience of people who read him faithfully: "Now entering his own dimension, Wodehouse brought with him a multitude with whom he could converse in a kind of mental short hand, as one does among friends." French points out that most authors would avoid a title like *Eggs, Beans and Crumpets,* used for a 1940 collection of Drones stories; yet Wodehouse's regular readers would immediately recognize its subject.[7] Perhaps by the mid- to late 1920s, Wodehouse was aware of this phenomenon, and his expansion of Jeeves's character and introduction of Bertie's linguistic learning process came in response to it. From the beginning, however, Bertie provided the opportunity for verbal play.

Before Bertie's learning process began, his language seemed incongruous principally because he mixed slang with ordinary phrasing. In the second story, "The Artistic Career of Corky," Bertie describes Corky:

> His principal source of income, however, was derived from biting the ear of a rich uncle—one Alexander Worple, who was in the jute business. I'm a bit foggy as to what jute is, but it's apparently something the populace is pretty keen on, for Mr. Worple had made quite an indecently large stack out of it.

Bertie's striking narrational style is already developed as well, as in his description of his first sight of Jeeves: "A kind of darkish sort of respectful Johnnie stood without" ("Jeeves Takes Charge").

More unexpectedly, Bertie was inclined to quote long before Jeeves began this habit.[8] Jeeves demonstrates little erudition until well into the middle period of the short stories. True, in "Jeeves Takes Charge" he calls Nietzsche "fundamentally unsound." Yet he does not quote here, and the next time his reading becomes an issue is again in that seminal story, "Bertie Changes His Mind" (the fifteenth in order of publication). There the familiar pattern of Bertie taking the source of the quotations to be an acquaintance of Jeeves's emerges full-blown:

> "Emerson," I reminded him, "says a friend may well be reckoned the masterpiece of Nature, sir."
>
> "Well, you can tell Emerson from me the next time you see him that he's an ass."

Later in this story, Jeeves again comments on a philosopher, though this time a fictitious one, and he quotes Kipling ("More deadly than the male, sir"). This is also the first story in which Jeeves uses foreign-language phrases, dropping "sine qua non," "finesse" and "contretemps" into his opening paragraph. Still, this seems merely part of Jeeves's stuffy prose style; he does not use less common foreign phrases and quotations until *Thank You, Jeeves,* where Latin phrases and sentences become a motif (for example, "*Tempora mutandur nos et mutamur in illis,*" chap. 15).

After "Bertie Changes His Mind," there is a gap in Jeeves's quotations, until in "The Inferiority Complex of Old Sippy" he wrongly attributes "Tired nature's sweet restorer" to Shakespeare. (This was presumably a mistake on Wodehouse's part, not intended as Jeeves's blunder; the phrase is from Edward Young's "Night Thoughts.") Jeeves quotes only occasionally in the late stories, referring (correctly) to Shakespeare for the first time in "Jeeves and the Song of Songs," with the "Patience on a monument" gag. Within the stories, we can identify a few points where Jeeves's character and verbal style took a quantum leap in complexity: "Jeeves Takes Charge" (1916), "Bertie Changes His Mind" (1922), and "The Inferiority Complex of Old Sippy" (1926). Not until the novels does Jeeves become a walking combination of Bartlett's and Roget's. As we might expect, the longer form gave Wodehouse more room for play with style.

Bertie, on the other hand, was a more complete character early on, and he developed only slightly during the short-story period. His important stylistic changes come only after these major developments in Jeeves. Even in the earliest stories, Bertie was quoting, mostly from the literature he would have been assigned at school. In "Extricating Young Gussie," he quotes "Pippa Passes" without hesitating: "God's in His Heaven/All's right with the world." Later he will often forget this one and call upon Jeeves to finish it. In these stories Bertie seldom quotes verbatim but gives a sketchy version of the original or simply refers to a literary work:

> It was like what somebody or other wrote about the touch of a vanished hand. ("The Aunt and the Sluggard"; from Tennyson's "The May Queen")
>
> The situation floored me. I'm not denying it. Hamlet must have felt much as I did when his father's ghost bobbed up in the fairway. ("The Aunt and the Sluggard")

Even the device of having Bertie render a poem, the words of which he has nearly forgotten, is already present:

> I remember, as a kid, having to learn by heart a poem about a bird by the name of Eugene Aram, who had the deuce of a job in this respect. All I can recall of the actual poetry is the bit that goes:
>
> Tum-tum, tum-tum, tum-tumpty-tum
> I slew him, tum-tum tum!
>
> ("Jeeves Takes Charge"; from Thomas Hood's "The Dream of Eugene Aram")

Some of Bertie's favorites make their first appearances early on:

> "Oh, I say, Jeeves," I said. "Sorry to interrupt the feast of reason and flow of soul and so forth, but—" ("Startling Dressiness of a Lift Attendant"; from Pope's "Imitations of Horace")
>
> Claude and Eustace looked at each other, like those chappies in the poem, with a wild surmise. ("The Great Sermon Handicap"; from Keats's "On First Looking into Chapman's Homer")

The device of quotation, then, stems originally from Bertie, and his learning vocabulary and quotations from Jeeves comes into the series quite late.

VOCABULARY

Once Wodehouse introduced the device of having Bertie pick up words, phrases, and quotations from Jeeves, he took care that the reader would notice at least some instances of the process. At several points Bertie refers to Jeeves's influence on him. In "Jeeves and the Kid Clementina," for example, Bertie and the other characters hear a loud crash:

> I'm never at my best at describing things. At school, when we used to do essays and English composition, my report generally read "Has little or no ability, but does his best," or words to that effect. True, in the course of years I have picked up a vocabulary of sorts from Jeeves, but even so I'm not nearly hot enough to draw a word-picture that would do justice to that extraordinarily hefty crash.

In *Thank You, Jeeves*, Stoker says he assumes Bertie will want to marry Pauline; Bertie responds with his usual "Oh, ah," which prompts Stoker to say:

> "I am not quite sure if I understand the precise significance of the expression 'Oh, ah!' " he said, and, by Jove, I wonder if you notice a rather rummy thing. I mean to say, this man had had the advantage of Jeeves's society for only about twenty-four hours, and here he was—except that Jeeves would have said 'wholly' instead of 'quite' and stuck in a 'Sir' or two—talking just like him. I mean, it just shows. I remember putting young Catsmeat Potter-Pirbright up at the flat for a week once, and the very second day he said something to me about gauging somebody's latent potentialities. And Catsmeat a fellow who had always thought you were kidding him when you assured him that there were words in the language that had more than one syllable. (Chap. 12)

We witness Bertie's own learning process, since Wodehouse introduces words and phrases in a remarkably systematic way.

The simplest (and least common) device is to have Bertie mention that he had picked a phrase up from Jeeves, without Jeeves having actually used the phrase earlier in the series:

> However, I was not accorded leisure to review my emotions, in what Jeeves would call the final analysis. . . . (*The Code of the Woosters*, Chap. 2)

> "Antagonistic."
> "What?"
> "I mean altruistic. You are probably not familiar with the word, but it's one I've heard Jeeves use. It's what you say of a fellow who gives selfless service, not counting the cost." (*Jeeves in the Offing*, Chap. 1)

Far more often, however, Jeeves uses a phrase and Bertie later repeats it. In *Right Ho, Jeeves*, Jeeves explains Gussie's misadventures on the way to the fancy-dress ball:

> "These aberrations of memory are not uncommon with those who, like Mr. Fink-Nottle, belong to what one might call the dreamer type."
> "One might also call it the fatheaded type."
> "Yes, sir." (Chap. 5)

But a page later, Bertie opts for Jeeves's term:

> "These dreamer-types do live, don't they?"
> "Yes, sir."

In *Stiff Upper Lip, Jeeves*, Jeeves explains why he summoned Plank to Totleigh Towers: " 'My heart was melted by Miss Byng's tale of her misfortunes, sir' " (chap. 21). This time Bertie uses the phrase after a longer interval, in the final scene, as he decides to give his Alpine hat to Jeeves's butler friend: "My heart melted. I ceased to think of self. It had just occurred to me that in the circumstances, I would be unable to conclude my visit by tipping Butterfield. The hat would fill that gap" (chap. 24).

These are simple cases, but the more common and complex uses of this device come when Bertie's repetition becomes a motif across two or more works in the series. In *Right Ho, Jeeves,* Bertie describes how Tuppy Glossop denounces him: "He also called me an opprobrious name" (chap. 15). We would hardly expect Bertie to know such a term, yet Jeeves had used it in "The Purity of the Turf," saying that Harold "made an opprobrious remark respecting my personal appearance." In the publishing history of the series, these two occurrences come eleven years apart. In "Bertie Changes His Mind," Jeeves for the first time supplies a word for which Bertie is groping; Bertie is trying to describe the schoolgirls he has just encountered:

> "Of course, I can imagine some fellows finding them a bit exhausting in—her—"
> "*En masse,* sir?"
> "That's the word. Bit exhausting *en masse.*"

In *The Code of the Woosters* (published sixteen years after the story), Stiffy Byng asks if Bertie does not loathe policemen, and he replies, " 'Well, not *en masse,* if you understand the expression' " (chap. 4). In *Jeeves and the Feudal Spirit,* Bertie sings to Aunt Dahlia: "I started to render the refrain in a pleasant light baritone. . . ." (chap. 9); in "Jeeves and the Song of Songs," this passage had occurred: " 'Mr. Wooster,' said Jeeves, turning to Aunt Dahlia, 'has a pleasant, light baritone.' " In this case, the publication dates are twenty-four years apart.

We might posit that such repetitions are mere coincidence, were it not for the fact that there are many cases where similar phrases become more pervasive motifs. In *Thank You, Jeeves,* for example, when Jeeves quits over Bertie's insistence on playing the banjolele, he tells Bertie:

> "No, sir. I fear I cannot recede from my position"
> "But dash it, you say you *are* receding from your position."

> "I should have said, I cannot abandon the stand which I have taken." (Chap. 1)

Shortly thereafter, Bertie tells Chuffy he cannot learn to love Sir Roderick Glossop: "No, Chuffy, I fear I cannot recede from my position" (chap. 3). Then, in the next novel, *Right Ho, Jeeves,* Bertie asks Jeeves how the awards ceremony went after his departure: "Did Gussie seem taken aback? Did he recede from his position?" (chap. 17). In *The Code of the Woosters,* Bertie initially disapproves of Stinker Pinker's stealing the policeman's helmet: "I could not recede from my position. At the Drones, we hold strong views on these things" (chap. 8). Later, when Stiffy is blackmailing him, he resists:

> I made one last appeal.
>
> "You won't recede from your position?" (Chap. 8)

The same sort of thing occurs with "contingency," which Jeeves uses in "The Inferiority Complex of Old Sippy" ("The contingency is remote, sir") and *Right Ho, Jeeves* (" 'The contingency is a remote one, sir," chap. 13). It returns twice, marked as something Bertie learned from Jeeves:

> I was about to laugh indulgently and say that this was what Jeeves calls a remote contingency. . . . (*Jeeves and the Feudal Spirit,* Chap. 6)

> I was thankful that there was no danger of this contingency, as Jeeves would have called it, arising. (*Stiff Upper Lip, Jeeves,* Chap. 18)

Other phrases that become motifs in this way are: "le *mot juste,*" first used by Jeeves in "The Ordeal of Young Tuppy" and repeated in all the novels up to *The Mating Season,* and "of the essence," spoken by Jeeves in *Thank You, Jeeves,* where it becomes a motif and is then repeated in most of the subsequent novels.

Probably the series' single most common phrase is "the psychology of the individual." Bertie knows the word "psychology" in "The Artistic Career of Corky": "I don't know why it is—one of these psychology sharps could explain it, I suppose—but uncles and aunts, as a class, are always dead against the drama, legitimate or otherwise." By Jeeves's first use of the phrase in "Jeeves and the Song of Songs," Bertie has conveniently forgotten it; Jeeves is explaining his plan to Aunt Dahlia:

> "In affairs of this description, madam, the first essential is to study the psychology of the individual."
> "The what of the individual?"
> "The psychology, madam."
> "He means the psychology," I said. "And by psychology, Jeeves, you imply?"
> "The natures and dispositions of the principals in the matter, sir."
> "You mean, what they're like?"
> "Precisely, sir."

Bertie assimilates this one quickly, and it soon becomes an element in his rebellion against Jeeves, when Bertie starts trying to outdo his valet in finding solutions based on the psychology of the individual. The phrase appears in each of the novels, often two or three times.

Wodehouse became adept at finding distinctive phrases the reader could remember from book to book and recognize as something Bertie had earlier picked up from Jeeves. Foreign phrases stand out in particular, and perhaps the most striking motifs of learned language come with Bertie's variants on *nolle prosequi* and *rem acu tetigisti*, which Jeeves introduces in *Right Ho, Jeeves* and *Joy in the Morning* respectively. Bertie picks up *nolle prosequi* and uses it often, initially in a straightforward way simply to signify a refusal. As the series goes on, however, he varies it in comic ways. In *Joy in the Morning*, he explains to Nobby that he could not stand up to Florence:

> "And if you think I've got the force of character to come back with a *nolle prosequi*—"
> "With a what?"

"One of Jeeves's gags. It means roughly 'Nuts to you!' If, I say, you think I'm capable of asserting myself and giving her the bird, you greatly overestimate the Wooster fortitude." (Chap. 12)

Here two slang renderings of the Latin term introduce repetition and comic variation.

Wodehouse could also combine this motif with others (in this case a scriptural one) to create a ludicrous effect, as when Bertie explains to Bobbie Wickham that it was Balaam's ass, not Jonah's, that was noted for stubbornness:

"Jeeves."

"Sir?"

"To settle a bet, wasn't it Balaam's ass that entered the *nolle prosequi*?"

"Yes, sir." (*Jeeves in the Offing*, Chap. 19)

Rem acu tetigisti provided even more possibilities for Bertie to twist language around in various ways. Jeeves introduces it in *Joy in the Morning*, when Bertie grasps the idea that Lord Worplesdon must make a deal secretly or the price of the stock he wants to buy will rise:

"Precisely, sir. *Rem acu tetigisti.*"

"Rem—"

"*Acu tetigisti*, sir. A Latin expression. Literally, it means 'You have touched the matter with a needle,' but a more idiomatic rendering would be—"

"Put my finger on the nub?"

"Exactly, sir." (Chap. 4)

Bertie takes more time to learn this one, but he soon tries to slip it into his conversation, talking to Nobby Hopwood:

"Exactly," I said. "You have touched the matter with a needle."

"Done what?"

> "One of Jeeves's gags," I explained. "*Rem* something. Latin stuff." (*Joy in the Morning*, Chap. 27)

The phrase returns in *Jeeves and the Feudal Spirit*, where Bertie asks Jeeves to refresh his memory on the phrase and its meanings, then begins using it himself in various ways:

> Aunt Dahlia seemed perplexed, like one who strives to put her finger on the nub. (Chap. 19)

> It was enough. I saw that, as always, he had *tetigisti*-ed the *rem*. (Chap. 21)

This phrase also appears in *Joy in the Morning* and *Aunts Aren't Gentlemen*.

Aside from learning vocabulary, Bertie also occasionally echoes Jeeves's speech patterns:

> "Then gradually, by degrees—little by little, if I may use the expression—disillusionment sets in." ("Jeeves and the Old School Chum")

> "I think there can be little doubt, Jeeves, that the entire contents of that jug are at this moment reposing on top of the existing cargo in that already brilliantly lit man's interior. Disturbing, Jeeves."
> "Most disturbing, sir." (*Right Ho, Jeeves*, Chap. 16)

> "I am not a disobliging man, Jeeves. If somebody wanted me to play Hamlet, I would do my best to give satisfaction." ("Jeeves and the Greasy Bird")

Such learning recalls Bertie's decision in "Jeeves Takes Charge" to let Jeeves do his thinking. At that early point, the juxtaposition of Jeeves's and Bertie's speech patterns had created a relatively simple contrast. Bertie becomes the means for gradually blending those two styles within the speech of a single character.

Bertie's adoption of Jeeves's quotations and language reflect the control the valet exercises over his master. In keeping with that relationship, the learning process goes in only one direction. Jeeves almost never learns a phrase from Bertie, and although his speech changes as he becomes a more complex character, he does not mix Bertie-style slang with his formal speech. The sole exception comes in *Much Obliged, Jeeves*; in chapter 12, Bertie asks Jeeves if the odds against Aunt Dahlia getting money from Runkle might be a hundred-to-eight:

> "A somewhat longer price than that, sir. We have to take into consideration the fact that Mr. Runkle is. . . ."
>
> "Yes? You hesitate, Jeeves, Mr. Runkle is what?"
>
> "The expression I am trying to find eludes me, sir. It is one I have sometimes heard you use to indicate a deficiency of sweetness and light in some gentleman of your acquaintance. You have employed it of Mr Spode or, as I should say, Lord Sidcup and, in the days before your association with him took on its present cordiality, of Mr Glossop's uncle, Sir Roderick. It is on the tip of my tongue."
>
> "A stinker?"
>
> No, he said, it wasn't a stinker.
>
> "A tough baby?"
>
> "No."
>
> "A twenty-minute egg?"
>
> "That was it, sir. Mr. Runkle is a twenty minute egg."

Note that the one time Jeeves tries to recall one of Bertie's phrases, he cannot do so, despite his usual excellent memory.

Later in *Much Obliged, Jeeves*, the phrase returns, turning the pair's verbal relationship on its head in a unique fashion; Bertie recalls that Jeeves had put the odds at a hundred-to-one:

> "Approximately that, sir."
>
> "Runkle being short of the bowels of compassion."
>
> "Precisely, sir. A twenty-minute egg." (Chap. 15)

The device underscores the reversal that the book creates between Bertie's and Jeeves's habitual positions: Bertie correctly predicting the use of the Club Book for blackmail, and Jeeves giving Bertie a reward in the final scene by destroying the eighteen pages he had written about his employer in the Book.[9]

Overall, however, Jeeves does not employ Bertie's vocabulary. Subtle hints in the series, though, might lead us to suspect that, given their mutual fascination with language, he is entertained by Bertie's slang and twisted quotations. "Bertie Changes His Mind" gives us the second of our two direct clues as to why Jeeves likes Bertie. (As we have seen, he considers Bertie to have a "heart of gold.") In telling of Bertie's uncharacteristic petulance, Jeeves remarks that he was "far from his usual bright self." "Bright" here obviously means sparkling and lively rather than intelligent, and restrained though Jeeves himself is, we can assume that he enjoys his association with Bertie specifically because of the contrasts between them. Bertie's language is surely one of the brightest things about him.

QUOTATION

The set of devices Wodehouse employs in relation to quotations resembles that used for the phrases and words Bertie learns from Jeeves. Again the quotations become motifs repeated and varied across the series; again Bertie translates Jeeves's erudite diction into slang terms; and again Jeeves teaches Bertie but does not learn from him. This wordplay suggests that for Wodehouse, units of language were interchangeable; that once he had repeated a motif a few times, it became an internal cliché of the series and that, whether or not it had started out as a cliché, it could then be combined with or substituted for other similar devices.

Indeed, for the most part Wodehouse sticks to very familiar quotations—exactly the type that would make their way into Bartlett's. Being so familiar, they can often be made strange through a simple change rendered by Bertie. In *Thank You, Jeeves*, for example, Bertie needs butter to get the boot polish off his face and appeals to Chuffy: " 'Butter, Chuffy, old man' I said, 'Slabs of butter. If you have butter, prepare to shed it now' " (chap. 14; from *Julius Caesar*). Of Aunt Dahlia's threat to withhold Anatole's cooking, Bertie says: "This is not the first time she had displayed the velvet hand beneath the iron glove—or, rather, the old way round" (*The Code of the Woosters*, chap.

2; attributed to Charles V). Bertie describes how Jeeves pressured him into telling Sir Watkyn that he is engaged to Stiffy:

> I don't know if you were ever told as a kid that story about the fellow whose dog chewed up the priceless manuscript of the book he was writing. The blow-out, if you remember, was that he gave the animal a pained look and said: "Oh, Diamond, Diamond, you—or it may have been thou—little know—or possibly knowest—what you—or thou—has—or hast—done." I heard it in the nursery, and it has always lingered in my mind. And why I bring it up now is that this is how I looked at Jeeves as I passed from the room. I didn't actually speak the gag, but I fancy he knew what I was thinking. (Chap. 8; the original quotation is from Sir Isaac Newton, "Said to a pet dog who knocked over a candle and set fire to his papers": "O Diamond! Diamond! thou little knowest the mischief done!")

Bertie describes Reginald "Kipper" Herring to Aunt Dahlia: " 'The muscles of his brawny arms are strong as iron bands, and he has a cauliflower ear' " (*Jeeves in the Offing*, chap. 6; Longfellow's "The Village Blacksmith"). As these examples suggest, Bertie's fascination with quotations provides another way for Wodehouse to juxtapose formal language and slang—whether Jeeves provides the quotation or Bertie recalls it (dimly) himself.

Similar juxtapositions arise from Bertie's tendency to render quotations in close to their original form and then to paraphrase them in more colloquial language:

> [Stoker] was one of those fellows who get their backs up the minute they think their nearest and dearest are trying to shove them into anything; a chap who, as the Bible puts it, if you say Go, he cometh, and if you say Come, he goeth; a fellow, in a word, who if he came to a door with "Push" on it, would always pull. (*Thank You, Jeeves*, Chap. 20)
>
> "[Poppet's] belligerent attitude is simple—"
>
> "Sound and fury signifying nothing, sir?"
>
> "That's it, pure swank. A few civil words and he will be grappling you . . . what's the expression I've heard you use?"

> "Grappling me to his soul with hoops of steel, sir?"
> "In the first two minutes." (*Jeeves in the Offing*, Chap. 11; *Macbeth* and *Hamlet*)

> There was no sense in beating about bushes. It was another of those cases of if it were done, then 'twere well it were done quickly. (*Much Obliged, Jeeves*, Chap. 13; *Macbeth*)

Wodehouse has a large repertory of techniques for defamiliarizing quotations. He can, for example, render poetry as if it were prose, as when Bingo describes Honoria Glossop to Bertie: " 'She walks in beauty like the night of cloudless climes and starry skies; and all that's best of dark and bright meet in her aspect and her eyes. Another bit of bread and cheese,' he said to the lad behind the bar" ("The Pride of the Woosters Is Wounded"; *Romeo and Juliet*). A quotation might be broken up and rendered as dialogue, as in *The Mating Season*, when Bertie asks Jeeves why the judge decided to let Gussie off with a fine:

> "Possibly the reflection that the quality of mercy is not strained, sir."
> "You mean it droppeth as the gentle rain from heaven?"
> "Precisely, sir. Upon the place beneath. His worship would no doubt have taken into consideration the fact that it blesseth him that gives and him that takes and becomes the throned monarch better than his crown."
> I mused. Yes, there was something in that. (Chap. 8; *The Merchant of Venice*)

Jeeves provides a subtle way of defamiliarizing standard quotations. He may break up the familiar rhythm of a bit of poetry by inserting "sir" or "madam" into it—as if it were necessary for him to maintain his respectfulness even at such moments. He particularly does this with Shakespeare, as in *Joy in the Morning*:

> "There's not the smallest orb which thou beholdest, sir, but in his motion like an angel sings, still quiring to the young-eyed cherubims." (Chap. 14; *The Merchant of Venice*)

> "What did Shakespeare say about ingratitude?"
> " 'Blow, blow, thou winter wind,' sir, 'thou art not so unkind as man's ingratitude.' " (Chap. 15; *As You Like It*)[10]

It seems safe to say that of all the devices Wodehouse uses in the Jeeves/Wooster series, quotation is far and away the most common. There are at least 800 quoted passages and references.

Surprisingly few quotations are used only once. Instead, quotations tend to be learned by Bertie and used, with variations, across the series. Many such motifs become internal clichés: God moves in a mysterious way/His wonders to perform (William Cowper's "Olney Hymns"), the toad beneath the harrow (Kipling's "Departmental Ditties"), the Assyrian coming down like a wolf on the fold (Byron's "The Destruction of Sennacherib"), the maddest, merriest day of all the glad new year (Tennyson's "The May Queen"), and on and on. I shall concentrate on a few of these motifs, to show how systematically Wodehouse changes them on each return in such a way as to render these outworn phrases vivid.

As with the verbal motifs, the quotations usually originate with Jeeves, who recites them to Bertie—often at the latter's request, since Bertie has forgotten them. Bertie typically uses them again within the same work and returns to them in subsequent books as well. Moreover, beginning with the late short-story period, Wodehouse tends to single out one or a few quotations to make a major motif for each work. These then return, less frequently, in subsequent works.

One of the earliest of these motivic uses come in "Indian Summer of an Uncle." Initially, Bertie quotes Burns but is corrected by Jeeves:

> "Well, as I was saying, I maintain that the rank is but a guinea stamp and a girl's a girl for all that."
> " 'For *a'* that', sir. The poet Burns wrote in the North British dialect."
> "Well, 'a' that,' then, if you prefer it."
> "I have no preference in the matter, sir. It is simply that the poet Burns—"
> "Never mind about the poet Burns."
> "No, sir."

> "Forget the poet Burns."
> "Very good, sir."
> "Expunge the poet Burns from your mind."
> "I will do so immediately, sir."
> "What we have to consider is not the poet Burns but the Aunt Agatha." (Burns, "Is There for Honest Poverty?")

Bertie dismisses "the poet Burns" (Jeeves's usual diction, picked up by Bertie) but tries to bring him up again in conversation with Aunt Agatha, rather as Jeeves would:

> "I have always known that you were an imbecile, Bertie," said the flesh-and-blood, now down at about three degrees Fahrenheit, "but I did suppose that you had some proper feeling, some pride, some respect for your position."
> "Well, you know what the poet Burns says."
> She squelched me with a glance.

Later in this story, Wodehouse shifts the quotations to another poet, using Burns as the transition. This transition also introduces a device that will be used throughout the series, as Jeeves and Bertie try to guess which poet the other has in mind. After Aunt Agatha departs, Bertie tells Jeeves that they will use Jeeves's scheme, which she rejected; he says they will

> "do Aunt Agatha good despite herself. What is it the poet says, Jeeves?"
> "The poet Burns, sir?"
> "Not the poet Burns. Some other poet. About doing good by stealth."
> " 'These little acts of unremembered kindness,' sir?"
> "That's it in a nutshell, Jeeves." (Wordsworth's "Lines Composed a Few Miles Above Tintern Abbey")

Later still, Jeeves quotes Tennyson to Bertie: "Besides, sir, remember what the poet Tennyson said: 'Kind hearts are more than coronets' " ("Lady Clara Vere de Vere"). At the end we get the pay-off, as Bertie and Jeeves decide to flee from Aunt Agatha:

"I'll get the car at once."

"Very good, sir."

"Remember what the poet Shakespeare said, Jeeves."

"What was that, sir?"

" 'Exit hurriedly, pursued by a bear.' You'll find it in one of his plays. I remember drawing a picture of it on the side of the page, when I was at school." (*The Winter's Tale*, which, of course, Bertie quotes incorrectly.)

All these poets return at intervals through the series.

The main motif of quotation in *Thank You, Jeeves* is initiated by Jeeves, at Bertie's request:

"Jeeves," I recollect saying, on returning to the apartment, "who was the fellow who on looking at something felt like somebody looking at something? I learned the passage at school, but it has escaped me."

"I fancy the individual you have in mind, sir, is the poet Keats, who compared his emotions on first reading Chapman's Homer to those of stout Cortez when with eagle eyes he stared at the Pacific."

"The Pacific, eh?"

"Yes, sir. And all his men looked at each other with a wild surmise, silent upon a peak in Darien."

"Of course. It all comes back to me." (Chap. 1; "On First Looking Into Chapman's Homer")

Bertie brings this passage up again and again, culminating in *Aunts Aren't Gentlemen*. There the sight of the stolen cat wandering in while Cook and Plank are on the premises leads to a mix of quotations and cliché:

I looked at it with a wild surmise, as silent as those bimbos upon the peak in Darien. With both hands pressed to the top of the head to prevent it from taking to itself the wings of a dove and soaring to the ceiling, I was asking myself what the harvest would be. (Chap. 19; "Oh, that I had Wings like a Dove!" is used frequently in the series; it is from Psalms, 55:6, and was part of a Victorian hymn.)

The Code of the Woosters is rife with motifs of this sort: Abou Ben Adhem and the Recording Angel, Archimedes and his discovery of the principle of displacement, the "native hue of resolution" passage from *Hamlet*, and Sidney Carton. It also introduces *Hamlet*'s "fretful porpentine" passage, the only motif I shall pursue through the series in complete form. It begins as a minor motif in this novel, when Bertie tells Gussie that Stiffy plans to give the notebook to Sir Watkyn:

> I had expected him to take it fairly substantially, and he did. His eyes, like stars, parted from their spheres, and he leaped from the chair, spilling the contents of the glass and causing the room to niff like the salon bar of a pub on a Saturday night. (Chap. 5)

Later, Bertie tussles with Spode and describes his adversary crawling out from beneath a sheet:

> His face was flushed, his eyes were bulging, and one had the odd illusion that his hair was standing on end—like quills upon the fretful porpentine, as Jeeves once put it when describing to me the reactions of Barmy Fotheringay-Phipps on seeing a dead snip, on which he had invested largely, come in sixth in the procession at the Newmarket Spring Meeting. (Chap. 7)

Still later Gussie runs in, chased by Sir Watkyn: "His spectacles were glittering in a hunted sort of way, and there was more than a touch of the fretful porpentine about his hair" (chap. 12).

The motif returns in *Joy in the Morning*, becoming more prominent (sharing top billing with the "still quiring to the young-eyed cherubims" passage from *The Merchant of Venice*). Bertie upbraids Jeeves for getting him into a scheme involving Lord Worplesdon:

> "Entirely through your instrumentality, I shall shortly be telling Uncle Percy things about himself which will do something to his knotted and combined locks which at the moment has slipped my memory."
>
> "Make his knotted and combined locks to part and each

> particular hair to stand on end like quills upon the fretful porpentine, sir."
> "Porpentine?"
> "Yes, sir."
> "That can't be right. There isn't such a thing. However, let that pass." (Chap. 20)

At the end of the same scene, Bertie says to Jeeves:

> "If I could show you that list Boko drafted out of the things he wants me to say—I unfortunately left it in my room, where it fell from my nerveless fingers—your knotted and combined locks would part all right, believe me. You're sure it's porpentine?"
> "Yes, sir."
> "Very odd. But I suppose half the time Shakespeare just shoved down anything that came into his head." (Chap. 20)

Bertie does ponder the things Jeeves says to him, however, as is evidenced by the motif's next appearance in the book; as Bertie and Boko are at breakfast, "I asked him if he knew what a porpentine was, and he said to hell with all porpentines" (Chap. 20).

Much later, Bertie is upset at the prospect of wearing Stilton's policeman uniform to a costume ball:

> "I am not a weak man, Jeeves, but when I think of what will happen if Stilton cops me while I am draped in that uniform, it makes my knotted and combined locks . . . what was that gag of yours?"
> "Part, sir, and each particular hair—"
> "Stand on end, wasn't it?"
> "Yes, sir. Like quills upon the fretful porpentine."
> "That's right. And that brings me back to it. What the dickens is a porpentine?"
> "A porcupine, sir."
> "Oh, a *porcupine*? Why didn't you say that at first? It's been worrying me all day." (Chap. 25)

After returning home from the fancy-dress ball, Bertie finds a hedgehog in his bed:

> Some hidden hand had placed a hedgehog between the sheets—practically, you might say, a fretful porpentine. Assuming this to be Boko's handiwork, I was strongly inclined to transfer it to his couch. Reflecting, however, that while this would teach him a much needed lesson it would be a bit tough on the porpentine, I took the latter out into the garden and loosed it into the grass. (Chap. 26)

Here, as a result of musing on the quotation, Bertie transforms a hedgehog into a porpentine—as if the motif of language has become so important that it virtually requires the introduction of the creature into the story.

Finally, Bertie tells Jeeves that Worplesdon is locked in the garage, and Jeeves gives his usual understated reply: " 'Most disturbing, sir.' " Bertie considers this too mild: "If Jeeves has a fault, as I think I have already mentioned, it is that he is too prone merely to tut at times when you would prefer to see his knotted and combined locks do a bit of parting" (chap. 28). By this point in the series, Wodehouse has become expert at weaving a quotation through a single book.

Bertie brings the porpentine back in three of the later books, working in comic variants in each case. In *Jeeves in the Offing*, he tells Jeeves that he is in trouble:

> "Do you recall telling me, once about someone who told somebody he could tell him something which would make him think a bit? Knitted socks and porcupines entered into it, I remember."
>
> "I think you may be referring to the ghost of the father of Hamlet, Prince of Denmark, sir. Addressing his son, he said, 'I could a tale unfold whose lightest word would harrow up thy soul, freeze thy young blood, make thy two eyes, like stars, start from their spheres, thy knotted and combined locks to part and each particular hair to stand on end like quills upon the fretful porpentine.' "
>
> "That's right. Locks, of course, not socks. Odd that he should

have said porpentine when he meant porcupine. Slip of the tongue, no doubt, as so often happens with ghosts. Well, he had nothing on me. It's a tale of that precise nature that I am about to unfold." (Chap. 11)

Later on in the same scene, Bertie fills Jeeves in on more of the plot: " 'I'll unfold the tale of Wilbert and the cow-creamer, and if that doesn't make your knotted locks do a bit of starting from their spheres, I for one shall be greatly surprised" (chap. 11). When Bertie tells Aunt Dahlia that Wilbert has stolen the cow-creamer, she is not surprised: "I had expected to freeze her young—or, rather, middle-aged—blood and have her perm stand on end like quills upon the fretful porpentine, and she hadn't moved a muscle" (chap. 12). Later, Bertie tells Aunt Dahlia, "I have a story to relate which I think you will agree falls into the fretful porpentine class" (chap. 20).

The same motif returns once in *Much Obliged, Jeeves,* where Bertie brings it in briefly when L. P. Runkle enters: ". . . the mere sight of whom, circs being what they were, was enough to freeze the blood and make each particular hair stand on end like quills upon the fretful porpentine, as I have heard Jeeves put it" (chap. 16). Finally, in *Aunts Aren't Gentlemen,* Vanessa Cook asks Bertie to hold Orlo's letters for her to pick up: "The idea of her calling at the cottage daily, with Orlo Porter, already heated to boiling point, watching its every move, froze my young blood and made my two eyes, like stars, start from their spheres, as I have heard Jeeves put it" (chap. 7). Bertie then tells Vanessa that Orlo is in the village:

> I have said that her face had hardened as the result of going about the place socking policemen, but now it had gone all soft. And while her two eyes didn't actually start from their spheres, they widened to about the size of regulation golf balls, and a tender smile lit up her map" (Chap. 7).

Near the end, Jeeves has just found Bertie bound and gagged, calmly freed him, and offered him some coffee. Bertie responds: " 'A great idea. And make it strong,' I said, hoping that it would take the taste of Plank's tobacco pouch away. 'And when you return, I shall a tale unfold which will make you jump as if you'd sat on a fretful porpentine' " (chap. 19).

Space permitting, we could trace such through developments of familiar quotations through the series with such items as the "cat i' the adage" (*Macbeth*), "Oh, woman in our hours of ease" (Scott's "Marmion"), and "the lark's on the wing, the snail's on the thorn" (Browning's "Pippa Passes"). Still, even without examining every occurrence of these phrases, we can see how, in addition to their other functions, they unobtrusively enhance the sense of Jeeves as an adult and Bertie as a perpetual child. Occasionally Bertie coaxes Jeeves to complete a familiar quotation, rather as a child insists that the parent tell the old story without omissions. In *Right Ho, Jeeves,* Bertie remarks on how Gussie cannot get up the courage to propose:

> "A marked coldness of the feet, was there not. I recollect you saying he was letting—what was it?—letting something do something. Cats entered into it, if I am not mistaken."
>
> "Letting 'I dare not' wait upon 'I would,' sir."
>
> "That's right. But what about the cats?"
>
> "Like the poor cat i' the adage, sir."
>
> "Exactly. It beats me how you think of these things." (Chap. 1)

At the end of *The Code of the Woosters,* Bertie's request for a familiar quotation irresistibly suggests a bedtime story:

> "This is the end of a perfect day, Jeeves. What's that thing of yours about larks?"
>
> "Sir?"
>
> "And, I rather think, snails."
>
> "Oh, yes, sir. 'The year's at the Spring, the day's at the morn, morning's at seven, the hill-side's dew-pearled—' "
>
> "But the larks, Jeeves? The snails? I'm pretty sure larks and snails enter into it."
>
> "I am coming to the larks and snails, sir. 'The larks's on the wing, the snail's on the thorn—' "
>
> "Now you're talking. And the tab line?"
>
> " 'God's in His Heaven, all's right with the world.' "

"That's it in a nutshell. I couldn't have put it better myself." (Chap. 14)

After Jeeves leaves, Bertie drifts off to sleep, turning the passage on its head as he does so:

> Jeeves was right, I felt. The snail was on the wing and the lark on the thorn—or, rather, the other way round—and God was in His heaven and all right with the world.
>
> And presently the eyes closed, the muscles relaxed, the breathing became soft and regular, and sleep which does something which has slipped my mind to the something sleave of care poured over me in a healing wave.

Here two juxtaposed quotations bring us full circle. The book had opened with Bertie waking up to Keats ("season of mists and mellow fruitfulness"); now it ends with him lulled to sleep with Browning and Shakespeare.

As we have seen, quotation is linked to the narrative stability represented by Jeeves. Only a few quotations in the series are spoken by characters other than Bertie and Jeeves, and other characters often misunderstand Bertie when he uses his shortened or twisted versions of familiar passages in conversation. Indeed, as Bertie picks up phrases, speech patterns, and quotations from Jeeves, the pair develops what almost amounts to a private language to which only they—and the habitual reader—have full access. This process enhances our sense of the pair's relationship as a marriage; even though they barely age in the course of the series, the frequent echoes from earlier works create the sense of a wealth of shared experience. It also suggests that they have access to a pool of clichés and conventions that only they, and the reader, recognize. Time and again characters ask Bertie to explain what he has just said, but usually these problems arise because Bertie has referred in elliptical or cryptic fashion to something learned from Jeeves. In contrast, Jeeves seldom has trouble understanding Bertie. He can supply the correct quotation when Bertie gives a bit of it or even when he gets it wrong, as when Bertie tries to describe Silversmith:

> "Forceful is correct. What's that thing of Shakespeare's about someone having an eye like Mother's?"
>
> "An eye like Mars, to threaten and command, is possibly the quotation for which you are groping, sir."
>
> (*The Mating Season*, Chap. 8; *Hamlet*)

In turn, Bertie often can translate Jeeves's more complex speeches into terms his friends and relatives can understand.

One of the subtlest devices that underscores this verbal rapport between Bertie and Jeeves comes in the occasional scene where Bertie drops his slang and speaks virtually as Jeeves would. Invariably his auditors grow impatient or fail to understand him—though in some cases these same characters listen respectfully to similar speeches from Jeeves himself. In "Jeeves and the Yule-tide Spirit," Aunt Agatha phones Bertie and tells him to behave himself at her friend's country home:

> "I shall naturally endeavour, Aunt Agatha," I replied stiffly, "to conduct myself in a manner befitting an English gentleman paying a visit—"
>
> "What did you say? Speak up. I can't hear.
>
> "I said Right-ho."
>
> "Oh? Well, mind you do."

In "Jeeves and the Song of Songs," Bertie assures Aunt Dahlia he will cooperate:

> "And you shall have it, Aunt Dahlia," I replied suavely. "I can honestly say that there is no one to whom I would more readily do a good turn than yourself; no one to whom I am more delighted to be—"
>
> "Less of it," she begged, "less of it."

In *Stiff Upper Lip, Jeeves,* Bertie tries to explain to Aunt Dahlia on the phone that it's not his fault that Gussie has shown up at Brinkley with Emerald:

> "Yes," I said, "I heard he was on his way, complete with freckled human Pekinese. I am sorry, Aunt Dahlia, that you

> should have been subjected to unwarrantable intrusion, and I would like to make it abundantly clear that it was not the outcome of any advice or encouragement from me. I was in total ignorance of his intentions. Had he confided in me his purpose of inflicting his presence on you, I should have—"
>
> Here I paused, for she had asked me rather abruptly to put a sock in it.
>
> "Stop babbling, you ghastly young gasbag. What's all this silver-tongued orator stuff about?" (Chap. 17)

Fortunately Bertie is not daunted by such misunderstandings and impatience. As long as Jeeves can understand (nearly) everything he says, he seems content. Here again we see why Jeeves is as important a character as Bertie. While he has not formed Bertie's entire narrational and speaking styles, he modifies them over the years. Bertie's narration and speech in the novels would not involve such a startling combination of slang, cliché, and quotation were it not for Jeeves.

CHARACTER AND LANGUAGE

Within this overarching pattern of change, Wodehouse uses many devices of repetition. Both Jeeves and Bertie provide ways of introducing repetition, ways which are appropriate to their contrasted characters. Jeeves is restrained and inexpressive, using a great many stock phrases. His command of language and his compulsion to provide information, however, lead him to become quite verbose at times. Bertie, on the other hand, is slow to catch on, and much of the repetition in the series comes from his efforts to understand what is happening. Finally, the pair's fascination with language leads them off on tangents, looking for the right word or quotation. The digressions and repetitions that characterize their dialogue set them apart from other characters, who are apt to become annoyed when listening to them. Again, the result is a sense of a private language arising from a lengthy, close relationship.

We have seen how Jeeves controls his idealistic employer and how he often manages to conceal some of his activities from Bertie. Jeeves's pragmatism and uncommunicativeness are also reflected in his language, which he can control as a tool or a weapon. Indications of this practical usage include his repressed diction, his repertory of stock phrases, and his occasional verbosity.

Jeeves, as we know from "Bertie Changes His Mind," reacts strongly to events but seldom betrays his emotion in his facial expressions. Similarly, his diction often suggests a reluctance to express himself openly, and indeed, indicates a considerable repression. He frequently inserts phrases like "I confess" or "I must admit" into his conversation. In the explanation at the end of "Clustering Round Young Bingo," he says (emphasis added in all cases), " 'I was somewhat baffled for a while, *I must confess,* sir. Then I was materially assisted by a fortunate discovery.' " When in *Thank You, Jeeves,* he inadvertently smiles at seeing Bertie in blackface and gets scolded, Jeeves replies, " 'I beg your pardon, sir. I had not intended *to betray* amusement, but I could not help being a little entertained by your appearance. . . . *I fear* I have forgotten what it was that you asked me, sir' " (chap. 13). In *Joy in the Morning,* Jeeves tells Bertie that, contrary to what he had just told Worplesdon, he has found a solution to the problem: " 'Yes, sir. *I must confess* that in our recent interview I intentionally misled his lordship' " (chap. 23). He is particularly apt to use such a phrase if he is expressing emotion. In *Come On, Jeeves,* he describes Bertie attending a school to learn how to fend for himself. Jeeves adds: " '*I must confess* it is not without emotion that I picture Mr. Wooster seated on a bed that he has made, in a room that he has swept and dusted, darning his own socks' " (act 1). Such qualifying phrases abound in "Bertie Changes His Mind," which Jeeves narrates. We can contrast this usage with that of the uninhibited Bertie when he reacts to Jeeves's solutions, as in the "Episode of the Dog McIntosh": " 'Jeeves,' I said—and *I am not ashamed to confess that* there was a spot of chokiness in the voice—'there is none like you, none.' "

Jeeves's linguistic repression also surfaces when he uses colloquial phrases. Typically he qualifies his usage in some way. For example, as Jeeves is explaining to Bertie how he solved the problem in *Right Ho, Jeeves,* he says, " 'After your departure on the bicycle, the various estranged parties agreed so heartily in their abuse of you that the ice, *if I may use the expression,* was broken' " (chap. 23). In *Jeeves and the Feudal Spirit,* when Bertie asks Jeeves for help, Jeeves's reply combines these two types of phrasing: " 'With a problem of such magnitude, sir, *I fear* I am not able to provide a solution off-hand, *if I may use the expression.*' " (chap. 12). The notion that telling one's thoughts and feelings amounts to confessing or betraying them marks Jeeves as secretive.

Many of Jeeves's contributions to the dialogue consist of stock phrases repeated so often that they become clichés internal to the series: "Very good, sir," "Most disturbing, sir," "I endeavour to give satisfaction," and so on. In the earliest stories these are used straightforwardly, but later on they often convey double meanings. For example, at the end of "Bertie Changes His Mind," Jeeves asks if Bertie still intends to invite his sister and nieces to live with him:

> Mr. Wooster shuddered strongly.
> "That's off, Jeeves," he said.
> "Very good, sir," I replied.

In many cases "Very good, sir" simply means yes, but here Jeeves uses it to approve Bertie's decision. Yet he does not want Bertie to realize that he opposed the plan. We, not Bertie, infer that Jeeves considers Bertie's decision "very good." Jeeves frequently uses the phrase in this way to approve of Bertie's actions, as at the end of "Clustering Round Young Bingo," when Bertie capitulates over the silk evening shirts. Jeeves also uses "Very good, sir" to avoid or cut off open conflict with Bertie. In his fight with Bertie over Bobbie Wickham in "Jeeves and the Yule-tide Spirit," Jeeves halts the discussion by retreating into meaningless repetition of this phrase:

> "Jeeves," I said, "you're talking rot."
> "Very good, sir."
> "Absolute drivel."
> "Very good, sir."
> "Pure mashed potatoes."
> "Very good, sir."
> "Very good, sir—I mean very good, Jeeves, that will be all," I said.

Jeeves pulls a similar move in "The Inferiority Complex of Old Sippy," when Bertie has acquired a new vase he detests:

> "How does it look?"
> "Yes, sir."
> A bit cryptic, but I let it go.

Bertie is not, however, always so easily fobbed off by Jeeves's stock phrases.

Jeeves's speeches are usually short and designed to convey information to Bertie (or to hide it from him). When he does become verbose, it is either in a deliberate attempt to confuse his auditor or in a gratuitous display of his learning. He is generally successful in using excessive verbiage as a weapon. In "Jeeves and the Unbidden Guest," which contains twelve scenes, almost one-third of the words Jeeves speaks come in the climactic eleventh scene, as he uses a series of speeches to reduce Lady Malvern to silence: "Lady Malvern tried to freeze him with a look, but you can't do that sort of thing to Jeeves. He is look-proof." He uses a similar tactic on the constable who tries to arrest Bertie in "Jeeves and the Kid Clementina"; even though the cop tells Jeeves to be quiet, Jeeves gets the last word:

> "I shall be delighted to accompany you, officer, if such is your wish. And I feel sure that in this connexion I may speak for Mr. Wooster also. He too, I am confident, will interpose no obstacle in the way of your plans. If you consider that circumstances have placed Mr. Wooster in a position that might be termed equivocal, or even compromising, it will naturally be his wish to exculpate himself at the earliest possible—"
> "Here!" said the policeman, slightly rattled.
> "Officer?"
> "Less of it."
> "Just as you say, officer."
> "Switch it off and come along."
> "Very good, officer."

The most spectacular instance occurs in *Thank You, Jeeves,* where Stoker enters in a rage over the fact that Jeeves has let Bertie out of the stateroom; Jeeves responds with a lengthy speech, during which Stoker is unable to interpose a word. As Bertie puts it, "You can't switch Jeeves off when he has something to say which he feels will be of interest. The only thing is to stand by and wait till he runs down." By the end of the speech, Stoker is mollified to the point where he thanks Jeeves for releasing Bertie (chap. 18). Jeeves continues to use this tactic on Stoker in later scenes, dragging in irrelevant information on the color of the two plotting sheds' roofs in describing how Sir Roderick has been incarcerated in one of them (chap. 21). In this case Bertie bemusedly defends Stoker by steering Jeeves onto the main track of the conversation. He is himself occasionally the victim of similar tactics, however. Jeeves's gratuitous speech about cultured pearls, the endoscope, and Moh's scale of hardness in *Jeeves and the Feudal Spirit* leaves Bertie dazed: "I was still blinking a bit. When Jeeves gets going nicely, he often has this effect on me. With a strong effort I pulled myself together and was able to continue" (chap. 12).

More often, however, Jeeves's sidetracks simply annoy Bertie. Jeeves first becomes gratuitously windy in "The Spot of Art":

> "Yes, sir. I telegraphed to Mrs. Slingsby shortly before four. Assuming her to have been at her hotel in Paris at the time of the telegram's delivery, she will no doubt take a boat early tomorrow afternoon, reaching Dover—or, should she prefer the alternative route, Folkestone—in time to begin the railway journey at an hour which will enable her to arrive in London at about seven. She will possibly proceed first to her London residence—"
>
> "Yes, Jeeves," I said. "Yes. A gripping story, full of action and human interest. You must have it set to music some time and sing it. Meanwhile, get this into your head. It is imperative that Mrs. Slingsby does not learn. . . ."

Later in the same story Jeeves brings up "the poet Scott" and is squelched by Bertie.

It might seem odd that Jeeves, with his carefully calculated use of language, should wander off onto tangents in this way, yet the device provides one of the few ways in which Wodehouse could make Jeeves funny in his own right. Jeeves seldom says overtly amusing things, but his main attributes—learning and intelligence—could be rendered funny through exaggeration. This tactic becomes more apparent in *Ring for Jeeves*, where Bertie is not present to provide a comic narrational style. Hence Jeeves must supply more of the humor, and his verbosity and tendency to quote are pushed further than usual, to the degree where he seems more pompous. Bill reprimands him frequently. Jeeves's verbosity again displays his mental file of language, for his longer speeches often involve anecdotes about his past experiences (with family members or former employers), information he had memorized in encyclopedic fashion, or quotations. These "recitations" accord with his overall approach to language, which is highly stable, based on already acquired knowledge rather than learning.

In contrast, Bertie's language is spontaneous. His naiveté and honesty make it difficult for him to use language to deceive or manipulate others. His conversation has none of the restraint Jeeves displays. Rather, it tends toward exaggeration and redundancy in descriptions of his reactions. In "Jeeves and the Old School Chum," Jeeves shocks Bertie by revealing that he had deliberately left the lunch behind: "I quivered like an aspen. I stared at the man. Aghast. Shocked to the core." His descriptions of the effects of Jeeves's pick-me-ups are also vivid:

> I swallowed the stuff. For a moment I felt as if somebody had touched off a bomb inside the old bean and was strolling down my throat with a lighted torch, and then suddenly everything seemed to get all right. The sun shown in through the windows, birds twittered in the tree-tops, and, generally speaking, hope dawned once more. ("Jeeves Takes Charge")

In keeping with this tendency to express himself freely, Bertie often disapproves of Jeeves's restraint, as in *Thank You, Jeeves*, when Jeeves tells Bertie that there is no butter available to wipe the boot polish off his face:

> "But, Jeeves, this is frightful."
> "Most disturbing, sir."
> If Jeeves has a fault, it is that his demeanour on these occasions too frequently tends to be rather more calm and unemotional than one could wish. One lodges no protest, as a rule, because he generally has the situation well in hand and loses no time in coming before the Board with one of his ripe solutions. But I have often felt that I could do with a little more leaping about with rolling eyeballs on his part, and I felt it now. At a moment like the present, the adjective "disturbing" seemed to me to miss the facts by about ten parasangs. (Chap. 16)

As in this case, it is usually Jeeves's stock phrases that annoy Bertie. In "Episode of the Dog McIntosh" Bertie asks if Jeeves remembers the obnoxious Blumenfeld boy:

> "Very vividly, sir."
> "Well, prepare yourself for a shock. He's coming to lunch."
> "Indeed, sir?"
> "I'm glad you can speak in that light, careless way. I only met the young stoup of arsenic for a few brief moments, but I don't mind telling you the prospect of hob-nobbing with him again makes me tremble like a leaf."
> "Indeed, sir?"
> "Don't keep saying 'Indeed, sir?' You have seen this kid in action and you know what he's like."

Bertie also comes to realize that Jeeves uses stock phrases to suggest what he cannot state openly. Hence Bertie may object to Jeeves's diction during a disagreement, as in "Episode of the Dog McIntosh," when he tells Jeeves he has received a letter from Bobbie Wickham:

> "Indeed, sir?"
> I sensed—if that is the word I want—the note of concern in the man's voice, and I knew he was saying to himself, "Is the young master about to slip?" . . .
> "She wants me to give her lunch, to-day."
> "Indeed, sir?"

> "And two friends of hers."
> "Indeed, sir?"
> "Here. At one-thirty."
> "Indeed, sir?"
> "Correct this parrot complex, Jeeves," I said, waving a slice of bread-and-butter rather sternly at the man. "There is no need for you to stand there saying 'Indeed, sir.' I know what you're thinking, and you're wrong. As far as Miss Wickham is concerned, Bertram Wooster is chilled steel."

As Bertie becomes more rebellious, he objects more and more to such phrases. These objections grow milder again after *Right Ho, Jeeves,* but they never entirely disappear from the series.

In general, though Wodehouse's stories and novels are not long and are usually carefully plotted, they contain an astonishing amount of repetition and redundancy. This extra material is not padding, but almost inevitably works in one way or another to let the reader linger over language. As a result, ordinary language can become strange and incongruous, and the repetitions themselves become humorous.

LINGERING OVER LANGUAGE

> "And it is for this," said Miss Mapleton, "that we pay rates and taxes!"
> "Awful!" I said.
> "Iniquitous."
> "A bally shame."
> "A crying scandal,' said Miss Mapleton.
> "A grim show," I agreed.
> ("Jeeves and the Kid Clementina")

Wodehouse's tactics for creating verbal repetition range from the obvious to the complex. The simpler devices direct our attention to the device of repetition itself; once noticed, the device can then be traced in its more subtle forms.

Perhaps the most obvious case is the familiar one of repetition between Bertie's narration and his dialogue. For example, in "The Spot of Art," Jeeves tells Bertie that Gwladys has become engaged to Lucius Pim:

> After the poster nothing seemed to matter.
> "After that poster, Jeeves," I said, "nothing seems to matter."

At most Wodehouse can vary this by adding a bit more repetition, as in "Jeeves and the Old School Chum":

> I couldn't follow him. The old egg seemed to be speaking in riddles.
> "You seem to me, old egg," I said, "to speak in riddles. Don't you think he speaks in riddles, Jeeves?"

I find only seventeen instances of such straightforward repetition between narration and dialogue in the entire series. Yet because the device is so obvious, every return becomes noticeable, and I suspect that many readers think of it as one of the more prominent methods for creating humor in Bertie's prose.

There is a considerable amount of repetition within the dialogue itself, but here the functions of the repetition are more varied than in the narration/dialogue echoes. Bertie's early "dude" burble is characterized by repetition, as with his typical "Hullo, hullo, hullo" and lines like "Oh, I don't know, you know, don't you know" ("A Letter of Introduction"). Later in the series, repetition becomes far more flexible. It can suggest Bertie's mood, as in "Jeeves and the Impending Doom," when Bertie contemplates a visit to Aunt Agatha:

> "Jeeves," I said, "I am not the old merry self this morning."
> "Indeed, sir?"
> "No, Jeeves. Far from it. Far from the old merry self."
> "I am sorry to hear that, sir."

It is notable that the second pair of lines in this passage was not in the original 1926 magazine version of the story but was added for the 1930 book collection. In general Wodehouse's revisions tended to expand the dialogue by adding repetitions.

Wodehouse became skilled at creating subsegments within the dialogue which have their own nearly self-contained structures based on repetition and variation—motivated by Bertie's slowness in grasping a situation and Jeeves's patience in explaining it. Jeeves's stock phrases can be crucial to the rhythm of these passages, as in this exchange from "Jeeves and the Song of Songs":

> "Yes, Jeeves? Say on."
> "Mr. Glossop, sir."
> "What about him?"
> "He is in the sitting-room, sir."
> "Young Tuppy Glossop?"
> "Yes, sir."
> "In the sitting-room?"
> "Yes, sir."
> "Desiring speech with me?"
> "Yes, sir."
> "H'm!"
> "Sir?"
> "I only said 'H'm.' "

Other characters display less patience than Jeeves in such situations, however. Aunt Dahlia reacts with annoyance when Jeeves delivers a note to Bertie in *Right Ho, Jeeves*:

> "A note for you, sir."
> "A note for me, Jeeves?"
> "A note for you, sir."
> "From whom, Jeeves?"
> "From Miss Bassett, sir."
> "From whom, Jeeves?"
> "From Miss Bassett, sir."
> "From Miss Bassett, Jeeves?"
> "From Miss Bassett, sir."
> At this point, Aunt Dahlia, who had taken one nibble at her whatever-it-was-on-toast and laid it down, begged us—a little

> fretfully, I thought—for heaven's sake to cut out the cross-talk vaudeville stuff, as she had enough to bear already without having to listen to us doing our imitation of the Two Macs. (Chap. 20)

Here Aunt Dahlia's objection points up the fact that the dialogue is not only internally repetitious but that the use of repetition as such is itself a cliché of stage comedy.

The contrast in Jeeves's and Bertie's vocabulary and diction leads to a pattern dependent upon what I shall call the "translation device." Often Jeeves says something that Bertie then repeats in less high-toned language to be sure he has it right. In other cases, Bertie grasps the point but translates for another person less accustomed to Jeeves's diction. The comic language in the early stories is particularly dependent on this device, as in "The Aunt and the Sluggard":

> "The crux of the matter would appear to be, sir, that Mr Todd is obliged by the conditions under which the money is delivered into his possession to write Miss Rockmetteller long and detailed letters relating to his movements, and the only method by which this can be accomplished, if Mr Todd adheres to his express intention of remaining in the country, is for Mr Todd to induce some second party to gather the actual experiences which Miss Rockmetteller wishes reported to her, and to convey these to him in the shape of a careful report, on which it would be possible for him, with the aid of his imagination, to base the suggested correspondence."
>
> Having got which off the old diaphragm, Jeeves was silent. Rocky looked at me in a helpless sort of way. He hasn't been brought up on Jeeves as I have, and he isn't onto his curves.
>
> "Couldn't he put it a little clearer, Bertie?" he said. "I thought at the start it was going to make sense, but it kind of flickered. What's the idea?"
>
> "My dear old man, perfectly simple. I knew we could stand on Jeeves. All you've got to do is to get somebody to go round the town for you and take a few notes, and then you work the notes up into letters. That's it, isn't it, Jeeves?"
>
> "Precisely, sir."

The inevitable joke in these situations is that Bertie's version is far shorter than Jeeves's.

Jeeves's habit of transposing Bertie's slang into more formal terms is also present from an early stage, as in "Jeeves and the Hard-Boiled Egg":

> "I suppose it bowled the poor fellow over absolutely?"
> "Mr. Bickersteth appeared somewhat taken aback, sir."

Wodehouse could motivate the translation device in various ways. It might occur when Bertie fails to understand Jeeves:

> "I can conceive that after what occurred in New York it might be distressing for you to encounter Miss Stoker, sir. But I fancy the contingency need scarcely arise."
> I weighed this.
> "When you start talking about contingencies arising, Jeeves, the brain seems to flicker and I rather miss the gist. Do you mean that I should be able to keep out of her way?"
> "Yes, sir."
> "Avoid her?"
> "Yes, sir." (*Thank you, Jeeves,* Chap. 1)

Or it might result from Jeeves's reluctance to seem to be accepting Bertie's slang terms as his own by simply answering "Yes, sir" to a question:

> "The chap I know wears horn-rimmed spectacles and has a face like a fish. How does that check up with your data?"
> "The gentleman who came to the flat wore horn-rimmed spectacles, sir."
> "And looked like something on a slab?"
> "Possibly there was a certain suggestion of the piscine, sir." (*Right Ho, Jeeves,* Chap. 1)

> "You agree with me that the situation is a lulu?"
> "Certainly a somewhat sharp crisis in your affairs would appear to have been precipitated, sir." (*The Code of the Woosters,* Chap. 2)

The basic point in all these cases is to allow the repetition of the same information in two or more ways. The phrases "face like a fish," "looked like something on a slab," and "a certain suggestion of the piscine" all describe the same attribute of Gussie, but the concentration is on language rather than on a steady flow of new narrative information.

The same is true of the series' frequent use of alternative words, mainly in Bertie's narration and dialogue. Bertie's interest in language leads him to link two virtually synonymous words, a tendency which begins early in the series, with "Jeeves Takes Charge": " 'This infernal kid must somehow be turned out eftsoons or right speedily.' " Such synonyms' relation to the general repetition in Bertie's dialogue becomes apparent in "The Rummy Affair of Old Biffy," where the device is doubled as he talks to Sir Roderick:

> "Old Biffy had some sort of fit or seizure just now and knocked over the table."
> "A fit!"
> "Or seizure."

He uses three equivalent terms when describing a maid's clumsiness: " 'The one now in office apparently runs through the *objets d'art* like a typhoon, simoom, or sirocco' " ("Clustering Round Young Bingo").

By the mid-1920s, the alternative words begin occasionally to be suggestions brought up by Jeeves or Bertie to each other in conversation, as in "The Episode of the Dog McIntosh":

> "I fancy, sir—"
> "Yes, Jeeves?"
> "I rather fancy, sir, that I have discovered a plan of action."
> "Or scheme."
> "Or scheme, sir. A plan of action or scheme which will meet the situation."

Increasingly, Bertie and Jeeves are concerned to find the precise word; in *Thank you, Jeeves,* Bertie decides to accept Stoker's invitation to dinner:

"I regard it as . . ."

"The *amende honorable*, sir?"

"I was going to say olive branch."

"Or olive branch. The two terms are virtually synonymous. The French phrase I would be inclined to consider perhaps slightly the more exact in the circumstances—carrying with it, as it does, the implication of remorse, of the desire to make restitution. But if you prefer the expression 'olive branch', by all means employ it, sir."

"Thank you, Jeeves."

"Not at all, sir."

"I suppose you know that you have made me completely forget what I was saying?"

"I beg your pardon, sir. I should not have interrupted. If I recollect, you were observing that it was your intention to accept Mr. Stoker's invitation."

"Ah, yes. Very well, then. I shall accept his invitation—whether as an olive branch or an *amende honorable* is wholly immaterial and doesn't matter a single, solitary damn, Jeeves. . . ."

"No, sir." (Chap. 11)

Bertie occasionally has to choose between two interchangeable words and settles on both, just to be on the safe side:

"Can't you see? It's all very well for old Stoker to talk—er—"

"Glibly, sir?"

"Airily."

"Airily or glibly, sir, whichever you prefer."

"It's all very well for old Stoker to talk with airy glibness about marrying us off, but he can't do it, Jeeves." (*Thank you, Jeeves*, Chap. 12)

Later in the book, Bertie plays it safe again: "Jeeves had spoken airily—or glibly—of busting in and making myself at home for the night. . ." (chap. 16).

As Bertie learns more elaborate language from Jeeves, his alternative words come to involve more consistent contrasts between somewhat esoteric words and colloquial words. Of Madeline, Bertie comments, "The Bassett-Wooster imbroglio or mix-up will, of course, be old stuff to those of my public. . ." (*The Mating Season*, chap. 4). Later he mixes a foreign phrase and a cliché in describing her: "She remained *sotto voce* and the silent tomb, and I carried on" (chap. 15).

Jeeves's reaction to all this is to allow Bertie the choice between terms in most cases, and if Bertie decides to use both terms, Jeeves respectfully does so as well. In this case, Bertie is describing Corky Pirbright to Jeeves:

> "And her manner was evasive. Or shall I say furtive?"
> "Whichever you prefer, sir."
> "It was the manner of a girl guiltily conscious of being in the process of starting something."

At this point Jeeves begins a digression, causing Bertie to lose the thread of the conversation:

> "Well, what *was* I saying? I've forgotten."
> "You were commenting on Miss Pirbright's furtive and evasive manner, sir." (*The Mating Season*, Chap. 20)

By late in the series, the use of alternative words becomes quite elaborate. At times Wodehouse calls our attention to it explicitly, as in this conversation between Sir Roderick and Bertie:

> "Mrs Travers impressed it upon me with all the emphasis at her disposal that the greatest care must be exercised to prevent Mr and Mrs Cream taking—"
> "Umbrage?"
> "I was about to say offense."
> "Just as good, probably. Not much in it either way." (*Jeeves in the Offing*, Chap. 7)

In *Much Obliged, Jeeves* we learn that Jeeves has a relevant reference book; Bertie uses it to come up with a flood of synonyms to emphasize Bingley's effrontery in the dramatic scene in the Junior Ganymede Club:

> As to his manner, I couldn't get a better word for it at the moment than 'familiar,' but I looked it up later in Jeeves's Dictionary of Synonyms and found that it had been unduly intimate, too free, forward, lacking in proper reserve, deficient in due respect, impudent, bold and intrusive. Well, when I tell you that the first thing he did was to prod Jeeves in the lower ribs with an uncouth finger, you will get the idea. (Chap. 4)

Overall the alternative-word device proved far from fruitless (or bootless) as a flexible source for much humor and defamiliarization of language.

One of the series' most noticeable devices is Bertie's habit of using abbreviations in place of words. Wodehouse may have picked this device up from *Great Expectations*, where Wemmick refers to his father as the Aged P., short for Aged Parent. (Bertie occasionally uses "aged relative" when referring to or addressing Aunt Dahlia. In *The Code of the Woosters* he speaks to her: " 'Let me explain, aged r.' " [Chap. 5]) The device neatly sums up Wodehouse's insistence on repetition and cliché, for, in order for us to be able to understand what the abbreviation stands for, Bertie must use one or the other.

In many cases, Bertie uses a word or phrase and then abbreviates it within the next few sentences or paragraphs. This version of the abbreviation device first appears in "Jeeves and the Yule-tide Spirit," where the repetition comes almost immediately: "But I had hung up the receiver. Shaken. That's what I was. S. to the core." It is then dropped until the novels, reappearing in *Thank You, Jeeves*, when Bertie looks downstairs:

> . . . a shadowy form was in the far corner, wrestling with the grandfather clock. . . . A sudden twist of the combatants had revealed to me the face of the shadowy f., and with a considerable rush of emotion I perceived that it was Brinkley. (Chap. 13)

These examples are relatively simple, but the device could become complicated, forcing the reader to glance back along the preceding paragraphs to figure out what Bertie's abbreviations stood for. Such backtracking necessarily fosters repetition, as in *Joy in the Morning*:

> "Well, then, sir, his lordship informs me that he is in the process of concluding the final details of a business agreement of great delicacy and importance."
>
> "And he wanted you to vet the thing for snags?"
>
> "Not precisely, sir. But he desired my advice."
>
> "They all come to you, Jeeve, don't they—from the lowest to the highest?"
>
> "It is kind of you to say so, sir."
>
> "Did he mention what the b. a. of great d. and i. was?" (Chap. 4)

As Wodehouse realized from the start, however, Bertie would not have to use the words in full at all, if the abbreviations stood for standard phrases. The reader would quickly recognize abbreviations for familiar phrases and clichés. The first use of abbreviations in the series comes in "The Aunt and the Sluggard," when Bertie says, "Mix me a b-and-s, Jeeves. I feel weak." Much later, in "Jeeves and the Impending Doom," Bertie describes, by means of hyperbaton, his listlessness as Jeeves serves breakfast: "He uncovered the fragrant eggs and b., and I pronged a moody forkful." About a page later he reverses the phrase: "He shimmered out, and I took another listless stab at the e. and bacon."

Abbreviated clichés multiply in the novels. In *Thank You, Jeeves,* Bertie says he "emitted a hollow g." (chap. 12), and in *Joy in the Morning,* he describes the conversation among himself, Nobby, and Boko after Jeeves's departure: "He oiled off, and we settled down to an informal debate in which the note of hope was conspicuous by its a." (Chap. 25) When, in *Stiff Upper Lip, Jeeves* Madeline tells Bertie she is in love with Gussie, he remarks: "Her words, as you may well imagine, were music to my e." (Chap. 5) In all these cases there is no use of the abbreviated word or phrase in full; we realize what Bertie means by the fact that the phrase is a familiar one.[11]

Some cases of abbreviation combine repetition with cliché. In *Jeeves in the Offing,* Bertie says: "I passed a hand over my fevered brow," and a few lines later remarks, "I passed another hand over my f.b." (Chap. 3) A similar passage occurs in *Stiff Upper Lip, Jeeves,* when Bertie hears that Gussie and Emerald have eloped: "I sank forward in my chair, the face buried in the hands"; he describes his hopelessness, since now he cannot reconcile Gussie and Madeline: "So now, as I say, I sank forward in my chair, the f. buried in the h." (Chap. 16) Such abbreviations not only induce us to look back to the original passage but also point up the similarity between the original phrasing and its return in the passage containing the abbreviation(s).

Abbreviation becomes far more common as the series progresses. Of the 143 cases of abbreviations or shortened words ("the old metrop"), only eleven occur in the short stories. Well over half come in the postwar novels (that is, *Jeeves and the Feudal Spirit* and after; there are none in *Ring for Jeeves,* since only Bertie uses such abbreviations). This development suggests that as Bertie's mixture of slang and language learned from Jeeves becomes more prominent, his use of abbreviation increases as well. The device of abbreviation relates to Bertie's fascination with the sound of language as well as with its meaning. His use of letters instead of words never causes any misunderstanding on the part of other characters, but it deflects the reader's attention from the narrative flow to the verbal level—and inevitably the result is to call attention to formulaic language. By the late period, the effect is quite baroque, and the reader can only fully appreciate the style by being familiar with Bertie's typical usage. A passage from *Aunts Aren't Gentlemen* uses the abbreviation device three times in connection with two clichés (and also returns to the device's probable source with the reference to the "aged relative"):

> So far, I said to myself, as I put back the receiver, so g. I would have preferred, of course, to be going to the aged relative's home, where Anatole her superb chef dished up his mouth-waterers, but we Woosters can rough it, and life in a country cottage with the aged r just around the corner would be a very different thing from a country c without her coming through with conversation calculated to instruct, elevate and amuse. (Chap. 3)

This is not a linguistic quirk Bertie picks up from Jeeves. It is his own from the start. He uses it increasingly in the course of the series, and, like so many of the other stylistic devices, it adds a complexity to the late novels that compensates for their loss of narrative density.

Finally there is the case of that innately repetitive term, "gentleman's personal gentleman." It is first used by Jeeves himself in the opening of "Bertie Changes His Mind" as a synonym for valet, and it becomes pervasive thereafter. (Previously Bertie had usually referred to Jeeves as "my man.") The phrase indicates how Wodehouse managed to weave his dominant device into the most small-scale of elements. In effect, "gentleman's personal gentleman" encapsulates the series' central relationship, since Bertie is the first "gentleman" and Jeeves the second, and the verbal echo suggests at once their equality, opposition, and union. Wodehouse was well aware of the possibilities the phrase held for further repetition and exploited them in the ingenious lyric, "Lament of a Gentleman's Gentleman" in *Betting on Bertie*. There repetition is carried to absurd lengths in the refrain, as Jeeves describes his mortification at Bertie's having become a bookie:

> Why even an unsentimental man
> Would surely be touched to the core
> By the sight of a gentleman's gentleman
> In the plight of a gentleman's gentleman
> When a gentleman's gentleman's gentleman
> Is not a gentleman any more! (Act 1, scene 2)

I shall close with two representative passages of what Alexander Cockburn has called Bertie's "dense allusive utterance":[12]

> It is pretty generally recognized in the circles in which he moves that Bertram Wooster is not a man who lightly throws in the towel and admits defeat. Beneath the thingummies of what-d'you-call-it his head, wind and weather permitting, is as a rule bloody but unbowed, and if the slings and arrows of outrageous fortune want to crush his proud spirit, they have to pull their socks up and make a special effort.
>
> Nevertheless, I must confess that when, already weakened

> by having to come down to breakfast, I beheld the spectacle which I have described, I definitely quailed. The heart sank, and, as had happened in the case of Spode, everything went black. Through a murky mist I seemed to be watching a negro butler presenting an inky salver to a Ma Trotter who looked like an end man in a minstrel show.
>
> The floor heaved beneath my feet as if an earthquake had set in with unusual severity. My eye, in a fine frenzy rolling, met Aunt Dahlia's, and I saw hers was rolling, too. (*Jeeves and the Feudal Spirit,* Chap. 21)

> "It may be fun for her," I said, with one of my bitter laughs, "but it isn't so diverting for the unfortunate toad beneath the harrow whom she plunges so ruthlessly in the soup." (*Jeeves in the Offing,* Chap. 10)

One can add little to this, except to point out that most of the books' titles are clichés (or, in the case of *Joy in the Morning,* a quotation).[13]

CONCLUSIONS

> INTERVIEWER: So readers looking for profundity will be disappointed?
>
> TOM SHARPE: Disappointed?! They'd be mental to start![14]

I have suggested from the beginning that Wodehouse is a distinctive case of an author who achieves the same sort of self-conscious awareness of literary conventions usually associated with modernist writers, yet simultaneously remains firmly within the sphere of popular publication. The complexity of his plot constructions and the brilliance of his style would in themselves make him worthy of respect and extended analysis, but beyond that, his blending of high art and popular tendencies lend him considerable interest.

Two traditional criteria for literary significance are obvious formal innovation and the expression of a major theme or world view. (These two would not necessarily be part of the same critical approach, however.) Neither seems to serve us well when looking at Wodehouse. As we have seen throughout this study, he did not participate in the massive changes in literature created by other authors of his generation. His decision to publish in mass-market fiction magazines placed his work in a context which ordinarily did not invite readers either to linger over stylistic complexities or to expect anything in the way of innovation. And yet, we have seen, he did develop an oddly original approach, that of pushing cliché, repetition, and quotation to absurd lengths in a way that calls attention to the conventions of literature in general, rather than changes it in any innovative way. This approach informed his work at every level: genre, narrative structure, characterization, and style.

Critics looking for thematic significance in Wodehouse will likewise dismiss him out of hand. Again, he was aware that from the beginning of his career important meanings were lacking:

> From my earliest years I had always wanted to be a writer. I started turning out the stuff at the age of five. (What I was doing before that, I don't remember. Just loafing, I suppose.)
>
> It was not that I had any particular message for humanity. I am still plugging away and not the ghost of one so far, so it begins to look as though, unless I suddenly hit mid-season form in my eighties, humanity will remain a message short.[15]

Yet if we assume that significance does not lie simply in meanings that the analyst can summarize baldly in a critique but in the sum total of the work's overall form, then Wodehouse can be seen to have created something complex indeed. As a young professional writer, he consciously absorbed the conventions of a vast range of literature, from the classics to newspaper journalism, and he saw something absurd in all those conventions.

Perhaps that range of citation and reference helps define how Wodehouse overrides the traditional distinction between high and popular literature. The teaming of Jeeves and Bertie balances the two, with Jeeves's quotations coming primarily from banal but high literature of the sort taught in Victorian and Edwardian schools and with Bertie knowing all the latest hit songs and slang. Wodehouse found it just as funny to have Jeeves exasperate Bertie by quoting Marcus Aurelius on "the Great Web" as to lampoon a cliché about a "faceless fiend" in a thriller Bertie reads.

Similarly, the overturning of traditional class associations further stresses the collapse in distinctions between high and popular literature. Jeeves, the lower-middle-class servant who ordinarily would be reading pulp fiction (as do virtually all other servants in Wodehouse's works, most notably Beach in the Blandings series), is the one who speaks with the precision of an Oxbridge-educated Edwardian gentleman. Bertie *is* an Oxford-educated Edwardian gentleman, but talks like a jazz-age upper-class twit. Both traditions are gently, and equally, mocked.

Wodehouse renews familiar aspects of many sorts of literature, not by overturning them with avant-garde devices but by pushing them just a bit further—hyperconventionalizing them, as it were. For in the end, Wodehouse's humor is not aimed at destroying the mundane in literature—an impossible goal. Instead, if we read a great deal of Wodehouse, we may become just as aware of the conventional as Jeeves is, and as delighted with it as Bertie.

APPENDIX A

INITIAL MAGAZINE AND BOOK PUBLICATIONS OF THE JEEVES/WOOSTER SERIES

TITLES OF INITIAL SERIAL PUBLICATIONS	DATE OF FIRST US PUBLICATION	DATE OF FIRST UK PUBLICATION	BOOK PUBLICATION
Early Short Stories			
"Extricating Young Gussie"	Sept. 1915, *Saturday Evening Post* (*Post*)	Jan. 1916, *Strand*	*The Man with Two Left Feet* (UK: Methuen, Mar. 1917)
"The Artistic Career of Corky"	Feb. 1916, *Post*	June 1916, *Strand* (as "Leave It to Jeeves")	*My Man Jeeves* (MMJ) (UK: George Newnes, May 1919), *Carry on Jeeves* (COJ) (UK: Jenkins, Oct. 1925; USA: Doran, Oct. 1927. Incl. "Fixing It for Freddie," prev. unpub.)
"The Aunt and the Sluggard"	Apr. 1916, *Post*	Aug. 1916, *Strand*	*MMJ, COJ*
"Jeeves Takes Charge"	Nov. 1916, *Post*	Apr. 1923, *Strand*	*COJ*
"Jeeves and the Unbidden Guest"	Dec. 1916, *Post*	Mar. 1917, *Strand*	*MMJ, COJ*
"Jeeves and the Hard-boiled Egg"	Mar. 1917, *Post*	Aug. 1917, *Strand*	*MMJ, COJ*

Middle-Period Stories			
"Jeeves and the Chump Cyril"	June 1918, *Post*	Aug. 1918, *Strand*	*The Inimitable Jeeves* (*IJ*), (as "A Letter of Introduction"/"Startling Dressiness of a Lift Attendant") (UK: Herbert Jenkins, May 1923; USA: as *Jeeves*, Doran, Sept. 1923)
"Jeeves in the Springtime"	Dec. 1921, *Cosmopolitan* (*COS*)	Dec. 1921, *Strand*	*IJ* (as "Jeeves Exerts the Old Cerebellum"/"No Wedding Bells for Bingo")
"Scoring Off Jeeves"	Mar. 1922, *COS* (as "Bertie Gets Even")	Feb. 1922, *Strand*	*IJ* (as "The Pride of the Woosters Is Wounded"/ "The Hero's Reward"
"Sir Roderick Comes to Lunch"	Apr. 1922, *COS* (as "Jeeves the Blighter")	Mar. 1922, *Strand*	*IJ* (as "Introducing Claude and Eustace"/"Sir Roderick Comes to Lunch")
"Aunt Agatha Takes the Count"	Oct. 1922, *COS* (as "Aunt Agatha Makes a Bloomer")	Apr. 1922, *Strand*	*IJ* (as "Aunt Agatha Speaks Her Mind"/"Pearls Mean Tears")

TITLES OF INITIAL SERIAL PUBLICATIONS	DATE OF FIRST US PUBLICATION	DATE OF FIRST UK PUBLICATION	BOOK PUBLICATION
"Comrade Bingo"	May 1922, *COS*	May 1922, *Strand*	*IJ* (as "Comrade Bingo"/"Bingo Has a Bad Goodwood")
"The Great Sermon Handicap"	June 1922, *COS*	June 1922, *Strand*	*IJ*
"The Purity of the Turf"	July 1922, *COS*	July 1922, *Strand*	*IJ*
"Bertie Changes His Mind"	Aug. 1922, *Post*	Aug. 1922, *Strand* (as "Bertie Gets His Chance")	*COJ*
"The Metropolitan Touch"	Sept. 1922, *COS*	Sept. 1922, *Strand*	*IJ*
"The Delayed Exit of Claude and Eustace"	Nov. 1922, *COS* (as "The Exit of Claude and Eustace")	Oct. 1922, *Strand*	*IJ*
"Bingo and the Little Woman"	Dec. 1922, *COS*	Nov. 1922, *Strand*	*IJ* (as "Bingo and the Little Woman"/"All's Well")
"The Rummy Affair of Old Biffy"	Sept. 1924, *Post*	Oct. 1924, *Strand*	*COJ*
"Clustering Round Young Bingo"	Feb. 1925, *Post*	Apr. 1925, *Strand*	*COJ*
"Without the Option"	June 1925, *Post*	July 1925, *Strand*	*COJ*

Later Short Stories			
"The Inferiority Complex of Old Sippy"	Apr. 1926, *Liberty*	Apr. 1926, *Strand*	*Very Good, Jeeves* (*VGJ*) (UK: Jenkins, July 1930; USA: Doran, June 1930)
"Jeeves and the Impending Doom"	Jan. 1927, *Liberty*	Dec. 1926, *Strand*	*VGJ*
"Jeeves and the Yule-tide Spirit"	Dec. 1927, *Liberty*	Dec. 1927, *Strand*	*VGJ*
"Jeeves and the Song of Songs"	Sept. 1929, *COS* (as "The Song of Songs")	Sept. 1929, *Strand*	*VGJ*
"Jeeves and the Dog McIntosh"	Oct. 1929, *COS* (as "The Borrowed Dog")	Oct. 1929, *Strand*	*VGJ*
"Jeeves and the Love That Purifies"	Nov. 1929, *COS*	Nov. 1929, *Strand*	*VGJ* (as "Episode of the Dog McIntosh")
"Jeeves and the Spot of Art"	Dec. 1929, *COS*	Dec. 1929, *Strand*	*VGJ* (as "The Love That Purifies")
"Jeeves and the Kid Clementina"	Jan. 1930, *COS*	Jan. 1930, *Strand*	*VGJ* (as "The Spot of Art")
"Jeeves and the Old School Chum"	Feb. 1930, *COS*	Feb. 1930, *Strand*	*VGJ*

TITLES OF INITIAL SERIAL PUBLICATIONS	DATE OF FIRST US PUBLICATION	DATE OF FIRST UK PUBLICATION	BOOK PUBLICATION
"Indian Summer of an Uncle"	Mar. 1930, *COS*	Mar. 1930, *Strand*	*VGJ*
"Tuppy Changes His Mind"	Apr. 1930, *COS*	Apr. 1930, *Strand*	*VGJ* (as "The Ordeal of Young Tuppy")
	Jan.–June 1934, *COS*	Aug. 1933–Feb. 1934, *Strand*	*Thank You, Jeeves* (UK: Jenkins, Mar. 1934; USA: Little, Brown, Apr. 1934)
	Dec. 1933–Jan. 1934, *Post*	Apr.–Sept. 1934, *Grand Magazine*	*Right Ho, Jeeves* (UK: Jenkins, Oct. 1934; USA: as *Brinkley Court*, Little, Brown, Oct. 1934)
	July–Sept. 1938, *Post*		*The Code of the Woosters* (UK: Jenkins, Oct. 1938; USA: Doubleday, Doran, Oct. 1938)
			Joy in the Morning (USA: Doubleday, Aug. 1946; UK: Jenkins, June 1947)
	Dec. 1949, *Long Island Sunday Press*		*The Mating Season* (UK: Jenkins, Sept. 1949; USA: Didier, Nov. 1949)

	Oct. 1953, *Long Island Sunday Press*		*Ring for Jeeves* (UK: Jenkins, Apr. 1953; USA: as *The Return of Jeeves*, Simon and Schuster, Apr. 1954)
			Jeeves and the Feudal Spirit (UK: Jenkins, Oct. 1954; USA: as *Bertie Wooster Sees It Through*, Simon and Schuster, Feb. 1955)
"Jeeves Makes an Omelette"	Aug. 1959, *Ellery Queen's Mystery Magazine* (as "Jeeves and the Stolen Venus")	Jan. 1967, *Argosy*	*A Few Quick Ones* (UK: Jenkins, Oct. 1959; USA: Simon and Schuster, Apr. 1959)
	Feb. 1960, *Playboy* (as "How Right You Are, Jeeves"; abr.)	Aug–Sept. 1959, *John Bull* (as "How Right You Are, Jeeves")	*Jeeves in the Offing* (USA: as *How Right You Are, Jeeves*, Simon and Schuster, Apr. 1960; UK: Jenkins, Aug. 1960)
	Feb–Mar. 1963, *Playboy* (abr.)		*Stiff Upper Lip, Jeeves* (USA: Simon and Schuster, Mar. 1963; UK: Jenkins, Aug. 1963)

TITLES OF INITIAL SERIAL PUBLICATIONS	DATE OF FIRST US PUBLICATION	DATE OF FIRST UK PUBLICATION	BOOK PUBLICATION
"Jeeves and the Greasy Bird"	Dec. 1965, *Playboy*	July 1972, *Argosy*	*Plum Pie* (UK: Jenkins, Sept. 1966; USA: Simon and Schuster, Dec. 1967) *Much Obliged, Jeeves* (UK: Barrie & Jenkins, Oct. 1971; USA: Simon and Schuster, Oct. 1971) *Aunts Aren't Gentlemen* (UK: Barrie & Jenkins, Oct. 1974; USA: as *The Catnappers*, Simon and Schuster, Apr. 1975)

APPENDIX B

A TIMELESS WORLD?

As innumerable commentators have pointed out, the characters in the Jeeves/Wooster series do not seem to age. Wodehouse told interviewers that he did not try to keep a consistent chronology in his writings to match their dates of publication. Speaking in 1960 of *Jeeves in the Offing*, he described his attitude:

> The critics often hold this time element against me. In my latest Jeeves novel, published this year, I referred to something as having happened "the previous summer"—it was, in point of fact, the presentation of prizes at the Market Snodsbury Grammar School by Gussie Fink-Nottle—and a reviewer in the *Times Literary Supplement* pointed out that it had happened twenty-six years ago, but I can never see that this matters; Perry Mason never gets any older.[1]

Wodehouse, then, conceived of the characters as not aging at all.

A few critics have, however, tried to work out "real," plausible chronologies. Maha Nand Sharma, working largely on the basis of the series' references to *Milady's Boudoir* and Aunt Agatha's second marriage, comes up with a 3.3–year time-span for the novels. Some of this is plausible, but, because Bertie mentions in *Jeeves and the Feudal Spirit* that Aunt Agatha had recently remarried, Sharma assumes that *Joy in the Morning* takes place after the action of both *The Mating Season* and *Jeeves and the Feudal Spirit.* Yet this is clearly impossible, since *Jeeves and the Feudal Spirit* is a sequel to *Joy in the Morning,* with the plot revolving around the production of an adaptation of Florence's novel *Spindrift,* first mentioned in *Joy in the Morning.*[2] Using similar kinds of clues to determine Bertie's age, J. C. Morris concludes that the series as a whole covers at least five years and that Bertie ages from twenty-four to twenty-nine (based largely on the fact that four Christmases are mentioned and another must have occurred during Bertie's approximately year-long stay in the United States in the early-period stories).[3]

Such attempts to treat the series as though it takes place in real, consistent time are doomed to failure. As with the Sherlock Holmes series, there are many inconsistencies if one tries to work out a strict chronology. Going by references to the amount of time Dahlia has been trying to make *Milady's Boudoir* profitable, along with explicit references to the temporal gaps between certain works in the series, we can develop only a very sketchy chronology. Here "Clustering Round Young Bingo," where *Milady's Boudoir* is introduced, defines year one (there being no set of clues that would permit the creation of even a rough chronology for the earlier stories):

YEAR 1: "Clustering Round Young Bingo" (no time of year specified)

YEAR 2: Jeeves and the Yule-tide Spirit" (December, takes place months before *Right Ho, Jeeves*)

YEAR 3: *Right Ho, Jeeves* (July, two years after "Clustering")
The Code of the Woosters (autumn, a few months after *Right Ho, Jeeves*)
Stiff Upper Lip, Jeeves (autumn, about one month after *The Code of the Woosters*)
"Jeeves and the Greasy Bird" (December, takes place shortly after *Stiff Upper Lip Jeeves*)

YEAR 4: *The Mating Season* (spring, *Right Ho, Jeeves* was the previous summer)
Jeeves and the Feudal Spirit (July, three years after "Clustering")
Much Obliged, Jeeves (probably summer, *Jeeves and the Feudal Spirit* is "recent")

YEAR 5: *Jeeves in the Offing* (ca. July, occurs one year after *Jeeves and the Feudal Spirit*)

There are insuperable difficulties here. *Much Obliged, Jeeves* takes place shortly after *Jeeves and the Feudal Spirit,* yet it is also specified as coming directly after the events of *Stiff Upper Lip, Jeeves,* which is almost a year earlier. It is impossible to fit *Joy in the Morning* into this scheme at all; it takes place in July, and it must precede *Jeeves and the Feudal Spirit* by one year. Year 3 is out, however, since *Right Ho, Jeeves* takes place in late July, and Bertie has just returned from two months in Cannes. Year 3 is hopelessly crowded, anyway, with four major narratives (or five, counting *Much Obliged, Jeeves*)—and Jeeves and Bertie go off on their round-the-world cruise "almost immediately" after *The Code of the Woosters. Aunts Aren't Gentlemen* also supposedly takes place "some months after" *The Mating Season,* yet there is not much room for it in year 4 either. Similarly, *Stiff Upper Lip, Jeeves* takes place one month after *The Code of the Woosters,* both being set in autumn. In *Stiff Upper Lip, Jeeves,* Bertie knows that Spode has "recently" succeeded to a title and become Lord Sidcup. Yet in *Jeeves and the Feudal Spirit,* set in the following July, he has no idea who Lord Sidcup is until meeting him. There is no clue as to when *Thank you, Jeeves* occurs, beyond the fact that it is a "year or so" after "Clustering Round Young Bingo." *Jeeves in the Offing* takes place a year after *Jeeves and the Feudal Spirit,* so it would seem to take place after all the others. As a final example, in *Jeeves and the Feudal Spirit,* Jeeves says Bertie has eleven pages in the Club Book, and he still has eleven at the beginning of *Much Obliged, Jeeves*—yet Jeeves is just adding eight on the events of *Stiff Upper Lip, Jeeves.* Why has he added no material on Bertie's doings in *Jeeves and the Feudal Spirit?*

Clearly in some sense Wodehouse did think of Jeeves and Bertie living in a world where time passed, but, just as the characters do not age, the events in which they participate do not take up fixed, real time spans. Richard Usborne has claimed that Wodehouse avoided references to time: "There are virtually no dates in Wodehouse's books, and all his recurrent characters remain the same ages throughout." Usborne points to an exception in an early Blandings novel: "Lord Emsworth is stated to have been at Eton in the 1860s. The statement was made at a time when Wodehouse had not learnt to avoid dates."[4] Yet there are actually many references to time in the Jeeves/Wooster series. It is easy enough to figure out Bertie's age, since in "Jeeves Takes Charge" Bertie specifies that he had been fifteen at a point nine years before the story's action, making him twenty-four when he hires Jeeves. (He does, however, state that he hired Jeeves "about a half dozen years ago," so that, if we assume he really ages, Bertie would have to be around thirty at the time he begins writing up his adventures—and there is no hint as to when that might be in relation to the events of the series.) Moreover, although there may not be any mentions of actual dates, there are numerous topical references throughout the series that allow the reader to infer that the action takes place in a temporal setting roughly contemporaneous to the writing of the story or book in question.

Wodehouse was quite systematic about making his books topical. When in 1957 the Modern Library was preparing its Jeeves collection, he wrote to Bennett Cerf:

> If you use The Aunt and the Sluggard, how do you feel about the letter the fellow writes to his aunt about going to the Midnight Revels and meeting George Cohan and Fred Stone and Douglas Fairbanks? The story was written in 1916 or thereabouts, and these names date it a lot. Better change them to something modern, don't you think?[5]

In "The Aunt and the Sluggard," Jeeves visits two nightclubs, "Frolics on the Roof" and the "Midnight Revels"; both derived from Ziegfeld's popular "Midnight Frolics" on the Amsterdam roof in New York, a reference that would have been familiar to many of the story's original readers but is probably lost on most modern ones.[6] Wodehouse did update his topical references occasionally. The version of "Jeeves and the Unbidden Guest" in *Carry On, Jeeves* has Bertie keen on a "Broadway Special" hat, while Jeeves prefers the "White House Wonder" model. In the original *Saturday Evening Post* version of 1916, Bertie favored the "Country Gentleman" and Jeeves the "Longacre." (*Post* advertisements of the teens often give items of clothing names of this sort.)

The result of this topicality, when juxtaposed with the characters' agelessness, is a systematically contradictory time scheme that adds a subtle comic dimension of its own. Some critics have noticed this strange Wodehousian species of time. David Cannadine attributes part of Wodehouse's enduring popularity to this overlay of contemporary references on the basic Victorian and Edwardian conventions:

> His work is littered with references to contemporary film stars, household names, inventions, and world events. . . . The mechanics of the Wodehouse technique necessarily give rise to a world in which time does not function in the normal sense at all.[7]

R. B. D. French compares the Jeeves/Wooster books to a maze: "Inside there are two kinds of time."[8]

Dozens of references to contemporary events and personalities give the series its second kind of time, with the world changing around the unaging characters. Wodehouse's habit of inserting such references began early, as the examples above indicate. There are many film references in his works, and these are usually up-to-date. Jeeves goes to *Tiny Hands*, starring Baby Bobbie, in "Fixing It for Freddie"; it was probably derived from the Baby Peggy films, popular in the mid-1920s. The craze for "Sonny Boy," which plays such a large part in "Jeeves and the Song of Songs," was actually occurring in England in 1929, following the release there of the American talkie *The Singing Fool.* Bobbie Wickham is described as "constructed more on the lines of Clara Bow" ("Episode of the Dog MacIntosh"); Bow's brief career lasted from the mid-1920s to the early 1930s. In *Thank You, Jeeves* Seabury is influenced by seeing gangster films, a genre particularly popular in the early 1930s. Stiffy Byng is a "Smallish girl about the tonnage of Jessie Matthews" (in *The Code of the Woosters*)—a reference to the diminutive star of 1930s British film musicals. Bertie's description of Daphne Morehead as having a figure "as full of curves as a scenic railway" quotes the lyrics of "The Girl Hunt Ballet" from *The Bandwagon*, an MGM musical released in 1953, shortly before Wodehouse began work on *Jeeves and the Feudal Spirit*. In *Jeeves in the Offing*, Bertie refers to "those horrors from outer space which are so much with us at the moment on the motion-picture screen" (the science-fiction genre having come into prominence in the 1950s).

Other arts are mentioned as well, though not to such an extent. The popular songs Bertie plays on his banjolele in *Thank You, Jeeves*—for example, "Singin' in the Rain" and "My Love Parade"—were hits of recent years (again, both from successful Hollywood musicals). Upon hearing in *Jeeves and the Feudal Spirit* that Aunt Dahlia wants to sell *Milady's Boudoir*, Bertie remarks, "It was like hearing that Rodgers had decided to sell Hammerstein," and there is a reference to the "$64,000 question" in "Jeeves Makes an Omelette." Murder-mystery authors and characters are also mentioned frequently. Wodehouse seems to have kept tabs on the contemporary high literary scene as well. In *Jeeves and the Feudal Spirit*, Percy Gorringe's poem "Caliban at Sunset" is a reasonably accurate parody of 1950s free verse, and in "Jeeves and the Greasy Bird," Jeeves says Blair Eggleston is "one of our angry young novelists. The critics describe his works as frank, forthright, and fearless."

Similarly, despite his supposed unworldliness, Wodehouse was aware of current events. (Some of his early comic essays were satiric accounts of world affairs, as when he wrote extensively for *Vanity Fair* in the mid-1910s.) Such references crop up throughout his career. When Sippy is arrested in "Without the Option," he gives his name as Leon Trotzsky; in *Right Ho, Jeeves*, Bertie urges Tuppy to skip dinner by telling him to imitate Gandhi. Bertie reacts to Gussie's new self-confidence in *The Code of the Woosters* by remarking that "Mussolini could have taken his correspondence course" (chap. 3). By *The Mating Season* Alfred Duff Cooper (the British politician responsible for the BBC's attacks on Wodehouse following the Berlin broadcasts) had replaced Trotzsky as an alias when Gussie is arrested. Gromyko is mentioned in the "Jeeves version" of *Spring Fever,* Eisenhower in *Ring for Jeeves.*

Few of these references would date the plots exactly, but they are often topical enough to place the action within a few years. Cumulatively, they give a general sense of contemporaneity to the individual works and of passing time to the whole. We must assume that Bertie and Jeeves, having aged little or not at all, begin in the New York of Ziegfeld's "Midnight Frolics" and end there in the age of protest marches and street gangs.

A NOTE ON EDITIONS AND SOURCES

Ideally every quotation in this volume should be followed by a reference to a specific page number. Given, however, the enormous number of reprintings of P. G. Wodehouse's works, as well as the lack of a standard edition, it has proven impossible to cite any one set of editions to which most readers would have access. I have had to be content, therefore, with citing the titles of short stories and chapter numbers of novels quoted. Appendix A identifies the collection in which each of the short stories was republished. Thus anyone interested in looking at the quoted passages in their original contexts should face only a short search. In all cases I have used the British titles for the stories and books, since these were the ones Wodehouse provided; the American titles, where different, were usually invented at the magazines and presses. Appendix A also provides the American titles for the books, as well as variant short-story titles. Dates in the text, however, are those of the earlier publication, whether British or American.

To save space in the endnotes, I have given short names for frequently cited collections of primary documents as follows:

Dulwich—Special Collections, P. G. Wodehouse Library, Dulwich College, London
Heineman—James H. Heineman Collection
Ransom—Harry Ransom Humanities Research Center, The University of Texas at Austin
Reynolds—Paul R. Reynolds Collection, Rare Books Room, Butler Library, Columbia University, New York

Wodehouse Archive—P. G. Wodehouse Archive, Wodehouse Estate

Endnotes involving correspondence begin with the sender's name, followed by the place from which the letter was sent in parentheses, then the name of the addressee, the date, and the archival source.

Because Wodehouse collectors and experts are so kind, they often share their holdings by sending photocopies to each other. In some cases I read copies of letters and manuscripts in one collection, then encountered the originals in another. Going back and revising the sources on hundreds of notecards seemed an insuperable task. Thus in some cases my endnotes attribute a document to an archive or collection which holds only a photocopy. Such citations are not intended to slight the collectors who hold the original documents.

NOTES

INTRODUCTION

1. During the 1980s this opinion was voiced more and more openly in serious literary circles. See, for examples, Edward L. Galligan, "P. G. Wodehouse: Master of Farce," *Sewanee Review* 93, no. 4 (Fall 1985): 609–17, and Richard J. Voorhees, "Wodehouse at the Top of His Form," *University of Windsor Review* 16, no. 1 (Fall–Winter 1981): 13–25.

2. Don Ross, "P. G. Wodehouse Is 80," *New York Herald Tribune* (16 Oct. 1961), Dulwich.

3. James L. W. West III, *American Authors and the Literary Marketplace since 1900* (Philadelphia: University of Pennsylvania Press, 1988), p. 119.

4. Evelyn Waugh, "Journeyman to Master: Strange Case of Dr. P. G. Wodehouse," *The Sunday Times* (3 June 1956) Dulwich.

5. Evelyn Waugh (Gloucestershire) to Wodehouse, 29 Dec. 1947, and subsequent correspondence, Wodehouse Archive. The "Dr" comes from an honorary doctorate Oxford University conferred on Wodehouse in 1939.

6. Victor Shklovsky, "Art as Technique," *Russian Formalist Criticism: Four Essays*, trans. and ed. Lee T. Lemon and Marion J. Reis (Lincoln: University of Nebraska Press, 1965), p. 12.

7. Boris Tomashevsky, "Thematics," *Russian Formalist Criticism*, p. 95.

8. For a different analysis of the use of formulaic devices in Wodehouse, see the chapter entitled "Narrative Become Burble: P. G. Wodehouse," in Robert F. Kiernan's *Frivolity Unbound: Six Masters of the Camp Novel* (New York: Continuum, 1990), pp. 95–124. There (esp. pp. 118–21), Kiernan attributes the mix of metaphors, clichés, quotations, and other repetitious language to a camp quality in Wodehouse's art.

Similarly, M. A. Sharwood Smith treats the stylistic formulas of the

Jeeves/Wooster series as a manifestation of Wodehouse's irreverent approach to his English subject matter. See Smith's "The Very Irreverent P. G. Wodehouse: A Study of *Thank You, Jeeves*," *Dutch Quarterly Review of Anglo-American Letters* 8 (1978): 203–22.

9. Some may wonder if this "He reeled . . ." formula is not merely coincidental and if Wodehouse ever actually read *Dracula*. We need only compare another passage from Stroker's novel with some sentences from one of Wodehouse's Ukridge stories. In *Dracula*, Jonathan Harker tries to kill the sleeping vampire with a shovel: "But as I did so the head turned, and the eyes fell full upon me, with all their blaze of basilisk horror."

In "A Bit of Luck for Mabel," Ukridge's initial description of his Aunt Julia reads: " 'You know her, Corky, and you know just how she shoots her eyes at you without turning her head, as if she were a basilisk with a stiff neck.' " Later on in the same story, Ukridge describes his landlady: "Now, this Beale woman, I must tell you, was a slightly sinister sort of female, with eyes that reminded me a good deal of my Aunt Julia. . . . At this moment, by the greatest bad luck, her vampire gaze fell on the mantelpiece" (*Eggs, Beans, and Crumpets*).

Incidentally, a minor character in *Something Fresh*, the Bishop of Godalming, borrows his name from Lord Godalming, Arthur's title after his father's death, and Stoker's own name comes prominently into *Thank You, Jeeves*.

10. One of the best brief descriptions of this aspect of Wodehouse's style comes from Philip M. Thody: "Because he has such a total mastery of the English language, Wodehouse is able to play with it. He dislocates its clichés and explores its metaphors, making the reader more conscious of the wealth and potentialities of the words which everyone uses every day of their lives." See Thody, "P. G. Wodehouse and English Literature," in Eileen McIlvaine, Louise S. Sherby, and James H. Heineman, *P. G. Wodehouse: A Comprehensive Bibliography and Checklist* (New York: James H. Heineman, and Detroit: Omnigraphics, 1990), p. xxiv.

11. Those interested in Wodehouse's personal circumstances might wish to consult one of the four main biographical studies: Frances Donaldson, *P. G. Wodehouse: A Biography* (New York: Alfred A. Knopf, 1982); Benny Green, *P. G. Wodehouse: A Literary Biography* (New York: The Rutledge Press, 1981); David A. Jasen, *P. G. Wodehouse: A Portrait of a Master* (rev. ed., New York: Continuum, 1981); and Herbert Warren Wind, *The World of P. G. Wodehouse* (London: Hutchinson, 1981).

12. West, *American Authors*, p. 1.

13. Donaldson, *P. G. Wodehouse*, p. 4.

14. George Orwell, "In Defence of P. G. Wodehouse," in his *Dickens, Dali & Others* (NY: Harcourt Brace Jovanovich, 1946), p. 229.

CHAPTER 1

1. Quoted in David Jasen, *P. G. Wodehouse: A Portrait of a Master* (rev. ed., New York: Continuum, 1981), p. 86.

2. Major N. T. P. Murphy, "The Real Drones Club," *Blackwood's Magazine* 318, no. 1918 (Aug. 1975): 135; Leonora Wodehouse, "P. G. Wodehouse at Home," *The Strand* (Jan. 1929): 24; Jasen, *P. G. Wodehouse*, p. 103.

3. P. G. Wodehouse, *Performing Flea*, in *Wodehouse on Wodehouse* (London: Penguin, 1981), p. 361.

4. Wodehouse (New York) to William Townend, 11 Feb. 1950, Dulwich.

5. Wodehouse (Remsenburg) to Tom Sharpe, 7 May 1974. Collection of Tom Sharpe.

6. James L. W. West III, *American Authors and the Literary Marketplace since 1900* (Philadelphia: University of Pennsylvania Press, 1988), p. 5.

7. Evelyne Ginestet (née d'Auzac), "Le Monde de P. G. Wodehouse (1881–1975)" (Diss., Paris: L'Université de la Sorbonne Nouvelle, 1980), 1:62.

8. Jasen, *P. G. Wodehouse*, p. 14; Frances Donaldson, *P. G. Wodehouse: A Biography* (New York: Alfred A. Knopf, 1982), p. 53; Ginestet, "Le Monde de P. G. Wodehouse," 1:64.

9. P. G. Wodehouse, "Money Received for Literary Work," ms. notebook, Dulwich.

10. Wodehouse's 1907 autobiographical novel, *Not George Washington*, written with his classmate, friend, and collaborator Herbert Westbrook, is an interesting fictionalized account of this era; in it the hero writes the "On Your Way" column for *The Orb*. See *Not George Washington*, ed. David Jasen (New York: Continuum, 1980).

11. Cosmo Hamilton was coauthor of the book of *The Beauty of Bath* (1906), the second musical, after *Sergeant Brue* (1905), to which Wodehouse contributed lyrics; Pocock is presumably R. Noel Pocock, who illustrated Wodehouse's first three novels, *The Pothunters* (1902), *A Prefect's Uncle* (1903), and *Tales of St. Austin's* (1903). *Pearson's* was, after *The Strand*,

one of the most prestigious fiction magazines of the day; Wodehouse published there occasionally.

12. *By the Way Book* (London: The Globe Newspaper, 1908; repr. New York: James H. Heineman and Sceptre Press, 1985).

13. P. G. Wodehouse, *Over Seventy: An Autobiography with Digressions,* in *Wodehouse on Wodehouse,* p. 486.

14. Reginald Pound, *Mirror of the Century: The Strand Magazine 1891–1950* (South Brunswick: A. S. Barnes, 1966), pp. 10–74.

15. A. J. van Zuilen, *The Life Cycle of Magazines: A Historical Study of the Decline and Fall of the General Interest Mass Audience Magazine in the United States during the Period 1946–1972* (Uithoorn, The Netherlands: Graduate Press, 1971), pp. 11–12.

16. Pound, *Mirror of the Century,* p. 33.

17. Jan Cohn, *Creating America: George Horace Lorimer and The Saturday Evening Post* (Pittsburgh: University of Pittsburgh Press, 1989), p. 22; John Tebbel, *George Horace Lorimer and "The Saturday Evening Post"* (Garden City: Doubleday, 1948), pp. 16–18, 2, 5.

18. Tebbel, *George Horace Lorimer,* pp. 243, 43.

19. Ibid., 43.

20. Wodehouse (Paris) to Scott Feldman, 1945, Wodehouse Archive.

21. Zuilen, *Life Cycle of Magazines,* p. 20.

22. Theodore Peterson, *Magazines in the Twentieth Century* (2nd ed., Urbana: University of Illinois Press, 1964), p. 213.

23. Henry Seidel Canby, "Free Fiction," *Atlantic Monthly* 116 (July 1915): 61. This description suggests that the scenes of Jeeves packing or unpacking for Bertie while giving advice and criticizing the latter's clothing (most notably at the beginning of *Right Ho, Jeeves*) came from a recognizable convention involving mother doing somewhat the same for sons.

24. Quoted in James Hepburn, *The Author's Empty Purse and the Rise of the Literary Agent* (London: Oxford University Press, 1968), p. 58. Other information on Pinker from this source, pp. 55–57.

25. Jasen, *P. G. Wodehouse,* p. 38.

26. Ibid., pp. 44–45; Ginestet, "Le Monde de P. G. Wodehouse" 1:113.

27. This early period saw Wodehouse's first book publications, though before 1909 none of his books appeared in the United States. The school stories and the Psmith novels to 1915 were all published by A. & C. Black, and the adult ficiton of the same period, from *Love among the Chickens* (George Newnes, 1906) to *The Prince and Betty* (Mills & Boon, 1912) was published by a variety of small presses. By 1913, he moved to Methuen for a series of books, from *The Little Nugget* (1913) to *The Man With Two Left Feet* (1917). *Love among the Chickens* was the first Wodehouse book to appear in the United States, brought out by Circle Publishing in 1909. The following year *The Intrusion of Jimmy* (*A Gentleman of Leisure* in Britain) initiated a series of three books from W. J. Watt (not to be confused with A. P. Watt, later Wodehouse's British literary agency). Thereafter Wodehouse changed publishers, going from D. Appleton to Dodd, Mead and then Boni & Liveright (1915–19). The late teens brought more stability to his situation, both in England and the United States.

28. Jasen, *P. G. Wodehouse*, pp. 45, 48. King-Hall had been a fellow client of Pinker's, and Wodehouse had surreptitiously tried to help get her writing placed (as he did with others of his author-friends). See Eileen McIlvaine, Louise S. Sherby, and James H. Heineman, *P. G. Wodehouse: A Comprehensive Bibliography and Checklist* (New York: James H. Heineman, and Detroit: Omnigraphics, 1990), p. 376, no. N45.17.

29. Jasen, *P. G. Wodehouse*, p. 54; P. G. Wodehouse (London) to Paul R. Reynolds, 9 Sept. 1920, Reynolds.

30. Jasen, *P. G. Wodehouse*, pp. 59–60.

31. Paul R. Reynolds, *The Middle Man: The Adventures of a Literary Agent* (New York: William Morrow, 1972), pp. 13–18.

32. Paul R. Reynolds (New York) to Wodehouse, 19 June 1936, Reynolds. The 10 percent commission had been established by A. P. Watt soon after he opened his English agency ca. 1875, and it has remained in widespread use ever since. See Hepburn, *Author's Empty Purse*, p. 54.

33. Jasen, *P. G. Wodehouse*, p. 55.

34. Tebbel, *George Horace Lorimer*, p. 39; Otto Friedrich, *Decline and Fall* (New York: Harper & Row, 1970), p. 9.

35. John Tebbel, *A History of Book Publishing in the United States*, (New York: R. R. Bowker, 1978), 3:110. Interestingly, Doubleday, Doran was one of the first presses extensively to exploit the "Omnibus" form (initiated with *The Omnibus of Crime*, ed. Dorothy L. Sayers, 1929). Wodehouse

jumped on this bandwagon early with *The Jeeves Omnibus* (1931), and similar large collections of his stories are still being published. (See Tebbel, *History*, p. 36.)

36. Herbert Warren Wind, *The World of P. G. Wodehouse* (London: Hutchinson, 1981), pp. 52–53.

37. This was a common strategy for other authors as well, as when G. K. Chesterton published the "Innocence of Father Brown" series in the *Post* in 1910–11.

38. Tebbel, *History*, p. 33.

39. Wodehouse (Great Neck, N.Y.) to Leonora Wodehouse, 25 Dec. 1923, Wodehouse Archive; Paul R. Reynolds (New York) to Wodehouse, telegram, 17 Oct. 1933, and letter, 18 Oct. 1933, Reynolds.

40. Paul R. Reynolds (New York) to Arthur Levenseller, 6 July 1934, Reynolds.

41. Reynolds, *Middle Man*, p. 209; Tebbel, *George Horace Lorimer*, pp. 59, 71; Cohn, *Creating America*, p. 241; Wodehouse (Le Touquet) to A. P. Watt, 20 Mar. 1935, Wodehouse Archive.

42. Wodehouse (Great Neck, N.Y.) to Leonora Wodehouse, 25 Dec. 1923; Hepburn, *Author's Empty Purse*, pp. 2, 54; Wodehouse (Le Touquet) to A. P. Watt, 20 Mar. 1935, both Wodehouse Archive.

43. For details, see David A. Jasen, *The Theatre of P. G. Wodehouse* (London: B. T. Batsford, 1979).

44. Detailed accounts of Wodehouse's personal wartime experiences are given in Donaldson's *P. G. Wodehouse* and in Ian Sproat, *Wodehouse at War* (New Haven: Ticknor & Fields, 1981).

45. Donaldson, *P. G. Wodehouse*, p. 190.

46. Sproat, *Wodehouse at War*, p. 33.

47. P. G. W. [sic], "The Big Push," *Punch* (13 Dec. 1939): 642.

48. Robert Hall, "Was Wodehouse Anti-Jewish?" *Papers on Wodehouse* (Ithaca: Linguistica, 1985).

49. David Cannadine, "Another 'Late Victorian': P. G. Wodehouse and His World," *South Atlantic Quarterly* 77, no. 4 (Autumn 1978): 475.

50. Information supplied by Mrs. Ira Gershwin to James Heineman in 1987, and by Heineman to the author. An extensive set of letters from Wodehouse to Gershwin survives.

51. Wodehouse (New York) to William Townend, 22 Sept. 1947, Dulwich. This passage is one of many in Wodehouse's correspondence and writings that suggest he was not as ignorant of world events as is usually supposed.

52. It has never been clear how Wodehouse's notes from the 1930s (which we will be examining in the next chapter) survived. A remark in a letter gives a clue, however. Just before Wodehouse set out from Berlin to Paris in September of 1943, he wrote to his French translator: "With regard to *Summer Lightning*, I think I have a copy but it will be some little time before it reaches me in Paris, as my books are being sent from Berlin by freight." (Wodehouse [Berlin] to Benoit de Fonscolombe, 3 Sept. 1944, Wodehouse Archive)

53. Interview with Christopher Maclehose, London, 16 Oct. 1985. It may at first seem an anomaly that Jenkins would keep older Wodehouse books in print but not publish any new ones. We must presume that any new book might have been greeted with a public outcry, while quietly keeping older books in the stores would cater to those who remained faithful to Wodehouse.

54. Wodehouse (Paris) to Mr. Pritchett, 15 June 1946, Wodehouse Archive.

55. Wodehouse (Paris) to William Townend, 30 Aug. 1946, Dulwich.

56. Zuilen, *Life Cycle of Magazines*, pp. 22, 28; Friedrich, *Decline and Fall*, p. 11.

57. Friedrich, *Decline and Fall*, pp. 11–12; Cohn, *Creating America*, p. 161.

58. Paul R. Reynolds, Jr. (New York) to Wodehouse, 8 Sept. 1944, Wodehouse Archive.

59. Pound, *Mirror of the Century*, pp. 164–70.

60. Wodehouse (Paris) to Hugh Kingsmill, 17 July 1946, Wodehouse Archive.

61. Jasen, *P. G. Wodehouse*, pp. 205–7.

62. Four ("The Shadow Passes," "Up From the Depths," "Excelsior," and "How's That, Umpire?") were previously unpublished; one ("Bramley Is So Bracing") had been Wodehouse's penultimate story in the *Post* (18

Oct. 1939) and the last one in *The Strand* (Dec. 1940); four had been published after the war in relatively minor North American journals ("Birth of a Salesman" and "Feet of Clay" [as "A Slightly Broken Romance"] in *This Week* [1950], "Rodney Has a Relapse" in the Canadian *National Home Monthly* [1949], and "Success Story" in *Argosy* [1947]); only one had appeared after the war in a major fiction magazine: "Tangled Hearts" (as "I'll Give You Some Advice") in *Cosmopolitan* (1948).

63. Reynolds, *Middle Man*, pp. 106–8.

64. Ibid., pp. 110, 112.

65. Except where noted, information on Scott Meredith, Inc., comes from an interview with Scott Meredith, New York, 6 May 1986.

66. Wodehouse (New York) to Benoit de Fonscolombe, 18 Nov. 1947, Heineman.

67. Wodehouse (New York) to William Townend, 14 Mar. 1948, Dulwich.

68. Wodehouse (New York) to William Townend, 21 July 1949, Dulwich.

69. Wodehouse (New York) to William Townend, 6 June 1947, Dulwich.

70. Wodehouse (Paris) to Jack Donaldson, 17 Aug. 1945, Wodehouse Archive; Ethel Wodehouse (Paris) to Denis and Diana Mackail, 26 June 1945, Wodehouse Archive.

71. Wodehouse (New York) to Sheran Cazalet, 13 Jan. 1949, Wodehouse Archive; Wodehouse (New York) to Guy Bolton, ca. Jan. 1949 (second page only survives), Heineman.

72. Wodehouse (Paris) to Guy Bolton, 31 Mar. 1947 and 16 Aug. 1948, Heineman.

73. Wodehouse (New York) to Sheran Cazalet, 16 Oct. 1950, Wodehouse Archive.

74. Wodehouse (New York) to William Townend, 30 Oct. 1950, Dulwich.

75. Wodehouse's correspondence with Bolton, 13 Nov. 1950–21 Jan. 1952, Heineman.

76. Even as late as 1958, Wodehouse was still trying to get a production, or at least a script publication: "I have heard nothing from the chap at French's about *Phipps*. It really does seem extraordinary that a play as good as that should not get on, especially when you see some of the

things that do get put on." (Wodehouse [Remsenburg] to Guy Bolton, 1 May 1958, Wodehouse Archive.)

77. Wodehouse (New York) to Guy Bolton, 7 Apr. 1950, Wodehouse Archive.

78. Wodehouse (Remsenburg) to William Townend, 15 July 1952, Dulwich; Wodehouse (New York) to Guy Bolton, 20 Mar. 1953, Heineman; Wodehouse (New York) to Edward Cazalet, 27 Jan. 1955, Wodehouse Archive; Wodehouse (Remsenburg) to Guy Bolton, 4 June 1955, Wodehouse Archive; *Come On, Jeeves* program, Guildford Theatre, June 20–25, 1955, Heineman; Wodehouse (Remsenburg) to Guy Bolton, 27 June 1955, Wodehouse Archive; P. G. Wodehouse and Guy Bolton, *Come On, Jeeves* (London: Evan Brothers, 1956); Wodehouse (Remsenburg) to Guy Bolton, 21 June 1956, 7 Apr. 1958, 8 Aug. 1959, 7 June 1964, and 30 June 1965, Wodehouse Archive.

79. Wodehouse (Paris) to Frances Donaldson, 2 June 1945, Wodehouse Archive.

80. William Townend (Folkestone) to Wodehouse, 21 Nov. 1949, Wodehouse Archive.

81. Wodehouse (New York) to William Townend, 6 May 1950, Dulwich.

82. Wodehouse (New York) to James Penrose Harland, 12 Aug. 1951, Heineman.

83. Wodehouse (New York) to William Townend, 14 Apr. 1952, Dulwich.

84. Original program, "Review," 1971, excerpted in "Bookmark" series, program entitled "Plum, a Portrait of P. G. Wodehouse," BBC Television, 1990, directed by Nigel Williams.

85. Peter Schwed, *Turning the Pages* (New York: Macmillan, 1984), pp. 2, 8, 44, 118–19.

86. Ibid., pp. 173–75, 206.

87. Meredith, 6 May 1986; interview with Peter Schwed, New York, 17 June 1985.

88. Schwed, 17 June 1985.

89. Proposal to Publish, *The Ice in the Bedroom*, Simon and Schuster, 9 May 1960; Proposal to Publish, *Stiff Upper Lip, Jeeves*, Simon and Schuster, 22 May 1962, Heineman.

90. Schwed, *Turning the Pages*, pp. 178–80; Schwed, 17 June 1985. As this book was being written, Simon & Schuster was still growing by buying up smaller presses; by early 1988 it had become the world's largest book publishing organization. Its revenue for 1987 totaled $1.075 billion, of which only $115 million was in the trade division (into which category Wodehouse would fall). Its largest sections are now in educational and "professional information" publishing. "Simon and Schuster 1987 Publishing Revenue: $1.075 Billion," *Publisher's Weekly* 232, no. 27 (8 Jan. 1988): 23.

91. Meredith, 6 May 1986.

92. Zuilen, *Life Cycle of Magazines*, pp. 197–204.

93. Interview with Hilary Rubenstein, London, 16 Oct. 1985. In 1990, Granada Television aired its series "Jeeves and Wooster," in the United Kingdom and United States, which created a flurry of additional interest in Wodehouse.

94. Rubenstein, 16 Oct. 1985; Maclehose, 16 Oct. 1985.

95. Schwed, 17 June 1985.

96. Editorial Department Report, *How Right You Are, Jeeves* Simon and Schuster, 5 June 1959, Heineman.

97. Editorial Department Report, *Stiff Upper Lip, Jeeves*, Simon and Schuster, 11 May 1962, Heineman.

98. Rubenstein, 16 Oct. 1985.

99. Maclehose, 16 Oct. 1985.

100. Peter Schwed (New York) to Wodehouse, 12 Feb. 1971; Wodehouse (Remsenburg) to Peter Schwed, 18 Feb. 1971, both Heineman.

101. Wodehouse (New York) to Sheran Cazalet, 27 Mar. 1950, Wodehouse Archive.

102. Wodehouse (Remsenburg) to Lord Citrine, 24 July 1965, Wodehouse Archive.

103. Wodehouse (Remsenburg) to Guy Bolton, 4 July 1965, Heineman.

104. Wodehouse (Remsenburg) to Sheran Cazalet, 27 Mar. 1966, Wodehouse Archive.

105. Wodehouse (Remsenburg) to Guy Bolton, 4 Mar. 1968, Heineman.

106. Wodehouse (Remsenburg) to Guy Bolton, 3 July 1968, Heineman; Ian Carmichael (London) to author, 22 Oct. 1985; Harold Fielding (London) to Guy Bolton, 3 Sept. 1968, Heineman.

107. Teddy Holmes (of Chappell and Co., who had been representing some of the parties involved) (London) to Guy Bolton, 7 Mar. 1969, Heineman.

108. Wodehouse (Remsenburg) to Guy Bolton, 10 Aug. 1972, Heineman.

109. Wodehouse (Remsenburg) to Guy Bolton, 18 Nov. 1972, Heineman.

110. Lord Walter Citrine to Prime Minister Harold Wilson, 3 July 1967; Wilson to Citrine, 4 July 1967; Wilson to Citrine, 11 Apr. 1968; Wilson to Citrine, 17 May 1984, all four in Wodehouse Archive.

CHAPTER 2

1. Wodehouse (Remsenburg) to William Townend, 7 Apr. 1955, Dulwich.

2. For example, a typed list of ideas, undated but probably from the early 1930s, contains this entry:

> 13. For possible use in a novel, see NOTE 14 in the IDEAS FOR SHORT STORIES section. The one about the young man going to the fancy dress ball as Mephistopheles.

This has a penciled check and note "Used in Right Ho Jeeves." Dulwich.

3. Unless otherwise indicated, all manuscript note material is in the Wodehouse Archive.

4. Ms. notes, Dulwich. All other Jeeves/Wooster ideas listed here in Wodehouse Archive.

5. Wodehouse (New York) to William Townend, 29 Sept. 1951, Dulwich.

6. P. G. Wodehouse, *Performing Flea*, in *Wodehouse on Wodehouse* (London: Penguin, 1981), p. 265.

7. Wodehouse (Remsenburg) to Edward Cazalet, 26 Sept. 1961, Wodehouse Archive.

8. Quoted in Frances Donaldson, *P. G. Wodehouse: A Biography* (New York: Alfred A. Knopf, 1982), p. 115.

9. Wodehouse (New York) to William Townend, 11 Mar. 1949, Dulwich.

10. Wodehouse (Beverley Hills) to William Townend, 6 May 1937, Dulwich.

11. Interview with Scott Meredith, New York, 6 May 1986; undated note from Guy Bolton attached to Wodehouse's copy of *The Man Who Lost His Keys*, Wodehouse Archive. Emphasis in original.

12. Ms. notes, Dulwich.

13. Ms. notes, Dulwich.

14. Wodehouse (New York) to William Townend, 16 Oct. 1951, Dulwich.

15. All notes for *Jeeves in the Offing*, Ransom.

16. Ms. notes, *Service with a Smile*, 27–29 May 1960, Heineman.

17. Wodehouse (Le Touquet) to William Townend, 6 Apr. 1940, Dulwich.

18. Wodehouse (Paris) to Sheran Cazalet, 27 Mar. 1946, Wodehouse Archive.

19. *Jeeves in the Offing* material, Ransom.

20. Wodehouse (Harrogate) to William Townend, 23 Sept. 1923, Dulwich. Another account of this first scenario appears in a letter to Leonora written while Wodehouse was still working on *Bill the Conqueror*:

> Did Mummie tell you I was working on the new novel in a new way,—viz. making a very elaborate scenario, so that when the time came to write the story it would be more like copying out and revising than actual composition. It is panning out splendidly, but is, of course, the dickens of a sweat, because I can't persuade myself that I am really accomplishing any actual work besides just mapping the story out. I have reached about halfway now, and it has taken 30 pages, each containing 600 words as they are typed close [i.e., single-spaced] like this letter. That is to say, I have written 18,000 words of scenario, the equivalent of about three short stories!
>
> I must say I think when it is all finished, I shall be surprised at the speed at which I shall be able to polish off the story. There are whole scenes practically complete with dialogue and everything, and I am getting the beginnings of each chapter right, which always holds one up. I often spend a whole morning trying to think of the best way of starting a chapter, and now I shall be able to go right ahead. (Wodehouse [Great Neck, N.Y.] to Leonora Wodehouse, 14 Nov. 1923, Wodehouse Archive)

21. Herbert Warren Wind, *The World of P. G. Wodehouse* (London: Hutchinson, 1981), p. 68; Donald R. Bensen, "Exclusive Interview with P. G. Wodehouse," *Writer's Digest* 51, no. 10 (Oct. 1971): 23–24.

22. "Jeeves and the Greasy Bird" notes and draft, Ransom.

23. Wodehouse, *Performing Flea*, p. 247.

24. Ibid., p. 365.

25. Wind, *World of P. G. Wodehouse*, p. 66.

26. *Jeeves in the Offing* notes and drafts, Ransom.

27. Wodehouse (Remsenburg) to Tom Sharpe, 27 Sept. 1973.

28. Wodehouse, *Performing Flea*, pp. 274, 299; quoted in David Jasen, *P. G. Wodehouse: A Portrait of a Master* (rev. ed., New York: Continuum, 1981), pp. 137–38.

29. Peter Schwed (New York) to Wodehouse, 2 Feb. 1971, Heineman.

30. P. G. Wodehouse, *Over Seventy: An Autobiography with Digressions*, in *Wodehouse on Wodehouse* (London: Penguin, 1981), p. 497.

31. Wodehouse (Remsenburg) to Sheran Cazalet, 16 Dec. 1957, Wodehouse Archive; Bensen, "Exclusive Interview," p. 23.

32. Clarke Olney, "Wodehouse and the Poets," *The Georgia Review* (Winter 1962): 393.

33. Wodehouse (Remsenburg) to Lord Citrine, 25 Mar. 1960, Wodehouse Archive; Fred Swainson, "Acton's Feud," *The Captain* (Apr.–Sept. 1900). One character in this serial, Aspinall, provided the name of the jewelry store in *Joy in the Morning*.

34. Bensen, "Exclusive Interview," p. 23.

35. Wodehouse (Remsenburg) to Lord Citrine, 20 Jan. 1971, Wodehouse Archive; Meredith, New York, 6 May 1986; interview with Hilary Rubenstein, London, 16 Oct. 1985; interview with Christopher Maclehose, London, 16 Oct. 1985; Peter Cazalet (Kent) to Wodehouse, 3 Jan. 1967, Heineman.

36. Wodehouse (Le Touquet) to William Townend, 2 Dec. 1935, Dulwich.

CHAPTER 3

1. Quoted in Richard Robert Sheldon, *Viktor Borisovic Shklovsky: Literary Theory and Practice, 1914–1930* (Diss. University of Michigan, 1966), p. 113.

2. Boris Eikhenbaum, *Lermontov: A Study in Literary-Historical Evaluation*, trans. Ray Parrott and Harry Weber (Ann Arbor: Ardis, 1981), p. 13.

3. P. G. Wodehouse, Preface in *Something New* (New York: Beagle Books, 1972), n.p.

4. Patrick Brantlinger, *Rule of Darkness: British Literature and Imperialism, 1830–1914* (Ithaca: Cornell University Press, 1988), p. 235.

5. Indeed, the reaosn that *The Prince and Betty* is perhaps the least familiar of Wodehouse's novels today is that this central newspaper section of the plot involves one Rupert Smith—an American version of the more familiar Rupert Psmith. Here Smith is an American, a Harvard graduate who works as a newspaper editor. His dialogue and mannerisms are lifted directly from the "real" Psmith of *Mike* and *Psmith in the City*, and the plot, concerning yellow journalism and slum-lord gangsters, would later be elaborated as the basis for the 1915 novel *Psmith Journalist*, still in print and read today.

6. P. G. Wodehouse (New York) to Denis Mackail, 1951, quoted in Frances Donaldson, *P. G. Wodehouse: A Biography* (New York: Alfred A. Knopf, 1982), p. 287.

7. Jan Cohen, *Creating America: George Horace Lorimer and the Saturday Evening Post* (Pittsburgh: University of Pittsburgh Press, 1989) pp. 83, 85.

8. P. G. Wodehouse, *Performing Flea*, in *Wodehouse on Wodehouse* (London: Penguin, 1981), p. 319.

9. There has been little generic analysis of the turn-of-the-century romance, but a survey of the prominent authors of that period suggests that the current subgenres can be broken down thus: exotic contemporary (e.g., Robert Hichens, Maud Diver, C. N. and A. M. Williamson, and H. Rider Haggard), Ruritanian (e.g., Anthony Hope and George Barr McCutcheon), historical (e.g. Jeffery Farnol, Rafael Sabatini, Mary Johnston, Baroness Orczy, Marjorie Bowen, and, again, Haggard), Gothic and mystical (e.g., Marie Corelli, Marie Belloc Lowndes, and, yet again, Haggard), and straight dramatic (e.g., Madame Albanesi, Annie Swan, Mrs. George de Horne Vaizey, Baroness von Hutten, Charles Garvice, McCutcheon, and Farnol). (Based primarily on the invaluable reference guide, *Twentieth Century Romance and Gothic Writers* [New York: Gale, 1982].)

10. Wodehouse, *Performing Flea*, p. 313.

11. See, for example, Cecil Smith, *Musical Comedy in America* (New York, Theatre Arts Books, 1950), pp. 210–15; David Ewen, *Complete Book of the*

American Musical Theater (rev. ed., New York: Henry Holt, 1959), pp. 26, 182–85.

12. For more complete information on *Our Miss Gibbs*, see John Drinkow's *The Vintage Musical Comedy Book* (Reading: Osprey, 1974), pp. 105–06. Other musicals Drinkow covers that bear some resemblance to Wodehouse's work are: *The Belle of New York, The Dancing Mistress, Florodora, The Girl Friend,* and *No, No, Nanette.*

13. Wodehouse, *Performing Flea*, pp. 323–24.

14. Andrew Malec, "Early Wodehouse Doyleana and Sherlockiana," *Baker Street Miscellanea* 27 (Autumn 1981): 2. See also W. S. Bristowe, "The Influence of Holmes on Wodehouse," *The Sherlock Holmes Journal*, 12, no. 3/4 (Summer 1976): 109.

15. Barrie Hayne, "The Comic in the Canon: What's Funny about Sherlock Holmes?" in Earl F. Bargainnier, ed., *Comic Crime* (Bowling Green, Ohio: Bowling Green State University Popular Press, 1987), pp. 147–48.

16. Several critics writing on Wodehouse have noted the resemblance between the Jeeves/Wooster series and the Holmes/Watson series, though none has analyzed the specific formal principles which Wodehouse derived from Doyle. See Richard Usborne, *Wodehouse at Work to the End* (London: Penguin, 1978), pp. 194–95; R. B. D. French, *P. G. Wodehouse* (Edinburgh: Oliver and Boyd, 1967), p. 108; Richard J. Voorhees, *P. G. Wodehouse* (New York: Twayne, 1966), p. 111; and Marie-José Arquié, "Jeeves, héros comique de P. G. Wodehouse" (Diss., L'Université de Rouen, 1975), p. 103.

After finishing this book, I found an article by J. Randolph Cox, "Elementary, My Dear Wooster!" in the *Baker Street Journal*, 17 (June 1967): 78–83. Cox draws some fascinating parallels between specific passages in the Holmes series and various Wodehouse works. He also refers to Jeeves as "the world's first consulting gentleman's gentleman," thus anticipating my chapter title by many years.

17. Viktor Shklovsky, *Theory of Prose*, trans. Benjamin Sher (Elwood Park, Ill.: Dalkey Archive Press, 1990), pp. 103–05.

18. Hayne, "The Comic in the Canon," pp. 159–61.

19. Bargainnier, ed., Preface to *Comic Crime*, p. 2.

20. H. R. F. Keating, "Comedy and the British Crime Novel," in Bargainnier, ed., *Comic Crime*, p. 7.

21. Elaine Bander, "'What Fun!': Detection as Diversion," in Bargainnier, ed., *Comic Crime,* p. 58.

22. Wodehouse was undoubtedly familiar with the Hewitt stories. In a set of notes labeled "Jeeves Ideas" dated 1937 (Wodehouse Archive), he refers to the "Stanway Cameo idea." "The Stanway Cameo Mystery" is a story in the first Hewitt collection, *Martin Hewitt, Investigator* (1894).

23. Compare Lord Peter Wimsey's first greeting to Harriet Vane in chapter 4 of *Have His Carcase* (1932): "Good morning, Sherlock. Where is the dressing-gown? How many pipes of shag have you consumed? The hypodermic is on the dressing-room table." The Red House, which features prominently in *The Nine Tailors* (1934), may well be an homage to Milne's book.

24. P. G. Wodehouse, Foreword, in John McAleer, *Rex Stout: A Biography* (Boston: Little, Brown, 1977), pp. xv–xvi.

25. In his *The Comic Style of P. G. Wodehouse* (Hamden, Conn.: Archon Books, 1974), Robert Hall points out a number of other examples of this common device: "He uncovered the fragrant eggs and I pronged a moody forkful" ("Jeeves and the Impending Doom"); "through the aromatic smoke of a meditative cigarette" (*Thank You, Jeeves,* chap. 2); "though somebody had opened a tentative window or two" (*Right Ho, Jeeves,* chap. 17), "I balanced a thoughtful lump of sugar on the teaspoon" (*Joy in the Morning,* chap. 5); and "He waved a concerned cigar" (*Jeeves and the Feudal Spirit,* chap. 11), all quoted p. 86. There are many other examples in the series.

In his "The Wodehouse Effect," *English Studies* 56 (1975): 245–49, Magnus Ljung has criticized Hall's use of the term "transferred epithet." Ljung's case is not altogether convincing, however, partly because he concludes that such phrases derive their humor primarily from the relationship of verb and subject.

26. Julian Symons, *Bloody Murder: From the Detective Story to the Crime Novel* (rev. ed., New York: Viking, 1985), pp. 100–01.

27. Bander, "What Fun!" p. 48; see also Keating, "Comedy and the British Crime Novel," p. 13.

28. Ralph Lynn was a British stage and film actor of the 1920s and 1930s, specializing in young-man-about-town roles, complete with monocle.

29. H. Douglas Thomson, *Masters of Mystery: A Study of the Detective Story* (1931; New York: Dover, 1978), p. 71.

30. Jane S. Bakerman, "Guises and Disguises of the Eccentric Amateur Detective," in Bargainnier, ed., *Comic Crime*, p. 117.

CHAPTER 4

1. Benny Green, *P. G. Wodehouse: A Literary Life* (New York: The Rutledge Press, 1981), p. 218.

2. Marie-José Arquié "Jeeves, héros comique de P. G. Wodehouse" (Diss., L'Université de Rouen, 1975), p. 3. Evelyne Ginestet (née d'Auzac) points out that Bertie and Jeeves initially live at 6a Crichton Mansions, Berkeley Street, in *The Inimitable Jeeves*, but that later Wodehouse changes this to Berkeley Mansions. See her "Le Monde de P. G. Wodehouse 1881–1971" (Diss., Paris: L'Université de la Sorbonne Nouvelle, 1980), 2: 402.

3. Frances Donaldson, *P. G. Wodehouse: A Biography* (New York: Alfred A. Knopf), pp. 99–100.

4. P. G. Wodehouse (Remsenburg) to Richard Usborne, 13 Jan. 1965, Heineman.

5. Original notes, Wodehouse Archive.

6. The ending of *The Mating Season*, with Bertie going off to defy Aunt Agatha, is a slight exception, but we must assume that he succeeds and that no new problems are introduced after the last action of the book; certainly all the main plot lines have been resolved.

7. To Richard Usborne, "Why Jeeves, with that brain, and that confidence in his own brain, should remain a gentleman's personal gentleman is fairly mysterious." He goes on to suggest that Jeeves's skills would make him a successful gambler or financier. See Richard Usborne, *Wodehouse at Work to the End* (London: Penguin, 1978), p. 231.

8. The literary original of the Junior Ganymede may well have been the Valet's Club in *What Next?*, a novel which Wodehouse's friend Denis Mackail modeled on the Jeeves/Wooster series; the clever valet Lush descibes the club as "a very valuable source of general information." See Denis Mackail, *What Next?* (Boston: Houghton Mifflin, 1921), p. 226.

9. Data on servants' wages during the 1920s are difficult to find in secondary sources. A sampling of London *Times* want ads for valets in early 1929, however, shows their annual wages falling in this £65-to-£80 range (not counting room and board). For example, a "general manservant"

asking £65 described himself as wanting a position in London doing the "entire duties for one gentleman"; he could cook, drive a car, and speak French (*The Times* [4 Mar. 1929]: 3). Butlers and butler-valets received more, in the £80-to-£100 range. An agency supplying footmen, butlers, and valets listed the wage range as £35 to £100 (*The Times* [19 Mar. 1929]: 4). Even assuming Bertie had to pay Jeeves double the highest valet's rate (i.e., £200) to keep him from his friends' clutches, he would still only make around £4 a week. (In Sayers' *Whose Body?* [1923], Wimsey reveals that he pays Bunter £200 a year, implying that this is unusually high because Bunter assists him in his hobby of detection.) Thus £95 received in the period of two weeks would be a very substantial sum, with even the smaller £5 to £20 rewards Jeeves customarily gets being far from negligible.

10. We would not want to call this material "padding," a term usually applied to extraneous action obviously added solely for the purpose of delay. Typically Wodehouse's delaying action is carefully motivated in relation to the more basic actions, and those digressions which remain obvious to the reader systematically add humor. In this sense Wodehouse fits into the tradition of *Tristram Shandy*, where delay and degression become the main comic devices. (See Victor Shklovsky, "Sterne's *Tristram Shady:* Stylistic Commentary," in *Russian Formalist Criticism: Four Essays*, trans. ed. Lee T. Lemon and Marion J. Reis [Lincoln: Unviersity of Nebraska Press, 1965], pp. 25–27, for a model analysis of the delaying pattern of a novel.)

11. The name of Bertie's club seems to have been another case of literary borrowing by Wodehouse; in his library there is a copy of William Caine's novel, *Drones* (London: Methuen, 1917). (*Drones*, by the way, is an interesting example of a conventional novel of the Wodehouse type—but written in a non-comic vein.) The Drones club first figures in Wodehouse's work in 1920, in *The Little Warrior* (the American title of *Jill the Reckless*). In pre-1920 entries in the Jeeves/Wooster series, Bertie simply refers to his "club."

David Jasen claims in his "Index of Places and Things" that Psmith mentions the Drones Club on p. 226 of *Mike* (1909), but this is not the case. What Psmith says is actually: "We are, above all, sir, . . . a keen house. Drones are not welcomed by us. We are essentially versatile." Clearly Psmith is referring here to the word, not the name. (See David A. Jasen, *A Bibliography and Reader's Guide to the First Editions of P. G. Wodehouse* [London: Barrie & Jenkins, 1971], p. 285.)

The real-life source of the club has been examined at length, and a good case has been made for a combination of London clubs of the turn of the century: the Pink 'Uns (referring to members of the staff of the *Sporting Times*), the Pelicans Club, and the Bucks' Club (see Major N. T. P. Murphy, "The Real Drones Club," *Blackwood's Magazine* 318, no. 1918 (Aug. 1975): 132, 203).

12. n.a., "Plummie," *New Yorker* (15 Oct. 1960): 36–37.

13. The only earlier use of the word "code" I have found is in "Jeeves and the Song of Songs," where it is not capitalized.

14. Donaldson, *P. G. Wodehouse*, p. 11.

15. His original name was Brinkley in *Thank You, Jeeves*, but Wodehouse used that name again for Aunt Dahlia's country house in *Right Ho, Jeeves;* when he brought Brinkley back in *Much Obliged, Jeeves*, he changed the name, blithely passing the discrepancy off as Bertie's error.

16. Evelyne Gauthier, "Etude structurale du récit chez P. G. Wodehouse" (Diss., L'Université François Rabelais de Tours, 1975), p. 127.

17. Watson, of course, occasionally disapproves of Holmes's actions (most notably his cocaine use), but he does not defy his friend; the tensions between them are usually minor, while Jeeves and Bertie's conflicts become forces underlying whole narratives.

18. Biographers have established beyond a doubt that the name "Jeeves" comes from an actual cricket player, but the real-life source of Jeeves's first name is not mysterious either: it was Guy Bolton's middle name.

19. Perhaps the strongest statement of the case against this story comes in Richard J. Voorhees' insightful essay, "Wodehouse at the Top of His Form," *University of Windsor Review* 16, no. 1 (Fall-Winter 1981): 23.

20. It may seem odd that Wodehouse would think readers would keep in mind a 1922 story when reading much later entries in the series, yet we know that in general he made many references to earlier events without cueing us as to their sources. For example, in *Stiff Upper Lip, Jeeves* (1963), Bertie has to hide behind a sofa to avoid his enemies and says of life at Totleigh Towers, "One was either soaring like an eagle on to the top of chests or whizzing down behind sofas like a diving duck. . ." (chap. 20). He is referring to a passage in *The Code of the Woosters* (1938): "At the exact moment when I soared like an eagle on to the chest of drawers, Jeeves was skimming like a swallow on to the top of the cupboard" (chap. 7). *Stiff Upper Lip, Jeeves* is a sequel to *The Code of the Woosters;* both take place at Totleigh Towers, with the later book's events taking place "a month or so" after those of the earlier (chap. 23). Not only are we ex-

pected to recall the situation conjured up by the phrase "soaring like an eagle on to the top of chests," but we cannot grasp the full appropriateness and humor of the avian imagery in the later passage unless we realize that it echoes a pair of similes in the earlier. To take another case already mentioned, we will not detect the discrepancy in Bertie's notion of Jeeves's motto ("Service," given in *The Code of the Woosters*) and Jeeves's real motto ("Resource and Tact," given in "Bertie Changes His Mind") unless we make the connection between a story and a novel published sixteen years apart.

Certainly "Bertie Changes His Mind" contains one event to which Wodehouse refers many times: Bertie's humiliation in his address to the girls' school. It would appear that he especially wanted readers to remember this story.

21. Edward L. Galligan, "P. G. Wodehouse: Master of Farce," *Sewanee Review* 93, no. 4 (Fall 1985): 610.

22. P. G. Wodehouse, *Performing Flea* in *Wodehouse on Wodehouse,* (London: Penguin, 1981), p. 299.

23. Wodehouse (New York) to William Townend, 4 Apr. 1951, Dulwich.

CHAPTER 5

1. Interestingly, in the original 1916 version of this story, Bertie is financially dependent on Uncle Willoughby and so is reluctant to risk his anger by stealing the manuscript. "Jeeves Takes Charge" was not reprinted for a decade, by which time Wodehouse had established that Bertie is financially independent; at that point he revised the story. In its original form, it stuck closer to the pattern of the other early stories.

2. In reworking the original magazine stories to create a sort of rough, episodic novel in *The Inimitable Jeeves,* Wodehouse broke most of the original stories into two chapters each. It makes more sense in analyzing them, however, to treat the pairs of chapters as a single story, since they still recount virtually self-contained narratives. This makes annotation clumsy, but for brevity's sake I will use the following scheme:

Original Story	Chapters in *Inimitable Jeeves*	Short Title
"Jeeves and the Chump Cyril" (June 1918)	"A Letter of Introduction" "Startling Dressiness of a Lift Attendant"	"Letter/Startling"

Original Story	Chapters in *Inimitable Jeeves*	Short Title
"Jeeves in the Springtime" (Dec. 1921)	"Jeeves Exerts the Old Cerebellum" "No Wedding Bells for Bingo"	"Cerebellum/No Wedding"
"Scoring Off Jeeves" (Feb. 1922)	"The Pride of the Woosters Is Wounded" "The Hero's Reward"	"Pride/Reward"
"Sir Roderick Comes to Lunch" (Mar. 1922)	"Introducing Claude and Eustace" "Sir Roderick Comes to Lunch"	"Claude/Sir Roderick"
"Aunt Agatha Speaks Her Mind" (Apr. 1922)	"Aunt Agatha Speaks Her Mind" "Pearls Mean Tears"	"Agatha/Pearls"
"Comrade Bingo" (May 1922)	"Comrade Bingo" "Bingo has a Bad Goodwood"	"Comrade/Bingo"
"Bingo and the Little Woman" (Nov. 1922)	"Bingo and the Little Woman" "All's Well"	"Bingo/All's Well"

The other stories were originally published under the same names they bear in *The Inimitable Jeeves*.

3. Wodehouse had a lifelong fascination with servants. They figure enormously in his work as characters, but he also wrote occasional essays on them. His "The Lost Art of Domestic Service," (*Playboy* [January 1969]: 138ff) is a relatively serious treatment. Despite the frequent assumption that Wodehouse was oblivious to social injustices, here he gives a view of the inequities of servants' lives in pre-World War I England: "One would prefer not to dwell on the treatment of domestic servants by the middle classes in the Seventies, Eighties and even up to the time of the First World War. They kept them in damp basements and dark attics. They made them work 16 hours a day," and so on, at some length. Wodehouse's library contains a copy of Ernest S. Turner's scholarly history of servants, *What the Butler Saw* (London: M. Joseph, 1962), in which he has marked a number of passages on the exploitation and oppression of servants (and which he may have used in researching his *Playboy* article).

At any rate, ideological defenses of Wodehouse (such as Orwell's) based on such things as his inversion of roles between Jeeves and Bertie become more plausible on the basis of such evidence. In general, however, Wodehouse's politics were essentially conservative.

4. Owen Edwards rightly compares Aunt Agatha with Professor Moriarty in the Holmes series; in general she is

> only perceived through the lens of Bertie's overwhelming fear of her, much as Moriarty can only be seen through Watson's perception of Holmes's chilling account. And once he reached the novels, Wodehouse seems to have made a remarkable decision in literary economics: to retain her power, Aunt Agatha must never appear at all.

Edwards points to the eerily effective evocations of Agatha in *Right Ho, Jeeves,* where Bertie is startled by an owl that he momentarily takes for her, and *Joy in the Morning,* where he is transfixed by her portrait. (*P. G. Wodehouse: A Critical and Historical Essay* [London: Martin Brian & O'Keefe, 1977], pp. 98–100.) Whether Wodehouse consciously thought of Agatha as an arch-villain comparable to Moriarty is another question; given his modeling of the series on Doyle's stories, it is quite possible that she did play this role.

5. Harking back to the notion that Aunt Agatha's resentment of Jeeves stems partly from class bias, it is interesting in terms of the series' ideology to note that her conversation with Bertie involves the only application of the word "menial" to Jeeves, and it comes as quite a shock. This story as a whole concerns class differences.

6. Wodehouse (Remsenburg) to James Penrose Harland, 17 July 1959, Heineman.

7. At the end of *Jeeves and the Feudal Spirit,* Aunt Dahlia sold *Milady's Boudoir,* but Bertie specifies that this story's action takes place before that of the novel. This ploy suggests that Aunt Dahlia's newspaper was more important as a source of motivation than Wodehouse realized—or that he had trouble coming up with new motivations. *Milady's Boudoir* thus returns, though here it is not the focus of the action.

CHAPTER 6

1. Quoted in Frances Donaldson, *P. G. Wodehouse: A Biography* (New York: Alfred A. Knopf, 1982), p. 263.

2. "Notes for Jeeves novel," 29 Dec. 1939, Wodehouse Archive.

3. Ms. notes, 18 Apr. 1937, Dulwich.

4. P. G. Wodehouse (Le Touquet) to Leonora [Wodehouse] Cazalet, 12 Feb. 1938, Wodehouse Archive.

5. Meir Sternberg, *Expositional Modes and Temporal Ordering in Fiction* (Baltimore: The Johns Hopkins University Press, 1978), pp. 2–4.

6. This mystery novel turns out to be a real one; the passage has recently been identified as closely modeled on one in E. R. Punshon's *Mystery of Mr. Jessop*, published in 1937. See William A. S. Sargeant, "P. G. Wodehouse as a Reader of Crime Stories," *The Mystery Fancier* 9, no. 5 (Sept./Oct. 1987): 16.

7. "My Jeeves novel is coming out splendidly. I think it's going to be good. I hope so, as I'm afraid it will be my last, me being 89 next month." Wodehouse (Remsenburg) to Major N. T. Murphy, 23 Sept. 1970, Wodehouse Achive.

8. Surprisingly, most critics have failed to note the original aspects of this book. Richard Usborne dismisses it as:

> A tired book, full of misprints and misprisions—e.g. Bertie says that Arnold Aubrey, M. A. was the HM of his pre-school (of course he meant the Rev Aubrey Upjohn, HM of Malvern House, Bramley-on-Sea), Jeeves misquotes Lucretius and Brinkley has changed his name arbitrarily and without explanation. Wodehouse is writing very short now. (*A Wodehouse Companion* [London: Elm Tree books, 1981], p. 94.)

Such minor mistakes, however, are hardly enough to condemn a whole book, especially since both Wodehouse and Jeeves had misspoken before (e.g., when Jeeves wrongly attributes a phrase from Edward Young's "Night Thoughts" to Shakespeare in the 1926 story, "The Inferiority Complex of Old Sippy").

CHAPTER 7

1. Alfred R. McIntyre (Little, Brown) to Wodehouse, 28 Mar. 1934, Wodehouse Archive.

2. Draft deposition, Paul R. Reynolds (New York), (1934), Reynolds; Swepstone, Stone, Barer & Ellis (London) to Herbert Jenkins, Ltd., 4 May 1934, Century-Hutchinson Agreement File.

3. Contract, "Société Anonyme Siva, P. G. Wodehouse and Twentieth [sic] Century-Fox Film Corporation Agreement and Option," 16 Oct. 1935, Wodehouse Archive.

4. Wodehouse (New York) to Edward Cazalet, 24 Jan. 1955, Wodehouse Archive.

5. Wodehouse (Remsenburg) to Trevor L. A. Daintith, 25 Sept. 1966, Wodehouse Archive.

6. *Come On, Jeeves* has been reprinted in *Wodehouse: Four Plays* (London: Methuen, 1983).

7. As far as I know, the only page of any "Ponsonby" drafts of the play to survive is one on the back of which Wodehouse accidentally typed part of a letter to Townend. (Wodehouse [Remsenburg] to William Townend, 18 June 1952, Dulwich.)

8. See his "Author's Note," *Wodehouse: Four Plays*, pp. 235–36.

9. This late entry of Jeeves led to a rearrangement of chapters in the American edition, entitled *The Return of Jeeves*.

CHAPTER 8

1. Philip M. Thody, "P. G. Wodehouse and English Literature," in Eileen McIlvaine, Louise S. Sherby, and James H. Heineman, *P. G. Wodehouse: A Comprehensive Bibliography and Checklist* (New York: James H. Heineman, and Detroit: Omnigraphics, 1990), p. xxiv.

2. It seems doubtful that Wodehouse himself ever read Spinoza extensively or intended us to interpret Jeeves's character on the basis of his leanings toward this philosopher's beliefs. I suspect that Wodehouse chose Spinoza in order to create that memorable scene in *Joy in the Morning* where Bertie tries to buy a book by Spinoza in a bookshop and is instead given Florence Craye's *Spindrift* (after being offered *The Spinning Wheel* and *The Poisoned Pen* by a puzzled clerk)—thus setting up his involuntary reengagement to Florence.

3. See Owen Dudley Edwards, *P. G. Wodehouse: A Critical and Historical Essay* (London: Martin Brian & O'Keefe, 1977), p. 20; J. C. Morris, *Thank You, Wodehouse* (London: Weidenfeld & Nicolson, 1981), p. 4; Robert A. Hall, Jr., *The Comic Style of P. G. Wodehouse* (Hamden, Conn.: Archon Books, 1974), pp. 91–92; Richard Usborne, *Wodehouse at Work to the End* (London: Penguin, 1978), p. 202.

4. Ruth Inglis, "What Ho, Wodehouse," *Nova* (Oct. 1974): 82.

5. Usborne, *Wodehouse at Work*, p. 195.

6. Quoted on end sheet of first British edition of *The Mating Season* (London: Herbert Jenkins, 1949).

7. R. D. B. French, *P. G. Wodehouse* (Edinburgh: Oliver and Boyd, 1966), p. 85.

8. Critics, however, are unanimous in suggesting that Jeeves is the source of quotations in the series. This presumable stems from their examination of the stories in the order of their book publications rather than of their original magazine appearances. It seems probable that Wodehouse deliberately covered over the weakness of the earliest stories by delaying their republication in the United States. After the success of *Jeeves* in 1923, he used the early stories to put together another collection, *Carry On, Jeeves* (1925), but added some newer ones. Of the ten stories in that collection, five are from the 1916–17 period and five from 1922–25 (including "Fixing It for Freddie," an extensively rewritten version of a 1911 non-Jeeves/Wooster story). The differences between the two sets of stories are striking.

In 1972 Wodehouse wrote to Bennett Cerf, who was putting together a Modern Library collection of Jeeves/Wooster material:

> I have always felt about the Jeeves short stories that the ones in *Carry On, Jeeves* were not much good. The Scott Meredith people told me you were using some of those. Don't you think a better plan would be to use most of the first Jeeves book and the whole of *Very Good, Jeeves*? Just as you say, of course, but I do think *Carry On, Jeeves* is inferior to the other two. (Wodehouse [Remsenberg] to Bennett Cerf, 12 Aug. 1972. Rare Books Room, Columbia University Library)

Some of the material in *Carry On, Jeeves* is quite good, of course—especially "Clustering Round Young Bingo" and "Bertie Changes His Mind" (which Wodehouse strategically placed as the last two stories in the book). I suspect that Wodehouse was referring mainly to the five early-period stories.

9. As far as I know, only one other critic has singled out this unique bit of dialogue. For an analysis from a different vantage see Marie-José Arqué, "Jeeves, héros comique de P. G. Wodehouse" (Diss., L'Université de Rouen, 1975), pp. 84–85.

10. Monroe Beardsley has analyzed one instance of this use of "sir" to interrupt a quotation in the opening of *The Code of the Woosters*. See his

"Verbal Style and Illocutionary Action," in *The Concept of Style*, ed. Berel Lang, (rev. ed., Ithaca: Cornell University Press, 1987), pp. 213, 216.

11. In two isolated cases, the abbreviation is identifiable because it is part of a familiar quotation. The first instance of this sort comes in *Right Ho, Jeeves*: "Old Pop Kipling never said a truer word than when he made that crack about the f. of the s. being more d. than the m." (chap. 19). The other use of this device returns to this same passage; when in *The Code of the Woosters* Stiffy blackmails Bertie using the notebook, he comments: "Kipling was right. D. than the m." (Chap. 8)

12. Alexander Cockburn, "The Natural Artificer," *The New York Review of Books* 29, no. 14 (23 Sept. 1982): 22.

13. *The Inimitable Jeeves* was not, of course, a cliché when first used, but it has become one by now: it is one of two quotations from Wodehouse in the 15th edition of Bartlett's. The other exception, *Aunts Aren't Gentlemen*, was a title Wodehouse brooded over for some time. He wrote to Guy Bolton in 1948: "I've been saving up for years what I think is the best title ever invented." The title was *Women Aren't Gentlemen*, which he offered to let Bolton have for a Sacha Guitry play he was adapting. (Wodehouse [New York] to Bolton, 17 July 1948, Heineman.) Wodehouse modified and used the phrase twenty-five years later.

14. "Plum, a Portrait of P. G. Wodehouse," "Bookmark" series, BBC Television, 1990, directed by Nigel Williams.

15. P. G. Wodehouse, *Over Seventy: An Autobiography with Digressions*, in *Wodehouse on Wodehouse* (London: Penguin, 1981), p. 486.

APPENDIX B

1. n.a. "Plummie," *The New Yorker* (15 Oct. 1960): 36.

2. Maha Nand Sharma, *Wodehouse the Fictionist* (Meerut, India: Meenakshi, Prakashan, 1980), pp. 80–89.

3. J. C. Morris, *Thank You, Wodehouse* (London: Weidenfeld & Nicolson, 1981), pp. 3–6.

4. Richard Usborne, *Wodehouse at Work to the End* (London: Penguin, 1978), pp. 32, 131.

5. Wodehouse (Remsenburg) to Bennett Cerf, 12 Aug. 1957, Columbia University Library. The names in "The Aunt and the Sluggard" were not actually updated for later collections.

6. Jeeves was right about the club's being in fashion; "The Aunt and the

Sluggard'' was published in April of 1916, and in November of that year the management had to add tables to accommodate two hundred more people for the ''Midnight Frolics.'' Jeeves was seated alone at a table by the dance floor, which at that time went for three to four dollars per person with four people per table. ''Ziegfeld's Added Capacity,'' *Variety* 44, no. 12 (17 Nov. 1916): 3.

7. David Cannadine, ''Another 'Last Victorian': P. G. Wodehouse and His World,'' *South Atlantic Quarterly* 77, no. 4 (Autumn 1978): 486, 489.

8. R. B. D. French, *P. G. Wodehouse* (Edinburgh: Oliver and Boyd, 1966), pp. 94–95.

SELECT BIBLIOGRAPHY

PRIMARY SOURCES

James H. Heineman Collection.

Christopher Maclehose, interview, conducted by Kristin Thompson, 16 Oct. 1985, London.

Scott Meredith, interview, conducted by Kristin Thompson, 6 May 1986, New York City.

Harry Ransom Humanities Research Center, The University of Texas at Austin.

Paul R. Reynolds Collection, Rare Books Room, Butler Library, Columbia University, New York City.

Hilary Rubenstein, interview, conducted by Kristin Thompson, 16 Oct. 1985, London.

Peter Schwed, interview, conducted by Kristin Thompson, 17 June 1985, New York City.

P. G. Wodehouse Archive, Wodehouse Estate.

P. G. Wodehouse Files, Century-Hutchinson, London.

Special Collections, P. G. Wodehouse Library, Dulwich College, London.

SECONDARY SOURCES

Allen, Frederick Lewis. *Paul Revere Reynolds*. New York: Privately published, 1944.

Arquié, Marie-José "Jeeves, héros comique de P. G. Wodehouse." Diss., L'Université de Rouen, 1975.

Bensen, Donald R. "Exclusive Interview with P.G. Wodehouse." *Writer's Digest* 51, no. 10 (Oct. 1971): 22–24, 43.

Bonham-Carter, Victor. *Authors by Profession*. Vol. 1, Los Altos, Calif.: William Kaufmann, 1978; Vol. 2, London: The Bodley Head and The Society of Authors, 1984.

Cannadine, David. "Another 'Last Victorian': P. G. Wodehouse and His World." *South Atlantic Quarterly* 77, no. 4 (Autumn 1978): 470–91.

Carlson, Richard S. "An Analysis of P. G. Wodehouse's Team of Bertie Wooster and Jeeves." Diss., Michigan State University, 1973.

Cazalet-Keir, Thelma, ed. *Homage to P. G. Wodehouse*. London: Barrie & Jenkins, 1973.

Cockburn, Alexander. "Introduction." *The Code of the Woosters*. New York: Vintage Books, 1975.

———. "The Natural Artificer." *The New York Review of Books* 29, no. 14 (23 Sept. 1982):22–27.

Cohn, Jan. *Creating America: George Horace Lorimer and The Saturday Evening Post*. Pittsburgh: University of Pittsburgh Press, 1989.

Donaldson, Frances. *P. G. Wodehouse: A Biography*. New York: Alfred A. Knopf, 1982.

Edwards, Owen Dudley, *P. G.Wodehouse: A Critical and Historical Essay*. London: Martin Brian & O'Keefe, 1977.

French, R. B. D. *P. G. Wodehouse*. Edinburgh: Oliver and Boyd, 1967.

Friedrich, Otto. *Decline and Fall*. New York: Harper & Row, 1970.

Galligan, Edward L. "P. G. Wodehouse: Master of Farce." *Sewanee Review* 93, No. 4 (Fall 1985): 609–17.

Garrison, Daniel. *Who's Who in Wodehouse*. 2nd. ed. New York: International Polygonics, 1989.

Gauthier, Evelyne. "Etude structurale du récit chez P. G. Wodehouse." Diss. L'Université François Rabelais de Tours, 1975.

Ginestet, Evelyne (née d'Auzac). "Le Monde de P. G. Wodehouse 1881–1975) Diss., L'Université de la Sorbonne Nouvelle, 1980. 3 vols.

Green, Benny, *P. G. Wodehouse: A Literary Biography*. New York: The Rutledge Press, 1981.

Hall, Robert A., Jr. *The Comic Style of P. G. Wodehouse*. Hamden, Conn.: Archon Books, 1974.

———. *Papers on Wodehouse*. Ithaca: Linguistica, 1985.

Heineman, James H. and Donald R. Bensen, eds. *P. G. Wodehouse: A Centenary Celebration 1881–1981*. New York: The Pierpont Morgan Library, Oxford University Press, 1981.

Hepburn, James. *The Author's Empty Purse and the Rise of the Literary Agent*. London: Oxford University Press, 1968.

Inglis, Ruth, "What Ho, Wodehouse." *Nova* (Oct. 1974): 80–82, 84.

Jaggard, Geoffrey. *Wooster's World*. London: Macdonald, 1967.

Jasen, David A. *P. G. Wodehouse: A Portrait of a Master*. Rev. ed. New York: Continuum, 1981.

———. *The Theatre of P. G. Wodehouse*. London: B. T. Batsford, 1979.

McIlvaine, Eileen, Louise S. Sherby, and James H. Heineman, *P. G. Wodehouse: A Comprehensive Bibliography and Checklist*. New York; James H. Heineman, and Detroit: Omnigraphics, 1990.

Morris, J. C. *Thank You, Wodehouse.* New York: St.Martin's Press, 1981.

Murphy, Major N. T. P. "The Real Drones Club." *Blackwood's Magazine* 318, no. 1918 (Aug. 1975): 124–35.

"Plummie." *The New Yorker* (15 Oct. 1960): 36–37.

Pound, Reginald. *Mirror of the Century: The Strand Magazine 1891–1950.* South Brunswick: A. S. Barnes, 1966.

Reynolds, Paul R. *The Middle Man: The Adventures of a Literary Agent.* New York: William Morrow, 1972.

Schwed, Peter. *Turning the Pages.* New York: Macmillan, 1984.

Sharma, Maha Nand. *Wodehouse the Fictionist.* Meerut, India; Meenakshi, Prakashan, 1980.

Sproat, Ian. *Wodehouse at War.* New Haven: Ticknor & Fields, 1981.

Tebbel, John. *George Horace Lorimer and "The Saturday Evening Post".* Garden City: Doubleday, 1948.

———. *A History of Book Publishing in the United States.* New York: R. R. Bowker, Vol. 3, 1978, Vol. 4, 1981.

Usborne, Richard. *Wodehouse at Work to the End.* London: Penguin, 1978.

———. *A Wodehouse Companion.* London: Elm Tree Books, 1981.

Voorhees, Richard J. *P. G. Wodehouse.* New York: Twayne, 1966.

———. "Wodehouse at the Top of His Form." *University of Windsor Review* 16, no. 1 (Fall-Winter 1981): 13–25.

West, James L. W., III. *American Authors and the Literary Marketplace since 1900.* Philadelphia: University of Pennsylvania Press, 1988.

Wind, Herbert Warren. *The World of P. G. Wodehouse.* London: Hutchinson, 1981.

Wodehouse, Leonora. "P. G. Wodehouse at Home." *Strand* (Jan. 1929): 20–25.

Wodehouse, P. G. Foreword. In John McAleer, *Rex Stout: A Biography.* Boston: Little, Brown, 1977.

———. "The Lost Art of Domestic Service." *Playboy* (Jan. 1969): 138–39.

———. *Over Seventy: An Autobiography with Digressions.* In *Wodehouse on Wodehouse.* London: Penguin, 1981.

Wodehouse, P. W., with William Townend. *Performing Flea.* In *Wodehouse on Wodehouse.* London: Penguin, 1981.

Zuilen, A. J. van. *The Life Cycle of Magazines; A Historical Study of the Decline and Fall of the General Interest Mass Audience Magazine in the United States during the Period 1946–1972.* Uithoorn, The Netherlands: Graduate Press, 1971.

INDEX

NOTE: Wodehouse's writings are listed here only by their British titles; see Appendix A for the American titles of works in the Jeeves/Wooster series.

A. P. Watt, 25, 31, 38, 53, 55
"Acton's Feud," 87
Addams, Charles, 50
Admirable Crichton, The, 120
Adventures of Sherlock Holmes, The, 107
Alleynian, The, 20
Anderson, Sherwood, 3
"Another of Those Cub Reporter Stories," 96
Apollinaire, Guillaume, 16
Aristophanes, 120
Arno, Peter, 50
Arnold, Matthew, 15
Arsenic and Old Lace, 45
Arthur, 41
"Artistic Career of Corky, The," 124, 128, 164, 166, 168, 176, 285
Atlantic Monthly, 22
"Aunt and the Sluggard, The," 128, 165, 166, 168, 169, 287, 319, 325, 342
Aunts Aren't Gentlemen, 15, 18, 67, 70, 81–84, 106, 114, 127, 141, 212, 215, 217, 221–223, 225, 294, 301, 305, 306, 326, 341
Aurelius, Marcus, 330

Baerman, A. E., 25
Bakerman, Janet S., 117
Balzac, Honoré, 209
Bandwagon, The, 344
Barchester Towers, 209
Bargainnier, Earl F., 108
Barmy in Wonderland, 48, 66, 121, 157
Barrie & Jenkins, 53
Bartlett's *Familiar Quotations,* 16, 86, 286, 296
Battle of Dorking, The, 92
"Battle of Squashy Hollow, The," 52
BBC, 33, 34, 39, 46, 49, 53, 56, 57, 254, 270, 344

Bennett, Arnold, 25, 27
Bensen, Donald, 76
Bentley, E. C., 116
Berlin broadcasts, 32–38, 42, 43
Berlin, Irving, 37
"Bertie Changes His Mind," 65, 129, 131, 139, 155, 180, 286, 296, 327
Best of Wodehouse, The, 44
Betting on Bertie, 57, 58, 218, 271–273, 327
Big Money, 29
Bill the Conqueror, 30, 76
"Bingo and the Little Woman," 134
"Birth of a Salesman," 65
Blackwood's Magazine, 92
Bolton, Guy, 2, 26, 45–47, 50, 56, 57, 66, 101, 102, 256, 265, 268, 270, 273
Bow, Clara, 343
Bowen, Elizabeth, 66
Brantlinger, Patrick, 92
Braque, Georges, 16
Bring on the Girls, 50, 204
British Broadcasting Corporation *see* BBC
Bruce, Leo, 67
Buchan, John, 36, 37
"Building of the Ship, The," 9, 86, 109, 205
Bulldog Drummond, 120
Butter and Egg Man, The, 66
By the Way Book, 21
Byron, Lord, 299

Cannadine, David, 36, 343
Cantor, Eddie, 50
Capp, Al, 50
Captain, The, 21, 22, 87
Carmichael, Ian, 57
Carry On, Jeeves, 140, 176, 343 (*See also* individual story titles)
Caryll, Ivan, 102
"Case Against the Jew, The," 39, 40
Cather, Willa, 24, 27
Caught Short, 50
Cazalet, Peter, 88
Cazalet-Keir, Thelma, 34, 47
Century-Hutchinson, 53
Cerf, Bennett, 50, 342
Chaplin, Charles, 58
Chekhov, Anton, 205
Chesney, Sir George, 92
Chester, George R., 98
Chesterton, G. K., 96, 98
Christie, Agatha, 108, 209
Citrine, Lord Walter, 57, 58, 87, 159
Clicking of Cuthbert, The, 29
"Clustering Round Young Bingo," 135, 148, 154, 180, 321, 340
Cobb, Irwin, 24, 27, 96, 98
Cockburn, Alexander, 327
Cocktail Time, 54
Code of the Woosters, The, 3, 35, 62, 104, 119, 122, 125, 127, 128, 129, 130, 132, 138, 141, 151, 153, 210, 212, 213–216, 219, 226–229, 235, 248, 267, 276, 289, 290, 291, 296, 302, 306, 324, 340, 341, 344
Cohan, George, 342
Cohen, Octavus Roy, 98
Collier's, 24, 26, 27, 31, 48, 52, 86

Collins, Wilkie, 31
Come On, Jeeves, 15, 46, 47, 56, 57, 127, 200, 218, 256, 257, 265–268, 270–272, 310
Coming of Bill, The, 95
"Comrade Bingo," 170, 171
Conrad, Joseph, 2, 25
Conventions, 5, 6, 8–10, 12, 17, 67, 99, 103–105, 107, 110, 118, 122, 142, 159, 160, 208, 210, 223, 231, 270, 273, 279, 307, 328, 329, 343
Cooper, Alfred Duff, 34, 344
Cooper, Gary, 255
Cooper, James Fennimore, 23
Corelli, Marie, 24
Cosmopolitan, 24, 26, 27, 43, 44, 86, 110, 253
Cowper, William, 299
Crane, Stephen, 24, 25
Crescent Press, 53
Crossword Puzzle Book, The, 50
Cussen, Major Edward, 34

Damsel in Distress, The, 28
Death by the Lake, 67
Dehan, Richard, 100
"Delayed Exit of Claude and Eustace, The," 180
Dell, E. M., 1, 95
"Departmental Ditties," 299
"Destruction of Sennacherib, The," 299
Detective genre, 4, 7, 9, 105–117
Dickens, Charles, 22, 303
Dictionary of Humorous Quotations, The, 86
Dominant, 9, 12, 231, 232, 276, 327
Don't Listen, Ladies, 45
Donaldson, Frances, 13, 33, 38, 121, 135
Doran, George, 27
Doubleday, Doran, 28, 30, 38, 39
Doubleday, Page, 27
Doyle, Sir Arthur Conan, 9, 10, 23, 31, 98, 105–109, 112–117, 127, 145, 151, 159, 208
Dracula, 7, 8
Dreiser, Theodore, 2, 3, 24
Dulwich College, 19, 20, 26, 86, 112
Durant, Will, 50

Eggs, Beans and Crumpets, 285
Einstein, Albert, 16
Eisenhower, Dwight, 345
"Episode of the Dog McIntosh," 186, 188, 194, 310, 315, 316, 321, 343
Exploits of Elaine, The, 110, 117
"Extricating Young Gussie," 27, 28, 128, 163, 164

Fairbanks, Douglas, 342
Faulkner, William, 24, 209
Few Quick Ones, A, 201
Feydeau, Georges, 102
Field, Marshall, 50
Fielding, Harold, 57
Firm of Girdlestone, The, 9
Fitzgerald, F. Scott, 2, 27
Ford, Ford Madox, 25

Forrest, George, 57
French, R. D. B., 285
Frogs, The, 120, 216
"From the Collection of the Duke," 96
Full Moon, 38, 63
Fun in Bed, 50

Galligan, Edward L., 157
Garden City Publishing Co., 28
Gauthier, Evelyne, 140
Gentleman of Leisure, A, 93, 94
George H. Doran Company, 27, 28
George Newnes Ltd., 22
Gershwin, Ira, 37, 81
Gilbert, W. S., 20
Ginestet, Evelyne, 20
Girl behind the Gun, The, 102
Girl in Blue, The, 53
Girl on the Boat, The, 67
Glass, Montagu, 96
Graustark: The Story of a Love behind a Throne, 93
"Great Sermon Handicap, The," 174, 181
Gromyko, Andrei, 345
Grossmith, George, 120
Guthrie, T. A., 92

Haggard, H. Rider, 31
Half a Sixpence, 57
Hall, Robert, 36, 115
Hamlet, 287, 294, 298, 302–305, 308
Hammerstein, Oscar, 37, 344
Hardy, Thomas, 31, 148
Harper's, 23
Harte, Bret, 22, 31
Hayne, Barrie, 106, 107
Heart of a Goof, The, 29, 143, 296
Heavy Weather, 30, 242, 254
Herbert Jenkins Limited, 28, 31, 38, 39, 50, 53, 55, 83
Hibbs, Ben, 40, 52
Hodgins, Eric, 50
Hood, Thomas, 287
Hope, Anthony, 93, 96
Hope, Bob, 50
Hornung, E. W., 109
Hound of the Baskervilles, The, 23
How to Succeed in Business without Really Trying, 50
Hurst, Fannie, 96
Hutchinson Group, 53

I Never Left Home, 50
Ice in the Bedroom, 51, 205
Ideal Husband, An, 120
"Imitations of Horace," 287
"Indian Summer of an Uncle," 172, 186
"Inferiority Complex of Old Sippy, The," 130, 148, 186, 190, 197, 283, 286, 291
Inimitable Jeeves, The, 29, 51, 141, 160, 177, 209 (*See also* individual story titles)
"International Cup, The," 97
Iolanthe, 20

James, Henry, 22, 25
Jarry, Alfred, 10

"Jeeves and the Chump Cyril," 28
Jeeves and the Feudal Spirit, 3, 15, 68, 74, 103, 120, 125, 126, 137, 200, 204, 205, 212, 222, 223, 225, 228–230, 251, 279, 280, 290, 291, 294, 311, 313, 326, 328, 340, 341, 344
"Jeeves and the Greasy Bird," 61, 77, 78, 83, 115, 125, 127, 202, 217, 278, 294, 340
"Jeeves and the Impending Doom," 67, 134, 138, 186, 192
"Jeeves and the Kid Clementina," 183, 186, 199, 312, 316
"Jeeves and the Old School Chum," 186, 294, 317
"Jeeves and the Song of Songs," 121, 182, 190, 318
"Jeeves and the Unbidden Guest," 165, 343
"Jeeves and the Yule-tide Spirit," 136, 184, 186, 187, 197, 198, 282, 340
Jeeves in the Offing, 54, 69, 74, 75, 78, 84, 130, 200, 201, 212, 215, 217, 220, 223, 224, 281, 289, 293, 297, 298, 304, 305, 323, 325, 328, 339, 341, 344
"Jeeves Takes Charge," 165, 167, 170, 215, 247, 277, 285, 286, 287, 294, 314, 321, 342
Jenkins, Herbert *see* Herbert Jenkins Limited.
Jesus Christ Superstar, 57
Jill the Reckless, 29, 48, 269
Joy in the Morning, 3, 36, 38, 39, 67, 72, 87, 90, 103, 138, 141, 142, 215, 216, 219, 222, 225, 227, 261, 277, 280, 292–294, 299, 302, 304, 310, 325, 328, 340, 341
Joyce, James, 2, 10, 11, 16
Julius Caesar, 296

Kaufman, George S., 66, 158
Keating, H. R. F., 108
Keats, John, 280, 287, 301, 307
Kelly, Walt, 50, 51
Kern, Jerome, 2, 26, 37, 101
Kersh, Gerald, 65
King-Hall, Ella, 26, 27, 31
Kipling, Rudyard, 24, 25, 31, 270, 286, 299
Kismet, 57
Kissing Time, 102
Kyne, Peter, 98

Labiche, Eugène, 102
Ladies' Home Journal, 52
Lardner, Ring, 96, 98
Leave It to Psmith, 28, 29, 41
Lermontov, Mikhail, 91
Lester, H. G., 92
"Lines Composed a Few Miles Above Tintern Abbey," 300
Literary agents, 25, 25–27, 31, 42, 43, 45, 53, 162, 202
Little, Brown, 30, 254
Little Nugget, The, 95
London, Jack, 96
Longfellow, Henry Wadsworth, 86, 297

Lorimer, George Horace, 23, 24, 27, 39, 40
Love Among the Chickens, 21, 25
Lubitsch, Ernst, 10
Luck of the Bodkins, The, 31
Lynn, Ralph, 115

Macbeth, 298, 306
Mackail, Denis, 17, 204
Maclehose, Christopher, 53, 55, 88
Magazine publishing, 1, 3, 6, 9, 11, 13, 18–23, 24, 27, 29–31, 39–44, 48, 50, 52, 53, 92, 94–98, 100, 106, 149, 172, 176, 177, 283, 285, 317
Malec, Andrew, 105
Mame, 57
Man Upstairs, The, 95
Man Who Lost His Keys, The, 66
Man with Two Left Feet, The, 29, 66, 132
Marquand, John Phillips, 65
Mating Season, The, 14, 38, 41, 42, 73, 103, 113, 130, 131, 133, 139, 140, 149, 150, 153, 164, 200, 204, 210, 212, 216, 220, 223–225, 231, 232, 263, 280, 284, 291, 298, 308, 323, 340, 341, 344
Matthews, Jessie, 344
Maugham, W. Somerset, 27
"May Queen, The," 287, 299
McAleer, John, 111
McCall's, 43
McClure's, 23, 27
McCutcheon, George Barr, 93
Mead, Shepherd, 50
Merchant of Venice, The, 298, 302
Meredith, Scott, 37, 43, 44, 48, 50, 52, 54, 66, 88
"Metropolitan Touch, The," 174
Mike, 21, 26, 91–93, 261, 277, 278
Milne, A. A., 108, 110, 111, 116
Miss Springtime, 26
Mr. Blandings Builds His Dream House, 50
Molnar, Ferenc, 37, 41
Monckton, Lionel, 102
Money in the Bank, 38, 39
Morris, J. C., 340
Morrison, Arthur, 109
Mosley, Oswald, 35
Moyle, Seth, 26
Much Obliged, Jeeves, 55, 68, 71, 72, 78, 85, 129, 130, 133, 140, 150, 153, 205, 208, 211–215, 217, 223, 230, 247–252, 278, 279, 295, 298, 305, 323, 324, 341
Muggeridge, Malcolm, 53, 119
Muir, Frank, 57
Munsey's, 23, 92
Murder Must Advertise, 115
Murphy, Major N. T. P., 17
My Man Jeeves, 176 (*See also* individual story titles)

Nation, The, 22, 240
Newbolt, Sir Henry John, 36, 37
Newton, Sir Isaac, 297
Nietzsche, Friedrich, 285
Nimmo, Derek, 57
Niven, David, 254

Not George Washington, 26
Nothing Serious, 42

Ober, Harold, 43
O'Casey, Sean, 2
Old Reliable, The, 15, 42, 45, 46, 48, 52, 120, 255, 256, 260, 261, 262–265
"Olney Hymns," 299
"On First Looking into Chapman's Homer," 287, 301
Oppenheim, E. Phillips, 96
"Ordeal of Young Tuppy, The," 148, 150, 182, 186, 200, 291
Orwell, George, 13
Our Miss Gibbs, 102
Oxford Book of Quotations, The, 86

Pelican at Blandings, A, 205
Performing Flea, 49, 98, 104, 157, 204
Perrin, Michel, 66
Picasso, Pablo, 16
Piccadilly Jim, 28
Pigs Have Wings, 28, 49, 68, 204
Pinker, J. B., 25, 26
Plack, Werner, 33
Plautus, Titus, 120
Play's the Thing, The, 44, 45
Playboy, 52, 53, 78, 224
Plum Pie, 54, 83
Poe, Edgar Allan, 23, 205
Pope, Alexander, 279, 287
Pound, Reginald, 40
Priestley, J. B., 204
Prince and Betty, The, 93
Prisoner of Zenda, The, 93
Psmith in the City, 13, 21, 93
Public School Magazine, 20–22
Punch, 35, 53, 88, 106, 232
Punshon, E. R., 67
Purloined Paperweight, The, 54
Pushkin, Aleksandr, 91

Quotation, 8, 9, 20, 85, 122, 123, 276, 277, 279–281, 283, 288, 296–299, 301, 304, 306–309, 328, 329

Red House Mystery, The, 108, 110, 111, 116
Redbook, 27, 31
Reeves, Arthur, 110
Repetition, 5, 8, 11, 12, 19, 83, 97, 98, 100, 159, 171, 210, 231, 232, 248, 276–278, 281, 284, 290, 293, 309, 311, 316–319, 321, 324, 325, 327, 329
Reynolds, Paul R., Jr., 26, 30, 38, 40, 42, 43
Reynolds, Paul R., Sr., 26, 27, 30, 38, 42
Rice, Tim, 57, 58
Right Ho, Jeeves, 6, 7, 85, 87, 102, 104, 112, 120, 126, 139, 145, 149, 150, 172, 178, 207, 210, 214, 215, 216, 218, 219, 222, 224–226, 228, 230, 234, 238–247, 254, 278, 281, 282, 284, 289–292, 294, 306, 310, 316, 318–320, 340, 341, 344

Rinehart, Mary Roberts, 1, 24, 27, 31, 96, 98, 100
Ring for Jeeves, 15, 46–48, 114, 131, 200, 218, 257–260, 265, 266, 268, 269, 314, 326, 345
Roberts, Morley, 96
Rohmer, Sax, 27, 31, 254
Romance genre, 7, 99–106, 117
Romeo and Juliet, 298
Ruggles of Red Gap, 121, 122
"Rummy Affair of Old Biffy, The," 181

Sacking of London in the Great French War of 1901, The, 92
Sally, 44, 45
Sandow's Magazine of Physical Culture and British Sport, 106
Saturday Evening Post, 2, 3, 14, 23, 24, 26, 27, 30, 31, 39, 40, 42, 43, 52, 65, 88, 91–93, 95–99, 121, 127, 343
Sayers, Dorothy L., 115, 116
Schuster, Max, 50, 51
Schwed, Peter, 50–52, 54, 55, 85, 251
Scribe, Augustin Eugène, 102
Scribner's, 23
Scully, Frank, 50
Seizure of the Channel Tunnel, The, 92
Seldes, Gilbert, 123, 133
Shakespeare, William, 85, 148, 279, 286, 299, 301, 303, 307
Sharma, Maha Nand, 340
Sharpe, Tom, 84, 328
Shaw, George Bernard, 27, 49
Shimkin, Leon, 51
Shklovsky, Viktor, 5, 91, 107
Simon, Richard, 50, 51
Simon and Schuster, 15, 50, 51, 54, 257
Singing Fool, The, 343
"Sir Roderick Comes to Lunch," 172, 174, 176
Something Fresh, 26, 27, 29, 92, 95
Something New see Something Fresh
Song of Norway, 57
Spinoza, Baruch, 125, 279
"Spot of Art, The," 184, 186, 207, 275, 313
Spring Fever, 15, 38, 45–48, 218, 255, 256, 260–262, 264, 345
Stalin, Josef, 16
Stein, Gertrude, 2
Step Lively, Jeeves, 254
Sternberg, Meir, 208, 209
Stiff Upper Lip, Jeeves, 7, 51, 55, 64, 103, 125, 152, 201, 205, 212–214, 217, 221, 223, 225, 228, 247, 248, 280, 281, 289, 291, 308, 325, 326, 340, 341
Stoker, Bram, 7
Stone, Fred, 342
Story of Philosophy, The, 50
Stout, Rex, 106, 111, 112
Stout, Wesley, 39, 40, 42
Stowe, Harriet Beecher, 23
Strand, The, 9, 22, 23, 28, 31, 40, 41, 92, 105, 109
Strong Poison, 115, 116
Summer Lightning, 29, 84
Sunset at Blandings, 18, 71

"Susanna and Her Elders," 100
Swoop . . . A Tale of the Great Invasion, The, 92

Taking of Dover, The, 92
Tarkington, Booth, 27, 31
Thank You, Jeeves, 14, 29, 30, 85, 112, 136, 139–141, 143, 144, 149, 150, 156, 172, 184, 204, 213–215, 223, 224, 226, 234–240, 254, 260, 262, 263, 271, 279, 284, 286, 288, 290, 291, 296, 301, 310, 312–315, 320–322, 324, 325, 341, 343, 344
Theory of Prose, 91
Thody, Philip M., 276
Thomson, H. Douglas, 116
Time Magazine, 52
To-day, 22
Tomashevsky, Boris, 5
Toronto Star Weekly, 52
Townend, William, 17, 18, 37, 39, 44, 45, 47–49, 59, 61, 63–65, 68, 72, 84, 88, 157
Train, Arthur, 98
Travers, Ben, 67
Treacher, Arthur, 254
Treasure Island, 192
Trent's Last Case, 116, 117
Trollope, Anthony, 80, 209
Trotsky, Leon, 16, 344
Try and Stop Me, 50
Twain, Mark, 22

Uncle Dynamite, 38
Upson, William Hazlett, 98
Usborne, Richard, 282, 342

Van Loan, Charles E., 97
Velez, Lupe, 255
Very Good, Jeeves, 141, 160, 311, (*See also* individual story titles)
Viking Book of Aphorisms, 86
"Village Blacksmith, The," 297

Walpole, Hugh, 27
Watt, A. P. *see* A. P. Watt
Waugh, Evelyn, 4, 108
Way of an Eagle, The, 95
Webber, Andrew Lloyd, 57, 58
Webster, H. T., 50
Wells, H. G., 25, 27
West, James L. W., III, 11, 19
West, Rebecca, 27
Westbrook, Herbert, 21, 26
When a Man Marries, 100, 101
Whose Body? 115
Wilde, Oscar, 25, 120
Wilson, Harold, 58
Wilson, Harry Leon, 96, 121, 122
Win with Wooster, 57, 218, 270–273
Winter's Tale, The, 301
Wister, Owen, 96
"Without the Option," 182, 212
Wodehouse, Ethel, 33, 56
Wodehouse, Leonora, 17, 65
Wodehouse, Pelham Grenville
- and the theater, 2, 42, 45–48, 57, 58, 101–104
- wartime experiences, 32–41
- working methods, 12, 59–89
- writing career, 6, 11–14, 16–58

Woolf, Virginia, 2, 16
Wordsworth, William, 7, 300
"World of Wooster, The," 53, 56, 57, 254, 270
Wright, Robert, 57
Yeats, William Butler, 31
Young, Edward, 286
Young Men in Spats, 30
Ziegfeld, Florenz, 45, 342, 345

This book was composed in
Meridian and Peignot by
Jackson Typographers, Jackson, Mi.

It was printed and bound by
Arcata Graphics Company, N.Y. on
60# Sebago cream white antique paper.

The typography and binding were designed by
Beth Tondreau Design, New York